ROAD
OF
LEAVES

Written by
Eric Loren

Book 1
Ways of Camelot

Reader Hill
Yucaipa, California

Published by
Reader Hill
PO Box 490
Yucaipa, CA 92399
readerhill.com

Dedication

To my beloved wife. You are such a blessing in my life, enriching my days and filling them with laughter. Thank you so much. I will love you always.

Acknowledgments

I want to share my appreciation for the many people who helped to make this book a reality, including Irene, Traute, and Rena. I am also thankful for my fellow scriveners at the Writers' Gallery: Andrew, Joyce M., Judith, Ron, Robert, Cathie, Joyce L., April, and Michael.

All of you gave your honest critique and helpful suggestions. Thank you for your words of wisdom.

ONE

Royal Oak Inn

The coolness of the inn felt good after a hot, dusty hike. Thomas had been walking since before dawn, wanting to get to the Road of Leaves before midday. It was now about two hours before noon; enough time for a brief rest since the gates were not far off. Once his eyes adjusted to the common room's dim lighting, he looked around and spotted an empty table in the cavernous place. He trudged over and sat down with a sigh. Although he was only seventeen years old, he felt like an old man after a week of hiking across the countryside. He shrugged off his pack and set it between his feet to make sure no sticky fingers tried to pilfer it. It held travel food, a blanket, his gray apprentice robe, and his magician's box, all things he dearly wanted to keep. All magicians kept their knapsack close and he was no exception, even though he was a mere student with only ten years of training.

Thomas ran a hand through his long brown hair, knowing it was a damp and tangled mess even with the drab ribbon tying it back. Maybe he would get it cut when he arrived at the king's city, but only if it didn't cost too much or take too much time. He wanted to see the magical city of Camelot, with its Great Market, the Short Road fortress, the ornate Council Hall, and King's Haven harbor where the Road of Waters started. Frankly, if his choice was to be between an intriguing trinket at the market or getting his hair cut, he would probably forgo the trim.

A young serving woman stopped at his side, ready to take his order. She offered a slight smile, for he was just another customer, probably one of hundreds she would help today. This was the only inn at the entrance to the Road of Leaves, as well as sitting midway between two sizable towns, so the Royal Oak had a large and steady flow of customers. He didn't bother trying to flirt with her, for he knew she wouldn't be interested in a poor apprentice. Instead, he just asked for a mug of cider. He had heard that the Royal Oak's brews were especially good, but the cider was cheaper. He just wanted a cool drink after a summer's trudge.

She gave him a nod and hurried on.

As he waited for his drink, he looked around the large yet dim room. The place held dozens of travelers waiting for their turn to enter the Road of Leaves. They were quite the mixed crowd. At one table sat a party of nobles, at another sat merchants and their hired swords. Usually, such people would never intermingle, but there was not much choice if you wanted to get to Camelot. It was either the Road of Leaves or the Road of Waters for most, since Camelot sheltered within one of Merlin's great enchantments.

Thom was heading there to deliver a message from Wizard Levitanus and to retrieve a collection of magical supplies that his master had already purchased. He was going to the guild house, which his master described as more like a fortress than a home for magicians. As a visiting student, the guild would provide a bed and meals but they would probably limit where he could go inside the keep. Nonetheless, he planned to explore all of Clas Myrddin that he could, for it was the home of the magicians' guild. He hoped to climb up Sky Tower where the Road of Clouds came to the earth, but that spire might be off limits to a mere apprentice. If they kept him from wandering around the guild house, he still had much to explore throughout the rest of the fabled city and maybe even snoop around King Arthur's castle. He dared not dally in Camelot long, but he thought an extra day or two would not get him into trouble with his master.

His drink arrived and he paid. She gave him a nod of thanks and hustled off to some other new arrivals. Thom took a long sip, washing the dust from his throat. He had considered buying a meal, but thought the better of it, for his master was careful with the purse. Instead, he pulled out a firm plum from his knapsack and took a bite. As he chewed, he looked around some more. That was when he saw a familiar face. His green eyes locked on a person from his wild childhood in York then looked quickly away.

What was Ned doing here?

It had been ten years since Thomas had left his hometown to start his apprenticeship- a very long apprenticeship. His first year with Levitanus was spent listening with his inner ear for the various sounds of magic. The next three years he had to learn how to mix magical elements and then attune them to himself- skills essential when crafting an enchantment. Over half of his life he had now spent learning about magical elements, plants, and odd creatures. Being a magician's apprentice was like that. It could take decades to become a journeyman and then even more decades to reach the rank of master, and he had no assurance that he would attain it even then.

Thom had never gone back to York, for he had no sentiment for the place. His drunkard thief of a father was probably dead by now and he had no friends back there. His mother had fled when he was five, finally tired of his father's drunken rages. So, seeing someone from his hometown brought mixed feelings. He wasn't certain if he wanted to be recognized or not. Also, who would want to admit to being an apprentice still, when most his age were already settled down with a family?

Well, at least the fellow he saw would have no family. That was obvious from his garb. Trying not to be obvious in his attention, Thomas glanced across at the corner table again, to where a man in priestly robes sat clutching a wooden mug.

As a boy the fellow had been a thief's son also, only a few years older than Thom and quite a bit meaner. Yet now he was dressed as a priest. Well, if Thom could be a magician's apprentice, certainly Ned could become a clergyman. It was just that Thomas never would have thought him to be of that bent, for he remembered Ned as something of a randy youth, chasing the skirts when he wasn't swiping fruit from neighborhood gardens. More often than not, the girls had rejected Ned, but the lad had pursued them relentlessly nonetheless. Ned a celibate priest? That was a surprise. If anyone would have followed in his father's dodgy footsteps, he would have thought Ned would.

Thom considered going over to say hello, but his feet ached and he really had no fond memories about Ned. As children, they had fought more often than they had worked in concert, for Ned had always wanted to order the younger boys to do his dirty work. None of them had played together, for Thom didn't have that kind of childhood, but they had done some thievery as a team. Ned hadn't been the most reliable team leader, but he hadn't been the worst of the lot either.

Thom decided to simply ignore the unwanted intrusion from his past and savor his cider and plum instead. However, when a bishop joined Ned, Thom quickly looked away and did his best to hide from them. He recognized that man too. The elderly man in clerical robes was Ned's father, Joseph, and he was certainly no servant of God. Whatever their scheme, these two would not like having someone know their true selves. He needed to get away.

Thom chugged the rest of his drink, grabbed his knapsack and then hurried out the back of the inn. In his rush, he forgot the half-eaten plum on the table. He regretted losing the food as soon as the door closed behind him, but he was not about to go back and retrieve it. At least he had more plums in his bag, enough to tire him of the fruit over the next few weeks of travel.

He would have fled the area, but he still needed to register for his journey. Upon the king's orders, everyone who took the Road of Leaves had to register and pay the toll, so Thom headed toward the gatehouse.

Behind the Royal Oak Inn and its ample stables, a wide paved road headed into a narrow valley. Thom walked up the road, his feet complaining with each step. Being paved, the way wasn't as dusty or weather-worn as most paths he'd been on, but it was also less forgiving with each stride. To either side was dense forest, but the trees offered little midday shade with the sun so high in the heavens. As he walked, he caught an occasional glimpse of the rugged hills beyond the forest canopy, but mostly he saw trees around him.

He had to step to the side of the road once, when a party of nine riders came down the road. They were nobles, dressed in fine garments and sitting on their proud horses. The men rushed by, apparently eager to reach the inn after days of riding through the Road of Leaves, not even bothering to glance at Thom as they passed. He waited until the dust cleared and then forced himself to kept going.

The dark paving stones ended at a tall, stone wall that sat across the mouth of the small yet steep vale. Behind the rough stones towered a thick forest that he identified as Whisper Pines. He recognized the trees by their unique sound which he could hear through the open gate, a steady low murmur in his inner ear that was part of a greater symphony of the Road of Leaves.

It was the innate gift of magicians that they could hear the whispers of magic, and it was that untrained skill that had brought Thomas to the attention of Wizard Levitanus so many years ago when he tried to filch from the man but got distracted by the sounds of the enchantment the wizard had been crafting. In that moment of distraction, Levitanus completed his work and caught Thom in a *Vine Snare* enchantment. It was the greatest mistake he had ever made as a thief, but it was the one that resulted in his abandoning that trade and starting a life as a magician's apprentice.

For the last decade, Thom had been training to listen with his inner ear to recognize the unique cadences and sounds of many magical elements, but the sounds he was hearing from up ahead were unique in their richness and complexity. He had never heard such a masterful enchantment as the Road of Leaves.

His steps slowed as he became absorbed in the complex sounds that were whispering from beyond the wall. He tried to identify the various magical elements in use, but it was a confusing cacophony of both living elements and potent magics made from fabled creatures.

It took a moment before he realized that he was standing in the middle of the road with his mouth open, staring like a country bumpkin. He shook his head and instead focused on what was on this side of the wall.

The road ran up to huge wooden gates where two guards kept careful watch. Thom understood that they were opened only at proscribed times. His heart lightened when he saw people standing in front of the gate, waiting their turn to enter. The day's walking party hadn't left yet, so maybe he could join it.

He didn't approach the gates, but knew enough to go to the nearby a three-story building that was the gatehouse. The nearest door sat open, so he walked in and came upon two clerks at their desks and one traveler in the midst of paying his toll.

The unoccupied clerk looked up. "Come to register?"

"Yes, sir." Thom stepped forward. He stopped in front of the beaten desk, swinging off his pack and setting it at his feet.

"Well then, give me your name and occupation. Are you on foot or traveling on horseback? The fees are doubled for those riding." The man pointed at a wooden sign listing the rates.

Thom fumbled for the coin purse hidden within his shirt. "My name is Thomas, apprentice to Wizard Levitanus. I'll walk the Road."

His statement made all three of them look.

"Magician, eh? You know the rules of the Road?"

Thom nodded. "I'll work no magic while in there. I've no desire for the Road to turn on me."

"And turn it would," stated the clerk, pointing a bony finger at him for emphasis. "The leaves will swirl as if in a whirlwind and you would be lost inside Merlin's enchantment, so leave off any spells or rituals or whatever else your kind does."

Thom put the right number of coins on the desk, next to the man's other hand. "My master stressed all of that before I set out on my journey. When will my opening come?"

The man took the coins, inspecting each before dropping them into an iron money-box. He then scribbled Thom's name and position on a line of his ledger. The man spun the book around and held out the pen. "Sign your name or place your X right here."

Thom signed it. "When will my assigned group be leaving?" he asked again, unable to hide his eagerness to enter the magical route. He really hoped that the group outside had room, for he wanted to get far away from the scheming of Ned and Joseph.

The clerk raised an eyebrow, a whisper of a grin touching the corners of his thin-lipped mouth. "God smiles on you, for you won the last opening in tomorrow's walkers. Your party will be leaving at noon." The man slid a wooden token across his desk. "Hand this over when the soldiers open the gates, for it is your proof of payment. Do not lose it or you'll have purchase another. Do not be late or you'll forfeit your place and your coins, no matter how much you wave your token in our faces. Become too much of a bother, and we will banish you from ever using the Road. So remember your manners, magician, and be here at before noon tomorrow, for we make no exceptions."

Thom didn't like even that long of a delay, but it could have been worse. He had heard that during the heart of winter a man sometimes waited as long as a week for enough travelers to gather. He wanted to get on with his travels and away from those crooks from his past.

He thanked the clerk, then picked up his pack and turned to leave. As he stepped out into the bright sunshine, he came face-to-face with Ned.

TWO

Unexpected Encounters

Looking at Thom, Ned's mouth curled into a polite grin, but the smile never touched his eyes. "Bless you, my son. Pardon me, but I wish to enter."

Thom gave a mumbled apology as he hastily stepped past. He kept going, not daring to look back, but wondering if Ned had recognized him. He tried watching out of the corner of his eyes, but lost him. He was so focused on the false priest that he bumped into someone else. Stumbling, he barely kept from falling.

Unfortunately, the lass he had bumped now lay sprawled on the paving stones. He tried to help her up, but she was too quick, jumping to her feet and brushing off her skirts.

His face turned red. "Excuse me. I am so clumsy sometimes."

"I'll not argue that point," she replied tersely, but then looked up at him and smiled.

The smile lit up her faintly pockmarked face and made it beautiful. Her blue eyes danced with life. Thom suddenly realized how young and fine-figured she was, and then blushed even more at his gawking.

"My name is Adele," she continued, politely ignoring his stares.

He cleared his throat. "I… I am Thomas."

Adele brushed her disheveled black hair over her shoulders and let it cascade down her back. "Well, Thomas, you certainly know how to sweep a girl off her feet, or at least how to knock her down. Are you always so forceful with the ladies?"

She paused, just long enough for him to start stammering another apology, and then she interrupted with a laugh. "I know you didn't do it on purpose, for your eyes were elsewhere. Please try to be more attentive to where you're walking, Thomas, and maybe if we meet again on the Road of Leaves it will be less bruising for me." She smiled and then hurried past him, heading for the gatehouse to register.

Thom stared after her, awed. He was still looking that direction when Ned stepped back out and this time his old acquaintance gave him a long stare. The polite smile had evaporated. Ned sped up, obviously intending to confront him.

Thom turned and ran, ignoring the angry yell behind him. He dodged behind a coach that was now parked in front of the building, and kept going. He didn't want a confrontation, for Ned's costume would make him far more believable to any audience. He raced back toward the inn, doubting that Ned would dare run while disguised as a clergyman.

* * *

After a day of hiding in the forest beyond the inn, Thom slipped back toward the Royal Oak as the sun lingered low in the western sky. He kept to the long shadows, unsure of what he might find. When he saw nothing of Ned or his father, he slipped into the stable area and asked if he could pay to bed in the hayloft.

"The master would never allow it," replied a stable boy. "He says that if we let one person in, then we will have dozens every week dirtying the hay and peeing behind the stalls. If you can't afford a room or floor space in the common room, then go sleep in the travelers' field. Don't even think of trying to sneak in here. The last fool Stablemaster Heldon caught was sent running wearing nothing but a thousand welts and bruises."

Thomas nodded his understanding, turning to go, but the stablehand wasn't done with his warnings.

"And don't try making your own camp in the woods. Most of these lands belong either to the inn or to the Crown, and neither take kindly to trespassers mucking up their grounds."

Thom made no reply, but just walked out into the gathering gloom of sunset. He had seen the travelers' field already, where people sat around stone fire rings roasting whatever they had for dinner. He had wanted to avoid the place, but it looked like he would have no choice.

He hiked back to the meadow and saw that four of the fire rings were lit, with various groups around each. As he understood it, the innkeeper had to provide the wood so that travelers would not scavenge in the forest. Thom guessed the man could easily afford it, owning the only inn at the Road's entrance.

He picked a campfire where it looked like none would shun him. He apparently chose well, for no one objected to his squatting next to the fire to warm his hands. He didn't recognize anyone around the fire, but he hadn't expected to. Ned and his father would be at the inn, keeping up their appearances as respectable clergy. No, the folks at these fires were just fellow travelers waiting their turn to enter the Road of Leaves. Many were merchants with pack mules and surly guards. As he understood it, some lingered here for weeks, waiting for partners to arrive or wanting to make some final trades before entering the Road. The king forbade selling or bartering on the travelers' field to keep it from turning into a bazaar, but the merchants used the meadow as their base nonetheless, overnighting here and then traveling to some of the nearer villages to do their trading.

Thom warmed up some leftover rabbit he had by skewering it with a stick and letting it dangle over the flames. He then made a quick meal of it, along with a roll and a carrot. Afterward, he moved away from the others and found a soft patch of grass on which to lay his blankets. He sat down, swinging off his pack and setting it before him. He went through it, digging out a small wooden bowl and mixing spoon, setting both in front of him. It was time to craft a protective enchantment around his sleeping place.

When he was sure that no others looked his way, he pulled out of his knapsack the small lead-lined, wooden container. His magician's box. He knew that as soon as he opened its lid he would expose his presence to any nearby magician, but it couldn't be helped. He needed to protect himself tonight.

He lifted the container's lid and the rhythms of the magical powders filled his inner ear. Inside the box were a hundred felt-lined slots designed to hold narrow glass vials containing the magical elements. Being only an apprentice, most of the slots in Thom's box were empty. However, he had what he needed.

He selected the right elements from among the powders, picking them more by their sound than appearance. He chose the three magical elements necessary for the enchantment he wanted to create. He took some dried and pulverized ear of a Bearded Night Hare to recreate the impressive hearing of those extraordinary rabbits. He also took some powdered tongue of Western Tufted Martlet, for that magical bird was well known to whistle in warning whenever an intruder entered its territory. The final element was crushed leaves of a Whispering Elm to give the magic a softer sound. A sprinkle of each went into the bowl. Quickly, he stoppered each glass vial and returned them to the box, then shut its lead-lined lid to dampen the magical rhythms inside.

He stuffed the magician's box back into his knapsack. The powders in the bowl still sang in his inner ear, but it wasn't as loud as having his whole cache open. Next, he took out some of the mundane elements he needed to add to the mix: lodestone shavings, powdered glass, and a tad amount of silver dust.

Thom mixed it all in the wooden bowl and then spat into it numerous times, tuning the magic to himself. A magician always added something of himself when crafting an enchantment, using spit or tears or sweat or even urine. He once read of using blood, but his master had told him blood was a dangerous thing to work with.

He then added water until the mixture reached a soupy consistency. His inner ear picked up the change in sounds as the different elements intermingled. He was crafting an enchantment known as the Whisper of Warning. He listened to his work as it came together, making sure all remained in careful rhythm. Although he had crafted this particular magic often enough, it being one of the few enchantments taught an apprentice, he still wanted to make sure he crafted the magic correctly.

When satisfied with the concoction, he dabbed some on his ears and then took the bowl in hand and walked a circle around his blanket, dribbling the mixture on the grass. He listened to make sure the magic's rhythm didn't alter or weaken as he set it in place. Once the circle was completed, it gave off a beat so faint that most magicians wouldn't even hear it, although it was steady beat in his own ears. Should anyone or anything pass through the circle break that rhythm, Thom would awaken.

He wanted to make sure Ned did not try to sneak up on him during the night.

* * *

Thom woke with a headache, but at least he woke. Dawn was just touching the sky. A chilling dew covered his blanket and the grass around him. He let go of the magic and felt a slight lessening of the headache. Sitting up, he looked around the travelers' field and saw a pair of merchants packing their things and hitching a horse to a wagon. Everyone else was still sleeping. He guessed that the two were part of this morning's traveling party.

He stretched, wanting to sleep longer but knowing that he needed to get away from here. Thom feared that Ned or Joseph might falsely accuse him of something. They would do something like that to keep him from spoiling their scheme, and no one would believe a lowly apprentice over a revered clergyman.

With no time to stir up any of the fire embers to cook a warm breakfast, he had to make do with another roll, a plum, and a thick slice of cheese. He ate while packing his things, tying his blanket to the bottom of his pack. He shouldered the pack and then looked around for a likely direction. The stableboy's warning about trespassing didn't worry him too much, but he would be careful to not gather or disturb anything. He picked a thicket at the meadow's edge and set off, barely aware that he had chosen a route that angled back toward the Road's entrance. Even as he walked, he could hear the enchantment's faint beat wooing him.

He planned to stay in the shadows until it was time for him to enter the Road. As he wandered among the trees, he practiced his plant lore, striving to identify each tree, shrub, and weed he passed. He didn't encounter any magical plants or creatures, but then he hadn't expected to. The woods were silent of magical sounds, leaving only the Road of Leaves' pulses to attract his attention. This close to such a busy route, the forest had been picked clean by merchants and magicians, no matter what the king's law prohibited. Though Thom had forsaken his thieving past, he was well aware how tempting it could be. The right handful of flowers or berries could bring a week's income. Without realizing it, he wandered toward the Road's gates.

Only when he heard the sound of people did he become aware of his location. He didn't turn away, but instead crept forward. The trees thinned and he saw those gathering for the morning opening of the gate. He saw Ned and his father, mounted on a pair of mules, their clergy robes drawing his eye even at this distance. The sight of them in this party brought him relief, for it meant he would not have to fear running into them on the Road. Riders would travel the route much faster than a walking party would.

He was about to slip away, when he saw a coach pull up and its door open, the one he had dodged behind yesterday. Adele stepped out and went over to Joseph, offering him a curtsy.

"What is this?" he muttered to the woods. "Surely she is not in cahoots with those scoundrels."

Old Joe listened to whatever Adele said and then looked over at the carriage and nodded. She stepped back as he dismounted. She then led him over to the coach's door. Joseph climbed in, while Adele lingered outside. Thom surmised that Adele's mistress wanted the supposed bishop's blessing or needed to make a confession. Either possibility assured him. Adele was only doing her duty as a noblewoman's maid.

He wished he could walk over and converse with her again. Although he doubted that a lady's maid would have any true interest in a poor apprentice, she had at least been polite and pleasant. He rarely encountered women at Levitanus' remote home, except for a middle-aged farmer's wife who sold his master needed produce, and a pair of old hags who came by once a season to barter magical elements.

After another lingering stare at pretty Adele, he slipped away until it was time for his own group to depart. He had noticed Ned looking around and he had no desire to have the man spot him again.

Eric Loren

THREE

Through the Gates

It was almost midday when he came out of the shadowy woods, walking into the hazy sunshine as he approached the gates. There were already four people gathered before the guarded portal, including one man on horseback. The mounted fellow was most likely their guide. As he walked closer, Thom studied the group. There was a middle-aged monk holding the reins of a pack donkey who was trying to start a conversation with the guide, but it seemed he was only getting grunts for answers. There was also a bored-looking troubadour leaning against the gatehouse wall, taking advantage of the eaves' shade. Although the fellow wore no motley, Thom identified him by his harp case. He was a lanky fellow with a finely trimmed beard and a pair of gold earrings. He wore a deep red cloak that bespoke of wealthy patronage. The final person was a big man in plain clothes, whom Thom guessed to be a common laborer. That one stood closest to the gates, eyes forward, waiting patiently for the gates to open.

Thom decided to join the laborer. When he came near, they exchanged a nod but no words, which was just what Thom wanted. However, his peace was shattered soon enough when the monk came up to the two of them, leading his donkey between them and the gates. The fellow's black robe displayed a collection of travel stains and a frayed hem. His thin hair stuck out in all sorts of directions, but his smile was neat and large and genuine.

"Hello, men! I am Brother Francis and it appears that we will be traveling companions for the week. May I ask your names?"

"Thomas," he volunteered.

The laborer grunted and then said, "Orem the bricklayer. You'll get no coins from me, beggar monk, so don't bother trying."

Francis laughed. "I have no need of your coins, good sir." He patted the slight bulge of a belly. "As you can see, I am well-fed. And I'll have you know that my order never begs in Camelot, for the king is a generous patron. Have no fear, Bricklayer Orem; I don't covet your purse."

Orem gave another grunt and went back to watching the gate, so Francis turned his attention on Thom. "What is your profession, sir?"

It was a question Thom never liked to answer, for so many were superstitious toward magic. Sometimes he just lied, but this time he chose to give a partial answer. "I have no profession yet, Brother Francis. I am an apprentice to Master Levitanus."

"Still an apprentice? At your age? You don't seem dim-witted, so that could only mean one thing. You train in the magical arts, which means this master called Levitanus is a wizard."

Thom raised an eyebrow, surprised at the man's knowledge. The monk might look jolly and foolish, but he had a sharp mind to guess Thom's profession so quickly. Orem gave a puzzled look, but didn't ask for an explanation. Thom was thankful for that.

He gave the monk a slight nod, not wanting to discuss it further.

At least the brother seemed to understand his hesitancy, for he went on to another topic. "I am a monastic librarian, myself." He pointed at his beast. "My faithful Ears carries the latest donations to the Saint Barnabas library. It is a fine collection of books and scrolls that I cannot wait to study."

Thom eyed the well-covered load. The monk might be sloppy with his own attire, but he was assiduous in packing his books. Thom tried to think of something to keep the conversation going, or else the fellow might start asking about magic. "Did it take you long to acquire your load?"

"Not at all. A mere six months of weaseling and begging nobles to donate things that only gather dust in their manors. It is hard to understand why they cling to books that are mere gibberish to them, in languages they do not even speak, let alone read. The books are like talismans or trophies." He shook his head, and then looked over at Orem. "Be glad you don't have a handful of books on you, bricklayer, for then you'd truly see my begging talents."

Orem ignored him.

"Ears and I have traveled our share of miles, we have. We've endured storms and bandits and wild animals." Francis looked behind Thom. "Ah, here come some more of our party."

Thom turned to watch. A finely-dressed man strode toward them, a large pack slung over his back. He seemed out-of-place, as if he should have been on horseback instead of getting his shiny boots dusty. The fellow stopped halfway between them and the lazing troubadour. He didn't seem eager to join any of them.

Next came a large, heavyset merchant and his guard, each of them leading a burdened mule. The merchant had a grand beard, bushy yet perfectly trimmed. His guard was clean shaved, with a prominent scar on his left cheek. The hired sword walked with a limp but it didn't seem to slow him down. The merchant and his hired hand came to a stop at the back of the group. The big man fussed with the bindings on the mules' loads while his guard watched everyone. The mercenary neither smiled nor frowned, just watched.

Behind them all walked an old woman in neat but well-worn clothes. She led a pair of goats pulling a small cart. Bells hung from their collars, jangling with each hoof step. The cart's wooden wheels rumbled on the paving stones as she led her pair of beasties to join the waiting party.

Thom wondered why she traveled to Camelot, for she didn't seem like a typical tradeswoman.

"We'll have quite the assortment around the fire," said the monk, "but there is still one missing."

Thom gave him a quizzical look.

"The typical party has nine travelers and a guide. Maybe someone has overslept."

Just then, their guide rode to the fore and turned his horse to face all of them. He wore a wide-brimmed hat that shadowed most of his face. A short grizzled beard covered his jaw and upper lip. "I'm Jake and I'll guide you through to Camelot. You're to follow my instructions as we travel, for the Road doesn't allow folks to wander off. You're not to fall behind or try to rush ahead, for I set a good pace that'll get us to each Waycircle in proper time. I know the Road far better than any of you, for I've been guiding folks along her for nearly a decade now."

He paused to look them over. "Since no one here is a pretty lass, I've no interest in knowing your names or your life stories. Keep your gabbing to yourselves, for I'm not your new friend. Neither am I your servant, so don't try to order me around like some lackey. While on the Road of Leaves, I am in charge. No matter your station in life, the king has decreed that the Road guides rule while inside the wizards' enchantment. If you have a problem with that, then go find some other route to Camelot."

One of the clerks came out and walked over to Jake. The guide bent over in the saddle to catch the man's whispered comments. He gave a terse reply. The clerk hurried back inside, but not before giving Thom a quick glance.

Jake pulled off his hat, revealing a weathered countenance. He rubbed his face and then pulled his beard, before looking Thom's way. A callused finger aimed at him. "Magic is forbidden while on the Road. Is that understood?"

Thom nodded, disliking that he had been called out in front of the others.

The guide then looked around to sweep everyone else into the command. "No magics or potions, even from a healer-hag. The Road of Leaves is a powerful enchantment, so it reacts to other magic. She'll get mad at any competition, so to speak."

He met eyes with each person, waiting until they either spoke their agreement or nodded. Everyone did.

Jake then paused again, as if considering what else to share. "The last member of our party won't be coming, so we might as well start. Hand your wooden token to the gate guards as you pass through."

He turned his horse toward the gates and gave a nod to the men on watch. They pulled back the large crossbar and opened the twenty-foot-tall doors, revealing their route.

Beyond the gates lay a green glen surrounded by a ring of tall Whisper Pines still dripping from the morning's dew. Thom unconsciously took a step forward as the enchantment's sound grew louder to his inner ear. The complexity of the rhythm almost overwhelmed him. He recognized a few of the elements that had been used to craft this grand enchantment, but it was all so confusing. It wasn't loud; the sound of magical elements was never loud, which explained why most people didn't hear them. But to the trained ear, the enchantment gave off a symphony of muted sound.

"I have walked the Road many times, and yet it still awes me," said Francis to no one in particular.

"Everyone move forward," ordered Jake. "As you start on the road, look around and you will see your first Waycircle, for the road starts and ends in such circles."

"Half-circle, to be precise," corrected Francis in a whisper too low for the guide to overhear. "The Waycircles at either end are much smaller than those we'll be camping in during our trip."

Thom did not respond, for his focus centered on the magical land in front of him. As he passed through the gateway, the world seemed to shift and mist over. He felt the familiar tingle of passing through an enchantment's perimeter. The temperature dropped noticeably, feeling more like cool spring than a humid summer morn. He entered a living hall of green, the trees soaring skyward all around him. It was dim in here, yet it felt airy. The trees stood as straight as sentries and as close as the pickets on a fence for the first thirty feet of their soaring height. A man might be able to squeeze between the massive trunks, but no horse could. He could not help but stand there gawking up at the towering giants for a moment, breathing deeply of the cool, tree-scented air.

Behind him, the others passed into the enchantment and exclaimed at the tingling sensation.

"Keep moving," barked their guide from up ahead. "The magic will do you no harm."

Thom did as told, following Jake through an opening in the encircling trees, under a wide stone archway. Within the archway the air shimmered a grayish-silver, like some misty curtain. Once again, he felt a tingle as he passed through, but it was due to a change in the enchantment rather than crossing the magic's boundary. He did his best to block out the normal sounds of the travelers around him and listened to the magic. Its beat had changed into a steady, yet lively whisper. It sounded more like the rush of a waterfall, almost as if the Road were encouraging them to hurry on like water racing downstream.

He now walked on the actual Road of Leaves, a wide lane that meandered between the trees. He recognized some of the trees as being magical: Gold Oaks, Royal Birches, Tertullian Sycamores, and even a few Blood Rowans. All were rare, but they seemed an integral part of the enchantment. Between them stood other, mundane trees, forming the leafy tunnel that would be their route for next few days. Magic hummed all around him, in the trees and from an invisible shield just beyond their trunks. The fact that he could hear the trees' magic told them that each tree was wounded somehow.

Stepping close to a Royal Birch, he spotted the circle of taps hammered in at eye level, each one dripping sap. Instead of flowing into catch buckets, the sap trickled down the trunk along hardened amber rivulets. The tree's magical essence was exposed this way, providing its element to Merlin's enchantment. Thom stepped back, admiring how the trees were being used as an ongoing source of magic. Standing in the middle of the route, he slowly spun around to look and listen to all the magical trees giving their sap for the Road's magic.

"He told us to keep moving," muttered the trader, coming to a halt behind Thom. The man shifted his large knapsack on his shoulders, waiting. When Thomas didn't move fast enough for him, the man stepped past. The way was wide, so the trader's pausing had been more of a subtle rebuke of Thom's dallying than because the Road was blocked.

A bit embarrassed, Thom started walking again, keeping to the side even though the Road was wide enough for two carriages to pass each other. As he strode along the Road, he became nearly mesmerized by it. Leaves covered the path, showing the fall colors of brown, gray, yellow, and rust even though most of the trees overhead were still in summer-green foliage. He kicked at the debris and it scattered, but that only revealed more leaves underneath. He heard the pulsing of active magic coming up from the leafy debris, so much power that he had the sudden desire to drop to the ground and roll in it, to cover himself with the leaves like a blanket of magic. He fought off the urge, knowing it would look foolish and would probably anger their guide, but he kept staring at the ground.

Never before had the detritus of trees felt so alive to him.

Levitanus had taught him about using the bark, sap, or roots of magical trees, but he had never heard about using leafy litter as part of an enchantment. It intrigued him. Thom noticed crushed leaves from where Jake's horse had stepped and wondered how often new leaves replaced those trampled. Unaware, he drifted closer to the center of the Road in his desire to look at the leaves stepped on by the guide's horse. He could not help but stop again, bending over to pick up a whole yellow sycamore leaf. It felt like a normal fallen leaf in his hand, even crumbling like one, but his inner ear heard the magic contained in it, the pulse still alive even though the magical tree had discarded it some time ago. He dropped the crumbled mess and watched the pieces drift back on top of all the others.

"Can you hear Merlin's magic?" asked Brother Francis.

Thom finally looked up. "Can't you? The magic is so strong that it distracts me. It pulses like a heartbeat. I can hear it in the trees to either side and in the debris on the road. It is especially strong among the fallen leaves."

"Most people are deaf to such things," said Francis. "Could you do something like this Road enchantment with your magic?"

Thom shook his head. "Not I. You mistake me for a master magician. I am nothing more than an apprentice, but should I ever reach the level of master I still doubt I'd be able to do anything like this. I suspect that there are few wizards capable of crafting such a complex enchantment." Thom shook his head in wonder. "I can't even imagine where to begin on such a huge undertaking. It would be like trying to empty a lake with a spoon or trying to rope a cloud."

Francis laughed. "I think Merlin has done both of those."

Thom nodded. Besides the Short Roads, there were only two other ways to reach Camelot, which were the Road of Waters, traveled by boat, and the Road of Clouds, which only wizards could walk. Merlin's enchantment encompassed the whole city, so that it never stayed in the same location for long. One month, Camelot might be sitting close to some vassal lord's town, connected by the pair of Short Roads, and the next month it could be a hundred miles away, connected to some other town. Thom thought it an extravagant use of magic that must require the help of many magicians to maintain. And yet, King Arthur deserved such extravagant protection, for he had united the land and brought it peace.

The merchant interrupted Thom's thoughts.

"Get to one side, if you're going to just stand there. Make way. Every trip it's the same, someone who has never seen the Road before gapes at the place like a simpleton." He pushed past them, leading his laden mule. Right behind him strode his guard with the second animal. At their heels came the musician.

Road of Leaves

"Bumpkins," muttered the troubadour as he walked past, caressing the gold ring in his right ear. "You would think you had never seen a leaf before."

Thom realized that they were almost at the back of the group now, with only the goat woman still behind them. He started walking again, as did the monk. "Do you know what happens to anyone who falls too far behind?"

"During the day? I would think nothing much except an angry rebuke from the guide," replied Francis, "but at night that would be a different story. I don't think anyone has lived through a shifting of the leaves."

"Has anyone ever been able to leave the Road?" he asked, pointing off into the dense woods.

The monk shrugged. "I have never heard or read of it. You should know more about magic than I do, but I have read that the Road has invisible walls preventing anyone from wandering off its route and stopping any from trying to sneak onto it. The only area where the enchantment is somewhat open is overhead. It lets in sunshine and wind and rain, but it does filter things somehow. The temperature is always autumn-like along the Road, no matter what it's like out there. The snow turns to a cool rain when it falls on the Road, even if there's a harsh blizzard outside. I suppose a person could try to climb in, but I would expect that the wizards' magic would catch the sneak in mid-air."

Thom nodded agreement, for that made sense from what little he knew of the greater enchantments. It would be like a bug falling into a spider's web and most likely just as deadly.

They walked on for a time in silence. Thom listened with his outer ears to the Road around him. Overhead, the trees whispered and sighed in a breeze, while beneath his boots the leaves crunched with each step. The breeze only grazed the tree crowns, not reaching any of the travelers. No winds ever did during the day. Thom knew that much. It was at night that the winds came, stirring up the leaves and moving the Road to a new location. His master had told him that the Road of Leaves never crossed the same countryside twice; it always chose a new route. Thom wondered if the magical trees moved with the leafy roadbed or if the enchantment found a new line of trees as its anchor points. He wondered, but doubted that he would learn the truth anytime soon, for he was just an apprentice who still had decades more of training ahead of him. So much of this magic was beyond his comprehension.

Thom listened some more and heard the sounds of his fellow travelers, especially the ringing bells hanging on the nanny goats. What he did not hear were birds or squirrels, for they apparently avoided the unnaturalness of the area. It was quiet in here when Thom ignored the whispered rhythms of magic.

* * *

Thom wasn't certain when they left the confines of the narrow valley, but the Road of Leaves began to wander, going over or around hillocks, so that he often lost sight of Guide Jake riding at the fore. The surrounding forest was still dense, hiding most of the countryside beyond the Road.

He walked alongside the monk, finding the man's company enjoyable. As they walked, Francis talked, even though Thom was often too distracted to listen. Thom caught only some of the details as his companion shared tales about the various estates he had visited during his latest manuscript hunt. If the monk noticed Thom's lack of attention, he was probably too polite to mention it.

The Road enchantment kept distracting him. In truth, his master had explained that although the Roads had been Merlin's idea, it took dozens of magicians to originally craft them and still more to keep the enchantments going. Levitanus had even mentioned the Founders who were the keystones of the Roads, although he never told Thomas their names except for Merlin's.

He found himself daydreaming about what it must have been like to participate in such a vast enchantment, for this stretched over an ever-changing number of vales and hills. What part of the magic would he have crafted if he had been a master in those days? Would he have been responsible for one enchantment covering the length of the Road or would he have been responsible for a mixture of enchantments in one specific area?

While Thom wondered quietly, Francis kept talking. He probably would have talked even if the mule were his only companion.

They passed most of the afternoon that way, the monk chattering as they hiked at a steady pace. Jake rode back twice to make sure that no one had fallen too far behind, but neither time did he say much. The goat woman remained out-of-sight, somewhere behind them, yet they knew she was still there from the sound of the goats' bells.

At times, the forest around them thinned enough to let in streams of light but Thom never saw any meadows or fields, let alone any settlements. He wondered if the Road of Leaves actually crossed the countryside or if it ran its entire length in some magical world of its own. Finally, he asked the monk what he thought.

"Oh, the Road crosses through normal lands. That much I know, for I have seen it shimmering in the distance a few times during my travels. There are tales of common folks stumbling on it, flattening their noses against the barrier. One story tells of a virtuous knight crashing through to the Road in pursuit of a dragon, but that tale seems woven from mist instead of solid thread. I doubt that anyone can enter the Road anywhere along its length, but you still might see it if you travel much. Maybe you will, during your time as a journeyman magician. As for coming close enough to touch the Road from the outside, I would compare the task to trying to catch a rainbow."

The monk gestured broadly at their surroundings. "While walking on the leaves, you will see some settled lands, but always at a distance. You will never get close enough to distinctly recognize any person or particular farm, though you might recognize some village from afar. To those outside, the Road seems to be a ghostly thing, ever on the horizon and never in the same location from day-to-day."

Francis looked over his shoulder. "Maybe we should pick up our pace, for those annoying bells seem to be getting louder. Goats are not the best of musicians."

Thom smiled agreement and they sped up. However, they had not walked much further when a sudden shudder went through the Road's magic, a jarring of the rhythmic beat. Thom spun around to stare back down the way. "Did you hear that?"

Francis had also stopped to look back. "What happened?"

The shudder repeated and then seemed to rush towards them, growing louder. "It's coming this way," warned Thom, pulling out his belt knife. He would have taken out his magician's box too, but dared not try any magic in here.

"What is it, mage? Is it some magical beast you sense?" The monk had a wooden cudgel in hand.

Thom did not answer, for he was too focused on the disturbance rushing through the enchantment's weave.

Eric Loren

FOUR

Windstorm

Thom's heart beat rapidly with fear as he heard the discordance surge through the Road's enchantment, a disturbance rapidly approaching and growing more distinct to his inner ear. He feared that something awful was happening to the magic and wanted to escape it. He wasn't too proud to run, but he knew it would be folly to do so, like turning your back on a robber. So he stood his ground.

He began to hear a roaring sound with his outer ears now and recognized it as the sound of wind. Just wind, but that signified much on this enchanted roadway. "Wind? Is this normal on the Road?"

"No," replied Francis, staring intensely down the roadway as if he too could hear the magic's discord. "The winds are supposed to happen only at night, when the Road of Leaves shifts its location."

Thom swallowed his rising fear. Their guide had been clear that no one could survive through the nightly winds. "Where can we find refuge?"

"We're still hours from Bright Meadow Waycircle. Whatever is happening, we'll have to face it out on the Road."

Thom felt a breeze on his face now. He stared down the leaf-littered path, and saw a few of the leaves stirring. With his inner ear, he tried to make sense of the changing sounds of magic but failed to hear any rhythm. All of it worried him. He had the sudden fear that something more than wind might be approaching. It was said that magical beasts were attracted to the Road's enchantment. What if some monster was stalking their way, affecting the Road as it approached? He tightened his grip on the knife as he waited.

His inner ear filled with a jarring noise as the disturbance surged through the magic. The breeze stiffened and leaves began to move around his feet. He looked over at the monk, but the man didn't notice his gaze. Francis stared at what was coming. Thom looked back down the Road, wondering if he should run after all.

Then it came. A wind roared at them, funneling up the Road and whipping up its bed of magical leaves. In a rush, the winds swept over him and suddenly he could see nothing but leaves. Frantic, Thom stabbed out in all directions but hit nothing except air. He slashed at the flying leaves repeatedly, to no effect.

"Stop! Thomas! Stop!" Francis called again and again, desperation in his voice.

At last, he heard the monk over the roar of the wind. Heart still hammering, he stopped his slashing and allowed Francis to get close. The man was fighting with his balking donkey, but still he took the effort to approach.

"It is the Road itself that you sense!" yelled the monk into his ear. "The Road of Leaves is shifting! We must run to the next Waycircle!"

The windstorm lessened its frenetic swirling, becoming a steady blowing. The roadbed of leaves reacted to the wind, abandoning the right edge of the road and shifting to the left. The Road was moving.

The monk wrestled with Ears, for the beast still tried to break free. Francis called out again. "The Road shifts! We must flee!"

Suddenly, Thom heard bells rushing toward him and he thought of the Goat Woman. "What about the old one behind us? We must help her flee too!"

Francis nodded agreement. "It sounds like she will be on us soon!"

The goats came around the bend, running at them with their cart bouncing behind them. Their owner was nowhere in sight.

They let the animals charge past, making no attempt to stop their mad run. "We need to find her!" shouted Thom.

The monk frowned with concern, but nodded.

They headed back down the Road, fighting their way through the brutal wind. Ears brayed his objections, but let his master lead him. Francis held the donkey's lead in one hand and a cudgel in the other.

Thom looked for the elderly woman, leaning into the wind as he worked his way back along the Road. He searched along the path and among the trees to either side, expecting to find her collapsed somewhere. The Road seemed more twisted now, but he assumed that was an effect of the swirling debris.

Behind him, Francis called out, "Goat Woman! Where are you? Shout out for help! Woman, where are you?"

A branch crashed down, barely missing Thom. He stepped past it and kept going. All the while, the monk stayed with him, helping him search. They traveled back almost a quarter-mile and still did not find her.

Francis grabbed Thom's shoulder to stop him. "She's gone! If we don't find shelter soon, we'll also be lost!"

Thom gritted his teeth, not wanting to desert anyone. He was about to object, when Guide Jake rode up.

Jake reined in his horse. "Run, you fools! We must get to Bright Meadow

Waycircle!"

"But the Goat Woman," protested Thom. "We must find her!"

"There is no time! Run or die!" He glared at them through the swirling leaves, his horse dancing nervously.

Thom did not want to abandon the woman to this freak storm, for he never wanted to desert any woman. He was still haunted with the childhood memory of watching his mother flee into a rainstorm to get away from his drunken father. He never saw his mother again and, although he had only been five at the time, he still remembered his anger and feelings of helplessness. No woman should have to die alone in a storm.

Francis tugged on Thom's sleeve. "We must go! We will be of no help getting lost ourselves!"

Thom wanted to pull away, but the monk would not release him. Francis yanked him along the road.

With a sob, he finally gave in and started running with the monk. Tears ran down his cheeks as he and Francis staggered along the Road that was shifting beneath their feet.

Their guide yelled at them to keep going, but he did not stay with them. With a fearful look at the chaos all around, Jake ordered them to keep running and then rode off at a gallop.

* * *

They did not catch up with Jake again until they staggered upon the next Waycircle. Two stone archways stood over the Road. Between them, a third archway opened to the left. What lay beyond that opening was obscured by a gray curtain-like sheen. That was the entrance to Bright Meadow Waycircle. Jake stood inside that haven while leaning only his upper torso out into the roadway, his hand grasping the stone column for support against the wind's fury. He shouted his encouragement but he didn't come out to help them.

Thom and Francis lurched past him and through the grayish shimmer. They fell to their knees on the gentle grass within the refuge, as Jake followed them inside and stood over them. Both Thom and Francis bled from being hit by flying debris. In exhausted relief, the two hugged each other. The monk had dropped his donkey's lead, so Ears trotted over to an animal trough and began drinking thirstily.

It took some time for Thom to get his breath back. A new guide offered him a waterskin, which he eagerly took. The water was cool and refreshing as it slipped down his throat. He did not even wonder about this new face for a time, but then looked about and realized that another party had joined theirs.

"Let me help you to the fire," said the new guide. This man was shorter and heavier when compared to Jake, but with a face just as weathered.

Thom let him assist, for he found his legs wobbly from all the running. He was led over to the fire circle where all the other travelers huddled. The smells food cooking and acrid smoke tickled his nose. He noticed that Jake was helping Francis over to the same fire.

They sat near the blaze and accepted cups of stew, obeying the order to eat. Thom did so without comment, too exhausted to thank whoever shared the food. Francis was also quiet.

Thom was just calming down when Jake stepped between him and the fire. The guide's shadow covered Thom like a hawk over a mouse.

"What did you do, magician? Tell me now." Jake's anger was obvious. Though his arms were crossed, his fingers flexed as if anxious to wrap around Thom's throat.

Thom did not understand the question, so he stared up at him in confusion.

Jake swung his open hand, slapping Thom so hard that he fell backward. "Out with it! What did you do to the Road of Leaves?"

"I did nothing," he answered, glaring up at the man. He touched his stinging jaw.

The other guide held Jake back. "Careful, or he may use his magic again."

"I used no magic," protested Thom, scrambling to stand. "I wouldn't do such a thing."

He looked around and realized that everyone was staring at him. He saw no sympathy, only fear and anger.

"If not you, then who?" asked the other guide.

Thom was at a loss for an answer. He just stood there, gaping at the accusation.

Many of the other travelers began to mutter as they finally realized what the guides suspected Thom had done.

"He did no magic or sorcery," said Francis, wearily rising to his feet. "I was with him on the Road and would certainly have noticed. I give you my word, as a man of God, that Apprentice Thomas did no enchantments."

He stood up and hobbled over to stand next to Thom, resting a hand on his shoulder. "He sensed something behind us and warned me, but he did nothing to cause it. When the winds came, his first thought was for the elderly woman on the road behind us. He insisted on going back for her and he didn't want to stop the search even as tree limbs came crashing down around us. Look elsewhere for the cause of this."

"Who do you want us to blame?" asked the troubadour, joining the argument. He and others were now standing behind the two guides. "Should we blame your donkey? I think not. That man is the only magician in our party. Maybe we should throw him back out there."

Thom started backing away from the crowd. "I'd die out there."

"You shall do no such thing, troubadour," replied the merchant's guard, suddenly speaking up. He stepped between Thom and the performer. "Are you a murderer or a musician? I'll have no part in killing this fellow just because you're a scared little girl, harp player. Sacrificing him won't calm the winds any."

Jake apparently had a change of heart, for he turned to the people gathered behind him and motioned for them to disperse. "Leave him be. We may need him to do some magic if the Road does not calm down."

"That's the truth," muttered the other guide. "I can't wait to ride out of here tomorrow."

"Should we turn around?" asked the well-dressed man from Thom's group. "No grain deal is worth my life."

Jake seemed to consider it for a moment, brushing his beard as he thought, but then shook his head. "The Road knows when too many are going in a single direction. It knows and gets angry. There is a reason why parties cannot exceed ten in number."

"Your party must go on," agreed the second guide, appearing relieved that he was only a half-day's walk from an exit.

"The winds are still howling out there," said a man from the other party. "Can any of us leave tomorrow?"

"We will," said the man's guide. "Those are the normal winds of night that you hear now; the same winds we have heard for the last seven nights. They always start with evening and become their most fierce by midnight. Whatever disturbed the Road today, I know the Road will move away from it during the night."

Jake nodded in agreement. "Aye, the Road takes care of herself."

The guides urged everyone to finish their dinner and then find a place to bed down for the night. Jake ordered Thom to stay close to the fire so that the guides could watch him while he slept. Thom complied, though the brightness made it harder to sleep.

Jake offered no apology for his accusations. Thom doubted he ever would.

* * *

Thom dreamt of Adele that night, of holding her hand and even kissing her lips. It was a dream he didn't want to leave, for no woman would be so attentive to him in real life. However, the dream fled before the clamor of bells.

He woke to the wet nibble of a goat rather than a lady's kiss.

"Get up, magician," ordered a harsh voice.

Thom opened his eyes, pushed the nasty goat aside, and stared up at Jake. The sky behind Jake was already blue-gray with the coming of morning. Seeing that the guide was about to kick him, Thom rolled to the side and then sprang to his feet.

"I have two goats here that I can't leave behind, so you're going to lead them."

"Me? I know nothing about goats." Thom frowned at the two animals still tethered to their cart.

"Yes you, magician, and don't try removing those bells, for they will help me to know where you are." Jake walked away, leaving the beasts to Thomas.

A smiling Brother Francis strolled over nibbling on a large onion. He held out another to Thom. He took it with thanks as he sat down on the grass to pull on his boots. He had just put the onion down when one of the goats quickly snatched it away. The other goat protested and grabbed for Thom's blanket in revenge. Thom yanked back his blanket, but was not about to try reclaiming the onion.

The monk laughed. "Sorry, Thomas, but I don't have enough to share with your new family."

"I've lost my appetite, anyway." He stood up again and then set hands on hips as he stared at the Goat Woman's team. "What am I going to do with two?"

"They can be useful animals, if you like goat milk or goat cheese." The monk eyed their udders. "But these two may have dried up like the leaves on the Road. If so, then about the only thing they can still do is flavor a stew."

Thom was glad that he wouldn't have to try milking the beasties. It would be work enough to lead them along the Road. Well, at least he could make them carry his pack for him. He rolled up his blanket and tied it to his pack, and then went around to the back of the cart. He noticed that the Goat Woman's things were askew.

"The guides already pawed through her things," explained Francis, "looking for anything of value. It appears that she was a trader in herbs, vegetables, and powders, which didn't interest them."

Thom studied the load as he straightened it and was surprised to find some of the rarer herbs that his master used for medicinal tonics and poultices. Curious, he looked inside one of the bottom crates and was greeted by a swelling of magical sound when he lifted its lead-lined lid. His inner ear heard the distinct sounds of an array of magical elements. It startled him enough to straighten up and look around, but no one except Francis paid him any attention. The crate was like an oversized magician's box, holding overlarge vials- more vials than even his master Levitanus kept at the house. Had the woman been some kind of wizardess or just a dealer in exotic wares? Thom didn't know.

"What is that you've found?" asked the monk, walking over and looking over the side of the cart.

Thom paused, not sure how much to reveal, for it was a fortune's worth of magical powders and liquids.

"Those look like magical vials," added Francis in a whisper.

Thom closed the lid quickly to dampen the magical noise, wondering if the monk was one of those who could hear magic. "You are right; they are magical powders. The Goat Woman may have looked poor, but her wares must have cost more than a commoner's lifelong wages. Why would she be traveling with so much stock?"

"Obviously, you weren't the only one in our party on their way to Clas Myrddin," replied Brother Francis. "Wouldn't that be the place to sell magical supplies?"

Thom nodded, for the guild house would be the place to go if you were selling magical elements, yet somethings still didn't fit. "How did she acquire such a huge cache of magical elements? It would take me years to harvest so much, even if I knew where to go and how to properly render down each magical plant or beast."

"Or magical being," muttered Francis.

"What do you mean?"

"Is it rumored that some also render down magical beings for their elements, like merfolk or pixies."

Thom's eyes widened. "You think she might have been a dealer in the dark arts?"

Francis replied with his own question, "Did you hear anything in there that came from such a being?"

"I…I don't know. I didn't study everything in there, but I would say about half those vials hold elements that I didn't recognize."

Francis nodded but still frowned, obviously not assured by Thom's answer.

"Did she ever tell you her trade?"

Francis shook his head. "I never had the chance to talk with her. Frankly, I thought she was merely some crone moving to live with her eldest son."

"I talked with her."

They both turned towards the deeper voice. It was the merchant's guard, who come up on them rather quietly. The fellow came even closer, his limp a bit more pronounced this morning after running so much yesterday.

"She said that she was going to Camelot to start a new business, but didn't say what kind. I also heard her call the goats Nibble and Dribble, though don't ask me which one is which." The big fellow gave Thom a nod and then went to start loading his employer's mules.

Once the mercenary was away, Francis whispered some final advice. "I would suggest keeping those magical supplies well hidden. The guides must have seen them when they snooped through the old lady's things but they would have no idea what they were. If they learn you have a wizard's worth of supplies, they might expect you to perform like one too."

That gave Thom pause. He had no idea what to do with most of those powders. If they pressured him into crafting with them, he would likely cause an explosion that would kill himself and any nearby. "I think I will do as you suggest, for I'd rather not die today."

Francis nodded. "And don't worry about them tempting me, for I abhor magic. Not that I dislike you, you understand, but I do not like your chosen trade." He paused a moment, then looked over at a bleating goat and smiled. "I also do not like your temporary profession as a driver of goats either."

Thom looked at them also, crestfallen at his new role. "How do I even get these mangy things to move?"

Brother Francis shook his head. "Your choices are to either lure them with a treat or threaten them with a beating." He clapped Thom on the back. "Trust your instincts and you'll be a goat herder soon enough. Now excuse me, for I need to get my books packed on Ears."

The monk walked off, leaving Thom alone with the beasties. The two nannies eyed him suspiciously, their furry chins moving as they munched on grass.

"I never liked bearded women," he muttered.

He pulled out one of his plums and tried luring them forward, but they just chewed their grass and stared at him. Frustrated, he pocketed the plum and went to find a good stick.

FIVE

Shifting Leaves

Bright Meadow Waycircle lived up to its name once the sun's rays broke through the surrounding ring of tall evergreens. The light revealed rich grasses sprinkled with colorful flowers. Thom was not the only person tempted to linger here, for it was so calm after yesterday's windstorm. However, the guides were insistent that both walking groups needed to get an early start. The two parties stepped out onto a now docile Road and then went in opposite directions. Many in Thom's group looked over their shoulders with envy at the other party, but the guides hadn't allowed anyone to switch groups.

Jake had them marching at a fast pace and ignored any who dared to protest. His wrath fell the most on Thom for not getting the goats to behave. It took plenty of cajoling and cursing by the apprentice to get the beasties headed in the right direction. Even then, they needed regular prodding to keep moving. The animals didn't appreciate having a new master.

Thomas quickly realized that the others were avoiding him. He suspected that they thought him guilty of yesterday's storm and Goat Woman's disappearance. Everyone kept well ahead of him, speeding up whenever the goat bells warned of his approach.

Even Francis seemed to avoid him, leaving him to a lonely walk.

When Jake finally let them stop for a midday rest, Thom wrangled the goats to a halt. He stayed well away from the others in his party, but they still cast the occasional glare in his direction. Tired, he retrieved his pack from the cart and sat down among the leaves. Exploring his supplies, he found the carrots and started munching one, while handing out two more to the beasties.

They ate greedily and then eyed him for more.

"No more from me, Nibble and Dribble. Try some of the grasses at the Road's edge."

One of them tried to bite into his pack, but he yanked it away. "Enough of that!" He quickly pulled out two more carrots and surrendered them.

Sighing, he realized that he needed to find something heartier for his charges, so he got back to his feet and returned to the cart. He felt hesitant about using any of the Goat Woman's supplies, but he had no other resources. Going through the common vegetables in the top crates, he found a few more offerings and gave them over to the goats. They ate quickly and then one bleated for more, but he ignored it. The two were just being greedy now.

When Jake ordered them to start walking again, Francis waited until Thom caught up with him.

"I thought you detested the bells," said Thom.

The monk shrugged. "The clanging is less harsh than some tongues in our group."

"I suspect most of it is aimed in my direction. Does everyone blame me for yesterday?"

Francis ignored the question to ask his own. "Have you heard any more disturbances in the magic?"

Thom shook his head. "No, why do you ask?"

"We have not yet seen any other travelers on the Road. Today we should encounter one riding party and one on foot, but neither has appeared. In the winter there are gaps in the flow, but not now."

That worried the magician's apprentice, for if more had vanished then he would surely be blamed again. "Has our guide said anything about this?"

"Nothing, but he also said nothing about the original missing member of our party, the one who died at the Royal Oak. He is a taciturn one, that Jake."

It took Thom a moment to understand what the monk had just said. "What did you say? There was another death even before we entered the Road of Leaves?"

The monk nodded. "Murdered in his bed. I overheard the innkeeper reporting it to a gate guard. Something stirs, mage, and I confess that it worries me and it has sharpened my prayers. I have been beseeching the Lord, almost hourly, to deliver us safely to Camelot."

* * *

A little later, they finally encountered another party, a mounted party of three. They were nobles, though their once-fine attire was now sullied and torn. Thom came as close to the others in his party as he dared, for he wanted to hear their tale.

"Where is your guide?" asked Jake, setting his horse across the Road to stop the men from riding past.

"That fool? He lingers somewhere behind us," answered the oldest-looking of the trio. "He insisted on waiting when another's horse went lame, but we would have none of that. We want out of this accursed magical way. Let us through."

Instead, Jake moved his horse to block their attempt to ride around him. "You need to wait, for the Road doesn't like isolated travelers. If you get too far ahead of your guide, the leaves will stir."

"As if they have not already," dismissed another of the nobles. "Get aside, man, or I will tell the king of your interference."

Thom heard muttered protests among his fellow walkers, but none dared to speak up against a noble. Only Jake did, because he had the king's law on his side.

"What I do, I do in the king's name," replied Jake. "We'll wait here until your guide catches up."

One of the lords pulled free his sword, but the older one held up a restraining hand and then replied to Jake, "We shall tarry, but only for an hour. If Guide Horace does not appear, then we go on without him. I will not let the sun get low while on this cursed road. Not after what happened yesterday."

Jake nodded agreement and moved his horse away from the nobles, but he did not get out of the saddle until they did.

Francis stepped closer to Thom and whispered, "Most likely, his lordship peed in his pants yesterday. I don't blame him for not wanting that to happen again."

The apprentice smiled, but he looked around to make sure none besides the goats and donkey overheard the joke.

It was an awkward time waiting for the rest of the riders, for none of the commoners felt free to talk in the presence of their betters and the nobles were too peeved for any banter. Finally, the rest of their party caught up. They were now nine in number, with two men riding double while leading a limping mare. Thom wondered if they had departed one short of the usual ten, or if they had lost someone.

The guides talked briefly, away from everyone else, and then the two groups parted. The horsemen rode off at a canter, pressing the lame animal to her limits, while the walkers continued at a steady trot.

A puffing Francis stayed close to the magician's apprentice and his bell-ringing nannies. His nearness worried Thom, for maybe the monk was expecting more trouble today. Francis also seemed to be muttering under his breath. Thom realized the fellow must be praying, and hoped the interceding worked.

* * *

They had been walking another two hours when Thom heard a disturbance in the Road's magic. It was faint, as if far ahead of them. Some element seemed out of balance, like an off-beat drummer. It caused the rest of the enchantment to sound a bit odd. He listened intently with his inner ear, but the discord soon faded.

"I think something stirs," he shared with Francis. "It's ahead of us this time."

The monk frowned, looking off into the distance as if he had heard it too. "You should warn our guide. Tell him now, so that he can't accuse you of hiding something from him. Let the goats walk on their own; I will keep an eye on them."

Thom nodded, though he did not want to face Jake again. He hadn't forgiven the man for his threats and accusations. With a grimace, he hurried his pace to catch up with the guide. As he strode up to the front of their party, he strove to calm his feelings. He would report quickly and then get back to his place.

Jake greeted him with an accusing tone. "What are you doing here, magician? You have goats to tend."

Thom controlled the biting remark he wanted to say. "I'll make this brief. Something disturbs the magic of the Road again. This time it is happening further up the Road." With that, he turned away from the rude man and started walking back.

"Wait! Tell me more, magician. Is this like what happened yesterday? Should we turn back or try to race to our next shelter?"

He stopped walking and looked over his shoulder, meeting the man's eyes. "I can't tell how far away this is or which way to flee, but I would rather not linger on the Road too long. I would say take us to whichever Waycircle is closest."

Jake grimaced and tugged at an ear. "To Stony Hill, then. God, why must this happen when I have such a slow party?" The guide shook his head and looked the others, who were pressing close. "We must quicken our pace, for this is no stroll in the queen's garden. The Road stirs early again and I don't want to be caught in its wrath. Anyone who falls behind can bed in the leaves tonight, for all I care.

"Merchant, you and your man set the pace with those mules. You've walked the Road often enough; I trust you not to panic. I'll make sure we have no stragglers."

The race began, for no one wanted to be left behind. Thom had to use his switch regularly just to keep the goats at a trot. The experience made all three of them surly.

An hour later, just as the trees began to stir in a new wind, they met another party on foot. The two groups passed each other without stopping. Only the guides talked, and they did so away from the others.

Another hour went by, with Thom sweating from the pace and the work of keeping the nannies moving. Jake rode back, as he had many times already, and asked if the magician's apprentice sensed any more trouble with the magic.

"Only the disturbance ahead of us. It seems closer, but not around the next bend." The magical symphony ahead of them still suffered from a jarring disharmony; it was faint, but the rhythm was definitely off.

"Anything else?"

Thom was shaking his head no, when something did happen. He looked behind them, trying to see it.

"Bad?" asked Jake.

"It sounds much like yesterday's storm," admitted Thom, "and almost as close."

"Move it, everyone!" yelled Jake. "Run! I'll not have us caught on a shifting Road again."

It became a mad dash for Stony Hill Waycircle. As they ran, a breeze hit them in the face, something stirred by whatever had happened ahead of them. Beneath their feet, the leaves stirred.

Thom swatted at the goats with his stick. "Come on, Nibble and Dribble. Run, you beasties. Run." Whether it was his persuading blows or the blowing wind, the pair decided to run. The cart's edge hit him as they sprang forward, knocking him to the side. Thom rubbed his hip and then ran after the goats.

At first, he was running into a stiff breeze, but then the breeze died off. The leaves swirled before settling and a stronger wind began to push on his back. Thom's inner ear filled with a growing noise from behind and he expected another windstorm to engulf him soon. He fought off the urge to run even faster, to abandon the animals, for that would only exhaust him too early. He needed to endure until he could escape into another Waycircle, so he stayed with his charges and ran with the rest of his party, right behind Ears.

The wind strengthened more, sending leaves rushing past Thom. The air seemed to be urging him to speed up. The wind's voice rose from a whisper to a chaotic shout that never ceased. His ears filled with that constant roar, so much so that he could no longer hear things with his inner ear.

"Only one more mile!" shouted Jake, urging them to run faster.

Thom did his best to hurry the goats. His heart beat fast within his chest, his breathing labored, and he thought again of abandoning the animals. The only reason he did not was his fear that Jake would force him go back and retrieve the pair.

The entrance to the Waycircle suddenly appeared ahead, the stone archways noticeable even with all the debris flying in the air. Everyone sprinted toward the refuge, with even the animals finding new stamina to speed up. They ran under the first archway and then turned to rush through the gray shimmer into the shelter.

Thom almost fell as he stumbled into the Waycircle as the wind's constant pushing suddenly ended. The roaring had also stopped, making it seem as silent as a tomb. The others around him gasped, coughed, or just sighed. Someone let out a ragged cheer. They had made it to safety.

He looked around the brush-covered place, finding the refuge much larger than last night's stop. The land rose from where they stood, slowly climbing toward the center where a tall hill stood- a rocky hill, thick with tall trees. There were many corrals around the foot of the hill, ready to receive those traveling through. He noticed another party was already encamped on the left side of the mount. These people looked up at their arrival, but none approached.

"To the right, folks. We will camp in the area to the right," said Jake, sounding calm again. "Follow me."

Their guide led them up a well-worn path, through the brush, to a grassy area at the foot of the hill. He assigned enclosures for the two mules, the donkey, and the goats. "Keep the animals away from the stream or else they'll dirty the waters. Just get them into their pens."

Thom had some trouble coaxing the nannies inside their enclosure, but he finally succeeded. He then labored to unharness them. When Nibble (or was it Dribble?) tried to feed on the cart's contents, he realized that he needed to push the cart out of their reach. The goats almost escaped during that struggle, but the merchant's guard and Francis gave him some much-needed assistance. The guard gave the cart a mighty yank while Francis chased the goats back.

"My sincere thanks to both of you," said Thom with a sigh, leaning against the gate. He jumped with a yelp when a goat bit him through the slats.

Francis laughed. "They're angry that you took away their king's feast."

Rubbing his buttocks, Thom glared at the offending nanny. "I was going to offer them some of the vegetables, but now the ungrateful wretches will have to make do with the grasses." He tried to look at his backside. "They did not tear my trousers, did they? Can you see any rip?"

"I look at no man's butt," declared the guard, walking off. His limp didn't slow his retreat. The man wanted to get away from any butt inspection.

Francis laughed even more, wiping away tears of amusement. "Thank you, Thomas. I needed a good laugh after that harrowing run."

"But what of my trousers?"

"They seem fine." The monk wiped again at his wet cheeks. "Now, I need to unburden poor Ears and get him fed and watered. Thank God, my donkey has the patience of Job. You should care for your animals too. Water your girls and give them some vegetables in spite of their rude manners, for they ran well for you today." Still chuckling, the brother walked to the enclosure where his donkey grazed contentedly, despite its large load of books.

With another sigh, Thom saw the wisdom in the monk's advice and set off to fetch some water for his charges.

* * *

The sun was just starting to set as the travelers sat around their shared campfire. Thom was sucking clean the leg bone of a chicken, when the sound of riders distracted him. He stood up, absently tossing the bone into the fire pit, and shielded his eyes from the light. Barely, he made out five horses and their six passengers. He saw one horse stagger and then collapse, throwing its rider. The horse with two passengers also stumbled, causing its extra rider to fall off, but the horse kept its legs under it.

Jake reacted immediately, running over to help.

"I think some others will have greater need of my leftover chicken," remarked Francis to Thom. "Why don't you go help Jake, while I warm up the remains. Take Guard Marcus with you. Tell Jake that I will have some food ready for them."

Thom and the merchant's hired sword set off running while the rest of their party just sat and watched. In spite of his limp, Marcus easily set the pace as they ran down the dirt path.

As he approached, Thom heard hysterical sobbing. A woman in the party was trying to turn her horse back toward the Road but others were restraining her. He recognized her as one of the few women that had been lazing about the Royal Oak's common room the other day.

"Let me go! Take your hands off my horse! Do you not understand? He is still out there in that horrible wind. I must go back and find him."

She must have lost a loved one on the way in, thought Thom. He avoided that drama and instead went over to nearest of the two people who had been thrown. His healing skills were limited, but maybe he could offer some help here. The first thrown rider lay on the grass, moaning and cradling his arm. Nearby, his fallen horse thrashed on its side, its leg obviously shattered.

Jake was already at the man's side and he turned to Thom. "Have you any healing skills, magician? Not healing magic, but skills."

Thom shook his head. Although he knew a few of the simpler potions and poultices to alleviate pain or staunch bleeding, neither skill was called for here. This man needed his dislocated shoulder set and his arm splinted. Afterward, he could brew a medicinal tea to help the fellow sleep. "We will need to wrench his arm back into place, but I've never done that before. I'm willing to try, if you will help."

Jake nodded and the two of them did what was needed, in spite of the lord pleading for them to stop. Thankfully, the man passed out from the pain, so they were able to finish the task without any more of his screams.

"Thanks for your help," Jake said gruffly.

Thom nodded in return. "Brother Francis is cooking food for all of them and I'll brew a tea later that will help them sleep."

"That would be good, though make sure it's not so strong that they can't awaken early. I think everyone will want to leave at first dawn."

Thom didn't want to think of braving the Road of Leaves again. "I'll be careful in the dosage."

"Good. Now, let's go help with the second rider who tumbled."

They approached the young man who had slipped off the back of the other horse, but a noble was already helping him to stand. A few questions proved him to be dazed but otherwise uninjured.

Jake did not linger with him, but strode off to where the other two guides stood over the flailing horse.

Having no desire to watch a horse die, Thom hesitated. He looked around the group and saw that no others seemed injured, so he decided to head back to the fire and his interrupted dinner. As he walked off, a noble called out to him.

"Hold on, boy. I could use your aid in rubbing down my steed."

Thom turned to the elderly man and gave him a head bob of recognition. "Sir, I am a freeman and not a groom. I know nothing about caring for horses."

"I will pay for your help, boy." The man tossed three coins at him.

He made no effort to catch the offering, letting the coins disappear among the grasses. "No thank you, sir. However, I can offer you and your party some food and a sleeping aid. Come to the fire on the right side of the hill where Brother Francis is preparing your meal even now."

Thom turned away, ignoring the nobleman's crude reply, and walked back to the camp. The coins would have been a nice padding for his purse, but he had no desire to spend the night hopping around for a group of lords. If he gave into one, soon they would all be demanding his service, especially if they heard he was a mere apprentice. To nobles, an apprentice was the same as a servant, no matter what guild he belonged to. They would probably find extra satisfaction in commanding someone training to be a magician, so he dared not take their coins.

He heard someone striding after him and, for a moment, feared the lord wanted to confront him. But he soon realized that it was Guard Marcus, the man's distinctive limp apparent. The fellow said nothing; but fell in beside Thom and matched his pace. He wondered if the guard had turned down a similar offer.

Eventually, the nobles did come over to their fire and the commoners quickly moved aside to let them get close to the warmth. Thom's companions had given up their assortment of platters and bowls, so that Francis could feed the party. The lords took the food with barely an acknowledging grunt. The hysterical lady, now sobbing quietly, refused the monk's offers of food or prayer. Another lady in the group at least had the manners to give a sincere smile and a polite thank you.

Francis returned the pot to the fire's edge and then leaned close to Thom, who was brewing a tea in a pot that their guide had lent him. "Is your concoction done yet? They could use something stronger than a chicken stew."

Thom removed Jake's kettle from the fire and lifted the lid. All seemed ready, so he held it out to the monk. "It might be better if you serve, for some of them still resent me for not grooming their mounts."

Francis chuckled, taking the tea. "The nobles would know better if they had seen you wrangling with your goats. No man should trust you near any animal bigger than a dog. You wouldn't know the difference between a mane and a tail."

Thom was about to protest, when Jake called for him.

The monk motioned for him to go. "Tell them what you know, but make no bold promises," he suggested. "The guides are scared for their lives, so they may pressure you into trying to soothe the Road. I would think that would be worse than trying to groom a bucking stallion, and we both know you can't do that either."

He gave the monk a dark look, but Francis was correct. Reluctantly, he went over to where the three guides huddled.

Eric Loren

SIX

Hillside Creatures

Thomas, apprentice of Wizard Levitanus, stood before the three Road guides and waited for them to speak. He was no mighty magician, but he would offer what knowledge and skills he had, for he wanted to get out of this enchanted passage too.

"Rather old to be an apprentice, aren't ya?" asked the guide who had arrived with the nobles. Thom thought of him as the Rider Guide. "Something wrong with ya?"

"The apprenticeship of a magician goes longer than any other," he answered politely, though the question irked him. "Many don't become a journeyman until they are thirty."

The fellow shook his head. "Who'd want to wait so long?" He looked at his comrades. "I don't see how he can help us, being only an apprentice."

"He's all that we have," replied Jake calmly.

The Rider Guide turned back on Thom. "What of it, then? Can ya tell us what stirs the Road? Keep no trade secrets from us, for lives are at stake."

Thom answered cautiously, "What do you want to know?"

"What do we wanna know? Are ya truly that daff? Tell us what's causing all this havoc, ya dim-wit!"

Thom scowled, but still answered. "This is not a failing of the magic, that much I can sense. Someone or something is attacking the Road of Leaves. It has been weakened, I think."

"It jerks like a wounded animal," agreed the Rider Guide, looking to his fellow guides. "Like I told ya, the Road's in pain, not attacking us out of spite."

"Where's this attack coming from?" asked Jake.

"I have felt it ahead of us and behind us," said Thom, "so either the attacker moves quickly or there are multiple onslaughts underway."

"Are they sustained attacks, like a siege?" asked the third guide, finally speaking up.

Thom had considered that, but doubted the possibility. "I think each is a single thrust at the linked enchantments, but they cause a prolonged reaction."

"Like a wolf taking nips at a stag to weaken it," said Jake. "A rogue wizard does this, rushing from place to place."

"Not that swiftly," argued Thom, after further thought. "Each magical attack may take hours to prepare."

"Is he attacking from inside or outside?" asked Jake.

Thom was surprised by the question. He had never considered that someone might actually be on the Road of Leaves and causing this havoc. It raised all sorts of frightening possibilities. Exhausting an enchantment or cutting it off from the magician maintaining it caused the magic to weaken and dissipate, to die off. He had thought these attacks were such things, attempts to kill Merlin's greatest work. However, attacking an enchantment from within led to far more violent results, much like tossing oil into a fire. Who would risk such violence? It would likely kill the wizard exploding the enchantment, along with anyone nearby.

The others waited for his reply, then became impatient. The Rider Guide stepped closer, raising an accusing finger and pointing it at Thom. "Didn't ya hear? Where's he attacking from?"

"I...I don't know. Attacking from within the magic would be easier, but that would be like pulling a burning house down around you. Who would be so foolhardy? Also, I don't know who the attacker is, whether a man or a beast or a..."

"Phaw, ya avoid commitment like a maid teasing two suitors. Tell us who does this to the Road and tell us plainly."

"I don't know," he replied again, now through gritted teeth. "It's not like this has happened right in front of me. Have any of you actually seen one of these attacks?"

The Rider Guide threw up his hands in disgust. "I told ya he'd be no help."

"We haven't seen any attack in person," said Jake, answering Thom's question, "and I hope we never do. It's not our job to defend the Road of Leaves, but to protect and guide those on its leafy route. Tell us, magician, how can we safely get through all of this chaos? That's the question we need answered."

Thom wanted to give the desperate men an answer, but he didn't know. He doubted that even someone as wise as his master would be able to discern what was happening without seeing an actual attack in progress. "I've no good answers, except that the Waycircles seem unaffected by these attacks. I do know that the disruptions have happened in the afternoon, so maybe the attacks take many hours to initiate. I think we should try to reach each Waycircle as early as possible, to avoid the next windstorm. But I can't be sure that will save us. I've never experienced anything like this before."

"We can take refuge here until the guild sends help," said the third guide. "Surely, they're aware of the attacks on Merlin's magic."

"There is that," acknowledged the Rider Guide. "Stony Hill would provide us with plenty of fresh grass for our animals and the springs run ever pure."

"But what of food?" asked Jake.

"We've enough horse meat from the dead mare to feed us for some time," replied the Rider Guide.

Jake brushed his beard absently. "For our three groups, maybe, but what if more arrive? How many can Stony Hill hold? How many before Merlin's magic reacts to the overlarge crowd?"

"We could linger here at least one more night," suggested the third guide. "Perhaps your magician can study the Road for a day and tell us something more useful."

"He'll learn nothing," dismissed the Rider Guide. "He's like a babe in the magic, just learning to babble, so ya can't expect any answers that make sense. It's beyond him."

"Will you try getting us some answers in the morning?" asked Jake.

Thom nodded. "I'll do what I can."

* * *

Early the next morning, Thom gave the goats fresh water and then quickly moved away from their pen. They stank with that distinctive goat smell, which was especially distasteful this early. He had already decided to volunteer the nannies to be next in line for any slaughtering, though they would probably give him a bellyache as revenge.

"Come over here for your breakfast," beckoned Francis. The monk had taken it upon himself to cook up the group's share of the fallen horse and was now ladling out stew portions to all takers.

Thom retrieved his eating bowl and held it out to him. "Thank you. Did you take any vegetables or herbs from the cart?"

"Not this morning, for Jake and the merchant both gave over some tubers and then I found some good onions during my morning prayer walk."

Thom sniffed at the food, cautious after the thought of eating goats. The stew smelled delicious, so he took a tentative bite. It was good. "Prayer walk?"

Francis smiled. "Don't tell my abbot, but sometimes I miss the solitude and order of the monastery. It is peaceful there and easier to focus on the Lord, unlike this campsite that is full of noise and distraction. How can I hear God over the snoring of my fellow travelers? So I wandered off to pray."

Thom squatted next to monk, choosing not to sit on the dew-wet grass. As he ate, he asked about "Is the weather always like this in the Waycircles?"

"Like what? The morning dew? Yes, that's normal, for it is forever spring inside these refuges, as it is always autumn on the Road. The midway inn, the Root and Bough, sits on an island bathed in summer's warmth every day. The Founders' enchantment separates the seasons as part of its power, though I don't think they included winter. Did your master tell you none of this?"

Thom shrugged. "He spoke a little about it, but words didn't prepare me." The apprentice swept his free hand wide to take in their misty surroundings. "I can feel the magic all around me, an intricate weaving that's far beyond my ken."

"Does it seem right? Whole?"

Thom listened with his inner ear and found no flaw in the enchantment's rhythms. "Within this wide circle of trees it does, but I cannot sense the Road from here. Somehow the two are apart while still connected."

Francis nodded, but said nothing. Thom's belly growled, wanting more, so he focused on the hearty stew for a while, until he saw someone he'd rather not banter words with. The troubadour strode over to the fire.

"I'll take some of your stew, monk." The performer thrust his bowl in Francis' face.

While the monk filled it from the pot, the musician looked Thom in the eye. "You seem rather useless for a magician. Why haven't you enchanted the Road back into quiescence?"

"I haven't been trained in such skills."

The man smirked. "Blaming your master for your own shortcomings, eh?" He snagged his meal from Francis' hand. "Monk, you should pray that a real magician might appear amongst us. We could us such a man."

He laughed lightly, implying all was meant as a joke, and then left to eat his food elsewhere. Thom stared after him, his anger simmering like the breakfast pot.

"There's something strange about that one," observed Francis.

"You mean besides his rudeness?"

"Oh, most performers are rude to simple commoners, for we don't have the coins they desire. No, what is strange is that he hasn't ingratiated himself with the nobles. He ignored the party we encountered on the Road and, so far, has done the same during our stop here."

"Look at the richness of his clothes. He must already have a good patron."

Francis raised an eyebrow. "Even then, he should want to learn the latest court gossip to tell his lord or lady. He doesn't play or sing or even tell stories. I have yet to see him open that harp case to check on his instrument. Most musicians obsess over theirs."

"Do you think him an impostor?" asked Thom, now curious. "If so, then he's not the only one on the Road pretending to be someone he's not." He then told him of his encounter with Ned and Joseph, the crooks turned clergy.

Francis seemed incredulous. "Playing at bishop? That is foolish, for not many hold such an esteemed office. I've met false mendicants and country priests living off ignorant peasants in forgotten hamlets, but who would dare to pretend to be a church leader and do so in Camelot? Are these two so foolish?"

Thom shrugged. "It has been many years since I've seen either one. I think they are neither brilliant nor dense, but I would place them among the sly, as are most on the bent path."

"Well, I'll call those two out if I meet them in the city." Francis paused to offer food to the quiet Bricklayer Orem, who accepted it with an appreciative nod.

When the finely dressed man strode over and demanded his share, Francis gave him a cool look. He pointed to the pot, telling the man to serve himself. "The food would have been heartier with a bit of your grain, Trader Will."

The man ignored the monk's remark, taking his fill and walking off.

"He's a grain trader, that one is," explained Francis. "His large pack is filled with grain samples, but he won't part with even a tenth of it. It's not like they are his only samples either, for he admitted that he has more coming by boat on the Road of Waters. He just doesn't want to be inconvenienced with having to wait for the rest to arrive. Too cheap to hire a horse and too impatient to ride the slow riverboat."

Francis stood and moved away from the fire. He motioned for Thom to join him for a walk. "I usually enjoy serving others, but not when they are unappreciative. They act as if I am trying to foist unripe gooseberries off on them." He suddenly laughed. "Listen to me grousing as if I've somehow been abused. My Lord endures much worse and still showers us with love, so I have no call to complain. Would you not agree, mage?"

Thom was not sure what he should agree with: the abusiveness of people, God's suffering, or Francis' need to endure. He simply nodded and left it at that.

"I have something to show you, mage, something that a person of your training will appreciate."

"What is that?" asked Thom.

Francis merely smiled and beckoned him to follow.

When he realized that the monk wanted to take him away from the camp, Thom spoke up. "I shouldn't go too far; the guides want me to spy on the Road this morning."

"The guides are occupied elsewhere. They're busy with the young nobleman who lost his horse. It seems the gentleman was traveling alone so he has no companion to double-up with. None of the other nobles is willing to help a country lord's son, not after experiencing yesterday's murderous winds. No one wants to burden their horse with that boy's weight. The other unhorsed noble found someone to share a horse, but that lord is powerful. The young one, who calls himself Lord Geoffrey, doesn't have any influence among his own kind. They all rejected his pleas for help.

"Geoffrey tried finagling a mule off Merchant George but failed. He also tried to buy Ears from me. He offered his few coins and promised a small fortune from his father, which I doubt his sire would honor. I told him no. So now the guides are with him at the other party of walkers, trying to find him a mount over there."

"He can have a goat to ride," offered Thom, "or even better, let him take both goats and the cart as well."

Francis chuckled. "He's a big lad and would be too much for your lovely girls, though you're generous to make the offer. I think they'll find no mount for him, so that means he'll be joining one of the walking groups."

"I hope he joins the other party."

"Whatever is decided, it will take some time so let's go for that little walk."

* * *

The monk led him to a clear stream and followed it upstream toward the center of the Waycircle. Soon, they were hiking the wild Stony Hill, pushing branches aside and scrambling up the steep grade. The stream gurgled and laughed as it raced past them going the other direction. At last, Francis brought him to a small pool where the stream lingered before starting its plunge.

The monk looked around and then motioned for Thom to sit with him on a grassy bank. "Our noise will have frightened them but, if we are quiet, I think their curiosity will bring them back."

"I thought animals avoided the Road's magic…"

"Whisper now," suggested Francis, setting the example. "They might be fearful of our booming voices. Will you speak softly?"

Thom nodded.

Francis gestured at the surroundings. "Animals fear the unnaturalness of the Road, but plants do not seem to mind it. The beings we have come to spy on are magical in nature and seem to be part plant themselves. They apparently enjoy this magical place. Mage, have you ever seen a dryad?"

Thom caught his breath. "Here? Dryads live here?"

Francis smiled. "I should think you could hear them, mage. Let us be quiet and see if they come out to greet us."

Road of Leaves

Thom stopped talking and listened with his inner ear, but he heard nothing. The magic inside a being didn't reveal itself unless it bled. You needed to cut or crush a magical thing to release its inherent power, be it a berry, an insect, or a beast. That was true of magical beings too, though Thom couldn't imagine harming a smart creature just to obtain its power. To do so would be to practice dark magic.

So he didn't locate the dryads using his inner ear, but he did eventually hear them with his outer ears. He heard them all around, soft chirps from beings hidden among the foliage. It was Francis who spotted the first one. The monk pointed her out, a petite, shy thing as brown as bark yet as lovely as a summer sunset. She was a tiny being, about a knee's height.

Thom watched with intensity as she tentatively stepped out from behind an oak. This was the first time he had ever seen one besides as a drawing in a book. When she stood still, he could easily have mistaken her for a woodcarving, but when she moved it was with litheness and fluidity. She wore green leaves and her hair seemed almost moss-like, though still lovely in its flowing.

He could sense the magic that was part of her essence and he understood another temptation. To a magician, a dryad was a lodestone of power. A magician of the dark arts- a sorcerer- might lust for that. It gave him pause that they would trust Merlin enough to enter his enchantment for shelter. He wondered if this one would soon sense his profession and flee. Magical creatures seemed to be aware of those who could listen with their inner ear.

The dryad stepped closer, her large green eyes sparkling with curiosity. Her dainty hand brushed aside an intervening branch. She stopped when she had a clear view of them, her head tilting to one side quizzically.

Thom held his breath. For some reason, the little one reminded him of Adele, the maid he had run into before entering the Road. Maybe because both of them seemed so certain of themselves. He saw no fear in this tiny dryad. Curiosity, yes, but no fear.

After studying them a bit longer, she turned her head slightly and let out a series of whistles that sounded much like a bird's call. Entranced, Thom wondered if she was calling to the others of her kind.

"Make no sudden move," whispered Francis, slowly pointing out some newcomers.

It took a moment for Thom to pick them out against the foliage, for they blended in so well, but another half-dozen dryads had appeared. However, these were male and armed with tiny bows. Thom imagined that being hit by one of the little arrows would feel much like a bee sting.

Francis seemed to know his thoughts, for he said. "I have heard their arrow tips are poisoned, so do not provoke them. We want to be their friends, after all."

More female dryads also appeared, many of them hesitant to come all the way out into the open. They looked at both of the humans but Thomas felt they might be looking more intensely at him.

"They sense your abilities," stated the monk in a whisper. "I have read that magic attracts them."

"Do they talk?"

"Yes, but it sounds like forest animals, like bird whistles and squirrel chatter. I haven't heard of any human actually holding a conversation with a dryad, at least no reputable tale of such."

Thom twisted his torso to watch another little one approaching from behind. "Are they peaceful?"

"They're shy creatures who prefer to hide rather than fight, but they will defend themselves so don't try to touch or hold them."

Thom remained very still, letting the dryads grow comfortable with his presence. His training had not covered magical beings yet, only magical plants and beasts, so his knowledge of dryads was barely more than that of a village healer. He studied them avidly, just as curious as they were.

"Merlin's magic is certainly wondrous," he sighed to the monk.

"Merlin didn't make these little beings; God did," stated Francis in a whisper. "As a matter of fact, Merlin didn't make this enchantment we are traveling through. It took all three Founders to craft the Roads, but then you would know that better than most…"

Thom looked at him quizzically, wondering what the monk was implying.

"You are the apprentice of Levitanus, are you not?"

"Yes, for ten years now. What does that have to do with it?"

The monk smiled but said nothing more, instead concentrating on the dryads again.

Thom shrugged, wondering if maybe the monk had once met his master or had heard of his reputation as a strong mentor. Thom had met less than a handful of other magicians himself, because his master preferred the life of a country hermit over the camaraderie of the guild house, but he had seen how the others respected Levitanus for his knowledge and skill. Nonetheless, his master had not taught him much about the Roads or how they were made. Now Thom wished he had pressed for more answers.

The tiny beings came closer, whistling and chattering to each other as they became more comfortable. They seemed to be commenting on the gigantic humans.

Road of Leaves

Suddenly, one of the female dryads sang out a series of whistles like that of an upset lark. Thom looked over at her as she repeated the strident call. When he looked away, all the other dryads had disappeared into the foliage. He looked back at the caller and found her gone as well.

"What happened?" he asked in a whisper.

"They sense danger," answered the monk, standing up to look back down the hillside. "Maybe their hearing is more acute that ours."

Thom stood up too. "What danger could there be in a Waycircle? Are there dangerous magical creatures in here?"

The monk answered without looking back. "There may be other creatures hiding here, but that's not what frightened them. They hear another human approaching. Now I can too, for someone just cursed at a root that caused him to stumble."

A few minutes later, Guide Jake pushed through the trees and marched into the clearing. He strode past the monk without a comment and stopped mere inches from Thom's face. "Why are you hiding up here? You're supposed to spy out the Road for us, magician. Are you afraid?"

The comment peeved Thom, but he still answered calmly. "I'm not hiding. I'm taking an early morning walk with Brother Francis. I don't recall anyone giving me a certain time for entering the Road, but if you want to do so now then let us get going."

Some more thrashing in the bushes occurred and the troubadour appeared behind Jake. "I told you they went this way." The performer looked at the small pool and the surrounding wilderness. "It's quite a climb for a measly waterhole, so what are you two doing here?"

"We're leaving," said Francis. "It is time for Thomas to spy on the Road and see if he can learn more about what is happening. You should go back down too, Troubadour Iago. You can provide some music to lighten the mood in the camps while we await his report."

Iago looked down his nose at the monk. He flourished his red cloak as if to show how well his current patron had rewarded him. "I am no commoners' clown."

"Then who's clown are you?" asked Francis with a smile.

The performer's eyes widened and he stepped closer to the brother. "Monk, you must be wearing your robe upside down, for I heard your arse talking."

"Enough of this," said Jake, wearily. "You two can linger here to argue, but the magician and I are leaving."

Thom saw that the man would not tolerate any more delay, so he started walking. He understood the burly guide's concerns, though the fellow's rudeness still grated.

Thom was gladdened when Francis joined him.

The monk gave one final look at the still-angry musician. "I'd rather not keep arguing with a man gifted in wordplay." He came close and gave their guide a friendly slap on the back. "Lead the way back down, dependable Jake."

Surprisingly, Jake did so without protest. Thom and Francis fell in behind him. Troubadour Iago seemed to hesitate and then came after.

SEVEN

Burnt Leaves

The musician followed only as far as the camp, but Jake and Francis accompanied Thom all the way to the Waycircle's entrance. The other two guides were already waiting there.

"About time ya got here," groused the Rider Guide, urging them to step through the archway.

All five of them walked through the grayish shimmer in the stone archway, coming out on the Road of Leaves.

The first thing Thom noticed was the stench. He looked to the left and saw the horse carcass now lying on the side of the Road, at least what was left of it after the butchering. There were no flies, for even insects avoided the magical route, but the smell of blood and guts wafted through the still air.

Thom looked away. "Why is that out here?"

"When the Road shifts tonight, the body will vanish," said Jake.

"And appear in someone's field or on the edge of a wood," added Francis.

Jake nodded. "That's true."

"Enough with the chatter," complained the Rider Guide. "What do ya sense out here? Is the magic stirring again?"

Thom walked up the path of leaves for a bit and then just stood there, listening to the rhythm of the Road. He heard nothing unusual with his inner ear, but used his normal senses to verify that. He looked, he smelled, he listened, and he tasted the air. Even though it was high summer beyond the Road's enchantment, it was a cool autumn day here and a very quiet one too, but for the various noises from his companions. Not even the whisper of a wind moved the still air.

Thom waited, worried that he might have missed some subtle difference in the enchantment's sounds, but all seemed in harmony. The magic formed an intricate pattern that spoke to his inner senses much like a melodious chorus might fill his outer ears or a beautiful meadow of flowers might please his eyes. It felt right.

He lingered, enjoying the sensation of such a powerful magic, but knew he needed to get back to the others. Finally, he returned to those waiting on him.

"What can you tell us?" asked Jake.

"The enchantment sounds strong," he answered. "I sense no attacks or disturbances."

The Rider Guide nodded, "See? The Road moved itself out of harm's way during the night. It's smart that way. I'll set off as soon as my group can mount up. I want to get my group to the Isle of Sun as early as I can." He left them, walking back into the Waycircle.

"Are you sure there will be no more attacks?" asked the third guide.

"I said nothing of the sort," replied Thom. "I can't see into the future. I don't know what will happen today."

The man frowned. "Then I am keeping my party at Stony Hill for one more day. I'll not risk another walk in a windstorm." He also returned to the Waycircle. That left Thom with just Jake and Francis.

"Magician, what should we do?" asked Jake.

"I have no magic to tame the Road or to defend us against attack. If we go on, then we go on unprotected."

Jake nodded understanding. "But remaining does not assure our safety either, for Merlin's magic will not tolerate us lingering along the route. I would rather go forward than huddle in fear."

"Let's get going then," suggested Francis. "The longer we delay, the more likely the Road will become unsettled."

"That's the truth," agreed Jake, stroking his bearded chin. "We are two days from the Isle. Are you certain the Road ahead of us feels whole?"

"I hear no disturbance in its rhythm," replied Thom.

Jake's chin stroke turned into a beard yank as he muttered, "Well maybe the missing party has hunkered down somewhere like Terrence plans to do." He gave Thom a long look, then shifted his eyes to Francis. After a moment, Jake came to a decision. "Go and get your animals ready, for I want us to be on the Road of Leaves within the hour."

* * *

Upon hearing Jake's decision to go on and the importance of an early departure, everyone bustled to gather their things. Thom suggested to Jake that the remaining party might want the goats for a good stew but the guide nipped his generosity off, saying that they needed the goats to get the cart pulled along the Road. There were strict rules about discarding anything while traveling Merlin's enchanted way.

Thom grumbled, but went to battle the girls into their collars. He pulled the cart into the pen and was able to get one goat strapped into place. The other one, though, proved feistier. She ran away and then came around to the cart and peeked inside, standing up on her hind legs. Thom shooed her off before she could steal anything but he failed to catch her. He chased her three times around the cart, until he realized the futility of the chase. He resorted to luring the beastie into place with a carrot and a plum.

Finally done, he led the pair out to where the rest of the party waited. Thom noticed that the young lord was now part of their group.

"The pen should be mucked," noted Jake, "but we don't have the time to wait for you. See that you do better at our next stop." He turned to the noble youth and pointed at the cart. "Lord Geoffrey, you may place your saddlebags and blanket in the cart since you are unaccustomed to walking with such burdens."

The young man nodded understanding and did as suggested, though he offered no thanks to anyone. He seemed shaken by his new circumstances and maybe a bit addled too.

Their guide gave the campsite one last look over and then ordered them to head out.

As soon as they were all on their leaf-littered route, Jake set a brisk pace.

The eight travelers followed Jake without complaint. First came the bricklayer, with the troubadour right behind him. The merchant and his guard followed with their laden mules.

The grain trader walked beside the merchant, while the young nobleman followed the beasts. At least he did until he stepped in fresh mule dung and then he hastily sped up to walk in front of the animals.

Francis and his donkey came behind the merchant, with Thom still at the back. However, the others did not seem to mind that Thom stayed closer now, no matter how much the goats' gait jangled those awful bells.

The Road of Leaves remained calm all morning, but they didn't slow their pace. The Road turned and twisted, never letting them see far ahead. They didn't stop until they came to a sharp turn in the road, and then Jake called Thomas to the fore.

Thom walked around the bend and saw that the Road now ran straight as an arrow's flight for some distance.

"What causes this?" asked Jake, pointing. "Why is the Road acting like some clothesline stretched over an alley? I have ridden this route for over a decade and I have never seen it run so straight."

The magician's apprentice strained to listen to the Road's magic and noticed something odd, like a fading in the enchantment. "There's something ahead, something different to the magic."

"Danger?"

"I fear so, but I don't know what shape it takes. This doesn't feel like the other attacks."

Jake stared ahead and mumbled to himself. "Keep going or turn back? Which shall it be, Jake?" He then looked at Thom. "How far away is this?"

Thom considered. "We should reach it within an hour."

"Then we'll keep going. If it proves too dangerous, we can still turn back to Stony Hill."

Jake brought Thom to the front of the group, tasking Orem with herding the goats. Thom was glad to be free of the animals, but not that it inconvenienced the bricklayer. He gave the man his switch and mumbled his thanks, then hurried to Jake's side.

As they continued on, Thom imagined that the others were staring at him, but he dared not look back to confirm his suspicions. It seemed that most of the others suspected that he had a part in the Road's disruption. No one openly accused him or spat in his direction, but he still felt no warmth from the others. They were as chilly as the weather along this magical route. Even Jake seemed to endure him merely so that Thom would help guide them through.

They were about halfway along the straightway when he realized that the surrounding mist had a smoky scent to it. "Do fires ever start along the Road's path?"

"I smell it too," remarked Jake from up on his mount, "but I see no flames ahead. What does your magic tell you?"

He sensed the muting in the magic even more. The problem was definitely much closer. "We are near the oddity now."

Jake twisted in the saddle to look back at the others. "Everyone keep your eyes open for trouble. The magician says there's something amiss up ahead. Yell out if you notice any danger."

When they came to the end of the straightway, the road veered sharply to the left. Thom and Jake rounded the bend together and came to a startled stop. The Road of Leaves was a smoldering mess. The leafy way was now blackened ash and the trees to either side stood like charred skeletons. The burnt area ran for about a hundred yards and lay heavy with smoke, though it no longer burned.

Thom's fear rose in his throat, making him gag. Who had such power to attack Merlin's work like this? The magic felt close to failing, but there was a tenacity to it. The enchantment still persisted in bridging the burnt area, keeping the Road intact for now.

Jake spoke out, "Will this kill us like it did that other party?"

It took Thom a moment to notice what the guide had already spotted, for he had been focused on listening to the magic rather than actually looking at the devastation. In the middle of the burnt area, shrouded by the lingering smoke, lay the blackened remains of a carriage and the bodies of another traveling party.

For a moment, Thom's breath caught as he imagined Adele burning to death in the inferno, but then he realized that the carriage had been traveling in the opposite direction. These were the remains of the other rider party, the group that hadn't made it to Stony Hill last night.

"What of it, Magician?" asked Jake, his tone demanding an answer. "Will this kill us? Should we run?"

"There is no threat now," replied Thom, recovering his voice. He pointed to an obvious trail through the ashen mess. "Look, the riders that left Stony Hill this morning have already ridden through. However, we should hurry past this before another assault causes the enchantment to snap apart or unravel violently."

Jake ordered the group to get moving, urging Thom to set the pace. The magician's apprentice obeyed, striding through the blackened leaves that crumbled to ash under his boots. He walked quickly past the dead animals and people, being careful not to step on any but also trying his best not to look at them either.

"I do not like this," said Lord Geoffrey abruptly from further back in the group. "If the magic is weakened, then why not just break out of this troubling route?" He ran towards the side of the road, hands raised in front of him, aiming for an opening between two blackened trees. He hit the invisible wall of magic just beyond the tree trunks, rebounding off the enchantment's invisible wall and ending up on his rump in the ashes.

"You need a magician to push through," said Troubadour Iago, pointing at Thom, "and I think this one will not help us. He wants us to suffer on the Road."

"I don't have the power," protested Thom, "and even if I did, I wouldn't be so foolish as to try. If I slashed through the magic, then all of us would die."

The performer rolled his eyes in disbelief.

"I can pay you," said Geoffrey, getting back to his feet. "I may not have much in my purse, but I promise that my father will reward you for my safe return."

"We can all offer something, if you get us free of here," added the grain trader.

"He has already answered you," said Jake, waving Thom onward. "We are surrounded by the greatest enchantment in the land. No mere apprentice can undue all of this. So no matter your fears, you must keep going. You will find refuge at the Isle of Sun. One more day, folks. We will arrive there tomorrow."

He again motioned for Thomas to start walking.

Thom nodded and set off through the burnt leaves. Behind him, he heard some of the others mutter, but they followed. When he came to the end of the torched area, the Road took another sharp turn and once again ran straight as a plumb line. Thom rounded the bend quickly and kept walking. He wanted to get far away from the devastation. However, he had gone only a short distance when Jake called him back.

"You can return to your familiar place and relieve the bricklayer," the guide said. "You have the goats and the rear watch. I think it will comfort the others to have you at their back."

He wanted to object to getting the girls back, but he doubted anyone would support him, so he returned to his charges.

Jake insisted on an even faster pace and no one protested, not after having seen the burnt area.

As soon as Thom had the goats moving, Francis brought his donkey near. "The attack came from within the Road, didn't it?"

Thom met the monk's gaze. "Yes."

"Then we have an enemy magician lurking on the Road somewhere. That's not good. Could such a magician hide from us in plain sight?"

Thom nodded. "It is said that those who practice dark magic can shape-shift or vanish from sight."

Francis frowned. "You should tell Guide Jake all of this, but do so in private. No need to heighten the fears of others."

"I wish my master were here, for there's so much of this that I don't understand. What's happening is far beyond my knowledge."

Francis nodded. "If anyone would know what caused this, it would be your master. It is a shame he didn't travel with you."

* * *

That day the Road remained quiescent all the way to the next Waycircle. Thom sighed with relief when he saw the stone archways up ahead. The group ran the last stretch, entering the first arch and then passing through the gray mist into the opening on the left. Thom, like the others, breathed deeply once inside, glad to have survived another day.

The Blue Lake Waycircle sank toward its center, where a clear lake shimmered in the late afternoon light. This Waycircle seemed intimate after the much larger Stony Hill, but then it was meant to contain only two parties of walkers every night. The place lay empty before them and very inviting.

"I will need to bathe this evening and wash my robe," said Francis, sniffing at his sleeve. "The stench of smoke clings to me still."

Thom noticed the same thing about himself.

Jake brought them to a campsite on the right side of the lake, assigning pens for their animals. This time Thom was able to unharness the goats on his own. However, one escaped while he wrestled with the cart, so he had to spend an hour chasing her. She ran across the grass and among the lakeside reeds, where Thom slipped, falling face-first into the mud. The beast also sprinted through the camp, trampling blankets and trying to steal the grain trader's dinner. Thom shouted apologies as he chased her off.

When he finally had both animals safely caged, he found a freshly washed monk smiling at him.

"Feed and water them and then take your bath, mage, for now you need one more than ever." He tossed him a bar of soup. "Use it extravagantly, my friend, or else I will spend all day tomorrow pitying the goats for having to smell your stench."

Thom caught the soap with a laugh. "Since when have you become the sheriff of cleanliness?"

Raising an eyebrow, Francis gave a mock-haughty look. "I'll have you know that the Benedictine monks at Saint Barnabas are the land's finest soap renderers and candle makers. We add pure honey from our own hives and delicate blooms from our gardens. Camelot's most refined ladies only use our soaps for bathing as they wash by the light of our fragrant candles. No soap makes a finer lather than ours."

Thom sniffed the bar and pretended to swoon over its fine aroma. "Why are you spending months collecting musty books instead of laboring beside your brethren to make soap and candles, if you are so convinced of their efficacy?"

The monk gave a dramatic sigh. "Alas, I detest stirring hot cauldrons, so I get easily distracted. When a pot overflowed and coated the floor in wax, the chandler-monks sent me to help the gardener-monks. However, my gardening skills caused more death than growth. After the unfortunate demise of a half-dozen rose bushes, the abbot thought it best to give me another task, well away from my deservedly peeved brethren."

Thom, muddy and tired, could not help but feel light-hearted. The monk had that effect on him. "Maybe you should be the troubadour and not that sourpuss over there, for you are quite the storyteller."

Francis smiled. "I'd rather serve God than mere lords. Now finish your tasks and bathe, then you can join me for dinner. That is, if you will allow me to use some of the Goat Woman's vegetables."

So far, Thom had only used the lost woman's load to feed the goats or to help the rest of the party. It felt a bit like thievery to use her supplies on himself, though he probably deserved some compensation for bringing the load to Camelot.

Francis seemed to understand his hesitancy. "On second thought, I saw some promising herbs near the lake that will add a savory touch to dinner. We are allowed to harvest from the Waycircles' bounty as long as it's done in moderation. Go bathe and then we will eat."

Thom finished with the goats and then found a quiet spot among the reeds to clean himself. The warmth of the water surprised him and made bathing more pleasant. After washing, he joined Francis for a meal. They sat away from the fire and the others so that they could have some privacy. Night had settled in by the time they finished.

"Why do you think there was no attack today?" asked Francis, plucking absently at the grass.

Thom considered. "The enemy can now attack the Road at any time. There is no need to attack only during the day."

"What do you mean?" asked Francis, leaning forward with interest. "Has the Road's magic been compromised?"

"Before, the Road would move every night, settling its magic between new trees. Any attacker had only a day to undermine the Road before it shifted and wove itself a new path. The enchantment replenished and began anew every day…" He fell quiet, awed at the complexity of such magic.

"But now the Road has been nailed in place," said Francis, showing his understanding. "That was why the Road seemed to strain at either end of the burnt area. It can no longer shift there."

Thom nodded. "That's what I fear. The attacker can now take his time and plan the Road's destruction."

"But why destroy the Road of Leaves?"

"You would know that answer better than I, monk, for you are more traveled. Who would hate King Arthur so? Does someone seek to invade Camelot or simply cut the city off from the rest of the land? Without its four Roads, the king's capital would be lost in some nether land."

"Those are troubling thoughts," said Francis with a frown. "I am a confidante of neither the king's court nor Merlin's magic council, so I'm not certain of who would scheme against the realm. Your questions will need to be answered by men more knowledgeable than I am. Our concern is simply getting to Camelot." The monk paused, running a hand across his bald pate. "Tell me true, mage, what will happen if the Road is severed? Will all of this…" he gestured at the Waycircle around them, "cease to exist? Or will it just float off into some magical fog, forever lost?"

Either prospect terrified Thomas. "When an enchantment shatters, anyone or anything inside dies. That is how my master explained it to me, and I know of no exception."

"One other question. Are you more than an apprentice? If so, I will tell no one." Francis was looking at him intently.

Thom gave him a confused smile. "No. Why would you think that?"

Francis smiled back, his face losing that intensity. "You just seem to know more than most magician apprentices that I've encountered, although I haven't seen your crafting skills yet."

Thom shook his head. "Trust me, Brother Francis. I have no journeyman staff hidden anywhere. I'm just an apprentice."

Eric Loren

EIGHT

Night Visitor

Thom tried to talk about other things with the monk as night settled in around them, but his thoughts kept wandering back down the Road to the weakened area. The next attack might happen at any moment, shattering Merlin's enchantment. He wondered what his master would do to counteract such an attack. That thought brought another to his mind- there was a stash of magical elements nearby, buried under the common vegetables in the Goat Woman's cart. Maybe he could find something useful in there. "Francis, can you retrieve a torch from the fire and meet me at the cart? I just remembered a possible aid for us."

"Of course, Thomas."

Thom hurried over to the cart and began unloading the vegetables in the dark. By the time Francis arrived with a burning branch, he was ready to inspect the lower crates. He opened the one box that he distinctly remembered and then straightened with shock. "That can't be."

"What's wrong?"

"Some of the elements are missing." Thom looked over at the monk. "Did the bricklayer take anything while he watched the goats earlier today?"

"I don't believe so," answered Francis. "Did you inspect the load before we left Stony Hill? Might it have been tampered with during our time there?"

Thom had to admit that was a possibility, although he thought he would have heard the magical elements if the lead-lined crate had been opened. There were so many magical elements inside that its sound would have been obvious to anyone trained to listen with their inner ear. How could anyone have slipped past him to pilfer any of it? "I don't like this, monk. The items missing are often used when working powerful enchantments."

"But they are also valuable, so they may have been simply stolen."

"Let us hope that's all that happened," said Thom. If someone had these powders on them right now, he couldn't hear it. That meant they had a lead-lined container to hold the elements, making them either a prepared thief or another magician.

"Look quickly to see what else is gone before we lose our light," urged Francis, indicating his half-burned torch, "and take anything that might be of use to you."

That had been Thom's original idea, but now he hesitated. It felt too much like the thievery of his childhood.

"Don't be foolish, mage. If any of these powders are useful, add them to your personal supplies. You need to be equipped."

Thom gave in, though he now doubted that any of the magic he knew would help. If nothing else, he would have enough powders to create a Wizard Light and not have to depend on burning twigs. He took only those elements that he knew how to work with, even though more potent powders were present. He placed the vials into his box or refilled the vials he already had. He then sealed the Goat Woman's stash to silence its magical melody, putting the crates of vegetables back just as the makeshift torch burned out.

"What will you do now?" asked the monk as he tossed the blackened and smoldering branch onto the dirt where it couldn't ignite anything else.

There was nothing Thom could do to stop the assault on the Road, but maybe he could stop the pilfering from the now-dead Goat Woman. He decided to use the same enchantment he had crafted three nights ago. "I will set an alert over myself and the cart tonight. If anyone gets too close, I will awaken."

"The Whisper of Warning," muttered Francis with a nod of approval. "Even masters can't always sense that."

Thom was surprised. "How do you know of that enchantment?"

He raised an eyebrow. "I'm well read, mage. Haven't you noticed my donkey's load?"

Thom wondered if the monk had read a book of magic. That was a tempting thought, for Levitanus carefully limited his access to the enchantment sections in his magic book and had so far only allowed Thom to copy six of them into his own, mostly-blank tome.

The monk spoke up again. "Beware, Thomas. The rest of the group has been watching us go through the Goat Woman's supplies. If the burglar is one of them, then he will now guess that you know of his stealing."

"True enough, but most thieves can't resist a challenge. I saw it often enough with my own father. They revel in the excitement and the risk. Let them watch and wonder, but I will still craft a Whisper of Warning before I go to sleep. If our thief is cautious then he will keep away, but if he's bold then I will catch him tonight."

* * *

Later, as the campfire died down and most of his companions began to sleep, the magician's apprentice set up his trap. He mixed three magical elements together- powders made from Bearded Night Hare, Western Tufted Martlet, and Whispering Elm- then added in the necessary mundane powders as well. He spat in it to attune it to himself, and then added enough water to create a proper consistency. He dabbed some on his ears and sprinkled the rest in a rough circle surrounding the cart and the area where he had placed his blanket.

Thomas crafted his enchantment carefully, knowing that it had to be a subtle magic to remain unnoticed by another magician. It took some time, but he was finally satisfied that it was the best he could create. He then lay down and let sleep come, the half-sleep of a magician holding onto an enchantment. He would have another headache tomorrow.

* * *

He woke with a start, the magic warning him of an intruder. The enchantment sounded like a throbbing in his ear. He remained still, not wanting to alert the thief, but he was fully awake. The magic dissipated, the throbbing waning. Lying on his side, Thom had a clear view of the cart. A shadowy figure approached and began quietly unpacking the cart of its vegetables. Once the intruder had those out of the way, he kindled a faint Wizard Light and set it on the cart's lip. Thom hoped to catch a glimpse of his face, but the light was behind the intruder and the burglar's hooded cloak concealed his form.

Thom silently watched, careful to avoiding any movement or sound that might draw attention, as the cart was ransacked. The thief was fast yet quiet as he worked. He either knew exactly what he wanted or didn't care what he grabbed, for he wasn't in the Goat Woman's stash for long. When done, the intruder set the vegetables back on top and then extinguished the wizard light. Frustration swelled in Thom, for now it would be even harder to identify the thief.

As his eyes adjusted back to the darkness, he saw the intruder walk toward the pens and noticed the goats run over in greeting. Then another person walked over, someone from among the sleepers by the campfire. This man was half-hidden from Thom by the cart and he didn't speak. However, the first intruder did and Thom suddenly realized what about the thief had been nagging him. The voice gave away a secret: the intruder was a woman.

Thom started sweating under his blanket as he realized more. The goats knew her and were friendly with her because they recognized their owner. The Goat Woman. Not only had she survived that windstorm, she had probably caused it. Thom was spying on a wizardess or, more likely, a sorceress- a master practitioner of the dark arts.

The two didn't talk much longer. The Goat Woman dismissed her ally, who went back to wherever his blanket was spread. Thom wanted to stand up and look, but he couldn't risk the sorceress noticing him. She would kill him if she knew he was spying on her. Whoever the other person was, he slipped away without Thom learning his identity.

The Goat Woman lingered a bit longer to pet her animals and then she too slipped away.

Thom was too scared to move. He pretended to be asleep even while his mind raced around in panic. He considered destroying her cache, but feared he would never succeed. She was probably still in the Waycircle, waiting for the night's winds to stop, and would quickly swoop in if he tried to do anything as foolish as attacking her supplies. Thom felt overwhelm and uncertain what to do.

After three hours of inner turmoil, he decided that he needed to tell someone. This was not something to keep hidden, for the Goat Woman was using them. They were transporting her magical supplies and caring for her pets even while she was attacking the Road. It had to be her causing at least some of the disruptions.

Thom finally dared to sit up and look around. The campfire had died down to a sullen glow and everyone seemed asleep. He considered waking Jake and telling him everything, but what if the guide was her accomplice? It was Jake who had made him take care of the goats and the cart. Might he be the woman's hidden ally? Thom frowned. Who else could he share with? He decided Francis would be safer, for if the monk were her ally then he would have exposed Thom's magical trap.

He picked his way through camp to where the monk snored and woke him with care, making sure not to disturb the others. When he saw Francis' eyes open, he motioned for him to follow and led him away from the others.

"What is it? Have you found your thief?"

"I know who's been taking the supplies, but I wouldn't call it thievery. After all, how can you steal your own things?"

"What are you talking about?" asked Francis, still a bit sleep-befuddled.

"I saw the Goat Woman slip in and reclaim some of her belongings. She is the one who has been taking things and she's the one attacking the Road."

"Her? The one we thought dead on our first day on the Road?" The monk's surprise was obvious. "I hadn't expected that."

"I didn't either," admitted Thom. "She was careful not to craft any enchantments near me, or else I would have heard it."

"The Goat Woman." Francis' voice sounded frustrated, even angry. "She's been using us to transport her magical supplies. Unknowingly, we have abetted in the Road's destruction. How can we make this right, Thomas? Should we destroy the cart and its entire load?"

Thom shook his head. He had already considered that during his three hours of faking sleep. "It may be that the cart is the only reason why she hasn't killed us yet. She needs us to be her goat herders. Besides, she has an accomplice among us." Thom explained the rest of what he saw, finally concluding with, "It complicates matters. Who else can we trust?"

"Guide Jake," replied Francis without a pause. "We can trust him."

"What makes you say that?"

"The Road guides are a tight clan, like a small guild if you will. It would be hard to infiltrate their number. If Jake had been corrupt, then you would no longer be alive, for you are a rival magician. I think they only spared you so that Jake's suspicions wouldn't be aroused."

That wasn't a comforting thought, but Thom could see the logic in it. "So let us rouse Jake and tell him about all of this."

They did just that, finding the man and waking him. He willingly went aside with them and listened to their tale, but he didn't believe it at first. By the time they convinced him, dawn lit the sky enough that Thom could see the treetops whipping under a strong wind passing overhead. Francis noticed where Thom looked.

"Have you ever seen such winds in a Waycircle?" asked Francis, drawing the guide's attention to the disturbance.

Jake stared up for a moment. "Something else for us to worry about. Magician, do you sense any troubles around us?"

Thom tried, in spite of his headache, but he heard nothing wrong with the magic enveloping the area. "It seems normal. Maybe this is something outside of the Waycircle."

"The wind blows from the direction of the Road," noted Jake. "Do you think the woman wizard may have already done some mischief out on the Road?"

Neither monk nor apprentice answered, yet both looked toward the Waycircle's entrance. Without another word, the three of them started in that direction, knowing that they needed to investigate. They hiked up to archway, just beneath the trees most affected by this new wind. They paused, staring up at the whipping treetops. A light breeze brushed at them, soft yet foreboding. The silvery shimmer inside the archway offered no hint of what lay beyond.

Thom knew he should be the first to look through but fear almost overwhelmed him. He could guess that something had gone wrong beyond the Waycircle. He feared it, but he still moved forward. When he stepped through,

Eric Loren

a howling wind shoved to the side and snow stung his eyes.

NINE

Snowstorm

Thomas staggered against the wind, barely able to see through the blowing snow. Although he could still see the green countryside to either side, the Road's bed of leaves lay buried under two feet of snow. He longed to break through the enchantment's boundary and walk on normal roads that wouldn't shift or kill.

Jake and Francis joined him inside the archway.

"What do you sense with your magic?" asked Jake, raising his voice above the noise of the storm. "What's happening to the Road?"

Thom concentrated, listening down the magical tunnel that was the Road of Leaves. His outer ears filled with the roar of the wind, but he did his best to ignore that. Instead, he listened with his inner ear. He caught the subtle and intricate weave of magical sounds all around him, tracing the rhythms back toward Stony Hill until he detected a distant shrill. A disharmony in the magic. Although faint, the sound made him grit his teeth.

Once he noticed it, he could trace the jarring sound back through the enchantment and found that it even affected the magic at his feet and to either side. Something had twisted Merlin's work. "The magic sputters and flares. I would say the enchantment has been shattered but that can't be, for it still holds on."

"Is the Road still whole ahead of us, toward the Isle of Sun?"

Thom focused his inner listening skills in that direction. He was reassured when all seemed in rhythm. "It sounds normal to me."

Francis stepped closer, his look intense. "Thomas, you need to study the damaged area more, even though it hurts. We need to know if the Road is stable or collapsing further."

He was surprised at the monk's guess, for Thom hadn't even considered that the awful sound meant the enchantment might be in slow collapse. And yet, the idea rang true. It caused him to shudder. Although he didn't want to listen to that faint yet awful shrilling again, he realized that they needed to know what was truly happening. Bracing himself against the wind, he walked out into the snow to get clear of the archway and then reached out with his senses and listened along the magic's path. He had not recognized it before, but it did seem that the enchantment was damaged. From a distance, the magic screamed at him like some gravely wounded animal calling out in pain, but he kept listening with his inner ear.

He felt the enchantment shred more, losing its rhythm as it fell into a jarring screech that only those attuned to magic could hear. The Road's enchantment fought hard to stay intact, unlike any crafting he'd ever heard of, but the magic still faltered, unraveling bit by bit. The damage was advancing their way. He listened as long as could, but the noise of the storm and the chill on his face became too distracting. He looked around and realized that Francis and Jake were holding him up against the wind's incessant pushing.

"The Road is slowly collapsing toward us," he shouted over the roar, breaking free of their grip.

"Faster than we can walk?" asked Jake.

He frowned in consideration, answering hesitantly, "No, I think it's slower than that."

"How much longer before it reaches this far?" asked Francis, pushing him for a more certain answer.

"Maybe a half-day, if the unraveling remains constant."

Francis met Jake's eyes. "We need to run. We've no idea what will happen if the Waycircle becomes severed from the Road."

"Let's gather up the others," said Jake, leading them back into Blue Lake Waycircle.

The wind had picked up inside the refuge, though the worst still kept to the treetops, whipping their tips rather fiercely. Thom hurried to get the goats harnessed to their cart. For once, they cooperated, so he was not the last one to be ready. As he waited for mules to get packed, he took a moment to look around the shelter and wondered if it would survive. The clear lake remained calm and untouched by the winds now whipping the treetops. How much longer before the storm swirled through the calm and churned both water and grasses? Would all of this be shredded into nothing? He shivered, and not because of the dropping temperature.

They hurried out of Blue Lake Waycircle and up the Road, turning away from the freezing wind. Guide Jake watched them carefully to make certain all came out and then he rode at the rear to make sure none fell behind. Thom and his goats were given the lead. Francis kept at his side, a welcome companion in the chaos.

The amount of snow seemed less once they turned away from the magical breech, but there still was a powdering of snow mixed with the leaves that they walked on. The trees to either side showed a fine coat of white on the windward side. Thom and his companions stared at the sunshine-touched forest on either side, the warmth just out of reach, beyond the Road's magic. The Road of Leaves' separation from the world no longer seemed enchanting; now it seemed ominous. To Thom it felt like a tomb waiting for its occupants to stop struggling and lie down on the cold bed of debris.

Thom was thankful that the snow ended after the first bend in the Road but the wind continued to follow, a chilling wind that ran its icy fingers along his neck and down his spine. A small cloud formed every time he exhaled, a bit of warmth escaping with each breath. He wished he had gloves and thicker socks but he had packed neither, since it was warm summer just beyond the Road's encasing magic.

He kept the goats to a fast trot, applying his stick whenever they slowed. Thom couldn't help but look at the beasties differently now, knowing that they were the favorites of a sorceress, yet he still swatted them as needed. Coddling them might cost him his life, but angering their owner could kill him too. He hated having such dangerous choices thrust upon him.

After another mile of dips and turns, the Road's temperature rose, returning to a cool autumn feel. The wind eased to a stiff breeze. Thom relaxed a bit and let up on the goats, allowing them to slow down to a fast walk. He looked over his shoulder and saw that the others were still close on his heels. He could see no snow behind him.

"Can you sense trouble?" asked Francis.

"Not nearby," he replied. "Frankly, I fear looking too far behind us. What if the unraveling has sped up? We would have nowhere to shelter."

The monk patted the canvas that covered his load of books. "You should never fear knowledge. Better to know the danger approaching than to let it creep up on you unaware." Francis smiled encouragement. "You have done well in warning us so far."

Thom frowned. "But I'm powerless to stop the attacks. What good is knowing, when I'm too weak to do anything?"

"Knowing helps," replied Francis. "Knowing your weakness, you can run faster to escape or to find others who can help."

Their conversation was interrupted by Lord Geoffrey's loud complaint. "When will we stop for a noon meal? I grow famished and light-headed."

In all the disruption, Thomas had almost forgotten about their noble newcomer, a youth unaccustomed to walking so far.

"Eat while you walk," answered Jake from farther back.

Thom heard the noble youth grumble, but then Geoffrey strode faster to catch up with the goat cart. He tried to reach in for his saddlebags, but the cart's wheel rolled over the tip of his boot. With a yowl, he sprang back.

Hiding a smile, Thom went to help, snagging the bags and handing them over.

Geoffrey took the bags without thanks, probably used to being served, then walked on with his head stuck inside a leather satchel, rummaging for something to eat.

"Ware the dung," warned Francis, as Ears did his business.

His lordship gave an angry shout as he danced out of danger, almost dropping his saddlebags.

* * *

An hour later, the Road shuddered. Trees moaned and leaves stirred restlessly. Thom stumbled as he felt what had occurred ahead of them, a jarring sound in the magic's steady rhythm. Although everything calmed again, he looked around in panic.

"What is it, mage?" asked Francis, coming near.

He did not respond as he searched for answers. He sensed as far as he could, but everything seemed normal with the Road's enchantment.

Jake rode up. "What happened?"

Thom realized that all were looking at him now. He could not share this quietly with Jake and Francis only. The rest of the party would insist on hearing. "Something has disturbed the Road ahead of us."

"Ahead?" blurted out Trader Will. "I should have gone to Camelot by barge. I'll die just because I didn't want to sick-up on a boat. What will my wife and children think?"

"We're trapped," said Merchant George gloomily.

Jake leaned over in the saddle, the leather creaking. His eyes grabbed Thom's and held them. "Tell me more, magician. Are we now cut off?"

Thom shook his head, more out of uncertainty than denial. "It didn't feel like the other attacks and now the Road seems normal again."

Jake straightened in his seat and stroked his beard in thought. He then looked at the group. "We go on. Maybe it was a shuddering by the Road. Surely, all of you have shaken so when injured, reacting to the pain. She's in agony, that's all."

"You speak as if the Road lives," said Lord Geoffrey, sounding doubtful.

Jake pulled off his hat and ran a hand through his graying hair. "Aye, she lives. Ride this route for as many years as I have and you'll understand. She may not breathe, but I've seen the Road's temper and her whimsy. Only a fool wouldn't respect her." He put his hat back on. "Not that I'm calling you a fool, my lord. I meant no insult."

The young man seemed too scared to take insult. He didn't meet Jake's eyes, but instead looked down at the leaves. The guide turned back to Thom. "Lead on, magician. I want to be at the Isle of Sun by this afternoon, at the latest."

The Road of Leaves became a strenuous hike as they continued. It rose and fell, twisted and turned, as the countryside around it became wilder. Without the wind, Thom heard no noises besides his companions and the ringing of goat bells.

He realized the Road lay empty but for those with him. No, that was not right. One other person lurked somewhere along their route. The Goat Woman.

"Where do you think she is?" he asked Francis, lowering his voice so that the others wouldn't overhear. "How can I fight against her if I can't even find her?"

The monk gave him a knowing look. "She could be near us or far up the Road. Certainly, the Goat Woman is in disguise, most likely shape-shifted to appear as someone or something else. That's a favorite talent among those practicing dark magic, or so I've read."

"You know of the forbidden dark arts?" Thom kept his voice low. Dark magic was a twisted version of natural magic, where unsavory rites were done to gain greater power. His master rarely spoke of it, but he once talked to another apprentice who mentioned that the dark arts went beyond using magical plants and animals to sacrificing magical beings for their power, like merfolk and fairies and pixies. It was not a topic discussed among respectable magicians. You just didn't talk about any who became a hedge witch, let alone any who became a sorcerer or sorceress. How was it that the monk knew about this evil side of magic?

"I am well read, mage. What I know would surprise you." Francis smiled warmly, but then it faded to a frown. "She is beyond your reach, wherever she hides, for you can't match a sorceress' power. This isn't your battle, apprentice."

Thom knew that Francis spoke truth about his weakness, but that didn't relieve his sense of responsibility. He felt it was his duty to stand against anyone abusing magic, for his master had trained that responsibility into him. The monk wouldn't understand, but every magician was expected to stand up against any dark practitioners, no matter who it was.

* * *

Two hours later, the travelers entered a dense forest, the way turning gloomy from the shadows. It was early afternoon and they had taken no rests.

All of them wanted to get away from the collapsing Road, but now they no longer ran or even walked fast. They were too tired for that. They simply trudged forward, determined to escape. The only one spared from weary feet was the mounted Jake, but he had worn out his voice shouting exhortations at the others.

Thom was at the rear of the group again. He was trying hard not to listen to the magic around him, for he didn't want to sense the damage farther back. It was enough to know that they were staying well ahead of it. Instead, he focused his attention on the dreary woods just beyond the Road of Leaves. He tried to guess which shire they were passing through, but failed because the land was too densely wooded for him to see any landmarks.

He was concentrating so much on the surrounding forest, that he didn't notice when the others came to a stop. He almost ran into Francis' donkey. Startled, he sidestepped Ears and pulled the goats to a halt.

Looking ahead, he saw why the others paused. An enchantment blocked the Road. A darkness.

A dozen paces beyond where Jake's horse pawed the leaves, the Road vanished into a black void. It was more than just a greater shadow or fog; some enchantment filled their route, robbing it of light. There was nothing except blackness in front of them, with a distinct boundary where the daylight ended.

"I thought you said there was no attack on the Road," said Jake accusingly. "Is it collapsing here too? Are we trapped?"

"There hasn't been any attack," argued Thom. He focused his mind, searching for any signs of magic nearby, and felt both the Road and the darkness. "The Road's enchantment feels whole here. This is something else…" He stared at it as he tried to hear the different elements in use. "This is a magic set inside the Road's enchantment. The light-less area is something separate from the Road, though it's an enchantment unknown to me."

Jake dismounted and stepped up to Thom. He lowered his voice so no others would hear beyond the nearby Francis. "Is this thing dangerous? Did the Goat Woman set this as a trap for us?"

Thom guessed it to be the sorceress' work, but had no idea whether it was malevolent or not. Whoever had crafted the magic had done so with great care, setting it within the confines of Merlin's enchantment without touching it. "It's magic within magic, which is a perilous thing to do. If the enchantments were to mix, then terrible things could happen. Is it dangerous to enter? That I don't know."

Thom left the goats and pushed his way to the front of company. He stepped near the black void and knelt to look at the magic's edge.

Jake gave his horse's reins to the mercenary and ordered Lord Geoffrey to watch the goats as he came up behind Thom and loomed over him. This time he didn't whisper. "What are you doing, magician?"

"I'm studying this enchantment. Look how the black area keeps from touching the leaves underfoot or the trees to either side. There is a gap between the enchantments, though it's a small one."

Francis walked up too and frowned as he leaned close to examine it. "Such power and control," he muttered. "I wonder if it's safe to breathe in there."

He straightened and met Thom's eyes. "Watch and listen to what happens with the magic."

Unexpectedly, the monk walked straight into the enchantment, disappearing from sight.

Thom startled and almost chased after, but caught himself. Instead, he paid attention to the elements around him, listening for any change in their rhythm. Nothing seemed to alter, which might be a good thing. He had no idea what the darkness was meant to do, though, so he could not gauge its danger.

"Monk!" yelled Jake, stepping up the edge of the magic. "Come back out here!"

"Give me a moment," came a muffled reply. "I need to try two more things."

Francis soon reappeared, walking out unscathed. "It seems safe to breathe, so I think we can pass through. I also heard Jake's shouting, though it seemed to echo in the gloom. Thomas, did you see or hear any reaction to me?"

"No, but I don't know what the enchantment is meant to do besides steal light."

"You're foolhardy but brave," said Jake. "Could you see anything?"

"It's as black as a cave. I struck my flint but saw no sparks, so torches will be of no help to us. I also tried walking toward the side, but the enchantment seemed to thicken and resist, so it will likely keep us to the center of the Road. Nonetheless, we will have to go as if blind."

"The magician should light our way with one of his spells," said Iago the minstrel. "You can do that much can't you, apprentice? Or are you so incompetent that even a little light spell is beyond you?"

"I can craft a Wizard Light," replied Thom, miffed by the other's taunting.

He went toward the goat cart to retrieve his pack, but Francis put a restraining hand on his arm. "I thought you said that different enchantments can't mix. Wouldn't carrying a magical light into that darkness cause a bad reaction?"

Thom stopped, realizing his stupidity. "Yes, enchantments that aren't interwoven do clash. I can't light our way."

Iago sniffed contemptuously as he strolled to the side of the Road and leaned against one of the trees. "You gave him the excuse he needed, monk. He's too afraid to try."

Francis stepped closer to confront the troubadour. "Maybe you are the one who's afraid. If you need comforting against the dark, then ask for it instead of attacking others. One of our companions might be willing to hold your hand as we walk through, if that's what you need."

The musician raised an eyebrow with contempt and gave a little smile to show that Francis' words meant nothing to him.

"The darkness must be hiding something," argued Geoffrey. "I will not walk into that. What if some wild beast or monster lurks within?"

"Animals shun the Road's magic," scoffed Jake. "I can't even ride the same horse through for more than eight trips. How would a rogue magician get an animal in here and get it to stay?"

"It might be some magical monster," said Iago, raising a fine eyebrow at the noble. "I think the Road's magic attracts such things as dragons and griffins."

Geoffrey stepped back from the enchantment, his fear obvious.

"We can't stay here," argued Jake. "Not with the Road collapsing behind us."

"Could we not wait here for help?" asked Geoffrey. "Maybe one or two could go on to the Isle and bring assistance. Are there no wizards there?"

Jake tugged his earlobe. "I'd considered that, but there's no time. Even if help could be found, they couldn't return in time to help us. Do you want to linger here until the night winds sweep you away? No, we must press on."

Geoffrey shook his head at that, taking another step back. "How will we find our way through such darkness? I'll not want to be trampled by the mules, or even the goats for that matter."

"We should hold onto a rope," suggested Orem.

The others quickly agreed with the bricklayer's practical idea. Although no one had a long-enough rope, they were able to tie a few lengths together.

Jake tied one end to his horse's saddle and order Thom to bind the other end to himself. "I would say tie it to the goats' harness, but they might try to chew it."

Thom complied, although it meant he would be last again.

Jake set the order in which they would enter, placing the merchant and his guard directly behind him with their pack mules, followed by Francis and Ears. After them came the trader, the bricklayer, Iago, and finally Lord Geoffrey just ahead of Thom.

"Is everyone ready to go on?" Jake asked.

"Wait," protested Geoffrey, not having grabbed hold of the rope yet. "How far does this magic go? Should we hold our breath while we walk through?"

Jake looked to Thom for an answer.

"I've no idea of its length," replied Thomas.

Jake tugged the end of his beard. "Then we'll have to assume it runs all the way to the next archway. Don't bother holding your breath, my lord, for we could be in darkness for another hour or two." He pointed at the rope lying at Geoffrey's feet, waiting for him to pick it up.

The young man finally grabbed hold.

Jake turned in the saddle to face the lightless enchantment and adjusted his hat. "We're going in."

He sent his horse straight at it. The mare tried to pull back at the enchantment's edge, but Jake kept a steady hand on her reins and forced her into it with a slight kick. Horse and rider vanished, but everyone heard Jake's calm words to both the horse and them. "Keep moving. We'll make it through this and soon be at the Isle of Sun. Keep moving."

Jake set a slow pace, but the rope quickly became taut, forcing the merchant and his guard to face the enchantment. The mules resisted, so they had to yank them forward and into the darkness.

Francis walked calmly after them, his donkey going without protest after a few whispered words of encouragement from its owner.

The rest followed quickly, until only Geoffrey and Thomas were left in the muted daylight. The young lord looked back at Thom, fear in his eyes, but then the rope's slack vanished and he was pulled forward. A small whimper escaped Geoffrey as he stepped into the enchantment.

"Our turn, girls," Thom said to the goats, urging them to get moving. Surprisingly, they didn't balk at the darkness, making him wonder how familiar the nannies were with this particular enchantment.

With one step, he went from daylight to darkness. His skin rose in gooseflesh as he passed through the magic's perimeter and the sound of elemental music filled his inner ear. It was an odd rhythm, its unfamiliarity grating on him. Thom could hear the others ahead of him, but saw nothing of them. He couldn't even see the goats at his side, the cart rumbling behind them, or the Road beneath his feet. He looked behind him, hoping to see the sunshine he had just left, but still saw nothing. It was as if his eyes had totally failed.

Eric Loren

TEN

Dark Passage

Thom kept one hand on the rope and the other on the lead to the nearest goat. The enchantment stole away the light, but it didn't thicken the air or make it difficult to breath. The reason Thom was breathing hard had nothing to do with the air; he was blind now and that brought on a feeling of helplessness. He slowed down, trying to see something until the rope around his waist gave a steady tug, making him stumble along in the dark. His steps were uncertain, his boots dragging in the leaves. He kept his hand on the nearest goat's collar, not wanting to lose them. He kept going because he had to, but he was unsure about every step he took.

Noises seemed louder in here, and they did echo as Francis had said. He heard Jake encouraging everyone to keep moving, while the mules brayed in protest at their sudden blindness. Someone cursed. Iago laughed, whether out of nervousness or humor Thom couldn't tell. Thom stayed silent, trying to avoid stumbling.

The goats walked in the darkness without any hesitation, so he wondered if the enchantment affected animals differently. Maybe they could still see a bit. He didn't trust them to lead him through to safety though, for they were an ornery pair. He also found no comfort in their bells, for the ringing made it harder to hear the others in his party.

Thom tripped when he stumbled through a dip in the Road but didn't fall. He did lose his grip on the goats and had to scramble to get hold of them again. The pause was long enough to bring a strong and steady tug on the rope, and he almost missed the goats because of it.

He yanked the beasties to hurry them up and yanked Geoffrey to encourage him to slow down. Then he stumbled again, staggering against the animals. They bleated in protest and the nearest one butted him in warning.

Geoffrey pulled on the guide rope again.

Gritting his teeth, Thom tried to hurry up, but that wasn't easy in the darkness. He gave up trying to catch sight of anything around him and closed his eyes so that he could concentrate on his other senses. Eyes were useless in here.

He listened as he walked. Jake still encouraged everyone to keep moving, though he no longer sounded so confident. Leaves and twigs crunched beneath Thom's boots. The cart's wheels rumbled. One of the beasties shook her head, setting off a jangle of sounds from her collar. He looked over in response, but of course saw nothing. Just darkness.

He closed his eyes again and tried to listen to the magic around him. It remained steady, doing whatever the Goat Woman intended it do. That thought disturbed him enough to stop listening with his inner ear. He needed to concentrate on where to put his feet. Each step was tentative now, like testing the ice on a newly frozen pond.

"I don't like this," the merchant grumbled. Thom recognized the man's deep voice. "Did someone brush against me? Who just poked me? That hurt!"

"Leave off the complaining," someone else said. It sounded like the troubadour. "I can't hear our guide."

Geoffrey whimpered again, at least Thom thought it was the youth since it sounded closer than the others did. The goat bells made it hard to be certain.

Thom followed their route over a rise and around three turns, with the rope sometimes slack and sometimes urging him on with a yank. As Francis had found, the enchantment seemed to keep them toward the center of the Road, so at least he didn't run into any of the trees that stood on either side. He stumbled once in another unexpected dip and fell to one knee, but the soft bed of leaves cushioned him. He scrambled back to his feet and kept going, his fingers firmly curled around a goat's collar while his other hand held the guide rope.

Thom smelled, catching the scents of autumn as well as the stench of goat.

He was still concentrating on his steps, when Jake called out for him.

"Magician! I feel a breeze. What is happening with the Road?"

From somewhere up ahead, he heard Francis speak. "Maybe it is some trickery from the sorceress and not a problem with the Road."

Thom tried to make sense of the elements in use around him. The enchantment of darkness masked much of the Road's Magic, but he did feel a change. He sensed a different rhythm to the elements. "I'm not certain what's happening, but I think it's not the Road. Maybe there's a storm brewing outside or maybe the sorceress is altering the magic of this darkness…"

"I want answers, magician!" yelled Jake from the front of the line, although his voice echoed and seemed to come from somewhere to the left.

"I don't have any!" replied Thom, frustrated. The breeze hit his face harder, as if mocking his uncertainty.

Road of Leaves

"He lies! The Road collapses!" shouted someone.

"Run!"

The rope around Thom yanked hard, almost pulling him off his feet. He had to scramble to grab hold of the goats again, even while the rope kept pulling. He resisted as he tried to get the nannies to speed up. Still the rope tugged at him. "Calm down, Lord Geoffrey!"

Suddenly the rope snapped back at him. He ran his fingers down its length to discover that its end had been cut. What had the fool done? Thom shouted to the nobleman but received no answer.

He wound the now-useless length around his waist, too thrifty to discard it even in his distress.

"Come on Nibble and Dribble. We must run to catch up with the others."

He got them to a trot as they hurried blindly along the Road.

There was more shouting from up ahead, though it echoed all around him. Someone yelled in anger and then came a scream of agony.

Heart beating wildly, Thom pulled out his knife.

More people yelled and there was the sound of fighting. He heard Francis and Jake pleading with the others to remain calm, but the others' yelling drowned out most of the words.

Thom slowed now, restraining the goats to a walk as well, for he was not about to rush between two combatants. What was happening? Was the Road collapsing or were they being attacked?

The breeze had not strengthened, but still blew steadily.

He brought the goats to a halt as the noises became even more confusing. Sounds still echoed in here, seeming to come at him from every direction now.

He needed to find out if the Road of Leaves was unraveling around them. He wished he could get out of this darkness so that he could inspect the Road at his feet. His feet! Thom dropped to his knees and pressed his face to the ground. The smell of damp earth and old leaves filled his nose. He pressed closer. There, just above the leaves, the dark enchantment ended and he had his sight again. It was shadowy here under the sorceress' magic, but not pitch black. To either side he could see the light of day. Better yet, he could now sense the Road again and it felt whole. At least it did here, where he had his face pressed against the cold leaves.

Thom rose to his knees and yelled to the others that the Road was fine, but no one heard him over the ruckus. He suspected that they were fighting each other in their panic and was about to rush forward and intervene when he heard a change in the sorceress' enchantment. There was a surge in the elements, too quick and complex for him to recognize, as the sorceress did something very close by. It had to be the sorceress, for the new magic didn't disrupt the darkness.

He flinched, ducking close to the goats in the hope they would offer him some protection. He doubted she wanted to harm her pets, so maybe they could serve as his shield. He looked in all direction, but still there was nothing to see. Only the black of blindness.

Thom wondered if they were all going to be killed in here.

Holding the goat's collar in one hand, he pulled free his belt knife. It would be of little help against magic or another weapon, but at least he wasn't barehanded. He crept forward, pulling the goats along.

The fighting sounds became fainter, as if the others were moving away from him. He had the sudden thought that he might be left behind in the darkness while the others escaped. Left alone in here with the goats and the sorceress. The thought caused him to speed up.

He walked as fast as he could while blind, and almost fell on top of someone. Stumbling against the goats, he barely kept his feet. The other person moaned, so it wasn't a corpse. Thom reached down and touched a fur-lined cloak. Geoffrey.

"Lord Geoffrey. I'm Thomas, the magician's apprentice. Can you hear me? Are you injured?"

He sheathed his knife and tried to pull the youth up while still holding onto the goats.

The noble resisted his tugging. "Who?"

Thom tried to grab the man's hand, but found it pressed against the back of Geoffrey's head, rubbing at some injury. "I'm the man who was walking last in line, right behind you. Who did this to you?"

"You did this! Why did you sever the rope? I was not yanking that hard."

"The rope?" Thom was confused. "You're the one who cut it."

"I did no such thing. I had turned to give you a good yank for being so slow, when suddenly the rope gave and I went flying back into the leaves, hitting against some fallen branch or something."

Thom doubted his story. "You have been lying here on the ground since the rope severed?"

"Of course not. How could I, with the ones up ahead dragging me through the dirt? I left you behind and kept going until someone cut the rope in front of me. That's when I fell down the second time. So why did you cut the rope?"

"I swear that I didn't," said Thom. He began to worry that something else was happening in here, something that he was just too dense to grasp.

Geoffrey scooted on the ground, almost breaking free of Thom's grasp.

Apparently, one of the goats tried to take a nibble of the noble, for Thom felt him push one of the beasties away. Then Geoffrey spoke up, sounding unconvinced by Thom's claim of innocence. "Who else would have severed the rope? Don't try blaming your goats."

Thom thought of the sorceress and felt a chill that had nothing to do with the coolness or breeze. He tried to look around but could see nothing of course. She might be listening to them right now. "On your feet, my lord, for we have to find the others."

He asked Geoffrey to hold on to the side of the cart as they moved on. Although he had the distinct impression that the young man wanted to hold his hand or cloak's hem, Thom didn't want to be hindered. He would have set the fellow inside the cart, but the weight would have overwhelmed the beasties.

A bit further and he heard an animal shake its head and clomp its foot. Was it horse, mule, or donkey? Carefully reaching out he found its lead and, after running his hands over the animal, realized it was one of the mules. He called out for the merchant and his guard, but neither answered. Although Geoffrey protested the delay, he tried to walk that whole area of the Road to see if either man lay in the leaves. He found no one.

Thom gave up, realizing the futility of searching for anyone in this darkness. He called out again, but no one answered except Geoffrey and he pleaded for Thom to lead them onward. Thom tied the mule's rope to the back of the cart and continued with his growing train.

The Road took another turn so that Thom walked too close to one side and felt the magic urging him back to the center. At least he wasn't walking in circles.

The Road began to descend, the drop seeming to urge him to quicker pace.

"Can we not go faster?" pleaded Geoffrey, echoing the urge. "I want to see again."

"Any faster and you'll be kissing leaves again, my lord," he replied, trying to sound polite but failing. He also wanted to run, but knew it would only trip them up. They needed to keep going at a steady pace, for there was no one behind them to help should either of them fall.

"Where are the others?" asked Geoffrey. "Surely they are near. Help! Help me! Where is the end of this cursed blackness?"

Thom cringed at the other's shouting; he didn't want to attract the sorceress' attention. "Hush, my lord. The one who crafted this magic is in here somewhere."

"What? Your rogue magician is here?" His voice raised in panic. "I am too young to die. Do not kill me, sorceress, for I have meant you no harm."

The youth let go of the cart and fumbled up to Thom's side. Thom nearly nicked him with the knife when Geoffrey latched on to his arm, but he was able to turn the point away from the desperate youth in time.

"Let go," he hissed at the nobleman. "I need my arm free in case we are attacked."

"Is she planning to attack us now?" he asked, gripping even tighter. "Leave us alone, whoever you are! We mean you no harm!"

"I said to hush." Thom considered asking Geoffrey to brandish his sword but he feared the man might skewer him or one of the animals by mistake. Better to handle any fighting himself, even though he wasn't that skilled with a knife. "Please be quiet. How do you expect me to defend us if I can't hear her approaching?"

That silenced the nobleman, though he still clung to Thom's arm. As the young man stopped his shouting, Thom realized that it had grown much quieter in here. He began to wonder what had happened to the others. Were they now dead or were they merely so far ahead that he couldn't hear them anymore?

Thom kept moving, straining to sense any changes in the magic elements in use around him. He also listened with his outer ears for anything unusual, but all he heard was the goats' bells and the heavy breathing from Geoffrey. His own breathing sped up. Where were the others? Just when he was nearly certain that all were gone or dead, he heard a voice.

"Keep moving!" The shout was distant and echoing but Thom heard it. It was Jake. "There is an end to the blackness. Everyone, keep walking toward my voice."

The words encouraged Thom and he increased his pace, but Geoffrey's reaction was much stronger.

"Oh God, it ends." The nobleman let go and ran ahead, stumbling off blindly.

Thom resisted the urge to chase after, for he did not want to leave the animals behind. It wasn't out of any new affection for the goats. He did it to keep the animals and their load out of the sorceress' hands. He realized that she might be trying to get back her supplies and he wanted to deny her those. He just hoped his stubbornness didn't lead to his death.

He pulled out his knife again, finding a little comfort in its cold handle. Thom was determined to fight for his life, even against a master magician.

Every few minutes, he heard Jake yell out again, urging everyone to keep going. He wondered how many were still inside the enchantment of darkness with him.

Closer by, Geoffrey shouted out as Thom heard him trip. For a moment, Thom thought the Goat Woman might have the youth, but then he heard the squire curse, whimper, and run on. The sound of Geoffrey faded as the youth ran, dying to a faint echo. Soon, the only things Thom heard were his own footsteps and the animals with him. He urged the beasts to a faster pace, worried about being left behind. If Geoffrey made it through, the fellow would probably forget to tell the others that Thom was still inside the darkness.

He was making good time when suddenly the goats resisted. Both beasties pulled back, nearly sending him flying. The pair came to a stop, complaining loudly. The mule tied to the cart's rear also complained. Thom tugged at their collars, but the stubborn things wouldn't budge.

"What is it with you two? Move it!"

Suddenly, he thought they might see or sense something he did not. Was something on the Road in front of them? His mouth went dry as he turned and tentatively probed with the knife. He encountered nothing but air. He listened, but heard nothing except his own breathing.

"Girls, what made you stop? Is there trouble ahead?"

The goats ignored him. They tugged on their harness, as if to look over their shoulders. He thought it odd, after they had walked so calmly through the darkness up to this point. But then he remembered that the beasties had nothing to fear from the sorceress. They had hurried to her that night she had pilfered from the cart. The hairs on the back of Thom's neck rose as he realized the sorceress must be behind him and very close.

He wanted to run but he didn't want to leave her the cart's contents.

Scared and furious at the same time, he yanked at the goats, trying to get them moving. They would not budge. Instead, the nearest one turned its head, pulling Thom along with it.

The mule protested some more, as if a stranger came too close.

Desperate, Thom took his knife and pricked the nearest beast in the hindquarters. "Run! Flee, you moth-eaten goats!"

The goat kicked out and then jumped forward. Thom gave a mighty heave on the cart's trace and got the two moving. Bleating in protest, the goats ran with the cart bouncing in tow. Thom kept at their side, tugging them on. The clamor of the bells covered any sound of pursuit, but he feared she had to be at his heels.

He heard Jake's voice again, but couldn't make out what he said over the clamor. The guide seemed no closer.

Thom almost fell as the Road's descent became steeper, but he didn't slow down. He had to get away.

He began to have some hope when the sorceress didn't strike at him immediately. Maybe she couldn't keep up, considering her age. But then he reconsidered. Maybe she had stopped to craft some other magic or to make the darkness do something horrible to him. Thom imagined the blackness becoming poisonous or solidifying or even the air being sucked out. He didn't sense any change in the nearby elements nor did he hear any new crafting with his inner ear, but his fears still raged.

Suddenly, Jake spoke up and it sounded much closer. "You're near the end, magician! I can hear your bells clearly. Keep coming! The rest of you, keep coming too."

He urged the goats to go faster, poking the nearest rump again. That goat bleated in protest but sped up, with the other trying to keep up. The cart weaved about on the Road as the pair fell out of rhythm. He heard a wheel thud hard on the ground after lifting off.

The mule brayed loudly. Bells jangled. The goats bleated, and then something stabbed him in the arm. He thrust out his knife in defense but hit nothing. It ached terribly and he realized it had been a poisoned blade, for he became light-headed and lost the ability to sense his inner ear. He could no longer hear the magic around him.

He tasted bile as his stomach churned.

And then she spoke, a laugh in her tone, and it sounded like she was racing right next to him. The words were right in his ear. "You are not really escaping. No, you are doing my bidding, apprentice. Flee to your companions, for that is what I want."

Her mocking laugh seemed to come from ahead of him now, but he didn't slow down. He was determined to get out of here, even if it meant chasing after a sorceress.

ELEVEN

Sudden Summer

Thomas came out of the darkness right behind Orem and Geoffrey. He and his train almost ran those two over, but they sprang out of the way. The sudden daylight made him blink and squint as he looked around for the Goat Woman. She was nowhere in sight, so it had probably been some trick of the enchantment that made it sound like she was ahead of him. He gazed back at the lightless passage and wondered if she was somehow watching them from its shelter. It unsettled him that he could no longer hear any of the magic around him.

He didn't pause long, but looked for Jake and Francis and spotted them nearby. "She's in there! The sorceress is in there. She whispered a taunt just before I broke out of her enchantment."

Jake didn't question, but started yelling orders to get everyone moving again. They responded to their guide's urgings, getting to their feet and gathering their things. Some glared at others, causing Thom to wonder what had happened inside the darkness. He noticed that both the grain trader and the merchant showed recent injuries, some already darkening into solid bruises.

Thom approached Merchant George, trying not to stare at the gashed forehead that still oozed blood or the blackening eye, and gave him the mule he had rescued. The merchant muttered thanks but then turned his back on the apprentice.

His hired guard, Marcus, strode over and gave a more heartfelt thanks, pressing three coins into his hand. "I would pay you more, but that's all that I got."

"But it wasn't your mule that was lost," he answered with confusion, trying to give the money back.

Marcus ignored his attempt to return the coins. "True, but George would have taken the loss from my earnings nonetheless, since it is my job to protect him and his cargo. Again, my thanks." The big man hurried to get his mule in line behind his master's, his limp a bit more pronounced.

"Come on, mage," said Francis. "Let's put some distance between us and that awful magic."

Thom realized they were at the back again and he didn't like it. He and the monk hurried after the others. As they walked, Thom began to worry that he might be dying, for he was now dizzy and finding it difficult to walk straight. "Francis, the sorceress did something to me." He rolled up his sleeve to show the ugly red mark where she had stuck him. "She poisoned me with some needle or blade tip. Whatever was on it, it has robbed my ability to hear the enchantments"

Francis drew up the sleeve of his dark robe to show a similar mark. "She poked all of us, Thomas. Some, like me, are dizzy, while others are just sore. It worries me that it has robbed you of your ability to hear magic, but I think it is just temporary. I recall something I read a while ago about a potion that can dull a magician's inner hearing for a day or more. Maybe she stuck us with a needle soaked in that potion."

"Why stick all of us? I'm the only magician."

Francis shrugged. "Maybe she wanted to make sure that there were no hidden magicians in our group or maybe she worried that you weren't with her goats while passing through that dark enchantment."

Thom frowned. Even if this was just temporary, it still presented a serious problem. "I can no longer warn our party of any traps or problems with the Road…"

"You have already done so much," said Francis, trying to reassure him. "Without you, we wouldn't have made it this far and we don't have much farther to go. I doubt the Goat Woman will have time to set another trap for us, so let's just make it to the Isle of Sun.

Thom found a little comfort in knowing all the others had been poked too. Either they would all live or all die.

* * *

The Road of Leaves continued its descent through a thick forest. It was actually quite gloomy on this stretch, though it had seemed bright after the enchantment of darkness. Thom kept looking over his shoulder, expecting to see her chasing them, but the Road remained empty except for shadows and autumn-colored leaves.

"We're close to the Isle," said Francis. "I don't think she will show herself openly now. Not after all that has happened."

"Have we gotten away?"

Francis had a hand resting on his donkey for support as he staggered a bit. The monk still answered him, though. "That I don't know, mage, for who can fathom the motives of those captured by dark magic? Her accomplice is still in our party and we haven't learned the reason for the attacks."

"So we're still in danger," deduced Thom, still worrying about the poison.

"Wisdom would assume as much," agreed the monk.

They walked awhile in silence, but something still puzzled Thom. He finally asked Francis. "Who shrieked in there? It sounded like someone dying."

"If it wasn't you, then I don't know. I've already asked the others and everyone denied screaming."

Thom humphed. "I'd guess Geoffrey, for he seems to panic easily."

"Maybe," said Francis, not sounding convinced, "but she was in there too and she cut the ropes between most of us. What if someone was killed in there?"

Thom gave him a questioning look. "All made it out."

"Did they?" asked Francis. "What if she replaced one of us? Didn't you tell me that dark magicians can shape-shift? The Goat Woman may have slain one of our companions and taken his place." Francis paused for just a moment, rubbing his eyes as if it was getting hard to see the Road clearly, and then continued. "Tell me, what was the first question I asked you when we met?"

Thom shivered with sudden gooseflesh. He lost his concentration and staggered, almost falling. Only his hold on the goats kept him upright. What if the monk was right? Someone had been killed and replaced.

"Can't you answer my question, Thom?" Francis spoke calmly, but he had stopped walking and was now looking Thom in the eyes. "What did I ask when we first met?"

"You asked Orem and me what our names were," he finally answered. The monk was verifying that he was indeed who he appeared to be. He realized that he should put the monk to a similar test. "What did we discover on Stony Hill?"

"Dryads, but that isn't a good question. You must assume that she could have listened to any conversation after her disappearance."

Thom thought of another one. "What did Orem say to you during our introductions?"

Francis smiled. "He accused me of wanting to put my hand into his purse. I told him my order benefited from the king's generosity and had no need to beg."

Thom let out his held breath, relieved.

Francis stepped closer and patted him on the shoulder. "Well, that proves two of us. That leaves seven others to worry about. One might be the sorceress and another is definitely her accomplice, so almost a third of our companions serve the dark magic."

He had no response to that. Instead, he stared at the people ahead of him, wondering who might be the impostors. There was the troubadour, the merchant and his guard, the trader, the bricklayer, Lord Geoffrey, and Jake.

"We're definitely not out of danger," said Francis, urging his mule onward and staggering alongside it, keeping a tight grip on its tack. "As for your temporary inability to hear magic, I think you shouldn't share that news with the others. It will only frighten them more."

Thom hoped the monk was right and that his sudden inner deafness was only temporary.

* * *

The Road of Leaves leveled out and they passed a series of small lakes on the right-hand side, the dark waters just out of their reach. Overhead, clouds were building, threatening rain. The temperature on the Road remained constant, but still many of the party raised their hoods against the overcast.

Jake kept them at what seemed a fast pace, although all of them were somewhat unsteady in their steps. Even though Jake swayed a bit in the saddle, he refused to slow down. Though many grumbled, no one really protested for they all knew the day was getting long. It was already late afternoon.

Thom thought that he and the monk might have gotten stronger doses of her poison, for the two of them seemed to struggle the most to keep up. The dizziness didn't subside and Thom still couldn't hear any of the magic of the Road or anything else that might be nearby. His inner ear was now deaf.

Finally, their route did a couple of twists and then straightened out to reveal a series of stone archways up ahead. The forest was dense here, offering no view of what lay beyond the archways. Nonetheless, the group let out a ragged cheer and some started running until Jake yelled for them to slow down.

"There might still be another surprise ahead. I don't want anyone dying so close to safety. Stay together. Magician, hurry up those goats and let me know if you sense anything odd with the magic around us."

Thom tried to hurry up his charges but he said nothing about his lost abilities. After Francis' warning, he dared not make such a confession. The sorceress already knew about it, but it would frighten all the others. He decided to remain quiet and just hoped no more attacks occurred.

When they made it safely to the first archway, Thom sighed with relief. Neither he nor the others hesitated there, but rushed through the shimmering gray, through another archway, and then a third, coming out on a huge wooden dock that thrust out onto a large river. There was room for everyone on the wooden planks, with plenty of space to spare.

It was markedly warmer now that they were through the archways. Even though the skies were still partially overcast, the cloud shadows no longer seemed threatening. Those in the party that had their hoods up, now dropped them. Merchant George took his cloak off, laying it over his mule. Thom loosened his own cloak but didn't want to try packing it in his pack so he left it on. With just a few footsteps, they had gone from autumn to summer and now he felt almost hot.

Jake dismounted and strode over to where a huge bell hung in a wooden stand. He struck the thing three times, the sound echoing over the waters.

"Thrice," whispered Francis to Thom. "Usually they ring it only once. If there has been a death, they ring twice. I am not certain what three rings announce."

"I hope it doesn't scare off our transport," replied Thom, suddenly worried.

"They will come, for it is their duty and that is something the pixies take seriously."

"What are you whispering about?" asked Troubadour Iago.

"We talk of the island's inhabitants," replied Francis, pointing at a rugged island in the middle of the flow. "The Isle of Sun is a beautiful place, but its inhabitants are a bit peculiar…"

Iago scoffed. "Peculiar, you say? I hear the pixies can be quite troublesome."

"You'll learn about them soon enough," Francis chuckled, "for they have a particular fondness for performers. Once they see your harp case, they'll pester you endlessly for a song or a ballad. Maybe we will finally hear you play, troubadour."

The musician sniffed his disdain and walked away, heading to the edge of the dock to gaze into the passing waters.

* * *

Thom's first sight of pixies came when the river ferry approached, poled by a crew of twelve small men. He stared at them as they neared, for they needed a long look. Their height compared to a child of seven or eight years, but they were bulkier. All had black hair and tan skin. Their exposed arms were covered with the blue tattoos announcing them as part of the Cruct tribe. The island's other tribe, the Pitheni, identified themselves with black tattoos. Thom had learned that much from his master. The crew looked to be strong and competent, aiming the ferry right where it ought to go.

As he understood it, the ferrymen were paid from the road tolls collected at either end. Thom was glad that he wouldn't have to dip into his purse again, for it was already too light even with the three coins that Marcus had given him. Although he would be staying at the magicians' guild house in Camelot, he still expected more expenses there, as well as having to pay the toll again for his return trip. Not having to pay for the ferry was definitely a good thing.

As the boat neared, Jake gave his final instructions. He doffed his hat and ran a hand through his unruly hair. "We are entering a land where the pixie elders serve as lords and masters. Break their laws and you will face a harsh justice, no matter your rank or occupation. These people may be the size of children but they are long-lived adults. Don't try to pick one up, no matter what tales you've heard of pixie-tossing."

"No pixie-tossing? What will I do for fun?" asked Iago in mock horror. Geoffrey snickered.

Jake gave the troubadour a cold stare, but continued. "Another thing to remember is that pixies aren't all thieves. Despite their reputation, they are mainly good folk and are sensitive about any such accusations. Therefore, be certain of it before calling 'thief' or you'll be the one to face punishment. The inn does offer pixie locks for your rooms and storage bins, but it costs extra."

Iago spoke again, this time in a falsetto voice. "We ain't thieves, so long as ya lock it up where we can't get it."

"Enough, troubadour," rebuked the guide.

The two exchanged a silent stare until Iago laughed and looked away.

"He's become bold in his insults," whispered Thom to the nearby monk, wondering if the troubadour might be the Goat Woman in disguise.

Francis whispered back. "Maybe it's from the relief of having survived our trip. Don't assume all odd behavior proves someone to be a shape-shifter. I expect everyone in our party to be a bit drunk on life after what we've endured."

Jake returned to his speech. "We'll overnight on the Isle. You can stay at the inn or camp on the field set aside for travelers, but you can't sleep anywhere else. You also can't gather wood, pick berries, or forage on the island. Any such actions are seen as theft from the community and may cost you your hand.

"Finally, a bit of warning. Although pixies are tiny people, they can probably out-drink you. Their Pix Ale is excellent and cheap but very potent, and anyone found drunk is considered fair game for their meanest pranks. Even the sober might have to endure some hijinks. It is considered poor manners to get angry over such pranks, so either repay them joke for joke or simply ignore their little games."

Jake paused to look at the party he was guiding. "That's my usual speech, however I'll add to it today... I still don't know what's been happening to the Road but I can assure you that the Isle of Sun offers us safe refuge. We may have to linger here for a short time, but I hope we're through with our troubles. Now we can wait for the king's magical champions to right the wrongs done against the Road of Leaves."

Their guide donned his hat to signal that he was done.

Road of Leaves

Thom turned his focus back on the ferrymen, fascinated by the deep voices coming from those child-like bodies. The pixies yelled and cursed as they poled the ferry into line with the dock. They knew their business and soon there came a solid thud as dock and boat kissed. Four of the small men jumped over and quickly tied the ferry tight. Another leaped across the diminishing gap and climbed up onto a wooden piling to confront the party.

He crossed his arms defiantly and gave the group their orders. "Animals load first. You'll take the pen we assign you and give us no lip. No unpacking of loads, unhitching of wagons, or any such foolishness. Wedge all wheels, for we won't stand for any shifting carts or wagons. No riding onto the ferry. No sitting in carts or carriages, or mounting a saddle while we're on the water. Wait until after you're on the far dock before doing such things."

"You little men sure do love making rules," complained Will the Trader, shaking his head. "Maybe we should let the troubadour toss a few of you to teach you some manners."

Two of the pixies dropped the ropes they were securing and ran at Will. They said nothing; the only noise was their bare feet slapping hard on the wooden dock. They knocked the man to the ground while the rest of the party watched in surprise. The trader's large pack fell off his shoulders and skidded along the rough planks, some of the grain samples spilling out. One pixie slugged him in the mouth while the other boxed his ear. It all happened too fast for the man to defend himself.

Just as quickly, the pixies left him and jogged back to their tasks without a glance or comment.

Will sprang to his feet, cursing and spitting blood. He took two heavy steps after them, but then reconsidered. For a moment, he just stood there glaring at the tiny men. When they simply ignored him, he bent over and retrieved his large pack, gathering some of the spilled grain and stuffing it back inside. He then walked to the far side of the dock to sulk.

Jake had done nothing to defend Will. Instead, the guide had been busy whispering with another pixie. Thom guessed he was giving a quick report on their troubles. Well, the guide had said that they would be under pixie law now.

The little man on the stump continued his speech as if nothing had interrupted him. "Passengers, you board last and disembark first. Keep out of the way of the polemen and don't sit on the rails. Fall into the water and there's no certainty that we'll fish you out. No matter your station in life, you'll obey any order given by a crewman." He paused until one of his crewmates whistled. "We're ready to board. Guide Jake, take your horse on board."

While Jake brought his horse onto the craft, the small man looked over the other animals. "The two mules next and then the donkey. What's that? Goats? I hate goats. They'd better not chew through any of my ropes, goat herder. Get them on after the donkey and keep an eye on that pair, or I'll charge you for the damage."

Thom ignored the insults, since they really weren't his animals. However, he looked around for any possible things he could use to wedge the cart wheels.

Francis seemed to know his predicament. "They have wooden blocks hanging on the ferry's railing as you climb aboard. Just grab a pair."

He nodded his thanks.

Thom led the goat cart onto the ferry without mishap and stopped the beasties in the middle on their assigned pen, well away from any of the pixies' precious ropes. He wedged a wheel and then gave each goat a carrot to munch for the ride. He dared not leave them alone, for fear they might cause trouble, so he stayed in the pen. He leaned against the cart, for his dizziness was still there, and hoped the river crossing wouldn't be too choppy.

His hope was misplaced. The boat rocked and shivered as it fought across the current. It was enough to churn Thom's stomach and he barely kept from vomiting on the pixies' boat. He struggled to keep it down, for he had the feeling the pixies would make him clean the deck if he threw up his last meal.

TWELVE

Isle of Sun

The ride over went smoothly, besides the rocking, and soon they were all unloaded on the far dock. Once they were off-board, the pixies lost all interest in them. They busied themselves with securing the ferry and then headed off to a nearby building to await any more calls to cross. The twelve laughed and jostled each other as they went up the side path, ignoring the humans milling on the dock.

Thom was just glad to be back on solid ground. It took a moment for his stomach to calm down. His equilibrium was still off, due to the Goat Woman's poison, which just added to his inner uneasiness. He hoped Francis was correct and that this was just a temporary dampening of his inner ear, for he could still hear nothing of the magic around him.

He looked at the large land in front of him and wondered where he should go. His master had taught him that the Road of Leaves, like all the other magical roads to Camelot, had a Keeper who helped maintain the enchantments and that the Keeper lived here on this island. He wanted to turn over the sorceress' cache to the master magician and report about all that had happened, but he had no idea where to find the Keeper's abode, so he pulled Jake aside before the guide mounted.

"Can you direct me to the Keeper of the Road?" he asked in a soft voice so that no one could overhear. "I need to hand over the sorceress' things and report about all that happened."

Jake held up his hand to forestall him. "Not yet, magician. First, I've been ordered to report to the pixie elders about what happened, but I will certainly tell them that you want to see the Keeper. He is likely occupied trying to repair the lower Road, though, so it may take a bit until you'll be seen, so keep the Goat Woman's magics secure for another day or so."

Thom nodded his understanding, although the delay worried him.

"Just a little patience, young man," encouraged Jake, ending the conversation by walking back to his horse.

Jake climbed onto his mount and raised his voice to the whole company.

"You're free to set your own pace to Pixvale and to make your accommodations for the night; however, you are expected to meet me in front of the inn at sunrise tomorrow for the next leg of our journey. Our party will meet under the oak to the left of the front porch."

"Surely we aren't going out onto that Road again," remarked Trader Will.

"We'll go on, if the upper portion of the Road's safe," replied Jake, "but I'll not be sure of that until I talk with the elders. Even if we're staying here for a time, I'll expect you for that meeting at dawn."

With that, he turned his horse and galloped off.

"He didn't tell me where to unload these goats," complained Thom to the nearby monk.

"Jake has bigger problems than your mangy pair," argued Francis. "Just keep them for now."

"But I've no spare coins for their care," argued Thom. He didn't want to be accused of theft should the goats decide to nibble the local plants.

Francis affectionately patted his donkey on the head. "I'll be going to the inn myself, for Ears has earned a night in a stall with some good grain and I want a bed. However, they do have a wide and lush travelers' field in Pixvale. Let the goats graze the meadow tonight, for that's allowed."

Thom was a bit reassured, but he still planned to hunt down Jake this evening and give him back the stupid goats. The guide could sell them to the locals. Surely, there were some pixies who didn't despise goats, as meat if not as live beasts. If all hated goats, then the innkeeper could butcher them for the humans traveling through. Thom was determined to be freed of Nibble and Dribble today. He had no desire to have a second profession; being a magician's apprentice was enough for him. Let someone else master how to herd goats.

As for the magician's cache of elements in the back, he hoped to turn that over to the Road's Keeper- the wizard who maintained the Road of Leaves from somewhere on this island.

* * *

The dirt road that climbed into the heart of the island felt good underfoot. No leaves. The road was merely a road and the trees were spread out on the slope, not lining the pathway. It still troubled Thom that he could not hear any of the magic around him, but he was glad to be away from that shifting forest debris. He looked back to the far bank of the river they had crossed but saw only the shimmering gateway to the Road; there was nothing to indicate the troubles that lay beyond that shimmer. Shaking his head, he turned back to the road ahead of him and walked slowly onward, letting the goats meander at their own pace because he was still light-headed.

Road of Leaves

The way climbed into the rock and tree strewn hills that formed the spine of the isle, towards a notch between the two highest mounts. Thom knew from his master that Pixvale perched in that saddle, offering human-sized buildings, including an inn and general store for the visitors. The pixies preferred to build their homes within the many small caverns and crevices in the crags overlooking the hamlet.

Summer was here. Thom felt it, starting to sweat halfway up the long slope. On the Isle of Sun, summer was always here. He already missed the coolness and shade of the Road, though not anything else of the trip.

"I can't wait to get away from that incessant ringing," said Iago, as he passed by with a glare at the goats and then hurried on up into the hills. He had his harp and pack hung on his back and they bounced a bit with every long stride he took. Thom watched after him enviously. Guide Jake should have made the others take turns leading the beasties.

* * *

Pixvale lay in the late afternoon shade of the tall hills that surrounded it. Looking through the trees, Thom saw that the peaks still glowed in golden sunlight. The craggy slopes pressed in close, thickly forested between the stony outcroppings. Here and there, Thom caught a glimpse of pixie dwellings among those rocks, each looking like a house partially swallowed by the hills. The pixies seemed to like painting their doors and shutters in bright shades, which helped to reveal them among the rocks above. Each cavern house had its own small garden plot at its door, for he could see the rows of staked vines and tall grain. He wondered how many harvests the pixies brought in, considering that summer never ended for them.

Thom entered the village, a small place where the pixies interacted with the many humans who traveled through. He crossed a wooden bridge over a babbling stream and then passed between a bakery and a smithy, both already closed for the day. Up ahead lay Pixvale's community green, where its fabled dancing nights and wrestling matches happened. Those grounds lay empty, but it was still early for celebration.

Beyond the green he passed a still-open general store, customers loitering inside. The sight of other humans, besides those in his own party, brought him a sense of relief. Maybe his troubles were behind him. When some of the people stared out at the pair of bell-ringing goats passing by, Thom remembered that two of his troubles were still very near.

The Root and Bough came into view just beyond the store, lanterns already shining on its wide front porch. Although the hill above it was still bright with sunlight, the inn sat in the hill's shadow. It was a low but sprawling building among wizened trees. The inn's garish colors of bright yellow with sly-blue trim shone even in the trees' shade. Its glowing windows promised a cheery common room. The place looked inviting, almost beckoning Thom to come in and enjoy the evening. The sounds of flute and harp spilled out the open front door, making him wish he had enough coins to stay there for the night.

Beyond the inn's skirt of pines, a grassy slope led down to a wide meadow where travelers could camp for the night. The field looked crowded in spite of its size, but it was his destination. He led the goats and their cart to an isolated corner of the meadow where the beasties were less likely to disturb anyone. It was far from the fire pits but it promised to be a balmy night, so he didn't need a warming blaze.

He stopped the goats and then realized he had another problem. There were no empty pens anywhere on the meadow and he doubted any other animals would endure their company. Thom couldn't just let the two roam, but then he remembered the scrap of rope that had been around his waist. He had tossed it in the cart after escaping the dark enchantment, so now he retrieved the length and wound it around the cart's axle, tying a goat to each end. It would have to do. He just hoped neither one decided the rope looked tasty.

He considered going over to the inn for a drink, but he didn't trust the steely-eyed pair to behave. So instead, he sat down in the grass out of the reach of Nibble and Dribble and watched the camps around him. He had been sitting for only a few minutes when he saw Francis walking over, leading his donkey.

"What? No room at the inn?" asked Thom when the monk came closer.

Francis stopped in front of him. "The place overflows with nobles and wealthy merchants. I've neither the coins nor the influence to displace any of them, so it looks like it will be another night sleeping under the stars. May I join you?"

Thom smiled and motioned to the grass all around. "Choose your bed, monk, and I'll not charge you anything."

The monk tied Ears to the other side of the cart and then unloaded him with some help from the apprentice. As he pulled the last stack of bundled books off, Thom asked something that he had wondered about. "Do you ever read any of the books you've collected?"

Francis took the bundle and placed it carefully with the rest. "I'm hesitant to undo any of these padded parcels, fearing that I might not retie it properly and expose the books to rain or dust. I'll do my reading once I'm safely back at the monastery." He went over to his faithful donkey and started brushing the animal's coat. "Ears will get a deserved rest and I will work to catalog these books into the library, with the help of Brother Theodoric. The old fellow will swoon when he sees my latest cargo."

"Are you worried about theft while we are here?" asked Thom.

Francis paused in his grooming of the donkey to look over and smile. "Not from the pixies, for they are an honorable folk, no matter what you've heard. As for the other travelers delayed here, that is more of a concern." He frowned a bit as he considered. "The upper Road is still open, so parties are still arriving from Camelot. In addition, the last few parties that came from the Royal Oak are still lingering here. The pixie elders kept them back for questioning and to allow everyone a chance to recover. Usually there are four groups staying here each night, about forty people, but this evening Pixvale is hosting five times that number."

He started brushing Ears again. "It's true that I'll have to keep a careful watch on my cargo tonight, but my greater fear is for your load. We already know that there is at least one person interested in that lead-lined crate at the bottom."

Thom hadn't wanted to think about that. Would the sorceress come back tonight to reclaim more of her goods?

Francis interrupted his worrying. "Look who else is room-less tonight."

Thom looked to where the monk pointed and saw Geoffrey trudging onto the traveler's field, appearing dejected. The youth looked around the meadow, spotted them, and headed their way.

"He's coming to us," said Thom with a slight frown. He had no desire to put up with that silly rooster.

"We're the easiest to spot, being away from the crowd. You should have hid among all the others if you didn't want to be noticed," said Francis cheerfully. "Just be glad it's not Iago coming over to sneer and insult."

The noble's son walked near but then stopped, apparently unsure if he would be welcomed.

"Lord Geoffrey, this is our camp," said Francis. "If you come as companion and fellow camper, then welcome. You may come and join us. If you are looking for servants to order around, then find some other group because we are freemen."

"I am simply looking for a place to sleep," replied Geoffrey, raising both hands in protest. "Have I ever tried ordering either of you? I do not expect to be waited on. I just don't want to be alone."

The monk strode over and put a welcoming arm over the youth's shoulder. "Then join us, my son. Set your saddlebags down and find some soft grass to cushion your blanket. You will have a more comfortable bed than most in that overcrowded inn, though maybe not as fine a dinner."

Geoffrey dropped his bags and all three settled in to eat a cold meal, sharing what they had. Afterward, an awkward silence settled on them until Francis made a suggestion. "Why don't the two of you go visit the pixie gathering? Tonight promises to be a boisterous one with such a large crowd of travelers. I will stay and watch our camp."

Thom wasn't certain he wanted to go carousing with a noble.

However, before he could demur, Geoffrey spoke up. "That is a wonderful idea. Always before, I have traveled by the Road of Waters to Camelot but this time I wanted to see a Pixie Eve. The other boys speak of it so highly. Let us go, Thomas."

"Have fun," said Francis. "I will enjoy some quiet for my prayers. But be wary of the Pix Ale, for it's potent enough to make a bear drunk, let alone young fellows like the two of you."

Geoffrey headed off, now excited, motioning for Thom to join him. The apprentice felt he had no choice but to go along.

"Oh, and one more thing, Thomas," said Francis as the two left. "Pixies are drawn to music and to magic, so if you don't want them pressing in on you, avoid crafting any enchantments."

"No matter how hard anyone begs, they'll get no magic out of me tonight," said Thom, even as he shouldered his knapsack that held his magician's cache. His ability to hear magical elements still had not returned, but he didn't want to say so in front of the nobleman.

Francis gave him a frowning nod, apparently understanding what he meant.

* * *

The walk helped to clear Thom's head, the dizziness fading. However, he was still deaf to magic. He tried his best to ignore that loss, concentrating on the darkened village they were passing through.

Sometime during their walk over to the Pixvale green, Geoffrey started treating Thom like a fellow squire. He shared his excitement of intermingling with pixies and experiencing their native customs. "I heard from David that a pixie girl's kiss is as soft as a puppy's fur but will set your lips to burning."

"Don't try stealing any kisses," urged Thom, imagining the young noble angering the whole assembly. "We are in their land now and not your father's."

Geoffrey giggled nervously. "I would not be so bold a thief even at my father's court. Do not worry, Thomas. I will not molest any pixie's lips, though I will certainly not refuse any kiss offered." Again he giggled with excitement.

Thom heard more outrageous stories about the powers and proclivities of pixies, all sworn true by various squires of the court and not one of them believable. As Geoffrey bantered, Thom listened without much comment. By the time they reached the commons, Thom was convinced that the Goat Woman was not disguised as the young noble, for he doubted anyone could keep up such an act.

On the community green, the pixies had already started their evening competitions. Thom heard music, singing, and laughter. Tall torches stood everywhere, giving the area an abundance of light. He saw pixie men sitting in a circle for some sort of drinking game. Apparently humans were welcome, for three men sat among them, towering over the smaller folk. A pair of pixies marched around the outside of the circle carrying a large pitcher and, whenever the singing stopped, they grabbed the nearest sitter and pulled his head back, pouring a dark, foamy beverage into his mouth.

"Look! A Draught Circle. Jacob claims to have won at that last year, winning a keg and a pixie's kiss."

Thom sensed that the squires of the royal court spent as much time dreaming about cuddling a girl as they did dreaming about becoming a knight. He had no such luxury. He was still just an apprentice and of no interest to any woman looking for romance. Following a few more years of total poverty, he had another two decades as a journeyman. The only women trying to kiss him wanted something, be it money or a potion to curse their enemy. When they learned he had neither to give, they quickly lost interest.

As they stepped onto the grasses, Thom noticed a line of canopies where the visiting nobles congregated. "Do you want to go over there, my lord?"

"Me? Not likely," said Geoffrey, frowning. "I would be spending the whole night running errands and fetching drinks. I might be a squire at Camelot, but here I would be just another lad to order around. Besides, some of them are the louts I was traveling with when my horse faltered. They denied me aid when I needed it, so I have no desire to be in their company. I am a gentleman, but they might provoke me to call them out for their boorishness."

Thom doubted that a mere squire could demand a fight from his betters, but he was no expert on noble customs. Frankly, he gave Geoffrey's words little hearing, for he was distracted by one of those walking among the canopies. She moved gracefully through the crowd, carrying a full carafe of wine but spilling not a drop. She took it to a middle-aged woman reclining on a campaign chair under the middlemost tent. The maid poured into a waiting cup, expertly anticipating her mistress' tendency to jerk the target as she watched the festivities. When done, the maid set the carafe on a side table and then stepped back out of the way to await her next order.

Thom remembered her face, her smile, her vibrant personality.

Adele.

Eric Loren

THIRTEEN

Keeper of the Road

That night Thom saw much of the pixies but only a little of Adele and then only from a distance. After a couple of hours, even Geoffrey noticed that Thom was focused elsewhere, but he mistook it for attention on Adele's mistress.

"So you know about Lady Ursula?" asked the squire, lowering his voice despite the loud cheering happening around a nearby wrestling match. "She is known among the squires for her…um… interests. The boys call her the Spider." He cleared his throat nervously. "She is considered a handsome woman, but she is old enough to be my mother."

"Where is she from?" asked Thomas.

"Her husband has lands to the north, but she spends most of her time at Camelot Castle among the queen's ladies. Thankfully, I rarely have duties in that part of the keep." He blushed. "Some of the others find the risks worth it, to chase the maids and spy on the young ladies, but I am not cut out for the intrigue. I am a mere country noble. I am most comfortable at the stables."

Suddenly Geoffrey frowned. "What will my father say when he hears that I lost the horse he gave me? I need one for my training."

Thom expected that the father would just buy another steed, but he did not say so aloud. Instead, he distracted the youth by pointing out a fair pixie maid selling cups of Pix Ale to the large crowd. "Why don't you buy a cup and share a smile with the maiden? It will ease your worries."

Geoffrey hesitated, obviously nervous at the prospect.

"I will go with you to keep you company."

Geoffrey gave a smile of relief and then eagerly set off to get a drink and a close look at the exotic maiden. Thom followed him over to the wooden platform that held a multitude of kegs and one tiny woman. The wooden structure let her face them at eye level. She stood the height of a seven-year-old, but she had the curves of a true woman. A finely tattooed black vine grew up the side of her neck and then kissed her one cheek with a fragile ink flower. When she turned her attention to Geoffrey, the boy became speechless. Thom had to rescue him.

"Hello there. I am Thomas and this is my companion, Lord Geoffrey. The gracious fellow wants to buy two cups of your Pix Ale." He had decided that a drink would be good now that his dizziness was gone, although he still couldn't hear any magic. He had never realized how much he used this acquired sense until now, and he missed it greatly. He hoped he would fully recover soon, for the loss made him feel incomplete. But there was nothing he could do but wait and maybe drink a little to help forget his temporary loss. If Geoffrey was willing to pay for his cup, so much the better.

"Want a drink, do you? Well, that is why I'm here, gentlemen." She aimed a bright smile towards both of them and then she looked to the youth expectantly. "Let me see your coins, fine sir, and I will get you those cups."

The young noble hastily dug out his money purse and paid. When she returned his change, her small hand lightly brushed his much-larger hand. She then handed over two large cups with a foaming crown.

"If this is your first taste of Pix Ale, drink it slow and savor the taste and the bite. We've enough drunks to tease this night, no need to add your fine faces to the bunch." She gave another flashing smile, aimed more at Geoffrey this time. Thom thought her reason had more to do with business than flirting, but he was not about to tell his companion.

"You are so pretty," blurted out Geoffrey, his first words to her. He looked at her longingly, then blushed and looked away.

"You're kind to say that," the tiny pixie replied with gentleness. "Most handsome lords like yourself wouldn't have noticed me, let alone thought such."

Geoffrey looked back, his eyes locked on her. "Only a blind man would be ignorant of your radiating loveliness. Would that I could marry someone as lovely as you."

She raised a fine eyebrow and gave a quick glance at Thom, showing discomfort with the lad's intensity.

Thom took the hint. "Come along, Lord Geoffrey. She has other customers and we have to sample this fine brew. Say good bye to the beautiful pixie."

Geoffrey mumbled his farewell, once again looking away in shyness. Thom pressed a full cup into his hand and then led him off into the crowd to find a spot where they could sit down and enjoy their drinks.

"I acted the fool," muttered the youth as he flopped onto the grass, not caring that he slopped some of the brew.

"They are magical creatures," replied Thom, sitting down with more care. "How could anyone restrain their tongue when someone so exotic pays them so much attention? I probably would have tripped over my tongue too, but she wasn't smiling at me. Think of the tales you will have to tell when you get back to Camelot. You rode a horse to death, walked through a tunnel of blackness, and flirted with a pixie maiden. The other squires will be envious. So let's add to the list and drink some Pix Ale."

Thom felt a little guilty for making the boy pay, but only a little.

Maybe after a cup of ale, he would find Geoffrey more bearable. Raising the wooden cup to his lips, he took a swallow. The Pix Ale slugged his stomach and then caressed his whole body. He drank over half a mug's worth much faster than he had planned, enjoying its torment with each gulp, and it was rather hard to stop himself from consuming it all. He could already feel its effect on him and he wasn't about to get drunk in a crowd of strangers. He had pick-pocketed too many drunks during his childhood to want to expose himself to that.

* * *

Thom never had a chance to get near Adele. One time he thought she looked in his direction, but he was not certain. He was considering abandoning Geoffrey and sneaking behind the canopies, but then he saw Ned and Joseph in their fake vestments, mingling with the nobles. He turned away quickly. He doubted the two were on the lookout for him but he dared not face them now, tipsy as he was.

"We should go back to our camp," he suggested to his companion.

"Sho shoon? Nonshense," slurred Geoffrey, trying to get up but making it only halfway before tumbling over and nearly landing on a sleeping drunk who had been tinted green and covered with some gruesome fake tattoos by pixie pranksters.

"Yes, it's time," insisted Thomas, helping the lad up. After returning their cups to the makeshift bar, Thom escorted the drunken lord back to the travelers' meadow. Part of the way, Geoffrey tried singing one of the pixie songs he had heard. The final leg, he just hung on Thom, barely awake.

Thom dropped the youth unceremoniously on his blanket and then went to sit next to Francis, who had been quietly gazing up at the stars.

"Have a fun night, did you?" asked the monk.

He wasn't about to admit that he was tipsy. "The pixies are a boisterous people."

Francis chuckled. "True. I've already chased off two groups of youth prowling the camps, looking for mischief. They won't steal, but they do cause havoc. One time they painted my whole donkey red."

Thom gave him a disbelieving look.

"Doubt me if you will, but the Lord knows it's true. It took a day of scrubbing to get Ears right again." When Francis paused, Thom could hear laughter and singing at one of the crackling fires and snoring from somewhere off to the right. The monk continued. "Did you see Iago at the commons? I would think the pixies would have insisted that he play."

Thom shook his head. "I saw no one from our group, though I did see those two impostor clergy that I told you about. I don't think they saw me, but I left as soon as I recognized them."

"It could prove to be a treacherous night," said the monk, "for the sorceress and her accomplice are on the island too. Maybe you should set that enchantment of yours around our little camp, if your abilities have returned. I think the pixies would sense it and keep their distance, but for any others it would provide a warning of their approach."

Thom grimaced. "I still can't hear the magical elements, so I don't dare try mixing any of them."

Francis rubbed his eyes. "I understand. Has your dizziness at least improved?"

Thom looked over at the goats, only partially glad that they hadn't chewed through the rope and run off. He paused because he didn't want to admit his folly, but Francis quietly waited. He finally confessed. "No light-headedness from the Goat Woman's stab, but that Pix Ale hit me more than I expected. I am a bit tipsy."

Francis chuckled again. "The pixies' brew sneaks up on a man, which is why I avoid it. It's a shame that your magical abilities haven't returned yet, but we'll have to make do tonight. I'll stay up to make sure no pranksters or thieves come near. Why don't you get some sleep now and then take over for the second half of the night's watch."

Thom wished Geoffrey could take a few hours too, but the young man was too drunk for that. So Thom agreed, telling Francis to wake him around an hour after midnight, and then lay down and dozed off.

The monk didn't rouse Thom until a few hours before sunrise. He was thankful for the extra hours of sleep but protested that he was the younger man.

Francis laughed, though he sounded tired. "Learn to simply say 'thank you' when someone gives you a gift, my friend. You needed the sleep more. Now take your turn at watch while I rest my weary eyelids."

A bit embarrassed, Thom did thank him and then settled in to watch for any intruders. His head had finally cleared, but his inner ear still seemed deafened.

* * *

Dawn caressed the Isle, as the sun's light slipped between two of the surrounding hills and brushed the traveler's meadow. Thom had been silently sitting on watch, but with the coming of the day, something stirred inside him.

He sprang to his feet and laughed so loud that the other two awoke. He ignored Geoffrey's groaning protest, for he was too happy. Thom could hear magic again. It was all faint and fuddled, but there was now hope that it would fully return. He hadn't realized how much the loss had affected him, but now he was smiling and trying to joke with the other two. Francis, though lacking in sleep, smiled and bantered with him, as if he could feel some of Thom's joy. Geoffrey, on the other hand, held his head, squinted at the day, and begged for him to only whisper or not talk at all.

The three ate a hasty breakfast, then gathered their things and their animals and went to meet with Jake at the inn. Thom walked with a bounce in his step, glad for the new day. He didn't even mind having to lead the goats and, even though Geoffrey begged for the ringing to end, he didn't despise the bells this morning.

They found Jake, on foot, waiting near the front porch near the tree he mentioned. The others showed up too, all of them wandering over from the commoners' field. Merchant George was missing half of his grand beard, but no one else seemed to have been victimized by a pixie.

There many people milling about the inn that morning, as other parties gathered to hear from their Road guides as well. Thom took a moment to look around but he saw no one he recognized beyond those of his traveling party, so he concentrated on his own group and wondered which one might be the Goat Woman in disguise. He caught snippets of some enchantment working nearby, but he couldn't tell exactly where it came from or what magic had been crafted. It frustrated and worried him.

If Francis' assumption was correct, the Goat Woman was in their midst disguised as one of their party. He circled the group, leading the goats behind the gathered men, but failed to find where the magic was coming from. His inner ear was still too muffled.

He glanced at each man, but no one acted like a disguised woman. No one seemed odd, but he did not know them well enough to spot behavior that was out of character. It made him uncomfortable to turn his back on anyone, so he stood at the rear of the group with the tree trunk behind him.

He wondered if the goats would react to her, but they just stood there chewing their cuds. Maybe they couldn't recognize her when she shape-shifted, though he would have thought they might be able to smell her. He watched, but they showed no interest in anyone. They proved no help, further frustrating him.

Jake spoke up. "We will be traveling on, but not for another day. As you have seen, there's a surprisingly large number of people in Pixvale. Apparently, someone failed to stop the traffic entering by the Rowan Gate. It has created something of a logjam here. But don't fret; we will be going on soon enough."

"What of the Road behind us?" asked Merchant George, scowling, almost daring anyone to comment on his half-beard. "Will I be able to travel back down this route when I finish my business in Camelot?"

"I've been told that Merlin's wizards are fighting off the attackers as we speak and will soon have the lower Road secured again, though not restored."

The merchant grumbled. "That means I'm stuck taking the Road of Waters all the way to the River Thames and that is far out of my way. This could devour all my profits for the season. What will the king do to help?"

"I'm but a Road guide, merchant. You'll have to take that question up with the court officials at the king's castle."

Jake took other questions from the group, mainly concerns about supplies and safety. He assured them that the island was safe and that there was no danger of running low on any food supplies other than meat. "The pixies are plant eaters, so there will be no beef stew or lamb pie until you reach Camelot. However, their breads and pastries and vegetable stews are delicious."

When there were no more questions, he dismissed them for the day. However, he asked Thom and Francis to remain. Geoffrey grabbed his blanket and saddlebags from the cart and said that he would look for them later. Thom would have told him not to bother, but that wasn't the way to speak to a noble, even one as young and awkward as Geoffrey. Instead, he just nodded as the youth strode off to spend a day inside the inn's common room.

"What is it, Guide Jake?" asked the monk.

"You two have been asked for," he replied. "I understand that the Keeper of the Road desires to speak with the two of you. Come this way and I will show you what path to take."

"Shouldn't I leave the goats somewhere?" suggested Thom, hoping to finally be rid of them.

"I understand he wants to see the Goat Woman's cart as well, so bring it with you." Jake turned his horse and led them behind the inn and up a small path among the trees. Finally, he stopped at a cross path and pointed up the right-hand trail. "Follow this up and around the hills. Whenever you come to a junction, pick the upper path. The wizard waits at the end of the trail."

Francis let Thom lead as they climbed in silence among the trees and rocks above the vale. Once they were in a more isolated area, Thom told the monk that he was starting to hear magic again.

"I'm glad for you," said Francis, but he seemed distracted. He eyes kept drifting toward the hilltop as if searching for the wizard they were to meet.

Thom shrugged off the others' preoccupation and turned back to the path.

Francis quietly followed with a compliant Ears. They passed numerous pixie homes and saw quite a few of the tiny people, most of them stopping to watch them pass. Thom suspected them to be curious and a bit suspicious, guessing that humans did not often travel these back ways. They did not stop until their path took them over a high pass and around to where they could look down at the distant dock they had landed at just yesterday. At that point, Francis called for a halt.

"Are you getting winded?" teased Thom.

"No, but I'm worried about what we'll face."

"Intimidated by a wizard?" asked Thom, with genuine surprise. "I wouldn't have expected that from you. Though powerful, that's no reason to fear them. You'll find a wizard to be like any grumpy old man you might encounter. Pay no attention to his idle mutterings but listen intently whenever he wants to share his wisdom. Don't fear him; just remember that you share a love of books with those in my guild. Surely a book lover can't be all bad."

"You don't understand, my friend," said Francis, the normal cheer lacking from his voice. "I have a past that I'm not proud of, one that I've buried to follow the Lord's calling. I fear that this wizard may dig it back up and show you its rotting grave clothes."

Thom smiled. So that was what was bothering his friend- an unsavory history. "Monk, I have a tarnished past too. What could be worse than being a thief, heir to a family of impoverished thieves? Now, come on. Let's get this meeting over with."

He pressed on, not really wanting to hear the monk confess his sordid past. He hoped the wizard wouldn't bring it up, for surely Francis' wild youth had no bearing on why the magician wanted to see them.

Francis tried to share his secrets a few more times, but Thom would have none of it. The path's narrowness helped with that, forcing the monk to keep behind the cart. The clanging goat bells prevented any polite conversation. He hoped that Francis would keep his past buried, for Thom liked the monk and didn't want to hear about any horrible crime. He would rather see him always as a good servant of God.

Thomas was also distracted by his reemerging ability to hear magic. Maybe it was the strenuous hike or just because of passing time, but the Goat Woman's poison faded quickly as he climbed the hill. He became aware of the enchantment that surrounded the Isle of Sun as well as an odd concentration on the hilltop where they were heading. He assumed it had something to do with the magician they were going to see.

He turned up the last stretch of the path, a narrow and steep way among the boulders near the top of the craggy hill. He had to concentrate on the trail and guiding the goats. Finally, he passed between two huge boulders and came upon a little dell just under the crown of the hill. There, tucked among some evergreens and up against a rock face, stood an overlarge pixie house. Where most pixie homes were painted in garish colors, this one was a muted gray with forest-green trim. It seemed a sober and serious place to Thom.

A gray-haired man stood before the house, staring at them. He wore the formal robes of a master magician, black in color, which made his skin seem rather pale in comparison. His face wore a frown, but it seemed to be there out of habit and not due to anything the two newcomers had done. He was greeting them barehanded, having left his wizard's staff somewhere else, and there was no magician's knapsack on his back.

The wizard watched intently as they followed the path toward him and Thom had the impression that the old man wanted them to hurry up. Out of the habit of wanting to please a master, Thom quickened his step and urged the goats to a faster pace.

The Keeper waited until they two stopped in front of him and then spoke in a raspy voice. "I am Wizard Cruthen. I hope I have not inconvenienced either of you by requesting your presence; I would have journeyed to you, but the Road's needs won't allow me to neglect it that long. I believe that I have met both of you before. Thomas, do you recall where I dined with your master, Levitanus?"

Thom nodded. He recognized this man from an encounter they had a few years ago. "The two of you met in Lancaster."

"You remember correctly; it was a meal of roast beef that was especially welcome on what turned out to be a dreary day," said the wizard with a nod, then turning to the monk. "And what of you, Francis? We have met more than once. Tell me about the last time we saw each other."

Francis frowned. "We spoke over a dead body."

"The corpse of your late master," agreed Cruthen. "Well men, we have confirmed that we are who we look to be, so I give you formal welcome to the Isle of Sun. I am its guardian as well as being the Keeper of the Road of Leaves. Come inside where we can sit and talk. The animals can wait in the pen over there."

He did not wait for their response, but turned and walked inside his place. Thom knew better than to keep a master waiting, so he headed over to the pen on the side of the building, knowing that Francis would follow. He led the goats inside but left them hitched to the cart. They did not protest when Ears joined them. Francis shut the gate and they walked over to the house.

The monk tried again to share his secrets, but Thom hurried his footsteps to avoid it. Let him confess to his abbot or some priest. He was too uncomfortable with the role.

Eric Loren

FOURTEEN

Confession of a Monk

They entered a cool and muted room that was meant to be a sitting room, but was instead cluttered with books, scrolls, potted plants, animal skulls, and other artifacts. The only items that seemed carefully placed were the wizard's staff and his knapsack, both carefully laid in a stand against the wall. Everything else seemed in mayhem, with only a few paths meandering through the piles and stacks, going to the front door, to the fireplace, to an overstuffed chair, and to a door at the far end. Even over their heads were things, with drying herbs and blooms hanging from the rafters, adding to the smell of dust and flowers. The master stood in the middle of this, looking around in puzzlement. "My pardon, but I rarely entertain visitors here." He used his foot to push aside a pile of scrolls and then bent over to move a potted plant, but stopped when that revealed a large pile of books stacked on the chair he had found behind the plant. He shook his head at the clutter. "I do not think it worth trying to find seating in here. Come, let us retreat to the kitchen. Lalippa won't let me leave any of my projects there; she insists on keeping her work area neat and orderly."

The house was surprisingly deep, going back into the mountainside. Even the hallway was cluttered with stacks of books and leaning map rolls and a stuffed bear that threatened them from a standing position, his fore claws sharp and his maw agape.

When they came to the kitchen, though, they entered a far different world. Everything was clean and in its place. Cruthen brought them to a spotless wooden table. He sat down on one of the unpadded benches, indicating for them to sit across from him.

They did so, with Thom setting his knapsack on the bench between them.

"As I said, I am the keeper of the Road, so I must know more about the attacks that have shattered the enchantment the Founders labored so hard to create. I have heard the reports of four guides already, including the one who led your group, but now I want the insight of a fellow magician. What happened on the Road, Francis?"

"I'm no magician," muttered the monk.

The wizard frowned, his forehead becoming as corrugated as a washboard. "No games here, Francis. You were but days from receiving your master's rank when your mentor turned dark. You are a wizard in all but formality."

"I'm no magician," he repeated. "I am not even a journeyman anymore. I am now Brother Francis, monk of the Benedictine order of Saint Barnabas' monastery. I have renounced my past."

Thom stared at Francis in shock, seeing him as a sudden stranger.

"You cannot really turn your back on who you are," argued Cruthen. "That your master chose the twisted path has no reflection on you or your training. The guild council agreed to that after you took your vengeance on him."

"It wasn't vengeance," answered Francis in a soft voice. "I killed Dorlain to keep him from doing more harm. He had already murdered a whole village of fairies to gain their power."

"And yet you were strong enough to stop him and find your way through the Road of Clouds on your own. That proves you worthy of the title Master Magician."

"Worthy? You think I denounced my training out of false humility?" Francis stared at the older man with fierce eyes. "I left that life because I realized the harsh truth. All magic ultimately leads to dark magic. Some are strong enough to fight off that temptation for a time, but it is always there. You cannot deny it, that subtle desire for more knowledge, more magic, more power. I saw how it corrupted my master and I have no desire to head down that road. Do not slander me by calling me a magician, for that is but a half-step from sorcery and witchcraft."

"You are the one who slanders, Francis," replied the wizard calmly. "I am no sorcerer and neither is Merlin or Thomas' master or dozens of others, from greenest apprentice to the most wizened wizard. We serve our land and our king with integrity. We do not dabble in necromancy or foretelling or any other forbidden art. It is unfortunate that your master succumbed to the dark magic, but do not color us to match his blackened soul. We are different."

Thom's mind raced with the implications of what Francis had just admitted. All that time on the Road, threatened by wind and death and a rogue magician, he had struggled to stay alive. Yet all that time there had been a magician at his side, secretly refusing to offer aid. Francis could have spared him. Maybe the monk could have saved the Road itself, but for his selfish denial of who he was. Thom's anger bubbled and boiled. He suddenly turned to the monk and blurted out, "You could have helped me, but you didn't. You played me for a fool."

"I didn't treat you like a fool, Thomas. I'm not a magician anymore, so I couldn't have helped. I haven't carried a magician's box in years and I haven't crafted an enchantment since the day I killed my old master."

"But you still know how to do things that are beyond my training," replied Thom, glaring at the monk. "You could have taught me things to stop her. You could have saved lives."

"Enough arguing," said the wizard, leaning over the table to break their stare. He continued once both looked his way. "Surely you can agree to help me stop these attacks. Tell me, Francis, what has happened on the Road of Leaves?"

The monk looked down at the table for a moment, silent in his thoughts. Thom wouldn't have been surprised if Francis refused to help the wizard too. But then he began to talk, his voice low and pained. Francis told the wizard about their harrowing days on the Road. Despite his anger, Thom listened. Francis revealed that the missing man from their party had been a magician's journeyman, apparently killed to prevent him from interfering with the plot. Francis had known the dead man, so overhearing about the death caused him to spend time ingratiating himself with the others in the group, looking for the murderer.

Thom couldn't help but interrupting. "You thought I was a killer?"

"Your confession to being a magician's apprentice certainly raised my suspicions, but I soon learned that you were too naive to be of the dark arts. You are a good man, Thomas."

"You could have helped me, but instead you left me to struggle against a rogue." He couldn't keep the hurt out of his voice. "You could have helped and maybe you could have saved the Road of Leaves. So many died and you just stood there doing nothing."

"Revealing my past would have done nothing except to get us both murdered. Why do you think they let you live? It was not because they feared your powers. The Goat Woman and her accomplices saw no threat in a mere apprentice. Instead, they found it amusing to have you act as their ignorant servant, caring for her goats and her cart."

"Who is this Goat Woman?" asked Cruthen, interrupting them.

"I had never seen her before," answered Francis.

"But it seems that you still think this person is a woman nonetheless," noted the wizard.

Francis nodded.

"And you suspect her of having accomplices?"

"Yes. Thomas saw her meet with another on the night we were at Blue Waters, so we know at least one other traveled with our group. Considering the many attacks on the Road, there may have been more dark magicians loose inside the enchanted way." Francis met the wizard's gaze. "You should also know that we think she killed someone in the group and took his form."

"I suspected as much when Guide Jake told me of that lightless passage you had to go through and of the unexplained screams, but that would not have worked unless the rest in the group had their magical senses hampered. When your guide mentioned that everyone was pricked by some needle or fine blade, then I was sure of it. Have either of you regained your ability to hear magic?"

"Then it was a potion to hamper magic as Francis said," noted Thomas, then realized where the monk had probably read about it: during his training to be a wizard. "Was it then an enchantment too?"

"No. It is but a plant turned into a paste or liquid, without magical elements. Some plants make us sneeze, others cause hives. This particular plant causes dizziness and dulls the ability to hear with our inner ear."

Thom was curious what plant it was but refrained from asking, for he knew masters didn't like being questioned by mere apprentices. Instead, he focused on the more urgent problem. "The sorceress and her henchman are now on the Isle of Sun."

"I anticipated that, Thomas. As soon as the Road began its pained writhing, I expected to see attacks along its whole length. I am not so foolish as to think this idyll place would be sacrosanct to them."

Cruthen offered no further explanation of how he would prevent any more attacks. Instead, he asked both of them more questions, drawing out many details about the Road's destruction.

Finally, after nearly an hour of conversation, the wizard called for a halt. He stood up and went to a side door, calling out for someone. Soon an elderly pixie woman entered. Her hair color was fading toward gray, but her blue tattoos were still colorful and intricate. She asked what she could do.

"Can we have some nourishment, dear Lalippa? We will wait outside and leave you to your cooking wonders."

The wizard led them back to the animal pen so that he could study the cart's contents. What he found disturbed him. He looked up at Francis. "You saw what she brought?"

"I saw, or more actually heard, since Thomas opened it at dusk."

Thom wondered what worried them, for he did not know any of the greater enchantments. He knew the cargo was worth a king's ransom to a master magician, but not how someone might use all of those magical elements. His own training had involved only a handful of them so far.

"Did you pocket any of this?" Cruthen asked of Thomas.

He had no qualms in admitting what he took, for it had kept them alive.

The wizard nodded his approval. "I would suggest you take more before leaving, for the cart and goats will stay here. I do not want the rest of it to get into her hands."

"You plan to send us on to Camelot?" asked Thom.

"Perhaps, but even if you linger in Pixvale, you will go back without the goats and their load. Come apprentice, take some of the elements now and you too, Francis. There is enough to supply five magicians' boxes in this trove, so you might as well take some in case you need it when you return to the Road."

The monk refused, but Thom obeyed. He took what he knew he could use, refilling the appropriate vials in his magician's box, and then would have stepped away but the wizard stopped him.

"Add these powders as well," said Cruthen, holding up a handful of vials. "If you cannot use them, then give them over to your master when you see him next."

Thom did as told, slipping the additional glass tubes into some of the empty felt-lined slots in his box. When done, he squatted over his knapsack and carefully stashed the box among his clothes. Cruthen waited, then motioned for Thom to close the Goat Woman's oversized box as well.

Thom straightened quickly from that duty when one of the goats came over and tried to nibble on his cloak. He pulled the cloth out of its reach and shooed the thing away. Although he realized that he would now be rid of Nibble and Dribble, he couldn't really enjoy the parting. His thoughts were still upset over how Francis had used him.

Just then, the cook came out to announce that their meal was ready.

"Thank you, Lalippa. Could you find Holvark and let him know that he has animals to tend? The donkey will be leaving with our guests, but the goats and their cart are staying."

She said she would do his bidding and strode off toward a small orchard on the far side of the dell.

Cruthen did not wait, but led his guests back to the kitchen where they found a simple meal laid out for them: warm bread, jam, cheese, grapes, pears, candied nuts, and mugs of cider. He bade them to sit and eat.

As he ate in silence, Thom's anger continued to simmer. The monk had called him friend and had seemed a person worth trusting, but Francis was nothing but a sham, as much of an impostor as Ned and his father. Maybe the abbot accepted Francis' sham of godliness, but Thom refused to. What a fool he had been to believe the claims that Francis knew so much about magic from merely reading books. The monk had let him take every risk, probably snickering into the sleeve of his robes all the while.

After the meal, the wizard began his questioning again, asking now about those in the group as he tried to assess which of them served the dark arts. They had just begun a conversation about Lord Geoffrey, when the pixie cook interrupted.

She barged in, face moist with tears. She ran up to her employer and spoke in a pained voice. "Sir, come quickly! It's Holvark! He's dead!"

"What?" The wizard sprang to his feet with such energy he rocked the table and sent his chair flying. "Where, Lalippa? Where is he?"

"At the animal pen. I went out to ask him to move a flour barrel and found him lying in the mud. It's horrible…" She broke into sobs.

"You two, come with me," ordered Cruthen, now acting as the master who would brook no dissension from underlings.

The three of them ran outside to find a pixie man surrounded by much blood. The pen lay open. The goats and their cart were gone, their bells now around the neck of the dead man. Ears stood quietly nearby, watching it all with big, sad eyes.

The wizard ran over to his worker and cradled the corpse, revealing to Thom that the magician had felt friendship toward the tiny fellow.

"The Goat Woman," said Francis, looking back down the hill. "She retrieved her cache of elements and her pets."

Thom chose not to respond to the monk, but instead watched the Keeper as Cruthen carried the body over to a grassy area, setting it down with tenderness and removing the offending bells, tossing them away.

"My poor Holvark. You did not deserve this." The wizard sighed. "I will need to inform your kin."

Thom waited near the house, uncertain what to do. The loss saddened him, but this was just one of many he had witnessed on this trip. Far too many.

After some time, the wizard stepped away from the body and looked over at his guests. "I have no more time for the two of you. Thank you for your candor in answering my questions. You are free to go. Keep an eye out for those goats, for she will be near them, but do not approach her yourselves. No need to come all the way up here to report it; just go to the inn and ask for a pixie elder. Now go, but be careful." He turned back to the fallen pixie and stood over the mangled body, obviously mourning.

Thom hesitated as Francis went to retrieve his donkey. He wanted to offer comfort to Cruthen, but how do you give solace to a master magician? Instead, he hefted his knapsack onto his shoulders and walked off, not waiting for the monk. He had no desire to talk with Francis ever again.

FIFTEEN

The Root and Bough

Thom strode down the hill trails as fast as he could, never looking back. He wanted nothing to do with the false monk walking somewhere behind him. He encountered no others along the way and was glad of that. He didn't even hear anything. No birds. No wind. No sounds, especially now that the goat bells no longer followed him. It reminded him that he was still inside Merlin's enchantment, a place that normal animals and insects avoided. His inner ear had now recovered enough that he could at least hear the background sounds of magic, the steady rhythm that was the encompassing summer-like enchantment of the Isle. It was the only thing he heard, besides his footsteps on the gravel path.

Thom realized how alone he was.

Against his own desires, he finally looked behind him, but Francis was nowhere in sight. He looked all around and couldn't even see any pixie houses at the moment. Nothing but trees and rocks surrounded him. He hurried on, wanting to get back among others. When the Root and Bough finally came into view, Thom decided he needed a drink.

The inn's common room ran long and low. One end held nicer tables covered by tablecloths, each encircled by a foursome of padded chairs. The other end held bare trestle tables with plain benches. Thom knew his place; he headed for the trestles.

He sat down at a half-full table, picking the empty end, and waited for one of the pixie maidens to take his order. The place seemed subdued this early, with no music or laughter, just the low hum of morning conversation provided a bit of noise. He still felt alone.

He placed his order and soon had his stone mug full of plain beer, having decided that Pix Ale would be too much this day. He took a big swallow and looked around the room some more, concentrating on the nobles' tables. He was glad that neither Ned nor Joseph was present. He was even more enthused when he saw Adele's mistress sitting with a nobleman. If Lady Ursula was here then maybe her servant would soon appear at her side. He wanted to catch another glimpse of Adele, for a look was about all he could expect.

Thom was so focused on the far end of the room that he didn't notice when someone sat down on the bench next to him.

"Hello, Thomas. Are you so fascinated by my mistress that you can't take your eyes off her?"

Startled, he turned and found Adele sitting beside him. She smiled, her blue eyes dancing.

"Adele. I... I was looking for you."

She laughed. "This is the second time that you haven't seen me, but at least this time I didn't end up with my rump in the dust. What must I do to get you to look at me?"

He cleared his throat. "You need only be near, for your beauty always catches my eye."

She scooted a bit closer on the bench. "Am I near enough now, or is your eyesight that poor?"

He opened his mouth to respond, but words failed him. He stared at her, not understanding why she would bother with him.

She laughed again. A pretty laugh. "You look like a fish, with your mouth open like that. Have you already lost yourself in your cup?" She grabbed his mug and gave it a sniff. "It's not Pix Ale, so you probably aren't drunk. What then? Do women scare you? Trust me; there is nothing scary about me. I'm just a noblewoman's maid who happens to be interested in getting to know you."

"Why?" he blurted out and then wished he could grab the word back.

Her face became serious. "It's not your looks, though you have a certain handsomeness about you. I guess you captured my interest the first time I saw you."

"Because I ran you down on the road?" he asked, puzzled.

"No, silly man, that wasn't the first time I saw you." She absently brushed a loose strand of black hair behind her ear. "I saw you the first time in Lancaster, when your master was meeting with another wizard. You were too focused on serving the two of them to notice anyone else in the room. However, I certainly noticed you."

"You were there?" He tried to remember who else had been at that inn, but it had been a few years.

"Oh yes. My mistress was traveling on her way home and had us stop at that same inn. I saw you serving those two great men. You did it with diffidence but no fear. You also listened carefully to their conversation and even joined in when they invited you to. I found that intriguing, for I like intelligent men."

He suddenly worried that she was cozying up to him in the hopes of getting some love potion or poison. Many commoners had such misconceptions about his kind. "So you know that I'm a magician's apprentice?"

"I do, and I find that intriguing, too. It takes a strong man to commit to such a course, for I hear that the rewards are decades away and then not even guaranteed. I understand not all make it to master magician, even after so many years of learning and serving." Her smile returned and she added, "Don't worry, Thomas. I have no intention of asking for a magical brew or a good luck charm. I'm interested in you, not your box of tricks."

He didn't know what to say in response so he simply looked at her, diving into her eyes and sinking deep.

She colored a bit at his attention. "So tell me, why are you traveling the Road? Do you have anything to do with the disturbances or the attempts to stop them?"

"I'm delivering a message from my master to the magicians' guild house in Camelot and retrieving some supplies for him." Absently, he touched his chest where the small leather satchel hung beneath his shirt. His master had sealed it with wax to guarantee that no one opened it besides its intended recipient. "As for the attacks on the Road, I'm neither the attacker nor the defender. I am but a mere apprentice trying to survive another day."

"I think you are no *mere* anything."

He smiled at her encouragement. "You're too kind."

"You could buy me a drink, apprentice, if your purse can afford it."

Suddenly embarrassed that he had not thought of that, he looked over his shoulder and motioned to the nearest pixie maid. She nodded that she would come over when free. Thom turned back to Adele and found her on her feet and climbing over the bench.

"I'm sorry, Thomas, but my mistress is looking for me. I must go."

Thom looked that way and saw that her mistress was indeed craning her neck and frowning. When he looked back, Adele bent over and gave him a butterfly-soft kiss on the cheek, making him blush. He noticed that she blushed, too.

"We are leaving with the noon group, but maybe I will see you in Camelot." She set a fine hand on his shoulder. "Look for me around the castle."

With that, she hurried off to her mistress' side. Thom watched her go, amazed at what had just happened.

"Ready for another, sir?"

He turned at the interruption and found the pixie lass at his side.

His eyes drifted back toward the quickly departing Adele and he frowned. "The young woman had to leave, so no thank you."

* * *

An hour later, he stood among the trees and watched the carriage pull away. Adele was hidden inside with her mistress, but he still watched. Ned and Joseph were also in the party, as he expected. What surprised him was seeing Troubadour Iago, now mounted on a mare. He wondered why the performer had switched parties and how he had found a horse in a place that kept no extra livestock. He watched as the riding group left Pixvale, heading toward Camelot. Soon, they were out of sight and he had nothing more to look at, but still his eyes lingered on the empty road.

For the rest of the day, Thom kept to the woods, avoiding the summer sun and the people milling about Pixvale. He no longer had goats to care for, so he was free to do as he pleased. He chose to avoid others. He wanted to be alone and daydream about a particular young woman.

Near sunset, he finally returned to the travelers' meadow looking for a place to sleep. He spotted Francis and his donkey at one of the fire pits with Merchant George and his guard, Marcus. Thom kept far away from them, picking a spot at the very edge of the field where he dropped his pack and sat down on the grass.

It felt odd not having to tend those annoying goats.

He spent the evening reviewing his master's lessons on enchantment limitations and the use of natural elements to augment magical elements. Thom wished he had Lamond's Book of Subtractions and Additions to Magic so that he could review it. But the book was back at his master's cottage, so he would have to rely on memory. It was a good exercise, taking his mind off everything else. He sat there quietly, almost in a trance, as he went through the various lessons.

Geoffrey found him that way two hours later, just as the sun gave its last caress to the high hills. Somehow the youth spotted Thom in the gloom and came over. "There you are. I almost did not find you without your goats. Where are they? And why are you over here and not with the monk?"

He looked up at the youth. "I gave the goats to someone else and then someone killed the pixie watching them and stole them away, so I have no idea where those beasties are. As for the monk, I have found him to be a bore and a charlatan, so I choose not to associate with him."

Geoffrey sat down uninvited. "That is a shame, for I enjoyed his company." He dropped his saddlebags to one side and then pulled out a pear. He looked it over by the moonlight and then took a loud bite.

"If you miss the monk, you can join him at one of the fires."

"I would rather stay near you, if you do not mind. I think the killers will avoid a magician."

"I think the pixie's killer has no desire for your neck."

Geoffrey kind of growled in frustration. "I am not talking about that killing; I meant whoever murdered the others."

"What others?"

"You did not hear? They found two people killed today, a man and a woman." Geoffrey shivered a bit. "I am so eager to return to court, no matter how much the other squires tease me. At least it is safe there. I thought going home for my sister's wedding would be an enjoyable adventure, but it has been nothing but trouble." He took another bite and chewed thoughtfully.

"Two dead?" He had missed the gossip while wandering the woods.

The youth nodded. "It was quite the scandal when they found the two this afternoon, both strangled and then stripped to their underclothes. Who would do such a terrible deed? They say it was not the doing of the pixies, but I still have my suspicions. Those wee folk are a wild bunch. What if they thought the two were trespassing or stealing? They might have killed the two for that and considered it merely justice. I say that the taking of the clothes proves it was pixies, for that is the kind of horrible trick they would pull on a dead person."

Thom had his doubts that pixies did their pranks on corpses, but he chose not to argue. "Have the two been identified?"

"I do not think so. When I left the inn this evening, the two bodies were still lying on the porch for people to look at. What an indignity. I never want to be put on display like that. Hopefully they are mere commoners, for no noble should be so humiliated, even after death."

Thom had a sudden fear. He had not seen Adele leaving, just the carriage. What if the Goat Woman had killed her and taken her form? Oh God, he thought, let it be someone else. Not Adele.

His heart began to pound as he sprang to his feet. "Show me where the two are, for I might know them."

Geoffrey grumbled about walking all the way back to the inn in the darkness, but he stood up nonetheless. They hurried to the Root and Bough and up onto the wide front porch. Geoffrey led him around the corner to the far side and there they found the two bodies covered by blankets. Someone had hung extra lanterns in that section, so the area was well lit. The youth would go no further than the inn's corner, saying that viewing the bodies once was enough.

Thomas stepped closer and pulled the first blanket down, revealing a dead man. He quickly stepped over to the other corpse and pulled back that blanket, revealing a woman he did recognize. Lady Ursula.

Thom sighed, glad it wasn't Adele. But then he realized that she was still in danger. The Goat Woman must be disguised as Lady Ursula now. Adele was riding inside a carriage with a dark sorceress. He stepped away from the bodies, not bothering to cover them up. He could only think of telling someone, of getting help for Adele.

"Where is Guide Jake?" he asked.

The youth shrugged. "I doubt he is at the pixie dance, for he is too dour for such frivolity. Perhaps he lingers in the common room." He glanced toward the corpses, now that they were mainly obscured behind Thom's back. "Did you recognize them? I will admit that I really did not look when they asked me to. Who has the stomach to view such horror?"

Thomas ignored the squire's questions and went inside, with Geoffrey trailing behind. He found the common room well patronized, but no Jake in sight. He approached the innkeeper who stood behind a counter drying freshly washed mugs with a white towel. The pixie stood on a platform that brought him to eye level with any humans on the other side of the counter.

"Excuse me, but do you know where I can find Guide Jake? I need to talk to him about the bodies outside."

The pixie set down the mug and rested his tattooed arms on the countertop as he focused on Thom. "What is this? You recognize the dead people? Stay here while I get the elders on duty and your guide."

* * *

Soon, he was in a back room with two pixie elders and Jake. Geoffrey had to wait out in the common room. Thom told them about Lady Ursula and watching her coach leave with Iago.

"I knew that the troubadour had joined the other party, but I hadn't realized he rode out on a new horse," said Jake. "I thought he had found someone to give him a ride on their wagon or in their carriage. Sounds like he killed some for their mount."

"I am glad to hear that the troublemakers have gone on without attacking our home," said one of the gray-haired pixies. Thom thought of him as Black-Arms Elder, for he had black tattoos covering his arms. The tattoos were an intricate weaving of vines that seemed to undulate as the old man flexed and moved his arms. The vine tattoos ended in detailed flowers on the back of his hands, tiny ebony blossoms that also wrapped around his wrist and stretched out along each finger.

Black-Arms continued, "But this means new danger for the upper Road. We will send word to Wizard Cruthen."

"Can you also send a warning ahead to Camelot?" asked Thom, hoping they could intercept the Goat Woman's party when it came out at the Rowan Gate.

Jake answered. "The messenger would have to pass them on the Road and then would beat their party by only a few hours. I don't think a messenger will help."

"Our greater problem is the possibility that they will collapse the upper section of the Road also," said the other pixie elder, whom Thom thought of as Blue-Arms Elder for the blue tattoos winding down to his hands. The pattern was as intricate and elaborate as that on the other elder, but these indigo vines were thicker and with deep-blue thorns. "They will isolate us from the outside."

"I hear that Cruthen could allow the Isle to connect to the Road of Waters…"

Blue-Arms dismissed his fellow elder's idea. "He would not do that, for fear that the attackers might gain access to that route too. We are alone in this battle, should we get cut off from Camelot."

"Why are they attacking the Road?" asked Thom. That question had been troubling him for a time.

"Does it really matter now?" asked Black-Arms.

"It matters," argued Thom. "Is their goal to isolate Camelot or to draw Merlin into battle? Is this the start of a war or is it a personal vendetta? So much is unknown."

"You're the one who traveled with them, apprentice," said Blue-Arms. "Did they reveal anything by their words or deeds?"

Thom shook his head. "Iago was a pompous one, claiming to be a troubadour but uninterested in entertaining any of the nobles we met. As for the Goat Woman, she was with us for such a short time that I never even heard what name the old hag claimed for herself."

"I believe she is Narissa, the former apprentice to Wizardess Liliana," announced Wizard Cruthen, barging into the room. Geoffrey entered behind him. "And if so, then she is not an old hag but closer in middle age like the dead woman outside." The elderly magician seemed haggard. "Guide, gather your comrades to the common room." He looked behind him at Geoffrey. "Young lord I was told you were party of Thomas' party. I need you to retrieve Francis the monk. You know who he is, so please bring him back here."

Once the guard and the noble were gone, the two pixie elders came close to the wizard and looked up at him earnestly.

"What has happened?" asked Blue-Arms.

"I have just learned that the queen has entered the Road and the passage has collapsed behind her. As far as I can tell, her party has found refuge at Twin

Hills, but she is now cut off from Camelot."

"Who would be so reckless as to let her enter?" asked Black-Arms.

"It seems someone was intercepting all of my reports on the attacks, leaving both the king's court and the magicians' guild house ignorant. I have not yet learned much, but I know the traitor in Camelot is now dead, though justice came too late. Guinevere is on the Road with only nine escorts and Merlin is not yet back in Camelot to try and bridge this newest gap in the Road's magic."

"Who would betray the king?" asked Black-Arms.

"The messenger who arrived was not so well-informed and the letter he carried from Wizard Thallus from the guild house was rather terse."

"How did a messenger get through?" asked Blue-Arms.

"The river," guessed Black-Arms, giving a knowing stare at Cruthen.

"Yes, the Road of Waters passed the Isle briefly at sunset," acknowledged the wizard, "but it has now moved on. Where the Road of Leaves shifts each night, the Waters can change course by the hour and I have no control over its flow. I have enough of a burden watching this Road."

"Did a magician deliver the message?" asked Thom, hoping the worn man now had help.

"It was an apprentice greener than you, Thomas." Cruthen looked around the room and spotted a stout chair in the corner. He trudged over and sat down with a sigh. The wizard looked even older than he had upon entering. "Apprentice, while we wait for the others to arrive, I want to hear your story. What were you reporting to the others?"

Thom told him but was done with his tale well before the others arrived, so for a time he and the two pixies waited quietly while the wizard took a brief snooze.

"He's exhausted from his work," whispered Blue-Arms. "Not only did he keep the Road of Leaves from completely collapsing, I think he has stabilized it and maybe even started its regrowth."

"Will he be able to help rescue the queen?" asked Thom, in his mind he added *and Adele.*

Blue-Arms looked long at the sleeping wizard. "I think not. The enchantment cannot be neglected that long and he is too worn to divide his attention."

Black-Arms nodded his agreement. "He cannot do more than he already has. Ask more of him and Wizard Cruthen will die of exhaustion."

SIXTEEN

Divided Parties

Wizard Cruthen opened his eyes when the others entered: six guides, the monk, and a magician's apprentice who introduced himself as Lance. Lance had delivered the message from Camelot. Thom guessed that the youth was in his first five years of training, for he was even younger than Squire Geoffrey.

The wizard stood up. "I do not have much time left, so I will ask Apprentice Thomas and the pixie elders to share the details of what has happened later. For now, let me just say that Queen Guinevere is in danger, probably stranded at Twin Hills Waycircle. The Road between Grassy Dunes Waycircle and Rowan Gate has been severed, so there will be no help coming from Camelot. We must rely on whoever is on the Isle of Sun, whether he be noble knight or lowly magician's apprentice."

Cruthen sighed, giving them all a mournful look. "I must get back to my post, for the Road enchantments demand it. Even now I can tell some are growing unstable again on the lower Road, while the upper half groans in agony." He moved towards the door.

Thom couldn't hear anything of the Road's magic, for the enchantment of the Isle blocked it. He wondered how the master magician could here through the portals and down the two Road lengths.

Jake blurted a quick question before the wizard could get away. "What are we to do?"

The wizard paused with his hand on the door's knob. "Save our queen. I cannot linger to organize this, so I am depending on you men." He looked up, as if he were able to see through the inn's walls and all the way along the Road of Leaves' tortured length. "I must go now. Pardon me, men, but I can delay no longer."

Cruthen opened the door to reveal a foursome of gray-haired pixies waiting for him in the hallway. Thom guessed them to be two husbands with their wives, for each pair held hands. Although well-wrinkled, the pixies stood straight in their pride and strength.

Speaking to the two couples, Cruthen said, "My friends, we must get going for the night grows late and we still have much to prepare. Thank you for being willing to sacrifice for the greater good. Let us go and gather some needed supplies, for I want to be at the lower Road's ferry by midnight."

Everyone stared as the door closed behind the Keeper of the Road and the four ancient pixies.

They were silent for a moment. But then, the six guides started talking all at once, tossing questions at Thomas. He did his best to answer them, though his story came out in bits and pieces as everyone demanded that their particular question be answered. He told them about the Goat Woman, whom he now knew to be the Sorceress Narissa, and about the many attacks on the Road. He was able to enlist Jake's help with some of the details, but he still ended up doing most of the explaining.

At some point, Thom glanced over at the pixies, but they ignored him. They were whispering with Francis. Apparently, they chose not to add anything to his story. Thom was stuck trying to satisfy the guides' demanding questions.

"This is a rat's nest," complained a guide- the very one that had led the mounted party out of Stony Hill three nights ago. This was the rude man Thom had thought of as the Rider Guide.

"Are you magicians capable of facing down a sorceress?" asked another of the guides.

Thom shook his head and muttered, "Not likely."

"I'd agree with that. Be foolish to depend on that one," declared the Rider Guide. "He has no magic worth spit."

"I will challenge her," announced Apprentice Lance. "She is just a woman, after all, and women are weaker than men. Let me go out to rescue the queen."

They seemed to accept the lad's boasting as fact and started plotting a rescue attempt with him. One of the guides took it upon himself to seek out some of the nobles and soon the room was full of men swearing that they would liberate the queen.

Thom found himself pushed to the side, for they saw him as too timid to help. Francis was still whispering with the pixie elders and ignoring all the others. Only Jake seemed to be aware of Thom and walked over to where he stood.

"Magician, what are your thoughts?"

"Everyone underestimates Sorceress Narissa."

Jake sighed. "I don't, for I endured that trip too. I saw her powers. So, is there any hope of rescuing the queen?"

"There is always hope," said Francis.

Thom hadn't realized that the monk had come over. He frowned disapprovingly at the robed man.

Francis continued. "Guide Jake, we will find a way to rescue the captives and defeat the villains. Good should always defeat evil."

"Nice words, monk, but this isn't the time for sentimentality. They'll not show their bellies like a submissive dog just because we claim righteousness on our side. More likely, they will tear us apart like hares caught by the hounds."

"I offer more than words," said Francis. "The pixie elders have convinced me that I must do all that I can."

"That is kind of you," said Jake. "You can pray during our mission."

Francis nodded. "Of course I will do that, but I will also share my knowledge of magic with the two apprentices. I'm no crafter of enchantments but I will help those who are." He did not explain further, but motioned for the pixie elders to join them and then indicated that they should all leave. "We should talk somewhere quieter, for the others are busy working themselves into a battle rage. Let them beat their swords against their shields while we plan the true rescue. Once their passion subsides, we will convince them of the best way forward."

"We will do that, Brother Francis, but I'm not so certain the others will be easy to convince."

Although Thom did not really trust the man any longer, he let Francis lead him away with Jake and the two pixies. The innkeeper provided them with a neighboring room where they met for most of the night, carefully considering how to rescue the queen and stop any more attempts at sabotage.

The noblemen could be heard the whole time, becoming louder as they bragged about accomplishments and argued over who should lead their party. They expected to win Arthur's favor by rescuing the queen and knew the greatest glory would go to whoever led the expedition. It became so heated that two of them dueled in the room, to the accompanying cheers and yells of their fellow nobles.

More than once, Thom and his group stopped their discussions and went over to the other room to try bringing some common sense to the arguing, but they were ignored. Most of these men had not endured the unraveling of the lower Road or seen the might of the sorceress. Being ignorant of the horrors, they saw this as some grand adventure and chance to prove their chivalry and prowess.

After three tries, the pixie elders refused any more attempts to talk sense into the nobles, saying that the humans were too excited to heed any words of caution. Francis agreed with them. When Jake also grudgingly admitted that the others were too heated to hear any logic, Thom asked for one more attempt and he was able to get the other apprentice aside from the others, facing him outside on the wide porch.

"You have to talk some sense into those noblemen," Thom argued. "If they charge up the Road haphazardly, they will be killed and the queen lost."

"What do you know about nobles or magic?" asked the youth. "I've never seen you at the guild house, let alone at Camelot castle. You can't be much of an apprentice if your master won't even send you to the guild house for further training or let you serve in the king's court. Most likely, you are little more than a hedge mage, with a bit of skill and some basic crafting knowledge, but they need more than that to aide them now.

"As for those brave men in there, they know what they are doing. I have seen them at court and many of them have the ear of the king and his ministers. They know how to plan a battle and how to rescue women in distress. This affront on the king and on Merlin demands a bold response. We will charge up the Road so fast that the sorceress and her allies will have no time to set any traps. Surely you know magic well enough to know that enchantments take time to craft. The lords leading our party know that as well, which is why they say speed will overcome any attempts to stop us. We plan to attack them before they can overwhelm the men guarding the queen, whereas the pixies and the monk are too cautious. They would have us taking days to get through and then it would be too late."

Lance was right about it taking time to craft any magic, but they were assuming that the sorceress hadn't already anticipated an attack from the direction of the Isle of Sun. Thomas suspected her to be far too cunning to not consider such, but when he tried to share that with the other apprentice, he was snubbed.

Someone from inside called out for Lance and the youth turned to go, adding one last comment. "You need to join us instead of talking with monks and little pixies. Let me guide you in how we can support these brave men."

Thom shook his head, not willing to join in their folly. They were treating it like some grand adventure rather than what it was- a desperate rescue effort in the face of a powerful foe.

Lance raised an eyebrow at Thom's hesitancy. "Are you afraid the mission will expose your ignorance of magic? You shouldn't be. They will understand that you are a sheltered apprentice; you just need to be honest about your shortcomings."

"That is not my concern. I'm afraid they are charging blindly into danger and they risk failure with their impetuousness."

"No need to fear," replied the youth, "for these are powerful and wise men who have faced dozens of armed foes and prevailed. They know what they are doing."

Someone shouted for Lance again, so this time the apprentice turned his back on Thom and hurried back inside. Thom just stood there, at a loss at how to convince these nobles to take this foe seriously.

* * *

The next morning, a force of twenty-four mounted men prepared to leave Pixvale. Apprentice Lance and three guides waited at the head of the group. The youth rode a borrowed horse and wore a metal helm that had been given to him by someone. It sat too low on his brow, but he still wore it proudly, playing the role of warrior wizard. Around his neck was tied a colorful cape that hung awkwardly over the lump of his magician's knapsack, but he wore it proudly. Lance was trying hard not to smile in his excitement.

The nobles had once again snubbed Thomas earlier this morning and they wouldn't listen to the pixie elders, for they were convinced that they knew better. Francis didn't even bother trying, having called them a pack of fools.

As Thom watched, four of the lords walked out of the inn wearing armor. Their noble squires, less-encumbered by heavy metal suits, hurried ahead to retrieve their mounts. The squires were not as finely or brightly attired, but they still looked impressive as they helped the knights mount up. The four squires then took to their own saddles, holding aloft banners announcing the mighty houses arrayed against the sorceress. The other dozen nobles were not so well armored, but they had their share of weapons at the ready.

The noblewomen gathered to wish them farewell, many of them proclaiming how grand the party looked. Some cried as their husbands prepared to leave, while others offered up favors of bright scarves and ribbons as a way to inspire their men.

More nobles came out to see the party off, men who were too timid or old to join in. Geoffrey stood among them, gazing longingly at the mounted party. An elderly lord dubbed the group the Queen's Mighty Men and expressed regret that his age prevented him from joining the expedition.

The commoners had come over too, though they kept farther back. Thom and Francis stood among them, though not together. Rumors ran rampant through the crowd over why the force was setting out. Thom heard talk of dragons and invaders and even about battling the Road itself.

Many of the pixies also came out to watch the group depart, apparently curious about the commotion. They kept even farther away, staying among the trees as they watched.

Finally, it was time for the two dozen men to leave. One of the squires raised a hunting horn and blew a slightly sour fanfare that echoed off the surrounding hills. With that, they rode off as the people shouted their encouragement, and soon they were lost from sight as they headed towards the Isle's ferry across to the upper half of the Road.

As the crowds dispersed, Jake came walking over to Thom. He had been checking on the rest of their original party. "Orem has disappeared."

The bricklayer had been a quiet and steady man, going to Camelot to find new work. Thom had no idea if he had any family. If Orem was the one missing, then he had been the Goat Woman's victim; the one killed inside that lightless enchantment and then replaced by the shape-shifting sorceress. "So he was the one who screamed when we were in the darkness."

Jake nodded. "I would have sworn it had been that little lordling, for he frightens easily. Unless you think that more than one man was overtaken in the dark…"

Thom considered this but it seemed unlikely. "Orem was the one that she shape-shifted to imitate."

"To think she fooled us all. Next time, I'll have everyone line up, drop their trousers and piss on a target. No woman can shoot like that, no matter how good she is at pretending to be a man."

Thom thought a sorceress would find a way to fool them that way too, but he chose not to mention it. "Have you been able to gather supplies?"

"The pixie elders are seeing to the supplies." Jake looked over as Francis came near with Ears. "The innkeeper has a stall in his stable for your donkey, monk, and he promises a dry spot to stack your books. Go over to the inn's side entrance and the pixies will help you store your load."

"That's good, for I would rather not drag either into this fight." He kept his donkey moving, now heading toward the inn. "Thank you for making the arrangements, Guide Jake."

Jake gave a slight nod in return and then added, "We leave in an hour, so don't tarry over your tomes."

Francis chuckled. "I'll try not to read more than two."

Thom watched as the monk walked on, frowning as he recalled the man's secret. Francis could have helped him so many times, but he had left Thom to flounder through it on his own. Thom gave Jake a warning. "Be careful with him, for he thinks only of himself."

"I think you misjudge him. He hid his past for his own reasons, but he's always been a generous fellow."

Thom disagreed, but realized that he wouldn't be able to convince Jake of the truth. "Who else will be joining our party?"

"The pixies are sending four of their hunters. Guard Marcus insisted on joining, though his master objected at first. He's an experienced fighter."

"No one else?"

Jake pulled off his hat and ran a hand through his unruly, graying hair. "Truth be told, I wouldn't want most of the others on the travelers' field. They are merchants, tradesmen, and pilgrims. The only weapon they've handled is a dinner knife. I wouldn't want them underfoot even if they were brave enough to volunteer."

"What of the other two guides?" Thom had noted that only three had ridden out.

"We decided among ourselves that at least two have to remain behind, for we still have our duty to those remaining in Pixvale. When all calms down, they will need to be guided out of here."

Thom thought it wrong that three went with the nobles and only one would go out with the second party, but it was too late to protest.

"One other thing, we found the sorceress' cart, but the goats and that lead-lined crate are still missing."

Thom guessed that Narissa took the supply of magical elements with her. He had no idea about the goats, for they certainly weren't tied to back of the lordly carriage when it left yesterday. He would certainly have noticed that.

"I will see you in an hour," continued Jake. "Right now I must find us some extra horses. You can ride, can't you?"

Thom nodded, though his only experience had been on an old wagon mare that he and a couple of boys had stolen back before his apprenticeship started. It had been a wild ride through the alleys of York and had ended with him tossed onto a pile of crates, but he had kept on the horse's bare back for a good distance. They got away with the animal, but then his father had beaten him for stealing something so hard to fence. Dad had never been satisfied with any of Thom's heists, even when he prospered from them.

Thom remembered that his father found a use for the wagon horse, nonetheless. Dad took revenge on a horse dealer who had once spat on him by sneaking the nag into the man's stable and then sending a snitch to tell the city watch. Dad had fallen over laughing when the horse dealer had to spend an hour in the stocks and pay the deliveryman recompense for the apparent theft. That night his father drank an extra half-bottle to celebrate and then beat Thom some more.

Thom could sit on a horse, but he had to admit to himself that he was no horseman. He would just have to pick the tamest of whatever collection Jake brought together.

* * *

When they gathered an hour later, the only horse in sight was Jake's. Francis, Marcus, and Geoffrey were there. A small group of pixies stood off to one side, encircling the two elders for some private conversation.

As Thom walked up, he heard Francis speaking. "No horses at all? Have the nobles no desire to help the queen?"

"They see our mission as folly," explained Jake. "They think their nobles will do the rescuing. Although I tried asking, begging, and ordering, it was all to no avail. Not only did everyone refuse to surrender their mounts, a handful of the more brash ones have taken it upon themselves to guard the stables against us. They might be wrinkled and fat, but they are well-armed and the doors are now barricaded."

Francis sighed. "They soothe their hurt pride by playing the tough with us. Fools."

"I could take my master's mules," suggested Marcus.

"He'll not surrender them willingly and what good would the two of them do us?" asked Jake. "We have no tack for them, even if they'll endure being ridden." He ran a hand over his face in frustration. "It looks like we'll be a walking party."

"What are you doing here, Lord Geoffrey?" asked Thom softly, stepping beside the youth. "You needn't go with us, for we head into danger."

"My queen is in need, so I must go. Please do not try to stop me, Magician Thomas." The young man looked at him pleadingly.

"You aren't doing this so that you can boast to the other squires later, are you?"

Geoffrey looked horrified. "No, no, no. This is no game to me. I believe that I can be of help, for though I am not yet a knight, I do know how to use my sword. Please take me along."

"You'll come," said Francis, interrupting. "We need men with your determination."

Geoffrey beamed at the monk, thanking him.

Thom scowled. He wasn't intending to refuse the boy, but he didn't appreciate the monk's interference.

"Yes, Lord Geoffrey, you will be one of our members," agreed Jake, "though you'll need to switch out those saddlebags out for a proper knapsack. Go find the innkeeper and ask him for something. Even a burlap sack would be better than those things."

Geoffrey hurried off to ask for a better pack for holding his belongings.

"We have food and supplies from the pixies," continued Jake, pointing to a collection of small bundles waiting on the inn's porch. "Go replenish your packs, and don't skip on the rope or tools. We have no idea what we might need on the Road."

* * *

Soon they were ready. Geoffrey returned with a decent pack, having traded his saddlebags for it. The pixies finished their conversation and the elders came close with their group.

"Which of you will be joining us?" asked Jake, giving the small folks a hard look.

"They will," stated Black-Arms, indicating four pixies, one pair tattooed black and the other blue. Two men and two women.

"Women? You send out your females?" Jake obviously had his doubts.

"We hunt as couples," replied Blue-Arms. "No hunters can do better. None can anticipate each other as well as a husband and a wife. Have no fear; all four are very competent. Silvala and her husband Krayne helped kill a baby dragon five years ago, while Theasa and Greler were part of the team who slew a griffin that tried to take up residence on the Road last year."

Thom had wondered what they hunted, since the pixies didn't eat meat and there were no animals or birds within these interwoven enchantments. So, they hunted magical creatures that were attracted by the Road's magic? Apparently, they helped Wizard Cruthen keep the route safe for its many travelers.

"I have read about this," said Francis. "Pixies are deadly accurate with their bows."

"But can they keep up with us?" asked Jake. "This is no stroll through the gardens. We will set a hard pace and the rest of us are long-legged."

"They will ride," answered Black-Arms, nodding to the four hunters.

Each whistled and in response a foursome of deer came running out of the woods, gold-colored deer with bright white speckled hindquarters and silvery antlers. Thom had never seen such animals before.

A deer stopped beside each hunter and waited. Thom noticed a small saddle on each as well as tied-up reins.

"Golden Harts," whispered Francis, enrapt. "What beautiful animals."

Eric Loren

SEVENTEEN

Return to the Road

They left Pixvale without any fanfare. The only ones seeing them off were pixies and they watched without cheers or shouts for they understood the seriousness of the situation. It was already late morning, with the sun warm and the air still. Thom hiked in the middle of the group, glad that they were soon under the cover of trees. The road followed a narrow defile through the hills and then down the far slope to the other dock. The ferrymen were ready by the time they arrived at the riverbank.

Once across, they passed through the triple archways and entered the autumn-cool of the Road. Thom stepped onto the bed of leaves with care, not fully trusting that the debris would stay put. He listened with his inner ear, but the rhythm of the magic seemed strong and steady. He kept looking at the trees to either side, watching for any stirring of the wind. But no matter how unsure he was of the Road, he was determined to go on. If there was any way he could help Adele, he would. And the queen. He wanted to see her rescued too.

They made good time that morning, not stopping until the late afternoon to eat a brief meal and to let the horse and the deer nibble on the grasses at the Road's edge. Sitting near the edge was uncomfortably close to the magic, so most just sat down in the middle of the leaves. Thom did so too, but could not relax. He was wondering if the sorceress would attack the Road again this afternoon. He almost asked Francis what he thought would happen, but decided not to even try talking to that one.

"Will we make it to the next Waycircle in time?" asked Geoffrey.

"Certainly," replied Jake. "It's tomorrow's destination that I worry about."

"What if she has laid traps to delay us?"

Francis spoke up. "I don't think you need to worry about that, Lord Geoffrey. The noblemen who rode ahead of us will kindly trip all those snares. I just hope young Apprentice Lance notices the traps before anyone is hurt."

They found their first corpse an hour later. He lay mangled in some kind of netting, his horse fallen nearby. It looked like a painful death, with ropes cutting deep into the body.

Jake, Francis, and the pixies all stopped to examine the trap while Marcus and Thom watched. Someone in the sorceress' party had decided to leave behind a mundane snare and it had worked. The corpse was one of the nobles. Geoffrey looked away from the mess and made a soft gagging sound.

When done examining the scene, Francis said a brief prayer over the departed. The others bowed their heads to join him in prayer, but Thom had a hard time focusing. It seemed hypocritical to hear the monk playing at holiness. They talked about taking the corpse with them, but it wouldn't be practical. They would just have to let the Road of Leaves purge it that night, most likely dumping the body in an overgrown meadow or among some tree copse.

They encountered a second body another hour later, this one burned beyond recognition. Thom gagged at the stench that saturated the confines of the Road's magic. Geoffrey retched until there was nothing left in his belly. No one wanted to linger to study the trap this time.

* * *

Late that afternoon, Pixie Theasa called them to halt at a turn in their route. She had been riding ahead as a scout. "The archway is nearby and there are men guarding it."

"How many?" asked Jake.

"I saw four standing, plus another lying down in the leaves." She tapped the bow slung over her back. "It is too great a distance for our arrows, but it would be best to stop them from warning any inside."

"They are not from the first party?"

"No, these men were not among those who left the Isle of Sun this morning."

"I hadn't expected this," said Jake with a frown. "Why haven't they all moved on to Twin Hills?"

"This is their only escape route," answered Francis quietly. "They don't want any surprises when it's time to flee.

"It also means that their force is larger than we thought," observed Marcus. "They have enough men to feel comfortable dividing their force between two Waycircles."

"But where are the nobles?" asked Geoffrey. "Did they just ride past instead of facing this challenge? Is that possible?"

"Maybe," answered blue-tattooed Greler. "They may have decided to press on to Twin Hills to gain that Waycircle before sunset. It would not have been strategic of them, but in their passion they may have left enemies behind."

"Well, we can't offer them help if they went that far," said Jake. "We have no choice but to fight our way into this refuge and win it before tonight. Any ideas how?"

"I do," said Francis. "Let Thomas and I put our heads together and see if we can provide some magical sleight-of-hand."

Thom was leery, but he let Francis pull him aside.

"Can you raise the wind?" asked Francis in a whisper.

"Invoke the Road? Are you mad?"

Francis raised an eyebrow. "Don't be a ninny, mage. I want to create our own breeze so that the watch guards will flee inside in fear that the Road is shifting early."

Thom admitted he didn't know any magic that could do that, but Francis took the time to explain how a Twist of Air worked. The monk was thorough, explaining the parameters to keep within for the enchantment to work. When he was certain that Thom understood how to craft the magic, he asked whether Thom wanted to do it.

"Are you insane? The first time you create a new enchantment it is bound to go awry a little. My work would likely crash into Merlin's magic and then we'll have a far greater problem on our hands. You must do this."

Francis didn't look pleased at the idea, but he motioned for Thom to pull out his magician's box. "Then I'll need your powders, both magical and mundane, for I have none."

So Thomas supplied the elements while Francis crafted the enchantment. The monk waited a bit to start, letting evening settle in. When it was about an hour before the nightly winds would stir, he judged it time and began mixing, adding his own spittle to attune the magic to himself. Thom watched and listened, for this was the best way to learn a new enchantment.

Francis' last step was smearing some of the potion on his lips and hands so that he could direct the brewing breeze. A miniature whirlwind rose from the mixing bowl. The monk directed its shape with his hands and then blew it into motion, sending it up the Road and around the corner.

Monk and magician's apprentice hurried to peek around the corner, watching the tiny windstorm travel up the center of the Road, well above the leaf-covered path. Thom could see the guards up ahead. They were not particularly attentive, but instead were laughing as they poked at the one lying in the leaves, making him cry out in pain. No one noticed the two observers or the windstorm heading their way.

Francis kept the enchantment going long enough to get the still air into motion, and then let it go. The magic died out well before its target, but the air kept its own momentum, dipping down without Francis' push and picking up leaves from the roadbed, as it kept moving forward. The watchmen reacted as soon as they felt the wind's tickle on their skin. All four stared at the stirring leaves and then started shouting to one another. They ignored the man lying among the leaves as they hurried to get inside the Waycircle. The wind dissipated soon after the foursome vanished through the gray curtain of power.

In the new silence, Thom heard the man among the leaves moan a few times.

Francis turned and signaled the others that their route was clear now. Thom waited for the others, not wanting to walk beside the monk. The four pixies rode past, not waiting for the walkers. They stopped in front of the one person remaining and pointed arrows at him while calling for Francis.

When Thom came close enough, he saw that it was one of the nobles now mortally wounded. He did not know his name, but remembered seeing him among the first rescue party. It looked like the guards had been torturing him for their amusement.

Francis knelt at his side, cradling the man's head in his lap and asking if he could hear him.

The man opened his eyes. "I...I can hear you." A bit of blood dribbled out the corner of his mouth.

"Where are the others?" asked Francis.

"They rode inside to rescue the queen. Is she safe now?"

"Do not worry about the queen, my lord," said Francis. "She will be fine."

The bloody man sighed with relief.

"May I pray for you?" asked the monk.

The dying man gave a slight nod, so Francis began to pray over him. The pixies bowed their heads in respect, as did Jake, Marcus, and Geoffrey. Thom still had his doubts about the monk, so he simply waited quietly.

By the end of the prayer, the man was dead. Francis gently laid him out, for there was nothing else they could do for him. Thom begrudgingly admitted to himself that the monk had been compassionate toward the dying man, but he still didn't like or trust Francis. He never would again.

They moved away from the body and to the archway that led into the Waycircle.

"So what happened to the nobles?" asked Geoffrey in an unnecessary whisper. "He made it sound as if they attacked here."

"He may have been confused by the pain," replied Francis. "I don't think there is any fighting going on inside this Waycircle. Not with guards standing so calmly out here and torturing that fellow."

"We cannot worry about the other rescue party. Our focus is on winning the refuge in front of us," said Jake. "We have no way to retreat now. We must go in and defeat whoever is in there. For those of you who have not been inside Oak Vale Waycircle, it is rolling land covered by a wide-spaced grove. Three small streams trickle through the folds in the land. The trees are huge but there is not much underbrush to hide us. The area set aside for campsites sits in a dip toward the center."

"We should wait until the winds actually stir," said Pixie Silvala. "As night settles, we will be better able to come on them unawares."

"Indeed," agreed her mate, Krayne. "Let the darkness by our friend, for humans cannot see as well in the dark as we can."

"What do we expect to find inside?" asked Thom.

"I was trained to always plan for the worst and then you'll not be surprised," said Marcus gruffly. "We need to be ready for magicians and mercenaries both. Act as if they hold the queen inside there with that sorceress standing over her, ready to kill."

"You paint a bleak picture," complained Geoffrey. "It may just be a handful of men assigned to hold this Waycircle secure."

"Then we will make quick work of them," said Marcus, "but we shouldn't wish for a docile chicken coop when storming a bear's cave."

"We should expect at least one sorcerer," said Francis. "The Road near Camelot was severed according to Cruthen and the sorceress couldn't have done that. She has at least one fellow magician helping her."

"If we can get close enough, our arrows can take down anyone, be they mage or soldier," said Silvala. "Dryad poison is potent enough to take down a dragon once enough arrows hit their mark."

"Then we should plan on ways to get the four of you close to their camp," said Jake.

While Jake and Marcus discussed ideas with the pixies, Francis came over to Thom and asked for help.

"If you give me a bit of powdered Azure Fireflies, powdered Meadow Dragon wings, and crushed Glow Berries I will do what I can to help distract those inside the Waycircle."

Thom just stared at him, shocked at the man's gall. He had refused to offer any help during their travails on the lower Road, but now the black monk wanted the elements to make Wizard Lights.

"I do not ask this lightly, Thomas. I despise magic, but I may need to do something to save the others, for the pixies intend to divide us into two parties. Give me the elements and I will promise to use them only if absolutely needed."

The monk had some nerve to ask this now after he had refused the offer of full magical supplies from Wizard Cruthen just a few days earlier. Thom continued to stare at the older man's calm face. He wanted to deny him, but this was about far more than his own anger; if the monk was willing to help, they could all use it.

"They will hear the powders," muttered Thom, breaking his stare and slipping his knapsack off his back.

"I have a leaded-silk pouch that will deaden the sound," replied Francis, pulling out a small bag and also three smaller cloth pouches for the powders.

Thom said nothing as he set his pack on the ground and pulled out his magician's box. Opening the lid, he quickly picked the three items the monk wanted and poured a little of each powder into the small pouches which Francis then stored in the larger leaded-silk pouch while Thom closed his box and returned it to his knapsack. While doing so, he tried to hear the elements he had given to him but their sound was definitely muted.

"Thank you, Thomas. I will only use what is necessary and I'll return whatever remains."

Thom nodded understanding, but said nothing.

Francis nodded back, then walked over to the pixies.

Thom watched him for a moment longer, then went over to join Jake, Geoffrey, and Marcus in their discussion.

They talked until they heard the Road starting to stir. As the winds increased and the leaves began to move, they charged into the Waycircle and split into two parties, both heading along the right-hand side of the refuge and staying close to the evergreen wall of perimeter trees.

Thom was in the second party, with the black-tattooed pixies, Marcus, and Geoffrey. Silvala led them on her deer while her husband rode at the rear. Thom could see nothing except the evergreen wall of trees on his right and the huge oak trees that sprinkled the clearing. The land dropped away from the circle's edge but they had no good overview from here. The oak forest and the wrinkles in the dell hid too much. He couldn't even see any campfire light.

After a few minutes, Silvala angled their route to follow a dip in the land toward the center of the Waycircle. Thom had already lost sight of the other group but he knew they were not far off, following another ravine inward. He still couldn't see or hear their enemy. As he walked, Thom wondered what he could do to help the pixies get close enough to shoot any magic wielder in the camp. He had no delusions; he understood an apprentice was no threat to a journeyman or master magician. His biggest concern was that a protective ward guarded the camp, either keeping them out or warning the enemy of their approach, but he could hear nothing obvious.

Silvala stopped her deer at a curve in the depression they were following, waiting for the others to catch up. When Thom reached the spot, he saw what lay ahead. The light of a campfire.

"Can you sense any magic?" she asked Thom in a whisper.

"Magic is all around us. The Waycircle hums of Merlin's work, making it hard to hear anything else," he answered, but then took a moment to listen more intently. "I don't hear anything unusual or out of rhythm from the Road's enchantment, but there might be something subtle." He paused to listened a bit more. "There might be a rhythm of another enchantment, but I'm not certain."

"I hear no battle," said her husband Krayne, "so if there was any fighting, it is now done."

The pixie did not say it, but Thom understood that he implied the utter defeat of the nobles.

"Maybe the nobles are resting in their victory," said Geoffrey. "We should look over that rise and see who lounges by the fire."

"The magician's apprentice and I will look," said Krayne, though he didn't sound hopeful. He jumped off his deer and motioned for Thomas to follow.

The pixie led him up the slope, angling them into the night shadow of a large oak. They crept up to the hill's crest, with Thom on his hands and knees. Thom dropped to his belly for the last few feet, creeping through the green grasses until he and Krayne could finally see down the far slope.

Thom saw men sitting around a campfire, some with their backs to him and others with their faces lit up. The fire roared, crackled, and sent sparks into the sky. It was a huge fire that overflowed the ring of stones intended to be its boundary. The men talked and laughed as some of them threw even more wood on the blaze. Thom recognized one of the men, a noble that had been in the first rescue party, and it lightened his heart.

He almost stood up in response, but Krayne hissed a warning when he stirred.

"That's one of the lords," he whispered to the pixie as explanation. "They must have won this Waycircle after all."

"I think not," argued the little man. "Look closer at that man on the left side of the fire, the one in the black cloak."

Thom had trouble seeing the fellow through the glare from the fire, but then saw fire bloom in his palm. The man idly tossed a fireball into the campfire, causing another surge of flame and sparks. Thomas knew how to craft a simple Fire Starter enchantment, but this was something far more advanced and it looked far deadlier. He caught only a snippet of its sound and it had an odd tone to it, containing something that was probably forbidden. Thom was confused as to why this magician was among the rescue party. "I... I don't understand.

Why would such a man be allied to the nobles?"

"There is your enemy magician," said Krayne. "That noble you see must have been a traitor."

Thom understood now, and caught his breath at how close he had come to revealing himself to the enemy.

"What can you tell me about his magic?" asked Krayne. "I can sense its use, for such things attract my kind, but I can't tell what the actual enchantments are."

Thom took a deep breath to calm himself and then concentrated on the camp below. He almost missed something the man had already crafted, for it was a subtle thing that he would not have expected from a sorcerer. The camp was encircled by a Whisper of Warning, a simple apprentice enchantment, though it covered a much larger area than Thom ever had.

"The fire magic that he makes is unknown to me, but I think it may involve something of the dark arts. He has also crafted a Whisper of Warning around the camp that will let him know if anyone or anything crosses it. The whole floor of the vale is within it."

"Will he sense an arrow passing through the encircling magic?"

"Yes, but maybe not in time to avoid it. The enchantment will do nothing to stop an arrow's flight." Thom knew there were greater wards that a master could use, but they also required more attention. The sorcerer's lack of concern meant that he expected no real threats tonight.

"Do you recognize anyone else?" asked Krayne. "Maybe some of the prisoners beyond the fire?"

Thom had not even noticed the captives, for they were away from the firelight. He shielded his eyes from the light so that he could see past it. Most were mere lumps on the ground, either wounded or tied into immobility. He thought he recognized the bright cloak from a lord who rode out with the first party. Only one person walked among them, the long hair and dress proclaiming her a woman. She appeared to be serving the others, bringing them water and food. Her walk, though hindered by leg shackles, was one he knew. The confident stride of Adele.

He would have risen to his feet again, but Krayne threw himself against Thom and they rolled back down the hill a ways.

"Foolish man," the pixie hissed when they came to a stop. "Twice, you almost gave us away."

Thom didn't care. "I saw Adele. She lives!"

"Lower your voice," ordered Krayne, "or you'll bring death on all of us. They must remain ignorant until we can kill that rogue magician."

Thom was chagrined at his own stupidity. "I apologize. Yes, I recognized some of the captives. They included some who were innocent companions of the sorceress and I think at least one other was a noble from this morning's group."

Krayne frowned. "There are also human corpses down there, off to the edges of the vale. It looked like the nobles charged directly at them after entering the Waycircle. I am sorry, Thomas, but I think they all died or were captured."

"So at least one of them turned on the others," said Thom. "How many allies does this sorceress have along the Road?"

"That is a good question. This is no lone madwoman we are dealing with. She has too many friends." The pixie stood and walked the rest of the way down the slope.

Thom followed the little man back to the others, but let the pixie share what they had observed. His thoughts kept going back to Adele. He would do whatever necessary to see her free.

Eric Loren

EIGHTEEN

Fire Sorcerer

The intervening ridge shrank as they went farther down the ravine. It would soon be too low to hide their mounts, so the pixies let their Golden Harts go free, then everyone continued on at a crouch and then a crawl. Thom didn't dare to raise his head, but he could now hear the men of the camp talking, though he couldn't yet recognize what they were saying. There were no more folds in the land to hide him, only a lone oak, so he headed in that direction. The two pixies crept on either side of him. Geoffrey and Marcus crawled behind him.

Thom stopped when he could touch the tree's rough bark. He heard the Whisper of Warning enchantment just beyond the tree and motioned to the pixies to let them know of its nearness. Carefully, he edged around the side of the tree and looked for the sorcerer.

The stranger magician still sat at the fire, once again fondling a fireball as if it were as harmless as an apple. Thom wondered what element coated the man's hands to protect them from the heat. The sorcerer gazed into the campfire as he tossed the fireball in. The fire roared higher, but the magician didn't flinch. He just stared into the light, his eyes following a particular tongue of flame upward as it licked the darkened sky.

Thom looked to the side when Krayne moved. The pixie rose to a kneeling position and took careful aim. Krayne was about to shoot when one of the men yelled and pointed somewhere off to the right. Krayne shot anyways, but the magician moved and the arrow flew past.

The pixie threw himself into the grass and Thom ducked behind the tree as the sorcerer whirled to glare in their direction.

A fireball splashed against the tree, washing over the trunk to either side.

Thom thought furiously about how he could strike back, but could think of nothing. None of the enchantments he knew were meant to attack people. His back against the tree, he hesitated and that was what probably cost Krayne his life. The pixie bravely rose out of the grass, loosed another arrow, and then sprinted to the side. The sorcerer was quicker to retaliate this time and Krayne became engulfed in flames. The pixie ran two more steps and then fell, setting the grass around him on fire too. Thom knew there was no hope for him.

Beyond the oak, he heard Silvala yell out for her spouse. Thom looked over and saw her shooting a barrage of arrows at the sorcerer. The magician tossed fireballs in their path, burning the arrows in mid-flight. The magician must have crafted them in advance, because he hadn't heard any new crafting, but surely there was a limit to how many fireballs he could keep lit without exploding them too early.

Thom knew this would be his only chance. He yelled for Geoffrey and Marcus to follow and charged at the magician, pulling out his knife because he could think of no other way to challenge him.

The sorcerer opened his magician's box and removed elements that he must have pre-measured and then quickly closed it again. Thom heard the elements being hastily mixed and knew they didn't have much time, but surely they could overcome the sorcerer before he could finish crafting a new enchantment. However, they only made it halfway when fire swept over the three of them. It was not like the fireball that had engulfed Krayne, but a line of fire that struck them down like a scythe cutting off wheat stalks. All three of them fell, blistered and moaning.

Thom heard Silvala scream as another fireball hit her. Where did that last fireball come from? How had the sorcerer kept it ready while preparing the enchantment he had thrown at Thom? Silvala tried to shoot again even as the flames burned away her life. She was probably dead before her body hit the ground.

Thom moaned again, this time more out of pathos rather than pain. They had failed. The queen wouldn't be rescued. Adele wouldn't be freed. He had been foolish to think he could defeat master magicians.

As men continued to shout and curse in the camp, Thom buried his face in the damp earth. He dared not get up again, fearing that he would attract the sorcerer before he could think of some way to beat him. His left side and arm pulsed with pain from where the fire had licked him. He laid there, tears of frustration filling his eyes. He would have remained there, unsure what to do, but he heard the sorcerer crafting and then flinging more fireballs and remembered that there were others still trying to attack.

Thom got up onto his hands and knees, looking around. He saw Geoffrey, his fine clothes smoldering, and Marcus beating them out while trying to stay low. The sorcerer was now focused elsewhere, sending fireballs at a line of Wizard Lights.

Thom stared at the lights and wondered if Merlin and his companions had finally arrived, but then was disheartened when the fireballs struck without any resistance, snuffing each Wizard Light and setting parts of the land on fire. The black-cloaked magician stepped around the fire to get closer to where the Wizard Lights had been, ordering some of his men to run up there and see who lurked among the trees. Thom hoped it wasn't Francis and the others, for it didn't look like anything could have lived through that firestorm.

He needed to do something, even if the dark magician was on the other side of the fire now. He decided to head around to where the prisoners lay and see if he could help there. He looked toward his surviving companions, but Geoffrey was still flat in the grasses, moaning over his injuries while Marcus was now running toward the center of the camp. There was no one else near that could help, so Thom headed off on his own, aiming to where the prisoners lay.

He would release Adele and find out if Queen Guinevere was among the captives. That was his plan, but two of the traitor lords had other intentions. They barred his way with bare swords and suddenly Thom was again at a disadvantage. Two against one and he only had a belt knife.

"Look, the little apprentice has shown his face after all," one of them sneered. "Ready to join the other one in the grave, are you?"

Thom's heart thumped harder. Francis was already dead? Or were they talking about Apprentice Lance? He had no way to know, so he ignored the remark. Instead, he tried to bluff them into giving up. "Drop your weapons now and I'll not kill you."

The other one laughed. "I doubt you know how to kill. Look at how the knife shakes in your hand. I think you are scared enough to soil yourself."

The two walked toward him, swords ready.

Thom reluctantly backed up, knowing that he was no match to trained fighters with superior weapons. He was about to turn and run, when the man on the left suddenly tumbled over, knocked down from behind. His attacker fell down with him and Thom realized it was a woman. A woman he knew. Adele had attacked the man from behind, taking a great risk to help him.

The other lord looked on as his companion wrestled with the woman and laughed at the scene. He ignored Thom as he enjoyed seeing Adele wrestle with his companion.

Moving quickly, Thom ran at the noble still standing and, before the man could bring his blade into play, knifed him in the belly and then the neck. The man fell over and gurgled his last breath.

Thom rushed over to where Adele had been struggling with the other, ready to rescue her, but found that noble grabbing at his throat and trying to breath. Somehow, Adele had wrapped her leg shackles around his neck and was strangling him. Thom used his knife to finish him off and then helped Adele to disentangle from the corpse.

"You're a fine sight for my eyes," she said, giving him a fierce hug.

"I'm so glad I found you," he replied, his voice husky with emotion.

They stood there amid the chaos, lingering in their hug, but danger kept the moment short.

Thom pulled free. "There are more to defeat. You should run and hide among the trees until the fighting is over."

"I'll not leave the others helplessly bound." She bent over the dead man and took his belt knife and sword, handing the longer weapon to Thom. "Take this sword and see if it works better at keeping the enemy away, while I go help the other captives. Go win this fight, Thomas."

"What of your shackles?"

"Don't worry about that; your friends need you now."

"Is the queen among those bound?"

"No. From what I overheard, they went to ambush her at the next Waycircle. The others are lords and ladies that I think they planned to ransom. I will get them cut free."

He paused to look at her, beautiful even though dirt-smeared and disheveled.

"You needn't stare at my tousled appearance, for I know I can't always look pretty. Stop gawking at my ugliness."

He couldn't help but smile. "You're lovely, Adele. Always lovely."

"Enough with the false flattery. Off with you, Thomas, and remember that your mind is your greatest weapon, even more than your magic." She turned her back on him and hurried to those tied up, her leg chain rattling as she moved.

The sounds of fighting pulled Thom's attention away. He spied the fire sorcerer on the other side of the camp, tossing more of his fireballs at someone over there. It seemed the pixies had all failed or else the man was immune to their poison, so Thom would have to stop him. But how? Once again, he reviewed all the magic he knew and could think of nothing that would harm a sorcerer. Nonetheless, he ran toward the magician, determined to find some way to stop him.

The large fire caught his eye as he ran. On impulse, he grabbed a burning brand and then kept going, sword in one hand and flaming wood in the other. He had gone a half-dozen steps when he reconsidered.

"You're a fool," he muttered to himself. What harm could fire do to a man who played with fireballs? He almost tossed the brand aside, but then another thought came to him. Some of the natural elements he carried could be used without creating an enchantment. Three of them, when mixed together and tossed into a flame, created a thick smoke.

Thom stopped, swinging his pack off his pack. He knelt, sticking the brand into the ground and setting the sword down. He started digging through the knapsack and would have died at that moment, if not for Marcus.

The sword swung out of nowhere, right at his head, but Marcus shoved the attacker and deflected the blade. Thom stared in astonishment, realizing that he had almost been beheaded. For a moment, he just stared as Marcus and the attacker began exchanging blows, and then he realized that he had better do what he had intended. That smokescreen was needed.

Thom looked around to make sure no others were close, and then he quickly pulled out his magician's cache, setting the wooden box on the ground and opening its lead-lined lid. As soon as it was open, he heard the collection of magical elements, each one with a unique sound and rhythm. He quickly found the three vials he was looking for and poured some of each into the palm of his hand then replacing the vials and closing the box with his other hand. He stirred the three powders together with his finger, no bothering with a mixing bowl, and then poured it onto the ground. It did not look like much, but it was all that he had.

He pulled free the torch and then dropped it onto the small pile of powders. Multi-hued sparks shot out and then billows of dark smoke rose. More smoke than he had expected. A smelly, eye-stinging smoke. While he could still see, he quickly shoved his magician's box back into his knapsack and swing the bag over his shoulder. He then retrieved the sword and covered his mouth against the smoke's foul odor.

He quickly lost sight of Marcus and his opponent, then he lost sight of everything else. The bonfire was now just a reddish glow off behind him, even that hidden by the sudden billows of smoke. Coughing, he hurried on, daring not to run but still trying to hurry. He wanted to sneak up on the fire sorcerer while the smokescreen lasted.

He didn't realize that he went in the wrong direction.

Eric Loren

NINETEEN

Heated Words

Thom stumbled over a body. Reaching down, he found a small arrow sticking in the corpse, so this was one of the pixies' victims. He moved on, avoiding the sounds of battle on his right.

He saw someone lurking in the smoke ahead of him so he raised his borrowed sword and crept closer, trying to make no sound. The man was looking the other way and didn't see the apprentice. Uncertain who this was, Thom came even closer. The smoke thinned a bit and he realized it was a stranger, so he lifted his sword in both hands and tried to hack into the man's back.

Some sound must have given him away for the fellow turned abruptly and caught Thom's blade on his own. The deathblow ended up doing nothing more than causing a small cut on the man's forearm. Thom stumbled off-balance from his swing and then had to jump back to avoid the stranger's response. Soon Thom was fighting for his life, awkwardly blocking a rain of blows from a far-superior fighter. He danced this way and that, doing his best to avoid the other's attacks.

He would have died then too, if not for the fire sorcerer.

The noise of their battle must have attracted the magician, because a fireball came roaring at them from out of the smoke. Thom heard it before either of them could see it, for its magic screamed in his inner ear, and he knew death was roaring toward him. Desperate, he ignored the fighter and threw himself to the ground. His opponent was not so fortunate. The fireball hit the stranger directly in the chest, turning him into an instant torch. The screams were horrible but short-lived.

Thom crawled away, fearing that the sorcerer might send a second fireball to finish him off. When nothing happened, he got back to his feet. He now knew where the sorcerer was. Though scared, he corrected his path and headed that way. The enemy magician had to be killed or they would never be able to win the Waycircle. However, the smoky darkness made it difficult to judge distances. More than once he slowed, fearing that he might have already passed the sorcerer, but each time another fireball screamed in his inner ear as it barely glowed through the smoke told him that the magician was still somewhere ahead. He was just thankful the fireballs were aimed in another direction.

The smoke began to break up some and he saw the fire sorcerer directly in front of him. Thom had no other magic tricks to try, so he raised his sword and charged.

The dark magician turned, his black cloak billowing. He locked eyes with Thom, showing no fear, and raised his hands. A new fireball formed, the bright glow highlighting the man's face and sudden smile. A grin of victory.

Determined, Thom ran harder. Even though he knew that he wouldn't get within reach, still he kept charging.

The fire sorcerer juggled the fireball from hand to hand, pausing to savor Thom's fear.

Desperate, Thom raised the sword with one hand and threw it. The blade spun and wobbled as it flew through the air.

The magician didn't even have to sidestep the sword. It fell harmlessly to the ground nowhere near him. He raised the fireball above his shoulder, ready to throw it like someone else would toss a mere river stone.

Thom kept running at him, now trying to get his belt knife free even though he knew it was too late.

But then the sorcerer jerked to the side. His smile turned into a look of pain and outrage. He spun around, now ignoring Thom. A tiny pixie arrow stuck out of his back. He threw his fireball at someone and then staggered. He conjured up another ball of flame but this time the flames burnt him and he dropped it. The man turned back toward Thom, a surprised look on his face, and tried to stagger off. He made it only four steps and then collapsed.

By the time Thom reached him, the sorcerer was dead.

* * *

They captured three renegades that night with twice that number dead, though some of those were killed by the sorcerer in his careless attacks.

The pixies suffered the brunt of the battle, with the death of Silvala and Krayne. The other couple had their share of open wounds too. Even in the smoky darkness, Thom could locate the pair of remaining pixies by the rhythms that emanated from their cuts. Open wounds revealed the magical essence of their nature, letting out a distinctive rhythmic beat for an inner ear to hear. When the pixies came closer, Thom eyed their injuries. Thankfully, none of their wounds looked deep enough to keep oozing much longer. That was good, for otherwise the two would be exposed to any magicians they might encounter.

The rest of the party had suffered a variety of wounds, burns, and bruises.

Geoffrey endured the worst injuries: a burnt arm and face. Francis mixed a paste and applied it to the young lord as a balm, but still the youth moaned. Francis then gave him a draught and the noble fell into a deep sleep.

While the pixies slipped away to perform some private rite over their two dead, the rest of the survivors gathered around a small fire. The blaze was in a different fire circle than the renegades had been using, well away from the corpses and lingering smoke. Thom sat looking at the fire, an arm over Adele's shoulders. Her leg shackles were off, but he had seen how chaffed her ankles had become. She didn't caress her sore ankles, though. Instead, she stroked a bow she had claimed from some dead noble, cleaning it of dirt and blood stains. When she expertly loosened its bowstring, Thom realized that she wasn't clinging to it just for comfort. She knew how to use the weapon. He kept his arm around her but made sure not to hinder her cleaning efforts.

He enjoyed her nearness, but more out of comfort. He was too tired to think of romance.

"The other rescue party died here, didn't they?" asked Marcus the mercenary, looking at two of the nobles that they had freed for an answer.

Neither answered or met his gaze.

Finally, Adele looked up from her cleaning and replied. "Yes."

Thom thought of the brash Lance, who would never attain journeyman status now. He recalled the proud nobles as they confidently left Pixvale. Only these two had lived through it, both severely injured. The other two nobles rescued, an elderly couple, had been in the party that had left with Lady Ursula's carriage.

Marcus looked to Adele as he asked his next question, his look intense in the firelight. "Where is the sorceress?"

"She and her pet goats rode the carriage to the next Waycircle where she planned to capture the queen."

Thom looked at her with surprise. "The goats? She brought along those two?"

Adele nodded. "She treats them like children, her Nibble and Dribble. She let them do whatever they wanted, from nibbling my clothes to fouling on the upholstery. She struck me when I dared to push one of them out of my face. She has more affection for those two than for any of her companions."

"Who fights on her side?" asked Francis.

"Among those still alive? The musician, two clergy, and a handful of thugs. I think there may have been more who joined her beyond this Waycircle, but I didn't see it. She dumped me out of the carriage as soon as she no longer needed a disguise. She would have killed me too, but I proved useful at caring for the captives."

Thom pressed her closer to his side. She had nearly died. The thought frightened him.

Adele gave him a warm smile, but then turned back to Francis. "I don't know much about their plans, brother monk, but I saw her disdain for those without magical skills. Even those she brought with her, that killer who pretended to be a troubadour and the pair of false clergymen, she treated as if they were mere servants. She wants to bring down Merlin and the king, and I don't think it's merely to put some other man on the throne. She wants a great sorcerer to rule."

"Who else in her party showed magical skills?" asked Francis.

"There was only the fire magician. She and the fire mage did speak of others though, including a Sorcerer Dalrake."

Thom saw Francis' sharp intake of breath.

"Do you know him?" Thom asked the monk.

"You should too, for he was one of the three Founders who created the enchantments that surround Camelot and sustain the magical Roads to it. None of this would have come into existence without Dalrake's help. But he couldn't stand the restraints on magic that the guild established and eventually broke away with some others to form a loose brotherhood of sorcerers. He was my master's master. My old master often bragged that Dalrake outshone even Merlin in skill and power."

The monk said no more, but Thom guessed that Dalrake had preceded Francis' old master into the dark magic. Instead, Francis looked at Thom. "I hate magic, but we must use it for this rescue. Mage, I know your list of enchantments totals to a mere handful but I will teach you how to vary each one into two or three other enchantments. Maybe that will help you in any coming battles."

"So we are it," stated Marcus, tossing a branch into the flames. "We are the queen's last hope."

Jake finally spoke up. "Though we're all tired, we should get ready for the morning. As soon as the Road settles, we'll want to move on. It'll be good to have everyone mounted now."

They had recovered enough horses for all of them, to Thom's rue. He would have to admit his lack of riding skills in the morning.

"Those we freed will have to stay here and hide among the trees," said Francis. "For we have no wagon to carry the wounded back to Pixvale. Maybe you can stay to tend them, Maiden Adele. Lord Geoffrey will probably be strong enough to offer some help, though his sword arm is useless."

"No," she answered, in a soft yet determined tone. "I'll go with you to rescue the queen."

Thom was shocked. He let go of her so that he could turn and face her directly. "It'll be too dangerous. You should stay here."

"You need all the help you can get. I see only the six of you. No matter the skills of the two remaining pixies, you don't have a large party. I may not have the bulk of a man, but I can handle a bow, a stave, and a long knife. My mistress liked to hunt, for it let her get away with her paramours. While she taught her young lovers a thing or two inside a hunting lodge or in her coach, I would spend the time learning from the huntmaster how to use various weapons. I mean no disrespect for the dead, but I want to make sure you understand that I have some skill. I'll protect her reputation later, but now I must be frank. I also learned how to fend off some of her frustrated suitors. I know how to stop a man, with a swift kick if nothing else is at hand."

Thom had no idea that she endured that kind of a life, yet he still meant to object. He didn't want her in the midst of more danger.

"You can join us," said Francis.

"She'll be a welcomed addition," agreed Marcus.

Jake grunted. "A pretty face will be a distraction but we need the help, just like she says."

Thom glared at Francis, considering this to be one more betrayal. How could the man be so callous toward a woman? Adele deserved to be sheltered, not shoved in front of a sword.

"So monk, are you a master magician or a journeyman?" she asked, ignoring Thom's obvious anger.

"Neither," replied Francis. "I denounced magic years ago. I'm merely a monk from Saint Barnabas who collects books for the monastery's library."

She laughed. "I saw you do some magic before that smoke hid everything." She pointed at Jake. "Are you claiming he created the magic lights and raised up the smoke?"

Francis didn't answer.

"Now isn't the time to be coy," said Adele. "This group is already too small, yet I sense resentment dividing the group further and I think your secrets caused some of it. What are you, monk?"

He finally answered her. "I am Francis, Benedictine brother and formerly a magician's journeyman."

"How can you be a former magician? I saw you do magic this very night."

"You want frankness? Fine. You shall have it." Francis stood up in his aggravation and started pacing in front of them. "Magic, even natural magic, is a treacherous thing. Any who practice it will be forever tempted to want more. Magic eats at your soul, calling you to manipulate others, to kill thinking magical beings just to get more power. Do you know how many magicians yield to the whispers and start practicing dark magic? A full two-thirds of those who start as apprentices either die early or succumb to the darkness. Be thankful that dark magic is a hard skill to master or we would be overwhelmed by hundreds like Narissa or Dalrake or that fire sorcerer." He stopped his pacing and pointed at Thomas while still looking at Adele. "You're attracted to him, aren't you? How do you feel knowing that there's a good chance that he'll become twisted by magic's power? Could you endure watching him become as cruel and uncaring as the sorceress? For that's what usually happens. It's one of the hidden secrets of the magicians' guild. Some try to hunt down those of their ranks that become corrupted, but it's a losing battle. Especially so, when many of them, like Merlin, refuse to admit the seriousness of the problem."

The monk looked around at everyone seated by the fire. "I watched my own master fall to the temptation. I started my apprenticeship to a wise and patient man, but in the end I killed him because he had turned into a monstrous person who stole lives and tortured innocents."

"I am not like your master," objected Thom, sick of this man's haughtiness. "I've no interest in dark magic."

"May you always remain so pure," replied Francis. He sounded sincere but Thom suspected more deceit.

"You still did magic," said Adele, returning to her original argument.

Francis met her challenging look. "I may not like Merlin, but I'm not ignorant of the good he has done for the kingdom. The Road of Leaves shouldn't be wantonly destroyed, especially since many magical beings have found refuge here. Camelot shouldn't be cut off from the realm, not when the king has brought peace to so many. I'll do what I must to protect this land, even if it means using something so vile as magic."

"I, for one, am glad you do," said Jake. "You saved my life this night, monk. You distracted that fire sorcerer when he would've burned me to a crisp. Thank you."

"I'm also thankful you have such powers," said Marcus, "and I respect your reasons for hesitating to use them."

Thom couldn't stand it. On the whole trip to the Isle, the others had been suspicious and distrusting of him for his magical skills and yet they now praised Francis for the same skills. They saw no problem with how the monk had refused to help, hiding his abilities while Thom floundered.

Furious, Thom stood up and walked away, ignoring Adele when she called after him.

Eric Loren

TWENTY

Crossroads

He walked off in anger. Francis had deceived him. The monk had let him struggle, even though he knew enchantments that might have stopped the sorceress or at least brought them through without losing anyone. And now, Francis was letting Adele come along, back into the danger. Thom thought it likely that most of them would die soon, but he could endure such thoughts if he knew that Adele waited in safety. But how could he endure it, knowing that she would likely die also?

He had wandered for about an hour, circling the central encampment, before Adele caught up with him. She stepped in front of him, forcing him to stop.

"He hurt you, didn't he?" she asked.

Emotion tightened his throat. "He can't be trusted."

"Can't you see why he did what he did? He has suffered great pain, though he hides it well. Imagine having to kill the man who has spent decades instructing you. You feel betrayed by a man you hardly know, but he was truly betrayed and it was by a man he'd served and respected for a long time. Can't you see why he hates magic?"

He didn't answer.

"Thomas, we are still practically strangers, you and I, but I already feel something for you. I can see that you're a good man and I hope we'll have the chance to become better acquainted. However, in this you're wrong. Francis deserves better from you, for he did you no harm."

He was about to object, but she touched his lips with a finger.

"And when it comes to me joining the rescue party, that decision belongs to neither Francis nor you. I'm going, for I owe the queen. Most in the queen's court snickered behind the back of my mistress, well aware of her lustful indiscretions, and most painted me with that same brush. Only they did not sneer behind my back. They openly insulted me and treated me like some whore just for being the maid of a randy woman. It was Guinevere who put a stop to it. The queen noticed an unimportant commoner like me and saw to it that I was no longer abused. I must help her now."

Thom's protests died. Once again, he was surprised by what she had endured.

"Will you hug me?" she asked. "I would rather have your comfort than your anger, for we may not live through another night."

Chagrined, he did what she asked. He hugged her, burying his face in her lustrous hair as tears filled his eyes. He felt his shirt dampening from her tears also.

He walked back hand-in-hand with Adele not much later, for they knew that tasks awaited them and the night was already growing late. Thom avoided Francis but otherwise did his best to be polite. The group sorted through supplies and chose horses. They picked out a hiding place for the injured and made it as comfortable as they could. Finally, they all lay down to rest for the few hours left until dawn. Thom set a Whisper of Warning around them as a precaution, knowing that Francis would never do so.

* * *

Dawn arrived quickly. As soon as Thomas awoke, he sat up and looked for Adele. She still slept nearby but was soon stirring. He was ready to let go of the enchantment encircling their camp for it gave him a headache, but he glanced around its perimeter out of habit. He saw one of the remaining pixies waiting patiently astride her Golden Hart just beyond the reach of the enchantment, so he quickly released it.

"We have more trouble," stated Theasa as she rode into the center of the camp. She didn't dismount. "One of the renegades survived and hid among the trees with his horse. We were sending off our fallen on their deer when he slipped past us and rode up the Road. Being in the middle of praying, we didn't see him at first. By the time we realized what had happened, he had gotten beyond an arrow's flight. Greler has ridden after him while I came back to give warning."

"Can your Golden Harts catch up with a horse?" asked Jake, looking doubtful.

"Greler will do what he can," replied the pixie woman. "If the fleer pushes his horse to its death then he escapes, but Greler's a determined hunter. If the fleer slows or stops to rest, then he'll die."

"Let us get the horses saddled then," said Francis. "We have another Waycircle to win and a queen to rescue."

Thom needed help getting the tack in place on his assigned horse. It embarrassed him. The fact that Adele and Marcus also needed help didn't soothe that feeling either. He was a city man uncomfortable around livestock but it seemed that on this trip he was always having to take care of some beastie or other. Even more unfortunate, it was Francis who came over to help him.

"Have you ever ridden?" asked the monk as he tightened the saddle's straps, "I mean more than a city block on some old nag."

Thom sourly admitted his ignorance, explaining his one time riding bareback on a runaway horse.

Francis chuckled. "Well, you'll find it much easier to stay on with a saddle under you. I'll tell Jake to set a steady pace, for you aren't the only inexperienced rider with us."

"Thank you," he replied, humbled. Something Adele had said to him came to mind. "Francis, do you hate magic?"

The monk lost his smile. He answered softly, "Yes, I hate it. The last time I used it, before this trip, was to stop my master from slaughtering a fairy village. I have no fond memories of magic." He bent over and offered his hands as a step. "You might as well climb up now, Thomas. Let the mare get familiar with you. Just sit on her, pat her neck, and talk to her some. The two of you need to become comfortable with each other."

Thom did as told, but his soothing of the horse was interrupted by a perturbed Geoffrey. The young lord had recovered enough from his burns to walk again, though he moved slowly and in obvious pain. He came over to make his anger known to Thom.

"You must help me with Guide Jake," he pleaded. "He does not understand that I must go on to rescue the queen."

Geoffrey was in no shape to do anything of the sort. His blistered sword-arm hung useless in a sling, wrapped tight by Francis. Half the youth's face still glowed an angry red and much of his hair was singed. "You are needed here," said Thom, trying to deflect him. "Who else can protect those helpless nobles, but you?"

Geoffrey frowned, apparently realizing that Thom would be of no help to him. Without another word, he turned and hobbled off to enlist the monk. That did not work either, for soon Geoffrey was heading back to where they had already hidden the four injured nobles. Thom felt relieved, for he didn't want to see the youth killed.

The horse frisked a bit, causing Thom to tighten with fear, but it calmed down. He adjusted his seat and moved his leg, finding it a bit uncomfortable to have a sword hanging off his waist now. It might prove a better weapon than his knife, but last night's attempt at sword fighting had proved disastrous.

* * *

Even though the Road of Leaves remained calm and dry this morning, the horse's reins still dampened from Thom's sweaty palms. He didn't trust the beast, though it behaved itself now. He also didn't trust the Road. Either one could turn wild without warning.

It was a miserable way to spend what might be the last day of his life. Thom wanted to talk with Adele and get to know her better, but instead the Road and the horse took all of his attention.

Francis rode near and tried to teach him more about magic, but he only partially heard. The monk spoke about ways to vary each apprentice-level magic into a new enchantment. He explained how to turn a Whisper of Warning into a Shout of Warning. The monk explained how to make mists and how to clear mists, how a Twist of Air could as easily blow toward him as blow away.

Francis shared quite a bit, but Thom failed to focus on any of the lessons He was simply too nervous about being on horseback. Thomas was also worried about what lay ahead. They numbered just six now. Jake and the pixie rode at the fore, followed by Adele, Marcus, and then Thom and Francis. A half-dozen against an unknown number of foes, and only Marcus had any sword skills. It didn't look promising to Thom.

After an hour of riding, he started to feel surer of himself in the saddle. He was just considering urging his horse to a faster pace to catch up with Adele, when Francis interrupted from behind him.

"The leaves stir," he said, loud enough for all in their party to hear.

Concentrating, Thom felt the light touch of air on his face. He listened with his inner ear, but didn't hear anything greatly amiss. "I hear no jarring in the Road's enchantment."

"Nor I," said Francis, "yet the Road stirs. It sounds somehow unsettled if you listen carefully."

The party came to a halt.

"Is it ahead of us or behind?" asked Jake.

"Ahead of us," said Francis. "Can't you feel the breeze yourself?"

Jake nodded with a frown. "Must we turn back?"

In response, Theasa urged her deer forward again. The others quickly followed, understanding that they had no choice if they wanted to rescue Queen Guinevere.

The breeze didn't increase, but it also didn't abate. They rode into the wind for another hour, until they encountered something that had never occurred on the Road of Leaves before. The Road split in two directions, with leaves shifted back and forth between the paths.

Theasa sprang from her deer and studied the ground, trying to spot which route her husband had taken but finding no revealing trail among the swirling leaves. The debris moved around her ankles, shifting restlessly between the two routes as if uncertain where to settle. "Which way is the true Road?"

Eric Loren

TWENTY-ONE

Winter's Chill

Thom looked up both roads with his eyes, listening intently with his inner ear, as a chill caressed him. He couldn't tell any difference between the routes. Both were narrower, no longer wide enough for two carriages to pass each other with ease, curving off in different directions. He was uncertain which way they should take.

"I have never seen such a thing," said Theasa.

"Nor I," muttered Jake, "and I have no idea which is the true path."

"We'll have to scout along the routes," decided Theasa, "for the magic doesn't reveal which is our route."

Thom had forgotten that magical beings like pixies could hear the enchantments as well as any magician.

Theasa mounted back onto her deer and chose the left road. "I will go up this one. Guide Jake, please take the other way, but for no more than a quarter-hour's steady ride. We will then come back here to the others."

Jake agreed.

Thom and the others had to wait only twenty minutes or so until Theasa returned. "My route narrows with each bend until it's too tight for even my deer to pass through. If Twin Hills Waycircle lays up that path, then we'll not make it through. Let us follow after Guide Jake."

They came upon the guide on his ride back and he assured them that this route remained stable in width, so they kept going up its leaf-strewn way.

They rode until they came to another intersection. The breeze was now stronger and colder, coming down both routes. Once again, Thom and the others waited while Theasa and Jake scouted each path and found that one quickly shrank to nothing. The other route narrowed and then stabilized again.

They came upon a third branching and this time found a surprise down the side road: a dead horse and rider. Jake discovered it and told the others.

Theasa spoke up. "Greler trapped him on the side road, so these branching paths have been here for many hours. I would guess that my husband has gone on to spy on the next Waycircle."

"Are these side roads caused by some magic of our foes or by some action of Merlin's?" asked Jake, looking to the Benedictine.

"That I don't know," said Francis, "but the Road of Leaves isn't under attack presently." He looked to Thomas for agreement.

Thom nodded reluctantly, not sure what to believe. The magic sounded different here. It changed to an odd rhythm, although not anything jarring or shrill.

"Why does it grow colder?" asked Adele of Thom, hugging her arms.

"It did that when the lower Road severed," he answered, "but that was far worse, turning into a snow blizzard. I don't sense the enchantment destroyed this time. Instead, the magic sounds… pulled and twisted… I'm not sure how else to explain it."

"Pulled and twisted is apt," said Francis, overhearing. "The magic changes around us but I don't know what it's changing into."

"Then let us keep going," said Marcus, speaking up for once. "Let's get to Twin Hills Waycircle quickly, before something worse happens. I, for one, am eager to end this. I want to see the queen freed and this sorceress killed."

Thom silently agreed, though he didn't know how they could kill such a powerful magician.

* * *

The Road of Leaves split twice more, the main route becoming so narrow that they had to ride single-file. With each crossroad, the air became cooler and the breeze stronger. The leaves became restless, with some now blowing through the air. Thom worried that it might start snowing soon or that their path might shrink to nothing.

The surrounding countryside became hillier, bringing more turns, dips, and climbs to the Road. A forest pressed in around the route, robbing much of the sunshine and making the way even darker and cooler. Thom could see his own breath and that of his horse. No longer was this forever autumn, for winter's nip had come even while it was still high summer beyond the Road's limits. He noticed a clearing to the right where bright sunshine fell on a colorful meadow and it enticed him, so close and yet impossible to reach. He was glad when the surrounding trees thickened and he could no longer see summer, for it proved a distraction to his chilly path. Here on the Road of Leaves, winter ran its icy fingers across his face and down his neck.

He worried, spending much of his time listening with his inner ear for any weaknesses in the enchantment surrounding them. It seemed like the magic was in trouble and they weren't making very good time to the next Waycircle. What had promised to be a quick ride had been delayed, as they were forced to explore every side path. Thom wondered if they would make it to Twin Hills before nightfall.

* * *

They came upon Greler in the late afternoon. The pixie hunter and his Golden Hart waited in the middle of the now-narrow Road. Theasa dropped from her mount and rushed forward. Husband and wife embraced. After a moment, they pulled back and then Greler turned to the others.

"The Twin Hills archway awaits us nearby. They have not been forewarned as far as I know, but three guards watch the Road so it will not be easy to get inside without the enemy learning about us."

"It is time for us to use some of this cursed magic," stated Francis, getting down from his horse and motioning for Thomas to join him. "Give us a moment to prepare the elements and we will create a Shield from Sight that will allow us to approach unseen."

The monk urged Thom to bring his cache of magical elements and the two walked ahead of the others, being careful to remain out of sight of those guarding the Waycircle.

As the two crouched over the lead-lined box, Francis spoke. "Thomas, I've observed that you are rather advanced for an apprentice, whether you are aware of that truth or not. Will you allow me to guide you in crafting one of the more complex enchantments? I think it will be useful in getting us inside the Waycircle without alerting the sorceress."

"What enchantment is it?" Thom couldn't think of what the monk thought he could craft, considering his limited experience.

"It will help hide us, when you successfully craft it."

"But if I fail..." he said no more but pointedly looked at the vast enchantment that surrounded them. A failed crafting often caused fire or an explosion, and that happening on the Road would be doubly dangerous. The magic conflict could kill them all.

"I will make sure you do not falter. I know you're still angry with me for hiding my knowledge, but now I'm willing to share. I hate magic, but I know that this is necessary. Come now, it is time to start crafting."

Thom looked into Francis' face and found it open and encouraging. He still had his concerns about the monk, but he nodded his agreement and opened his magician's box, the sound of the elements filling his inner ear. "I hope they don't have a magician as part of their watch."

"Greler is watching for that. He will note if anyone reacts to your crafting."

Thomas hadn't even noticed when the pixie slipped ahead of them.

"First element to add to your mixing bowl is powdered Shadow Worms, a finger-tip's worth."

Thom quickly set up his wooden mixing bowl and pestle, and then added the first element as told. What followed was a complex mixture of elemental powders and liquids until he ended up with a dark, bubbling goo. At times, the crafting sounded dangerously close to going rogue, but Francis remained calm and guided him through. Now that the monk said it was done, Thom stopped crouching over the mixture and sat down hard on the leaf-covered Road.

Wiping away a bead of sweat, Thom listened to the final rhythmic song of the enchantment and suddenly recognized what he had crafted. "Is this like the blind passage we came through earlier?"

Francis nodded. "It is, but it will be much smaller than what the sorceress made."

His first thought was amazement at having crafted such a complex enchantment. His second thought was that the monk wasn't as foolhardily brave as he had thought when he had walked into the sorceress' enchantment without hesitation. "You knew what you were walking into back on the lower Road."

"Somewhat. I knew it was a Dark Passage and that it wouldn't harm me of its own, but I had no idea what might have been lurking inside. She surprised me when she used it as cover to poison us and then kill one of our group."

Thom wished the monk had explained much of this to him back then, but he realized it wasn't the time to argue. "What next? How do I apply the enchantment?"

"You will be dipping your hands in it and then smearing it on us. Finally, you will splash the last of it over a set area, activating the enchantment before the droplets can hit the leaves of the Road. Give me a moment to get ready, for I want myself and the pixies to use the enchantment to get close to the guards. You will direct the magic from outside…"

"Not from within?"

Francis shook his head. "Magic is easier to control when you aren't in the enchantment itself. You will watch and guide the Dark Passage, letting it drift toward the Waycircle but not touch the sides of the Road or the archway. It will be a difficult task, but I have confidence in you."

Greler trotted down the Road to them. "No one reacted to the magic," he stated, his breath making a cloud in the cold air. "They are still four guards but they are more attentive than the ones that were watching at Oak Vale."

"We will sneak up on them cloaked in darkness," said Francis. "Can you get a decent length of rope so that I can guide your wife and you?"

"We can sense where magic is. We could probably walk the Road blindfolded and keep to its center."

"I know, but this will make it easier to keep in a straight line. We will leave our mounts with the others because all animals get skittish when suddenly blinded."

"I will tell Theasa and also get the rope."

Soon everything was ready. The monk had a rope around his waist and his stout club in his hand. The two pixies were also tied in the line. They left their bows over their shoulder and instead carried swords that were more fit to their diminutive size.

While Adele, Marcus, and Jake watched, Thom completed the enchantment by first spitting into the potion to attune it to himself. He then painted the thick liquid on each face with stripes as Francis directed. It looked like some weird war paint, contrasting strangely with the more intricate face tattoos on the pixies. Next, he dabbed it on their boots and then tossed what remained into the air over the trio, being careful not to splash too high or too far to either side.

Thom realized that the monk was creating the parameters of the enchantment on them instead of on the ground so that the magic could move with them.

When all was done, the monk and the pixies were hidden within a pocket of darkness. Smaller than the sorceress' enchantment, it was also less obvious. It almost seemed like an extra-dark shadow.

"Are they still there?" asked Adele.

Thom pointed to where the darkness lay. "They are already moving up the Road."

"May God grant them success," she whispered.

Thom nodded agreement to her prayer. They needed divine help, and not just to get into the Waycircle.

"Do you want some water to wash that gunk off your hands?" she asked.

Even though the residue had cooled to a sticky mess, he shook his head. "No, for it helps me maintain the enchantment. You could wash out my mixing bowl though and store it back in my knapsack."

He had to move forward as the trio came to the final bend in the Road, because he needed to keep a visual link to the magic to sustain it. He squatted low to keep the Dark Passage between him and the guards and he concentrated on keeping the enchantment going by the force of his will.

Adele tried to speak to him again, but he was too focused on the enchantment to hear her. He was barely aware of her cleaning his utensils for him.

* * *

What followed was about a quarter of an hour that felt ten times as long, as the trio slowly and quietly crept up on the guards, who somehow didn't notice the darkness coming toward them. Thom remembered a similar surprise when they had come up on the sorceress' enchantment and wondered if the magic somehow averted the attention of those outside of it. He felt/ heard the enchantment come up alongside the men and then the cudgel and two small swords came out of the darkness and hit the men.

It was over quickly, then Thom saw Francis wave his cudgel out of the darkness, signaling it was done, so he let the enchantment dissipate.

One of the pixies came running back. Greler's war paint had faded to a gray, adding an odd second pattern to his blue tattoos.

"Come quickly," he ordered, retrieving the two deer. "The guards are dead but we do not know how long it might be before someone else steps out of the Waycircle."

They mounted up and rode after him, with Marcus leading the monk's horse.

When the archway came into sight, Thom spotted four bodies fallen among the leaves but he saw nothing of Francis or Theasa- in the commotion the two had stepped through the archway. Just as the rest of the party came up to the stone arch the two reappeared, suddenly visible next to the shimmering curtain.

"There is no one between the archways; we did not go any further." He turned to Jake. "Guide, you know this Waycircle better than any of us. How can we best slip inside?"

"Between the perimeter circle of evergreens and the hills in the center there are only a scattering of trees. You may want to use that magical shield again once inside, for it's not like the thickly grown Oak Vale."

Francis shook his head. "Any magicians within would notice the magic immediately. Think of a way to enter without any magical aid."

Jake considered. "The Waycircle may not have many trees away from the central hills, but its grasses are lush and tall. Away from the wide path that has been ridden low, it will be high enough to hide anyone crawling in. If we ride in, we will be seen by anyone watching. You can't hide horses in that open Waycircle- at least not on the grassy outskirts."

"Should we wait until sunset again?" asked Marcus.

"No," replied Francis. "The guards talked of regular attempts to sever the Road. They were speculating about how many sorcerers would come out the next time. It seems the Road kept fighting back by growing new side roads to go around every severing of the magic. The three found that amusing, chuckling about frustrated magicians."

"So the sorceress has other magicians with her," said Thom, concerned.

They had enough trouble last night and that had been against only one magic wielder.

"Should Theasa and I scout the Waycircle?" asked Greler. They were all looking to Francis as their leader now.

The monk placed a hand on the small man's shoulder. "Thank you, Greler, but we'll need to go in together. There might be more guards just inside. I'll not want the rest of us waiting out here in ignorance while you are slaughtered. Instead, I think we should leave our mounts out here and try sneaking in on foot. Let us run inside in two waves. First to enter will be Greler, Marcus and I. Next, will come Thom, Jake, Adele, and Theasa. Give us a lead of five breaths. Once through the archway, dodge to the side and slither among the grasses."

No one argued with the monk, for his plan was the best that they had. They tied up their animals on long leads, so that they weren't too near the Road's border, and then took what they absolutely needed from their mounts. If they survived, they would come back for them before the night winds started.

Thom watched the first group run through and then counted five deep breaths before chasing after. With him ran Adele, Jake, and the pixie. He burst into the Waycircle and looked around for trouble. He saw Francis' group disappearing into the grasses to the right. It seemed the best route, so he led the others in pursuit.

He dove among the grasses, unworried about staining his clothes. Adele landed next to him. Jake and Theasa right behind them. Though the Waycircle was lush, it was still painful to crawl among its grasses, with rocks and nettles and rough ground. He kept his group closer to the perimeter wall of trees so that they would not be right on top of Francis' party. They hadn't crept very far when the first fireball crashed into the ground nearby, charring a wide circle to blackened ash.

Eric Loren

TWENTY-TWO

Twin Hills

Thom froze, uncertain what to do. He could hear men shouting from far off.

"Creeping is not the answer," said Theasa. "We need our mounts or else they will burn us before we can ever get near."

Before Thom could stop her, she rose and ran back for the archway. A fireball roared after her but missed. Whoever was throwing fire didn't try again for her, probably out of fear of hitting the archway.

"Keep moving," said Thom, setting the example. Adele and Jake kept up with him.

Another fireball soared their way, landing closer to where Francis' group most likely hid. It didn't look good. Thom could imagine everyone burning to death without ever seeing the captive queen, let alone setting her free. He crawled as fast as he could, hoping to get beyond the magician's aim. He didn't even know how close their foe was and he dared not rise up to find out. A fourth fireball hissed through the air and landed in front of him, bringing him to a halt. Desperate, he flattened against the ground and dug into the pack still on his back, pulling out his magician's box. He opened the lid and looked at the glass vials, trying to decide what to mix. Maybe some kind of distraction or a screen. Maybe smoke.

"What are you doing?" asked Adele in a whisper.

"I'll make some more smoke. It will shelter us from the fireballs."

Adele put a hand on his, and shut the box, smothering the sound of the elements. "Can this wait? We aren't close enough yet."

He wanted to protest but realized that she was right. Filling the perimeter of the Waycircle with smoke would provide them no worthwhile cover. "How can we get close? They already know that we're out here somewhere." Then a panicked realization came onto him. "And I just foolishly confirmed that I'm a magician by exposing my magical elements. If our attacker heard that, then our location is revealed."

"Then move it!" ordered Jake. "Stop the crawling and run while staying low. We need to get away from here."

The three of them ran until they came upon a depression in the land. Thom found the grass thicker and higher, offering them more cover. At Jake's suggestion, he turned down the gully, leading them toward the enemy now. They had gone only a little farther when a commotion occurred behind them. Two fireballs sizzled that way.

Thom climbed to the edge of the depression and then stood up to see over the greenery. Theasa was back on her Golden Hart, leading the horses and Greler's mount. Thom looked the other way and saw two sorcerers watching her and getting ready to toss more fire. He also noticed a handful of knights riding in their direction.

Theasa's herd broke into two, with the other Golden Hart leading half the horses unerringly toward Francis' party while she brought the rest toward Thom. He was amazed that the animals did not bolt from the fire and smoke, but they kept close to the deer as it ran. They didn't even swerve when two more fireballs splashed into the nearby grasses, leaving a blackened, smoky trail.

Theasa followed their trail and was soon upon them, ordering them to mount up. It took Thom three tries to get into the saddle as his normally docile horse danced about, but he finally made it up. Within seconds, they were charging across the grasses.

Thom looked around and noticed the pair of wooded hills that filled the center of this large Waycircle. Theasa lead them toward the far side of the hills, moving away from the sorcerers and their mounted men. Thom held on tightly during the terrifying race, for two days in the saddle hadn't done much to improve his riding skills.

He was vaguely aware of Francis' group charging in the same direction, one horse too few, which meant that the monk and the mercenary were now sharing a horse.

Thom tried his best to anticipate each jolt or jump, but still barely kept in the saddle. He would have yanked the horse to a slower pace, but she had the bit and the last fireball had landed too close to her hindquarters. The mare was not about to slow down.

As they raced around the Waycircle, the fireball attack lessened and then ended. Apparently, they were beyond the sorcerers' reach. However, the enemy knights were gaining on them. He had a short view of them, armored men riding under a crow banner, but then lost them from his periphery sight as they fell in behind Thom and the others. Thom knew they were being followed because Jake shouted the fact, yet he dared not look back out of fear that he would lose his seat and fall. He felt helpless while in the saddle and it frustrated him even while frightening him.

It was pixies who saved them from the knights, falling to the rear and taking aim with their dryad-poisoned arrows. Jake actually cheered when he saw the knights give up the chase and pull back. "The pixies have downed ten men rather quickly," he shouted. "The rest have reined in their horses and are letting us go."

Thom doubted that would give up on following them, but at least they would have some distance between them.

Their path brought them behind the steep hills that stood at the Waycircle's center, soon hiding them from the sorceress' force, but they didn't stop. Marcus and Francis now rode in the midst on their shared mount, while the pixie couple moved back to the fore.

As they raced around a cluster of empty corrals and pens, Thom wondered if there had been any travelers camping there when Narissa and her men invaded the Waycircle. If so, there was no trace of them now.

Marcus shouted and pointed behind them. As Thom had suspected, the warriors were still in pursuit, keeping back just far enough that the pixies couldn't shoot them.

Before the next area of corrals, the pixies swerved, aiming them for the trees at the foot of the hills, and soon they had to slow down among the pines. Branches slapped Thom's face but he didn't dare fend them off. Instead, he just held onto his horse and hoped the ride would soon be over. He sighed when Greler and Theasa finally brought them to a halt in a small clearing.

"We are safe for now," said Greler. "I doubt the soldiers will ride in here after us."

Suddenly, a voice boomed through the Waycircle, the same woman's voice that had whispered a taunt during his journey through the dark passage. Though loud, she didn't shout. She spoke calmly, letting magic amplify it for everyone to hear. "Apprentice Thomas, I know you are with the intruders. Do you really think that you can stand against three magicians? This is foolishness. Are you a stooge of Merlin and his puppet Arthur? Why put your trust in a mere man, with all his foibles and faults? Surely, you are wiser than that.

"You should join me, Thomas, and I will teach you real magic. Powerful magic. I do not tease my disciples with mere crumbs of knowledge, but teach them many enchantments and skills. Join me, and you will no longer be restricted in your learning. Join me and I will teach you about the Great Magic that the ignorant misname as dark magic. Your master has purposely kept you ignorant of it because he does not want you to grow more powerful than he is. That is truth Thomas, for I can tell that you will be a quick learner. It is one of my giftings in the Great Magic to sense others' potential in the arts. Join me and you will be a ruler in this land and not a mere apprentice for others to abuse."

Thom was surprised that she even knew his name, let alone wanted to lure him to her side. He became curious as to why she called it Great Magic. Had his master kept some of the truth from him? Why would he do that?

"She uses magic to make her words more appealing," said Francis, catching Thom's attention. "Even I can feel the enchantment's lure and I am not its target. You need to resist, Thomas."

The sorceress continued, her voice booming through the Waycircle and yet sounding sincere and guileless. "Come to me, Thomas, and I will teach you about the Great Magic. I will not hold anything back, for I want you to attain your full strength in the mind arts. Come to me and leave behind the chains of apprenticeship and the lies of the magicians' guild. Join me."

Without realizing he did so, Thom pulled on his horse's reins to turn it around.

He only stopped when Adele blocked his path. "Resist her call, my dear Thomas. Stay with me instead."

Francis came up beside her. "You must fight it, mage. She lures you like the hunter tempting a boar into the open."

Theasa came up to him, holding out some bits of cloth. "Plug your ears if you must."

Realizing how close he had come to giving in, he took the wool cloth and stuffed a piece in each ear. It didn't block out everything the sorceress said but it garbled enough to weaken her magic's hold.

Adele motioned for him to dismount so he did. They were all watching him carefully, probably afraid that he would try to rush to the temptress. Once assured that he would stay with them, they also dismounted and began to talk about what to do next. He missed much due to his plugged ears, but he comprehended enough to know they were debating whether to encircle the hills or try to climb over the steep pass between them.

He interrupted to share his thoughts, probably speaking too loud. "What about the dryads? Aren't there dryads in this Waycircle? Maybe they can help us find the best route or even help to spy out our enemy."

Adele stepped close to him and pulled out the cloth from one ear. "She's stopped her ranting."

He removed the other plug and tried handing the cloth back to Theasa, but she was busy looking skyward.

"Do you hear that?" she asked, finally noticing Thom.

The others strained to listen, while Greler quickly scampered up a tall oak to get a view over the tree cover. By the time he climbed back down the rest could make out a faint cawing.

"Crows. Thousands of crows are circling the hills. I think they are looking for us."

"How can that be?" asked Thom. "I thought animals avoided the Road?"

"One of the sorcerers called them here," replied Francis. "Even if they can't attack us, the birds will act as spies. We need to get deeper into the woods before the birds locate us."

"We'll have to abandon our mounts here, for the hillsides are too steep for them," said Theasa. "The bucks will lead them away to await us. Leave the saddle and tack, but tie up the reins so that they will not snag in any brush. Take only your weapons, your water, and any food you can stuff in your pockets for we need to travel light."

Soon they were hiking deeper into the murky woods, climbing uphill and keeping away from any clearing that would expose them to the enemy. The crows could be heard in all directions, cawing somewhere above the tree canopy. It was only a matter of time before the birds would find them.

Francis and the pixies talked about whether they should skirt the hilltops or climb over the pass between them. Either route promised to be grueling. They decided to go up and over so that they could at least avoid the mounted men if not the birds. The two pixies led the way, following a small stream up its course. The hills were thickly wooded, making for good cover but also forcing them to often detour around impenetrable brush. They scrambled over boulders, used gnarled roots as steps, and trampled through knee-deep water as they climbed higher and higher.

Thom hiked right behind Adele and found his eyes often resting on her, and not just because of her beauty. He admired her determination. Although he wished she had stayed behind at the last Waycircle, he respected her resolve to help the queen. To his eyes, she was brave and beautiful.

The crows still called out somewhere above the tree cover, persistent in their hunt.

They were more than halfway up to the narrow pass when the pixies called them to a stop.

"Two dryads watch us," said Greler. "Wait here while my wife and I talk with them."

Thom sat down on a log, glad to rest. Francis and Jake sat on a second log, while Marcus leaned against a tree trunk.

Adele remained standing, her mouth forming a silent O as she saw the dryads come out of the undergrowth. "They are so tiny," she whispered.

Thom looked over his shoulder to watch them too. "They are a small and shy people, but I wouldn't want to be their enemy. I just hope that they'll be willing to help."

He heard their distinctive bird-like speech of whistles and chirps. He was surprised to hear the pixies respond in kind, holding a serious discussion with the miniature pair. They attained some kind of conclusion, for the dryads disappeared back into the brush and the pixies returned to the humans.

"Terrible things have been happening here," said Theasa. "Dryads have been murdered for their magic. Those two don't trust humans, not after what magicians did to their kindred, so they will not join us." She glanced at both Thom and the monk. "However, they will help us. They want to see justice done."

Before anyone could reply, a crow dove through the trees and cried out at its discovery. Greler took quick aim and shot it out of the air, but the rest of the flock now knew where their prey hid. Without another word, the rescue party hurried on as crows began to call out on all sides, coming closer.

Thom gave Adele a helpful boost up a steep rock and then struggled to climb after her. He then reached back to assist Marcus, who was the last in their party. Through a break in the trees, Thom could see that they were much closer to the hilltops. Evening had arrived, stretching shadows and filling the pass with shade.

He hadn't seen the dryads again during the climb but he did hear their whistled messages to the pixies. Whatever they said, it guided the group into the pass. The trees thinned and now Thom could see some of the crows circling overhead. The pixies shot down two more, but the birds came in the hundreds and all were determined to caw about the rescuers' approach. It became obvious to him that they wouldn't be sneaking up on the sorceress.

Their path had only just leveled out when they heard a new cry overhead, far louder than any crow. Looking up, Thom saw the huge beast launch from one ridgelines of the other hill. He saw its large wings spread out over a golden-furred body. It was a griffin- part eagle and part lion. The magical beast swooped toward them, the crows scattering out of its way.

TWENTY-THREE

Attack from Above

Thom grabbed Adele's hand and yanked her after him, under a copse of thick trees. He pushed aside branches as he tried to get under sturdier cover. Others yelled out warning and scrambled to hide from the diving griffin.

The flying beast let out an eagle's cry as it swooped down among them, catching Jake in its fore talons. Thom and Adele looked back when Jake cried out. The beast landed on its hind legs and lifted Jake toward its vicious beak. It would have bit him in two but Marcus stabbed it in the side. Hot blood gushed from the wound, releasing the sound of the gryphon's innate magic. Thom's inner ear heard the deep, beating rhythm.

The beast tossed Jake aside and lunged for Marcus to avenge the wound, but its attack came up short. Francis slipped behind the griffin and hit him on the rump with his cudgel and then ran off. It was enough to distract the griffin and so that Marcus was able to scamper behind a large boulder. During all of this, the pixies grabbed a bleeding Jake by his two arms and dragged him among the brush.

Thom suddenly realized that Adele was stepping out from beneath the trees, her bow up and aimed at the monster.

"No! Don't endanger yourself."

She ignored his plea and let an arrow fly, hitting the griffin in the neck. The beast whipped around and glared at her while Thom pulled her back among the trees.

They both ran when the griffin charged their way, the huge eagle-lion crashing through the trees in pursuit. Thom pulled Adele behind a larger tree and then down into a defile, sliding on the dirt and leaves. They lost their balance and fell sprawling into a creek at the bottom of the shallow ravine.

Looking up, Thom could see the trees shaking as the griffin pressed after them and then its eagle-like head appeared, glaring down. He sprang to his feet and struggled to get his sword out. Next to him, Adele rose more gracefully, lifting her bow and notching another arrow. Neither of them had the chance to attack the beast, however, for it suddenly pulled back with a sharp cry. Thom guessed that someone else in the group had struck the griffin.

"Come on," said Adele, slinging her bow over her back and scrambling up the bank in pursuit.

Thom hurried after her, not certain why he was rushing to face such a monster. He slipped once during the climb out of the ravine and, although he didn't slide back far, it delayed him enough that he didn't catch up with Adele. He made it out of the defile and ran after her as she disappeared among the splintered trees.

He heard the griffin scream again as he stepped over crushed branches. Its magic was louder now, due to its many wounds, but its roaring cry didn't sound weakened at all. Although the nearby brush obscured it from his sight, he could tell exactly where it was by the noise of its exposed magical essence.

Thom tried again to get ahead of Adele, but she was too fast. He came out of the copse right behind her, to find the griffin still battling the others. It screeched, trying to attack with both its talons and its sharp beak. Its lion-like tail swished with aggravation. Adele shot it in the rump but this time it didn't turn. It was too distracted by the others in front of it.

Theasa and Greler stepped in front of the monster to shoot their poisoned arrows into its breast, and then the two pixies scrambled to get out of the way of its angry lunge. Thom was amazed that the thing wasn't dead yet, for he saw at least a half-dozen pixie arrows already in the eagle-lion.

Marcus and Jake came at it with swinging swords and Francis with his cudgel, trying to turn the beast away from the pixies. Adele also struck again with another well-aimed arrow.

Thom was the only one not attacking, as he tried to think of some way to use magic. He could think of nothing. Finally, he swallowed against his heavily-beating heart and ran at the thing, clumsily swinging his sword in front of him. The monster's rear haunches were as tall as he was. He looked for a likely target, ignoring the swishing tail, and decided he might be able to injure its leg. With a mighty swing, he hacked into the lower leg where the golden fur gave way to a wreath of feathers. His sword bit into the griffin's flesh, splattering a dark blood everywhere.

The animal lifted its head and let out a horrible cry of pain, although Thom wasn't certain if that was in reaction to his attack or not. He struck again, chopping at the leg once more before it was pulled out of reach. The beast retreated from him, the injured leg dragging a bit. The griffin moved slower now, as if the poison was finally catching up with it.

Thom stepped back as the griffin turned and snapped in his direction, but then he tripped and fell. He desperately kept the sword pointed up at the monster approaching. He held his sword with one hand while using the other to scoot back on the hard ground. A tiny whimper escaped his lips.

The griffin loomed over him, ready to snatch him in its maw. Its dark eyes were focused on Thom now.

He gave up trying to scoot away and held onto his sword with both shaking hands. Its beak opened as it lunged for him, but then it pulled up short. With an angry cry, it jerked its head back and looked over its shoulder. Someone had attacked it from behind.

At that moment, an arrow flew from Adele and hit within its open mouth, and then two more pixie arrows caught it in the back of the neck. The griffin shook its head violently at the darts, snapping in half the arrow in its mouth. The beast began to sway, finally succumbing to its many injuries and to the poison. Before Thom could crawl out of the way, the huge eagle-lion came crashing down, dying right on top of him. Thom smothered in musty feathers as its chest slammed him against the ground.

"Thomas! Thomas!"

Adele's shouts were muffled as if he were hidden under a dozen feather-filled quilts. The monster's chest covered him and he was having trouble breathing. He opened his mouth and it filled with foul-tasting feathers. He tried pushing the griffin away, but it was too heavy.

The others came to his rescue and heaved the carcass off him. Suddenly, the crushing weight was gone from his chest.

Gasping, he coughed out feathers and then gulped in fresh air.

Adele knelt beside him and lifted his head. "Thomas! Are you hurt?"

Francis knelt on his other side, checking for any serious injuries.

Embarrassed, Thom wanted no attention. He pulled away and sat up, though he gave Adele an apologetic smile. "I'm fine. Really, I am. The stupid beast just knocked the wind out of me. How is everyone else?"

Francis stood up as he replied. "Thank God, we are all well. Can you stand up?" He held out a hand to help pull Thom up.

Thom accepted the help as he struggled to his feet, wincing at some new bruises. He noticed the pixies climbing over the carcass and yanking out arrows. Jake and Marcus sat on a tree trunk that the griffin had knocked over, catching their breath. Everyone except the pixies seemed shaken up.

Theasa and Greler finished their arrow collecting and then came over to the others. Theasa handed to Adele all of hers that they were able to salvage. "Here, Maiden Adele. Greler and I must talk to the dryads again, for we need more poison for our arrows."

"Should I have mine poison-tipped too?" asked Adele.

"That would not be wise," replied Theasa. "We are resistant to its potency, but humans are not. An accidental touch and you would be dead. I would not want that to happen."

"Will this take long?" asked Jake. "We don't have time to hunt for hiding dryads."

"The dryads are close," replied Greler. "Close enough to have helped us bring down the griffin." He held out a handful of tiny darts. "This will not take long."

Thom hadn't seen any of the tiny folk, but he knew how well they blended into their surroundings. It was good to know that the dryads were brave enough to join the fight.

Greler and Theasa slipped into the woods.

While the others tended to wounds and refilled waterskins, Thom just stood there staring at the griffin carcass. It didn't seem quite so large now that it no longer moved. He had a hard time convincing himself that it was truly dead, for its innate magic still lived, letting out a deep beat from the spilled blood and open wounds. He knew that now would be the time to harvest the magical elements, but he couldn't bring himself to do that. Not after being nearly killed by the thing.

Adele came over to stand next to him. Her hand slipped into his, their fingers intertwining. He found that comforting.

"It doesn't seem quite dead yet," she whispered. "It's almost as if I can still hear its heart beating."

Thomas looked over at her. Maybe she was hearing its magic with her inner ear. "Maybe you hear the whisper of the magic clinging to it. It will fade away as the carcass decomposes."

Adele gave him a puzzled look. "I'm no magician. How can I hear magic?"

Thom shrugged, not really wanting to explain any theories of magic right now. He chose a simple answer for her. "Sometimes magic is loud enough for most people to hear it."

She nodded. "Like a death cry."

* * *

As promised, the pixies weren't gone for long. When they came back, Greler shared disturbing news from the little folk. "The sorceress has been sacrificing dryads as part of some evil rite on the far edge of the Waycircle. They originally wanted us to help them save the few still in her clutches, but now they say it is too late."

"What magic are they creating?" asked Francis. "Can you show me?"

Greler nodded. "There is clearing in the pass where we can see far. Come with us."

As the others gathered to follow the pixies, Marcus stepped over to the dead griffin and plucked a feather from its head, putting it in his pack as a souvenir. Adele watched him and then did the same. No one else did. Not even Thom, who knew the value of a griffin as a magical element. He had neither a desire for a memento of his near suffocation nor the time to render any part of the beast into a magical powder.

The pixies led them along a faint path through the dense forest choking the pass between the two hills, bringing them to a clearing where they could look down at the rest of the Waycircle. They saw the corrals and pens set aside for travelers on that side of the hills and the grasslands that swept all the way out to the encircling evergreens that formed the Waycircle's outer perimeter.

Overhead, the crows still circled and called out their location.

Greler pointed to where the sorceress practiced her dark magic. The place was against the far end of the Waycircle, where another archway sat. At first, Thom didn't grasp the significance of the structure.

"How is that possible? She has built a new door into the Waycircle," said Francis. "Somehow, she forced the magic to accept a new archway. I wouldn't have thought anyone could do that, but there it is. She was able to weave a new opening into the enchantment without causing all of it to explode. Dalrake must have given her some secret way to manipulate the magic, for only a Founder would know this intricate enchantment well enough to find a way to weasel into the Road's pattern."

"Founder?" asked Jake. "Is the Road not Merlin's creation?"

"It was Merlin's idea," replied the monk, "but it took all three of the Founders to craft the enchantment: Merlin, Dalrake, and Levitanus."

Levitanus? His own master was counted as one of the Founders? Thom looked away from the new gateway and stared at Francis. His mentor had never claimed that title, but then he had never taught Thomas the names of the Founders... he hadn't even mentioned how many there were.

"Sorcerer Dalrake was one of the Founders?" asked Adele. "And also Thomas' teacher?"

Francis nodded with a quick glance toward Thom, as if he had suspected some of this was new to the apprentice. "The three strongest magicians came together for the good of the realm and created a magical haven for the king, sheltering Camelot and the various approaches to the city. In those years, the land was dangerous with warring lords, bandits, and invaders from across the seas. King Arthur needed a protected city so that he could concentrate on bringing others to heel. Because of those great enchantments, the king was able to unite the land and keep it together for these many decades. But even the king couldn't keep the magicians united. Eventually, Dalrake rebelled from the magicians' guild to create his own band of dark art practitioners."

"And you think Dalrake gave the sorceress the secrets to do this to the Way?" asked Theasa.

"I think that is beyond the abilities of most, even the Keeper of the Road; it must be the work of a Founder or someone instructed by one of them."

"Let us hope that Dalrake is not over there," muttered Greler.

"Were the other attacks on the Road done for mere distraction?" asked his wife, hands on her hips as she stared across the grasses at the shimmering gateway.

"That is my guess," said Francis, making eye contact with the diminutive yet fierce pixie. "Actual masons are needed to build a gateway, so it took days to build this, even with magical help in curing the mortar. Very likely they started on this at the same time the attacks started. The jarring noise from the lower Road hid what was happening here."

"It is not long done," she replied. "I see the mason workers still resting in the grasses nearby."

Thom stepped closer to the pixie, but his eyesight wasn't sharp enough to see the people she did. He wondered where the workers came from and that brought another thought to him. "Where does it lead?"

"I hope nowhere," answered Francis, "or else we might have an invading army charging through soon. Two gateways need to be built with the aid of magicians and then the enchantment between those two archways is crafted. If this one was just finished then hopefully the actual passageway hasn't been crafted yet."

"Can we destroy it?" asked Jake of the monk.

"If we used magic to tear that down, it could shred the whole encircling ward. We would all die." Francis shook his head in apparent disbelief at what the sorceress had created. "Maybe it can be blocked..."

Marcus interrupted. "Before you worry too much about that archway, we need to deal with more immediate problems." He pointed to the foot of the hills, where a group of twelve men rode toward them. These were not the armored knights, but they were still well-armed."

Thom recognized Iago at their fore, his distinctive red cloak obvious even at this distance. Soon he lost sight of them as they passed under tree cover. The slope was just as steep on this side. The only route offering a way down from the pass was a deep ravine. Iago's men aimed at the mouth of that fold in the land.

"They'll not make it far on horseback," replied Jake. "It's too steep and wooded."

"That won't stop them," replied Adele. "I saw their red-cloaked leader butcher others with a cruel efficiency. He hunted down the few who tried to hide among the trees in the last Waycircle. He later bragged about being the best assassin in Britannia, at least he did until his mistress rebuked him."

"They will have no trouble hunting us down while on foot," said Theasa, "not when the crows act as their spies. We won't even be able to sneak around their flank, for our route looks to be forced into that narrow defile."

"Then we'll have to kill them all," said Marcus, slapping his sheathed sword in challenge.

Eric Loren

TWENTY-FOUR

Deep Ravine

Although the pixies' stride was much shorter, the two had no problem scurrying where the humans had to lumber through the undergrowth. Thom was hard-pressed to keep up with them, as were the others. When Marcus asked them to slow down, Greler refused, saying that they needed to get among the thicker growth quickly if they hoped to elude the black-feathered spies overhead.

Their route became steeper as the pixies led them downhill, through shrubs and under dense copses. The two seemed determined to pick the worst route just so that it would be harder for the crows to follow them from above.

Thom lost his footing and slid down a leaf-littered slope, barreling into Marcus and sending him sprawling too. He apologized as he regained his footing, pulling the guard up.

As Thom stood, a crow mocked him from a perch far overhead. He glared up at it, but it knew he could do nothing to it.

"Can't you light that thing on fire?" asked Marcus, sounding like he also took personal insult from its call.

"We don't need a forest fire to add to our troubles," said Francis as he stepped past them. "Let them squawk. It's the humans that we need to worry about."

"Keep moving," ordered Jake, stopping on the slope above them. He had assigned himself the rear guard. "The others are already disappearing among the trees."

Thom turned and saw that was true. The pixies and Adele were nowhere in sight and Francis was already partially obscured by a bramble bush. He stopped brushing his clothes and scrambled down the slope, being careful not to slide into a thorny shrub. He then scurried after the others, with Marcus and Jake right behind him.

The pixies kept to their determined pace. The small hunters found a small stream that leaped down the canyon in an altering series of falls and rapids and led them along its bank.

The crows still followed, but Thom saw little of them. He only knew they were near because he could still hear their caws somewhere above the trees. Anywhere else, he would have expected such a wild area to be full of other sounds: birds chirping, insects buzzing, maybe the scamper of a startled animal. But this was a Waycircle. Such things didn't exist in a Waycircle unless a human brought them in, like the ebony birds spying overhead.

Their rapid descent came to a sudden halt when four dryads stepped out in front of the pixies and signaled for all to stop. A soft conversation of chirps and whistles followed and then the dryads vanished again, blending into the foliage.

"The men are just below," interpreted Theasa. "They abandoned their horses further down the slope and are now hiking up to meet us."

"They are unaware of us?" asked Francis.

Greler pointed up at the latest crow cry. "They must know we are close, for their winged spies reveal that much, but the dryads think them ignorant of much beyond that."

"Why bother to chase after us among the trees?" asked Francis. "They have the upper hand away from the hills. I don't like this." He paused a moment to concentrate elsewhere, then looked at Thom. "What do you hear?"

Thom concentrated too and heard someone crafting magic nearby. "There is a magician among them."

Francis nodded. "They set a trap for us and aren't trying to be subtle about it. Our way is blocked."

"Can we go another way?" asked Adele. "We want to rescue the queen, not fight all of these men."

"We need to kill the magicians," answered Francis softly. He didn't sound enthused at the prospect. "I know you care deeply for the queen, Adele, but the greater problem is the rogue magicians killing indiscriminately. Sometimes death must be repaid for death. I pray that God will use us to bring justice to these lawless ones."

"Praying for success in killing, monk? You are a bold one," said Marcus, smiling.

Francis frowned. "I take no joy in it, but they must be stopped. I only hope that we can rescue the queen as well."

Theasa walked up to the monk and stood before him with her hands on her hips. "What magic will you use against this sorcerer? Greler and I cannot sneak up on him, for he will sense us." She held up a scratched arm. Everyone in the group had scrapes and cuts, but for the pixies it meant that their magical essence was now revealed. Thom hadn't noticed until now, but both pixies were noticeable to his inner ear. Their magic made a faint but distinct sound. Theasa continued, "So, Brother Francis, that leaves you and the apprentice. Prepare your elemental powders, magician and monk, for the two of you must lead this next attack."

Francis nodded and motioned for Thom to follow him over to where the stream formed a small pool. There on its edge the monk stopped and stared down at the water. He was quiet for a moment, then finally spoke. "I think we will need more than one enchantment this time. Have you ever crafted magic while still maintaining an enchantment?"

Thom's eyes widened. "Never. How can I do two at once?"

"I will direct you, Thomas. I will even help with the first one, if you'll me."

Thom nodded his agreement, so Francis quickly led him through his plan. "We'll use the water to create a Cloud of Mist. When the vapors fill the forest, I want you to start your second enchantment, sending Wizard Lights through the fog. Hopefully, they will think it is our party trying to sneak through."

"I've never made moving lights," admitted Thom. "I only know how to keep the Wizard Light in the palm of my hand. I don't even know how to set it somewhere, let alone send it dancing through a tangled wood. Will you be helping me with the lights?"

"I'll join in on the first enchantment to maintain it, so it will have to be you alone." Francis then explained how to alter the simple magic so that the lights could move away from the magician. It took Thom a few minutes to understand the details.

"Don't let your lights fall into the waters, for then the enchantments will clash. The fog will be harmless, but the stream will be alive with magic. More importantly, you need to realize that the sorcerer will feel your magic and might trace it directly back to you, so move after each Wizard Light is created. I thank God that Wizard Lights will wander and bounce off things with little or no harm, so you can release them to weave through the trees below us. The dark magic's fireballs are much more powerful, but they will no more float or drift than an arrow or spear. They fly in a straight line, which will not be easily done in this dense wood."

"What do we hope to accomplish with all of this?" asked Thom. Fog and floating lights might distract but they couldn't harm the enemy.

"We need to divert the sorcerer's attention so that someone… anyone can get close enough to kill him."

Thom was doubtful, but he had no better ideas so he agreed to Francis' plan. "Tell me what elements we'll need."

"To craft a Cloud of Mist, we will need some of the elements that Wizard Cruthen added to your magician's cache," stated the monk, crouching and setting his clean eating bowl on the ground in front of Thom's feet. "We'll use this so that you can save your mixing bowl for the Wizard Lights you'll be crafting."

Thom nodded at as he pulled off his knapsack and crouched next to the brother. He pulled out his magician's box, setting it near the bowl.

"We will need powders of Gray Dew Moth and Quaking Bulrush seeds, as well as a few drops of blood from a Wisp Grass Snake and some droplets of Cloud Dew."

Francis had to help with selecting two of the vials since Thom was unfamiliar with their sound, but soon he had the right vials on the ground and his cache closed to block out all the extra noise. The monk guided him through the crafting, telling him when to add each powder and in what quantity. Thom listened, both to Francis and the developing enchantment. Finally, when it came time to attune the magic to its welder, both Francis and Thom spat into the smoking potion.

The monk took the bowl and urged Thomas to get going. "You did that well. You crafted with confidence and a skill beyond any apprentice I've encountered. I will keep this enchantment going so that you can now create Wizard Lights."

Francis began drizzling the potion into the pool of water and a faint mist began to swirl over the waters. As he moved to another area of the pool, he looked at all the others who had gathered around them. "All of you go. Get away from me, for the sorcerer will soon react. Spread out and do whatever you must to get close to him. We need the sorcerer removed so that we can win through to the queen."

The others obeyed, silently moving off in separate directions as the mist continued to grow over the waters. At Theasa's insistence, they paired up: Jake with Marcus, Theasa with Greler, and Thom with Adele.

Thom looked back once more and saw that the mist was much thicker now and was spilling down the fall, following over the waterway for now. He could hear the magic building in the pool rather than dissipating. He still had a connection to the enchantment even though it was Francis who was actually sustaining it, and he wondered how many were connected to the Road of Leaves and heard when it was attacked. Had his master Levitanus sensed the vicious blows, even though his cottage was so many miles away?

Adele touched his shoulder to regain his attention. "We should go," she said. "The others are already vanishing into the forest."

He nodded, turning away from Francis and leading her downhill and to the side, well away from the enchantment brewing behind them. He found a sheltered copse that overlooked the now-steaming creek and knelt there. Adele stooped beside him, an arrow already notched in her bow, and kept a lookout. She didn't ask why he paused, apparently understanding Thom's need to collect his thoughts and prepare his magic. He took out his magician's box and set it on the ground. Opening it, he chose the powders he would need, picking them more by sound than by sight in this dim canyon. He worked quickly, for his open magician's box would be like a beacon to the sorcerer. He shut the box and then started mixing the elements in his mixing bowl. It would be enough to create a few Wizard Lights.

The mist expanded outward, filling the bottom of the ravine with a knee-deep soup. It was not enough to hide in yet, but enough to bring a response from the sorcerer farther down the canyon, a response that Thom more heard than saw.

Thom reflexively ducked when the fireball roared through the trees, but it wasn't aimed his way. It soared overhead until it slammed into a wide tree that had to be near where Francis worked. The tree burst into flame, a glaring light in the gathering dusk. Thom was too far away to feel the heat but he could hear the flames eating through the wood.

While Thom had ducked, Adele had jumped to her feet. She ignored his attempt to pull her to shelter as she stared down the ravine. "I didn't see exactly where he is, but I have an idea of the distance now. It's too far for my bow. I'll need to move closer."

"Not yet," objected Thom, fearing for her safety. "We need to wait for the mist to grow, then I will send off my first trio of lights and we can move on."

She nodded and gave him a smile, letting him pull her out of harm's way. She reached out with her finger and touched the tip of his nose. "I'll wait that long, but then we'll need to go on. I'll not have the others take all the risks."

Thom smiled back, though he didn't feel like it. He was nervous about his part in this charade, for he still wasn't certain he could create floating Wizard Lights. He reviewed Francis' instructions and wondered if he had forgotten any steps. The mixture in front of him was almost ready, lacking only two more powders, both of which sat in vials next to the bowl. How much should he add of each? What if he got the portions wrong? How much spittle was needed to attune the magic to himself?

The mists now hid the waterway, billowing up in cloudy waves to silently crash against the trees on either side. Where before it had grown slowly, now the fog billowed off the pool above them and rolled down the canyon, weaving through the trees. He felt the dampness on his face as one wisp floated past him and then another. Within two minutes he could barely see Adele even though she knelt next to him.

It was now time. The magician's apprentice added the last two elements, spat, and stirred up the concoction. He poured some into his hand and created a Wizard Light and then sent it off in the way Francis had explained. It wobbled away, bounced off a tree and then fell to the ground, flickering and dying. Thom was just glad to see it move away from his palm.

"Beware the stream," reminded Adele.

He nodded that he had heard but was concentrating on his second creation. This one flew better, careening off into the fog. A fireball came roaring past as he released his third one. Thankfully, the sorcerer was still aiming at Francis. As soon as the fireball passed, Thom grabbed Adele's hand and they hurried off in the fog. In his other hand he held his mixing bowl, trying to keep from slopping its contents as he strode across the rough terrain.

Thom chased after his released enchantments, though not following directly in their path. The mists now filled the ravine and thickened to hide much of the landscape. It was an eerie place to sneak through, for he had no idea where Iago and the other men hid.

Only the sorcerer revealed his location, doing so by holding aloft his now-glowing master's staff. A white light shown from it and engulfed the sorcerer for a moment, even as a wind stirred the trees around him and swirled up the dead leaves at his feet. Soon the fog swept toward him too, but the glow of his crafted magic still shone through the mist and Thom wondered what kind of enchantment he was crafting.

Suddenly, the sorcerer released his magic and it roared out from him, a furious wind. Thom and Adele were thrown to the side and the trees moaned as they bent to the onslaught.

By the time he was back on feet, Thom found the light extinguished and the fog gone.

"He overcame Francis' work," whispered Adele as she realized the clear air around them.

Thom concentrated behind them and could hear Francis still maintaining the enchantment. "Not fully. I think the fog will return shortly and I doubt the sorcerer can keep doing such extravagant magic to counter it."

"Where is the sorcerer now?"

Thom shook his head. "I cannot hear or see him anymore. Let us try to move closer, but not too close."

They carefully made their way further down the canyon, trying their best to move with stealth. It seemed that they should have been almost on top of the others by now, but they encountered no one. Finally, Thom stopped Adele and quickly prepared another Wizard Light. This one floated off on a surer path, and so he kept it going, bobbing down the canyon. He guided it with his thoughts and hand motions for a while and then let it go on unaided. He needed to focus on moving farther down the canyon. Its light had revealed none of the soldiers, but then it was started to become foggy again.

They hurried on, hand-in-hand through the returning misty wisps. Thom let Adele lead because he had to keep some of his attention on the Wizard Lights. Neither of them saw the rope strung between two trees at ankle height, so they tripped and fell hard.

Two men came out of the fog with swords raised, ready to finish them off.

Eric Loren

TWENTY-FIVE

Killers in the Woods

Adele had lost her bow in her fall and was now trying to crawl after it. One man followed her, chuckling at her struggles. Thom tried to unsheathe his sword as the second man towered over him, but was having a hard time getting it free.

Just then, another fireball sizzled through the mists. The sorcerer was trying for Thom now, tracing his magic use unerringly back to him because he had been carrying a bowl of pulsating paste used to form Wizard Lights. He threw a sizzling fireball through the mists toward where Thom had been, attracted by the sound of that half-used Wizard Light paste. However, Thom was sprawled on the ground now, with a soldier looming over him, so the conflagration struck the other instead, hitting him directly in the chest with such force that he was flung against a tree. The man let out a horrible scream and danced in flames for a moment before perishing. Thom watched the death throes in shock.

Adele finally grabbed a hold of her bow and swung it to strike the first man in the leg, sending him sprawling. The commotion brought Thom out of his daze and he sprang to his feet, freeing his sword in the process. He rushed over to help, and swung down on the man, catching him in the gut just before Adele's knife dug into his throat. The man struggled but soon lay still.

"Are you hurt?" Thom asked, helping her up.

"Merely bruised," she whispered back. "Can you tell if any more of them are near?"

Thom shook his head. "Let us move on before the sorcerer sends a second fireball our way. I need to create more Wizard Lights." He was getting closer to his opponent which greatly increased the risk, but that was unavoidable. His earlier lights had already died out so he needed to kindle more. The almost-done mixture he had been carrying was slopped onto the ground and useless now, its magical power spent.

He led Adele up the side of the ravine, leaving her in a more protected niche while he went to stand next to an old chestnut tree. He hastily wiped his mixing bowl clean and started over with his mixing. He worked as quickly as he could, well aware that the sound of the magic would attract the sorcerer. Finally, he finished his crafting and then shaped another Wizard Light and sent it sailing off into the thick mists. As soon as it left he leaped behind the tree trunk, hugging the patterned bark with one arm as he waited for an explosion. Nothing happened.

After waiting a moment, he looked around the tree and tried to hear if the sorcerer was creating any new enchantment. He was. Soon, another fireball came sizzling through the forest, but not in his direction. Thom quickly created another Wizard Light and sent it in the direction of the sorcerer, hoping that he could highlight the man for the others to find.

He and Adele moved on, now having to move slower because they couldn't see the ground at their feet. Francis' fog was thick as soup. Thom carried his half-full mixing bowl as he went. He knew it was a risk, for any magician would be able to hear the exposed elements he carried, but he mixed larger batches so that he could craft more Wizard Lights in rapid succession. He let Adele pick their next stop.

As Adele sheltered behind a wide oak, Thomas conjured another Wizard Light and sent it to hover over the sorcerer. This time, the magician responded. A fireball roared at Thom, forcing him to scramble away as fire washed over the tree. The trunk sheltered them from the worst, though both suffered a shower of sparks. Thom created another light, using the last of his mix, and sent it off to float over the sorcerer. He then took Adele's offered hand and let her lead him away, for he was too drained to think clearly. He could barely hold onto that little bit of connection to the lights that kept them working.

Another fireball roared their way, striking the hillside nearby and setting fire to some brush. There were numerous fires in the canyon now, adding a glow to the fog. The smoke intermingled with the mist, giving the air a charred taste.

Somewhere in the canyon, men were fighting. Thom could hear them as Adele led him back toward the stream. They were heading closer to the sorcerer, so he whispered a warning.

"I know that," she replied in his ear. "We need to get closer to the stream where the mist will be thicker. He won't expect us this close."

As if to confirm her guess, the sorcerer threw another fireball at the slope they had just left, setting fire to something in the murk.

Thom felt exposed even as he struggled to see anything in the fog. He had no idea who or what might be nearby. Even Adele faded from view, in spite of them having their fingers interwoven. In all directions, he saw only walls of darkening gray. Evening approached, making the fog even harder to navigate. He listened for the enemy, but heard nothing nearby, even with his inner ear. The sorcerer had paused in his magical crafting. There were shouts and curses elsewhere but it was hard to judge direction and distance in this cloud soup.

Adele found the stream by stepping into it. Thom heard the splash and felt her jerk back. He smiled a bit at her angry mutter. She paused and then turned to follow the water toward the sorcerer. Thom considered protesting her choice but didn't, for he realized it was his fear that made him want to hold back. Adele was surely braver than he was.

They noticed the shadowy movement at the same time.

Adele stopped, lifted her bow, and aimed an arrow.

They lost clear sight of the person as he blended into the fog and a tree's shadow.

Adele waited patiently. Thom stood silently at her side, not wanting to distract her or attract the enemy's attention.

The man moved away from the tree, a darker shadow among the mists.

Adele tracked his movement with her bow.

Thom saw a slight limp in the man's movement and suddenly realized who he was. He pushed Adele and her arrow flew wide. She whipped around to give him an angry look, while the shadowy man turned and froze.

Thom ignored her glare and called out in a loud whisper. "Marcus?"

The shadow came towards them and soon Adele recognized the merchant's guard too.

"You missed," he whispered. "Your aim seems a bit high and to the side." He said nothing more, but turned and resumed his stalking, quickly becoming an indistinct shadow again.

"Thanks for pushing me," whispered Adele as they followed after him.

Thom sensed his two still-burning Wizard Lights ahead, though he could not see their faint light. He didn't know if they still hovered over the magician but he guessed the man wouldn't be too far from that area. Surely, the sorcerer wouldn't be as foolish as they were to go stumbling about in this fog.

As they crept closer, he worried that they might stumble into another trap. He heard a twig snap off to the right but he didn't see anyone. Maybe it was Jake, who was supposed to be Marcus' companion on this foggy raid, but it could've easily been an enemy instead. He had to trust that the person couldn't see either Adele or him.

He was startled a bit later when someone called out nearby, in a voice he didn't recognize. "Where are they? I can't see a thing in this soup!"

"Silence!" hissed a second man. Thom could see neither one.

The first man made a gurgling reply.

"Robin? What happened to you?" asked the second man but received no reply. Thom heard the second man grunt and then heard distinctive clash of metal on metal. The fellow shouted a warning, "They're on us!"

A fireball blazed through the mist and crashed into the second man. Thom saw the man's opponent dive to the ground right before the impact. The magician had no qualms with killing his allies if it meant maybe getting a foe as well.

Thom wished he could send a fireball back at the sorcerer. Instead, he hurried over to the two men on fire. Once close, he recognized Jake rolling in the dirt to extinguish the flames. The other man was dead. Thom swept off his own cloak and used it the smother Jake's smoldering clothes. When done, he turned the guide over to see how he faired.

"Thanks, magician." Jake's voice was raw from smoke.

"Can you move?" he asked.

Jake stood to prove he was still able. He tried to disguise a wince as a mere grunt, but Thom saw through it. He helped the gruff man to limp behind a sheltering tree, using the light of the still-burning corpse to guide his steps. Adele joined them there.

As Jake leaned against the rough bark, Marcus suddenly appeared out of the fog to check on him. Jake sank to the ground, his back still against the tree. For a moment, he seemed unaware of any of them as he battled against obvious pain. Thom held a waterskin to his mouth and he drank.

Finally, Jake looked over at Marcus. "Go on without me. I need to rest here a bit and then I'll follow."

Marcus nodded and left to continue the hunt. Within five steps he had vanished into the fog.

Jake turned to the pair kneeling in front of him. "You two should also go. That sorcerer still needs to be dealt with."

The fire had died to an angry glow, so Thom couldn't see the man's face very well. He wasn't sure if Jake needed more immediate attention.

"I told you to go," repeated Jake with more force. "Kill him."

Thom offered to leave his waterskin, but Jake refused. Seeing no other choice, Thom left with Adele. Jake was right; they needed to stop their enemy.

Thom passed around a boulder and climbed over a fallen log, Adele right behind him. He was careful not to snap any twigs but their footsteps still seemed loud in the quietness of gathering night. The only other sound he heard was the stream gurgling nearby. The enemy could be anywhere.

He paused to concentrate on his magical senses and felt the enchantment Francis had placed on the stream. He also felt something off to the right. Although he knew the sorcerer was starting another enchantment, he led Adele in that direction.

As he walked away from the stream, the mist thinned a bit and he could finally see the glow of his Wizard Lights. The lights weren't directly over the magician but the pairs of lights hovered near enough to highlight the man's location. Thom tried to shelter behind trees as he led Adele closer. If it weren't for Marcus being somewhere ahead of them, Thom would have walked right into a trap. Instead, it was Marcus who did so.

Men yelled and swords clashed but Thom could see none of it. When the sorcerer kindled a huge fireball in both hands, it backlit the struggle, showing two men fighting Marcus.

Desperate to distract, Thom reached out with his mind and sent one of the Wizard Lights careening towards the magician. The sorcerer responded with a curse, tossing his fireball at the light that was just overhead. The engulfing fire destroyed Thom's weak magic. The man soon held more flames in his hand.

Adele stepped out into the open and drew her bow. She shot, but the arrow missed.

The sorcerer turned his attention toward her.

Thom panicked. He started running for Adele, wanting to push her out of the way.

The sorcerer smiled and raised his arm to throw fire, but then stumbled forward.

It was enough of a delay for Thom to reach her. He pushed her down and threw himself on top. He lay there for a moment, but no fire engulfed him. Instead, he heard Marcus still fighting and others yelling. He looked up and saw the sorcerer still holding his fireball, but now looking over his shoulder. One of Marcus' opponents was running to offer the sorcerer aid against whatever was attacking him from behind.

The magician turned to face his new foe but then stumbled again, flames spilling out of his hand and setting fire to the brush around his feet. He cursed, but it came out slurred. His legs gave out and suddenly he was kneeling in his own fires and feeling the scorching heat. He screamed in agony and then fell over, catching fire as he collapsed. It was only then that Thom saw the tiny dryads lined up behind where the sorcerer had stood.

The tiny creatures now took aim at the soldier running toward them. Before he could dodge, they pin-cushioned him with their dart-like arrows and he dropped dead.

Amazed, Thom stood and helped Adele up. He wasn't even needed by Marcus, for the merchant's guard had already killed his foe.

* * *

Apparently, the magician's men chose to flee rather than fight without him, because the attacks ended. The dryads also disappeared into the approaching night.

Realizing they had won, the group found each other in the fog by calling out to each other. They gathered around their injured guide. Realizing that Francis hadn't returned yet, Greler went to retrieve him while Theasa saw to Jake's burns. Thom, Adele, and Marcus watched Theasa minister, with Thom providing a Wizard Light for her to work by. The guide had some ugly burns on his arms and back, but the pixie slathered a poultice on the wounds and it seemed to provide relief. Jake sighed and then lost consciousness.

They made as comfortable a bed as they could for Jake, covering him with his own blanket to keep the damp fog off. When Greler returned with Francis, Thom was surprised that the monk's face was smudged with ash and one wisp of hair singed. One of the sorcerer's fireballs came very close.

Francis knelt over Jake and examined his bindings by the light of Thom's still-burning Wizard Light, frowning at the seriousness of the wounds. Satisfied with Theasa's ministrations, he stood up and gave her a sad smile. "Thank you for your care. I merely wish we could stay here and give him proper attention. However, we need to go on. We should place water and food within easy reach of him because it may be many hours before we can hope to return."

"How will we find him afterwards?" asked Adele, gesturing at the darkening forest around them. "Can we mark his place somehow?"

"We can find it without any problem," stated Greler, "but there is no assurance that Theasa and I will make it through the upcoming fight. We will mark the tree and also two more at the stream's bank. That should be sufficient to guide whoever returns to get Guide Jake. We are in a Waycircle, not vast a wilderness. There are no lions or bears here, so he should be safe until we come back."

"You didn't say anything about griffins," muttered Marcus.

"They do not dwell here either," replied Greler. "The one that attacked us was sent here by a magician."

The pixie moved over to the side of the tree and began hacking at it with his blade, cutting a series of slashed into the bark. Once satisfied with his mark, he nodded toward Thomas. "Bring your Wizard Light and let us mark two trees along the stream. While we are gone, the rest of you can place the food and water for Jake."

Thom went with the pixie down to the stream and he quickly marked two more trunks and then they hiked back to the others. Finally, Thom was able to let go of his enchantment and darkness seemed to rush in around them. Even though the fog had vanished, it was now too dark to see much around them.

"We need to get moving," stated Francis in the darkness. "Did anyone succeed in killing Iago, the assassin who pretended to be a minstrel?"

No one remembered facing the man but, if he had taken off his flashy cape, they most likely wouldn't have recognized him in the midst of the fog. The monk spoke to the pixies in the sudden darkness. "Do either of you know if the dryads hunted down the fake troubadour?"

"I doubt it," replied Theasa. "Though they might pretend at being tiny warriors, dryads detest killing. It was only their rage at the sorcerer that drove them to kill him. He was the one who captured most of their people for the sacrifices."

"Then Iago is not among the dead, so we will need to be wary. Adele has already warned us that he is an assassin."

Thom looked around the dark forest, wondering where the killer now hid. There were so many shadows everywhere.

Eric Loren

TWENTY-SIX

Swirling Mists

They checked on Jake one more time and then headed down the canyon. They went without lights, not wanting to warn anyone watching. Beyond the ravine it was not yet fully night, but in this fold of the hills the darkness prevailed, making any light noticeable from afar.

They were nearly down when they heard the horses gallop off. Apparently, four survivors had retrieved the mounts and were now fleeing to ground that was more open.

When they finally reached the forest's edge, they looked out on a land darkened by late evening. Some stars already shown overhead. The crows were finally gone, roosting somewhere for the night. Out on the grasses, they could see a small fire and a woman standing over it, gazing toward the newly made archway that was two or three ridgelines away. Even at this distance, her master staff was obvious, the jewels at its head adding a greenish glow to her flowing hair.

Four men rode toward her leading a train of riderless horses.

"There she is," whispered Adele.

"But where is the other sorcerer?" asked Thom.

"Maybe he is patrolling the other side of the hill with those knights," suggested Marcus. "Be thankful they aren't underfoot. So how will we sneak up on the sorceress?"

"Dusk is our aid," stated Greler. "The coming night will be our friend, especially with her staring over the fire like that. It robs her of any night vision."

"I do not see any captives," remarked Marcus, still looking.

"The land has folds in that area," stated Theasa. "Maybe she keeps them in one of those dells."

Thom watched as the horsemen swept past the sorceress and kept riding. She ignored them, concentrating on the new archway instead. There was no camaraderie among them. Apparently, they were beneath her notice and they knew it. The four riders and their extra horses swerved off and dropped into a fold of the land. He was surprised that the dip was deep enough to hide a man on horseback. Losing sight of them, he looked back at the sorceress, but she had not moved, her focus still on the magical opening.

"Why does she stand so far from the archway?" asked Thomas of the monk.

"Maybe the crafting requires it, or maybe there is a certain danger that makes her cautious," replied Francis. "Her staff is lit, which shows that she's in the middle of something, but I'm not sure what." He turned toward the pixies. "Can we send the dryads to scout the area?"

"I can try to enlist them, but dryads fear open country," replied Greler. He softly whistled, sounding much like a forest bird. No one responded.

"We have no time for their timidity," argued Theasa. "We must hurry on without them, for we need to reach the sorceress before the other magician returns."

"Then let us do the scouting," suggested Greler to his wife. "We are better suited to hide among the grasses."

When his wife consented, the small man turned to the others. "Give us a short lead and then follow after."

Thom watched the pixies sneak off toward the sorceress, soon losing sight of them in the gloom. He looked over at his companions and realized there were not many left to finish this rescue, just the four of them hunkered behind the last row of trees.

Brother Francis met his look. "Thomas, what do you sense of her work?"

Thom wondered why Francis insisted on having him listening when the monk knew so much more about magic, but now was not the time to argue. He slipped around the tree, keeping to the shadows, and did as asked, listening with his inner ear. After a moment, he came back and told the others. "She uses magic, but I don't recognize the enchantment at all. What is she doing, monk?"

"I do not recognize it either; it seems some sort of Dark Art. I'm not certain, but I think it has something to do with the archway she built. Maybe the magic is too dangerous to craft from close by."

Although his master had spoken briefly of such potent enchantments, Thom had never really considered the reality. The idea chilled him. He couldn't help but stare at the sorceress' outline. How could a magician be tempted to try such a potentially deadly enchantment? He was still mulling that question when Francis interrupted his thoughts a few minutes later.

"We've waited long enough. Time for us to sneak up on Narissa. May God grant us favor in our approach."

The others followed the monk's example of crouching, as Francis led them away from the trees and toward the sorceress. Thom kept careful watch as he went, using all of his senses. The only magic he heard was around the woman standing so still. The only person he saw, besides his companions, was the sorceress. Something sounded odd, but he wasn't certain what.

She never turned or moved. Instead, she stared off into the night, focused on the new archway and whatever she was conjuring there. There was no encircling magic to protect her, but Thom wouldn't expect that if she were crafting an enchantment. The sorceress apparently had no fear of others harming her.

The four humans walked in a single file: Francis, Thomas, Adele, and finally Marcus. Thom hoped to protect Adele if the sorceress attacked. He was unsure how he would protect her, but he would do so. They moved as quickly as they could while staying low to the grasses. They walked carefully, making no sudden moves that might attract attention and keeping in a row, even as they tried to make good time.

The pixies suddenly rose among the grasses ahead of them and shot arrows, hitting the woman four times in quick succession. The sorceress fell over and then the pair rushed up on her. But something was wrong. Greler yelled a warning, something about the woman being too young, but Thom didn't understand what he meant.

The other sorcerer rose from crouching among the grasses on the far side of the woman and completed some enchantment that he had already laid down in the grasses, unknown to the rescuers.

"The woman was a decoy! This is some kind of trap!" yelled Francis, running full speed and no longer crouching.

The pixies took aim at the sorcerer, but more men stood up from the tall grasses, acting to shield him. Some fell beneath the pixie arrows but the others stepped into the gaps to shelter their leader.

"Get out of there!" yelled Francis, but the pixies were focused on the magician who was crafting something.

Thom heard the new magic, something brooding and dark in its rhythm. He heard Francis yell out another warning just as a circle of mist began to swirl around the area where the decoy had stood. The monk was standing where the magic began to manifest and he desperately dove away from the mist. The clouds swirled and grew, becoming a wall of power that imprisoned Theasa and Greler. The mist became darker and thicker.

The pixies tried to dive through the enchantment but rebounded off it. They were stranded inside whatever was manifesting.

"Can you break them free?" asked Adele of Thom.

He looked for any weakness but saw nothing. He listened to the magic's song, but it was an unknown mix of elements. "I can't fight this."

Francis stood and motioned to Thom. "He crafts something deadly to encircle them. We must stop the sorcerer or the pixies will die."

The monk started running around the swirling magic. Thom ran after him, fumbling out his sword because he couldn't think of any magic that would help. Adele and Marcus chased after both of them.

The mist was now over eight feet in height and so thick that Thom could now longer see the two trapped inside.

When they came around the encircling magic, they faced six men led by Iago. The false troubadour flung knives, striking both Francis and Thom.

Francis stumbled when the knife struck him, tumbling into the grasses.

Thom was also hit. The thrown blade sliced across his shoulder, cutting the cloth and nicking the skin underneath, and then spinning off into the grasses. The sudden sharp pain caused him to grunt and grab his shoulder, but he kept running.

Iago's dark cape swirled as he reached for another pair of knives.

Thom considered throwing his sword at him but knew he would miss. Instead, he ran straight for the assassin, hoping to disrupt the next throw. He didn't even notice the other man charging at him until he glimpsed a long blade swinging at his head. Reacting instinctively, he raised his sword and caught the oncoming blade in a jarring clash that almost sent him to his knees.

The foe swung again and Thom barely deflected that blow too. The soldier would have killed him quickly, but the man stepped between Thom and Iago and got the assassin's thrown knife in his back as payment. The fellow staggered but kept fighting. Even weakened, he was better than a hapless Thom.

Thomas would have probably died, but Marcus came up and killed the man from behind. The merchant's guard gave Thom a nod and ran on to challenge another of the soldiers.

"Thomas!"

He looked over at Francis, who was getting back up on his feet.

"Leave off the swordplay. Instead, you need to toss Wizard Lights into the sorcerer's enchantment."

Thom's eyes widened at the implication, but agreed. Digging out the right elements, he hastily crafted a feeble light and then looked to Francis for direction, but the monk was caught in another battle, using his cudgel to keep away a swordsman. It was up to Thom now.

"Ware the mist!" he yelled, sending a Wizard Light into the maelstrom. There was a bright flash but the whirlwind held, continuing to compress on the pixies.

Thom quickly created two more Wizard Lights and sent them flying after the first. This time the flash caused lightning to crackle around the dark circle and the whirling magic began to wobble.

He was about to conjure a fourth light when another of Iago's knives caught him, this time in the side. The knife had been spinning as it flew and was mistimed. It was the haft and not the blade that hit him, but the impact still spun him. He fell into the grasses. That was probably what saved him, for suddenly the sorcerer's enchantment shredded in a rush of wind that flattened the grasses all around him. The roar of air deafened as it passed over.

* * *

He lost awareness for a time, and when he woke, the grasslands were silent. He thought at first it might be his hearing, but that wasn't the cause. When Thom staggered to his feet, he found no one else standing. He now heard a few faint moans, but nothing more.

He noticed the crushed pixies but had no time to mourn. He couldn't even search for Adele, for he needed to kill that sorcerer before the man could craft more magic. He staggered on, searching for the magician. He found the man already dead, killed by the backlash of his shredded enchantment.

Next, he looked for Adele and spied her getting to her feet not too far away. Seeing her in no imminent danger, Thom turned his attention to any remaining enemy. He looked for Iago and located the assassin beneath Francis. The monk had killed him with the assassin's own weapon. He bent over and found that Francis lived. He called out and shook him. The monk moaned.

Eric Loren

TWENTY-SEVEN

Only Three

Thom moved Francis away from the dead man and laid him gently on the grass. The monk let out another moan as Thom probed his injuries. Seeing that the worst was the knife wound in his side, he tried to staunch it with a piece of cloth.

Adele came over and knelt next to Thom. "How is he?"

"He has bled too much. Can you find some strips of cloth so that we can bind his wounds?"

She cut material from Iago's burgundy cloak and brought them over. Thom had Adele take over applying pressure while he mixed a poultice and then applied it. When done, they let Francis rest on the grass again.

The monk's eyes flickered open. "Thomas? Did we get them all? Have you found the queen?"

Thom looked around, wondering if any of the soldiers were still about, but he found only Marcus standing watch nearby. "We stopped the two magicians and the assassin, but I don't know where they have hidden the queen."

"Now I remember. Greler yelled out that it wasn't the real sorceress. When she fell under the pixie arrows, I saw her change into another person. I think the sorcerer had shape-shifted a queen's maid to look like Narissa as bait for his trap." Francis grimaced. "Narissa is still out there, with the queen as her hostage." The monk let out a regretful sigh. "I cannot go on. You must be the one to stop her. Although I hate magic, I regret that I can't show you all the enchantments that were taught to me." He fumbled for Thom's hand and gave it a squeeze. "You will need to depend on your wit instead, and on God's aid."

Francis looked over at Adele. "Do what you can to help him kill the sorceress Narissa and rescue the queen. I'm glad that you're at his side, for you are such a resourceful and determined woman."

He looked back at Thom. "Did any others survive?"

"Marcus stands watch."

Francis gave a weak nod. "He's a good man too."

"You act like you are about to die," protested Adele.

"I don't know about dying, but I'm certainly of no more use for this rescue. The three of you will need to go on without me." He tried to sit up, but the pain stopped him. He spoke through another grimace, "Can you call Marcus over?"

Thom did so, bringing the merchant guard to join them in kneeling over the gravely injured monk.

Francis looked up at them. "I want to pray for God's guidance and strength on the three of you. May I?"

When all agreed, the monk said his heartfelt prayer, asking for the Lord's help. Thomas never thought of himself as much of a religious man, having been raised in a thief's house, but he felt almost close to God while Francis prayed. The words comforted, having a power that was unlike any enchantment.

Francis' genuine sentiment also melted the last of Thom's bitterness towards the monk. Moisture came to Thom's eyes, which he quickly wiped away before anyone noticed. Francis really cared about them, in spite how Thom had treated him. He proved himself to be a true friend.

The monk sent them off with assurances that he would be fine resting there among the dead. He also urged Thom to recall their discussion on crafting variations. "You can turn your handful of enchantments into so many more with just a few alterations in mixtures. Remember this too, don't fear that woman, no matter how great her power. Fearful respect is meant for God, not mere humans. She can kill your bodies, but your souls aren't hers to touch. That is God's providence."

* * *

The three of them walked away, onto the dark grasslands of Twin Hills Waycircle. They now hunted for the last magician, the sorceress who started all this havoc. They had no more pixie scouts, dryad help, or even Jake's steadfast guidance. It was just them: Thomas, Adele, and Marcus. Thom reluctantly led.

Night blanketed the expansive Waycircle, making it hard to see much. The sorceress and the queen were out there somewhere. Thom looked for any revealing fire or Wizard Light, but all was dark under the canopy of distant stars. Narissa could be anywhere.

Having no certain direction, he chose to head toward the new archway.

Thom no longer tried to crouch, trusting the night to hide him, but he did follow one of the dips in the land that headed in the right direction. Right behind him walked Adele and then Marcus. As he walked, Thom listened with his inner ear. So far, he heard no other magic except the Waycircle itself.

His chosen route flattened as the land rose toward the encircling evergreen trees that marked the outer edge of the Waycircle. He noticed a small fire that he hadn't at first noticed because of the glow of the archway and because two shadowy figures stood before it, blocking much of the light. Carefully, Thom crept closer so that he could hear the pair talking. It was the father and son duo from his childhood, the two who had dressed as clergy.

"I don't like it, father. Why'd she send us to stand out here in the dark?"

"Shut up, Ned."

"But I wanna just sit by the fire…"

"I said to shut up. We're supposed to be watching for trouble and guarding the masons."

"What about the knights? They should be doing this. We ain't soldiers, so why does she have us watching?"

Old Joseph whacked the back of his son's head. "Do as told, Ned. You'll not anger her, understand? Play at priests, tend goats, or act as guards. We'll do whatever she asks, because she's our leader. Maybe she's worried that the masons might try to filch something, so we watch them and keep an eye open for trouble. What does it matter, when she promises to reward us handsomely?"

"You're one to talk about being nice to her. What'll happen if she ever finds out that you filched coins from her?"

Joe hit him again. "She won't find out if ya keep your mouth shut. I swear, Ned, sometimes ya act as dumb as your mum."

"Mum's not dumb," muttered Ned.

Their conversation died off as father and son gazed off in different directions.

Thom considered if he needed to kill these two. They were traitors to the land and accomplices of the sorceress. They were also fools. Rogues yes, but still fools. He decided to let them live, pulling back and picking another route that would take him past the two thieves. It wasn't hard to avoid notice because the two kept too close to their warming fire.

Adele and Marcus followed his lead without question as they silently slipped around the two fake ministers and kept going toward the magical portal.

He finally discovered Narissa when he heard a sudden welling of new magic. Following the sound, he found her standing directly in front of the new archway. There was a torch shoved into the ground nearby, further lighting up the area and showing the sorceress' features. She still looked like the Goat Woman she once pretended to be, but not so old or haggard. Narissa appeared to be a middle-aged woman, haughty in her power. She wore far better clothing now, a fine yet practical dress with a wide belt that had numerous pouches on it that hummed with ready-to-use magic. She looked competent.

She touched the new stonework with both hands and stared at it intently. Magic enveloped her already, but he was unsure what enchantment it might be.

He listened intently as he watched, just to make sure it didn't sound like the trap that had caught the pixies. It did not, and she seemed unaware of being watched.

Thom ducked below a hillock and then whispered to his companions. "She's in the midst of crafting an enchantment."

"Is she shielded by magic?" asked Marcus. "Or guarded by others?"

"No. She is alone and focused on the new archway."

"Good," whispered Adele, taking her bow in hand and notching an arrow. She looked to Thom for permission.

Thom hesitated, but then realized that Adele's skill was their best hope in catching the woman unaware. He nodded.

Adele stood, aimed, and shot.

There was a sudden change in Narissa's magic, too late for Thom to stop Adele.

The arrow flew unerringly at the sorceress, but then stopped mere inches from its target. It just hung there in mid-air.

Narissa turned, unhurried and with a bit of a smile on her lips. "The three of you might as well stop trying to hide, for I can see you clearly."

The arrow fell to the ground.

Thom hurriedly pulled out his magician's box and pulled vials by their sound, quickly closing it again. He filled his palm with a mix of powders and then kindled them. Only when the Wizard Light burned brightly did he stand. He didn't know why he created the light, but it felt right. This would not be a duel with normal weapons, but one with magic.

"I am impressed at your determination, apprentice. Although your master has been miserly at teaching you enchantments. Imagine what power you would have if you ever learned any of the greater magic. You should insist that Levitanus show you the rest of his book, for you are ready. Do you not think so?"

Her concern for his training seemed odd, but he had thought many of the same things. Maybe Levitanus was miserly with sharing enchantment as well as coins. Maybe his master shared things only grudgingly.

She continued to speak, her voice soft and reasonable. Her magic sang to him, an enticing rhythm unlike any he'd ever heard. "It is a shame that you are not interested in the Greater Arts, for we are much freer with our knowledge. Others malign us as practitioners of the dark arts, but they are envious of our power and freedom. Maybe you should consider investigating the Greater Arts."

Another arrow flew at her, but she waved if away with a flick of her hand. Thom didn't bother to look at his companions. He had eyes only for the sorceress.

Narissa gifted him with another smile. "What could it hurt to learn more and see whether you have skill in doing the greater magic? Would you like to learn more, apprentice?"

Adele spoke up, her voice sounding harsh. "Your honeyed words don't convince me, but then I'm not the target of your incantation, am I?" The maiden stepped in front of him, blocking his view of the sorceress. "She tries to bewitch you, Thomas. Resist her enchantment."

Thom leaned to the side to look past her.

Marcus stepped up behind him and stuck a beefy finger into each of Thom's ears.

Thom tried to elbow the man off him, but Marcus didn't budge. Thom's eyes were still on Narissa and he saw her lips move but this time he couldn't hear her words. It was enough of a break in the magic to weaken its effect. He stopped trying to fight off Marcus, anger growing as he realized how the sorceress had manipulated him.

He still held a Wizard Light in his hand, having maintained the simple enchantment unconsciously. With a heave of both his hand and his mind, he sent the light hurling toward the sorceress. As she dealt with it, he made another, spilling powders in his haste, and flung it at the new archway. It was a desperate move, but it was the only way he could think to distract the woman. She would have to stop the light or else the clash of magic might destroy the new opening. He noticed that the archway didn't shimmer steadily like the others, instead flickering. He wondered if it was active yet and where it was meant to lead.

Narissa easily deflect his first light and then scowled at the second. "You fool! Do you mean to kill us all?" She quickly sent a wind to shove the light aside. Thom had never seen anyone craft an enchantment so quickly and deftly, grabbing on the pouches at her belt. He wondered how she had pre-mixed them without activating the enchantment. Well, now was not the time to ponder that. He needed to retreat.

The Wizard Light struck the ground well away from the archway and the Waycircle's encircling evergreens.

In that moment of distraction, Thom and his companions ducked out of her sight, rolling down a slight embankment to get away. They had failed to stop her. As Thom came to a rest at the bottom of the dell, he heard a thundering sound and it took a moment for him to realize what caused it. Galloping horses.

Eric Loren

TWENTY-EIGHT

Archways

Narissa didn't chase them. Most likely, she no longer considered them a threat.

At the bottom of the slope, Thom sprang to his feet. He looked around for any shelter or high ground but they were in an open and grassy bowl, ready to be served up to the knights like a fine meal. He couldn't see them yet, but the sound of their approach grew louder.

Adele notched another arrow while Marcus hefted his big sword.

Thom created another Wizard Light and then threw it directly at the ground where it splattered in a burst of almost harmless sparks. The light didn't carry much heat to it, but it was enough to start a little fire. Hurrying before the flames could die out, he threw in another mix of powders and smoke began to fill the dell. By the time the knights crested the hollow's lip, the three of them were hidden in a smoky cloud that swirled within the bowl like a soup freshly stirred.

The riders weren't deterred by the smoke, but rode directly into it.

Thom heard them coming and tried to think of some other magic that he could use. Nothing came to mind. It was Marcus who saved them this time.

The guard tugged at Thomas and Adele, urging them to run to the side. They did, hoping to avoid the onrushing horsemen.

The riders barely missed them, charging through the bottom of the dell and up the far side.

Marcus brought them to a halt, but they had already gone too far. The smoke around them thinned to reveal the night and the six riders looking for them. One of the knights pointed and gave a shout. The half-dozen armored men now charged their horses around the lip of the bowl so that the smoke wouldn't obscure their targets this time.

Thom vaguely recalled an enchantment Francis had mentioned while they were riding that morning, an alteration of some magic he had just learned. If done right, the Teasing of Air would be able to send the smoke at the riders, but Thom was uncertain he remembered the whole enchantment. Fumbling in the dark, he opened his magician's box and selected the elements by their sound.

Having no time to dig a mixing bowl from his pack, he cupped his left hand and poured the elements into it, stirring the powder with his right index finger and adding his spit to attune the magic.

The riders came at them quickly.

Thom touched some of the moist powders to his lips and then threw the rest at the smoke. He made a sweeping motion with his arm and blew toward the charging knights. Surprisingly a wind stirred, sweeping up the smoke and enveloping the knights in its billows.

Marcus yanked them away from the dell and then down into the grasses. As he lay flat, Thom hoped that no horse would trample him or his companions.

The horses thundered through the smoke and then their riders pulled them to a stop. The knights looked around, then charged into the smoke still at the bottom of the dell.

While the riders were out of sight, Thom kindled a Wizard Light and sent it chasing across the grasses, away from where they wanted to go. When the knights rode up to the bowl's lip again, two of them spotted the light and soon they were all riding hard after it. Thom concentrated and gave the light a bit more speed even though that meant it would be out of his range sooner. He watched for a minute, and then allowed the light sputter out.

"They'll be back," stated Marcus, "so let's kill the sorceress quickly."

"We need to be careful though," said Adele. "The queen was not that far from her, tied up on the ground like some roped steer."

Thom had not noticed Guinevere, but if she was close then it complicated stopping Narissa. He didn't want to hurt the queen.

* * *

This time Marcus led them, taking a circuitous route to come at Sorceress Narissa from another direction. When Thom saw the new archway in the distance, he realized that her enchantment work was done and the entrance active. It was no longer flickering; now a gray shimmer steadily filled the opening. Twin Hills Waycircle held two exits now and maybe this one had no nightly windstorm beyond its sheen. He worried that maybe the sorceress had already fled with her captive, but then he saw her silhouetted against the faint-glowing archway. The woman was talking to two others. Thom realized that they were Ned and Joseph.

The masons who had built the archway were now leaving through the new archway, so apparently it was safe to use even at night. There was nothing to prevent the sorceress from following, but she didn't leave. Instead, she motioned for the two men to lift the tied-up queen. They followed Narissa as she stalked off into the night, leaving the archway unguarded.

Marcus stepped close and whispered into Thom's ear. "Do you want to attack the new opening?"

Thom shook his head, frightened by the idea. "No. If I were to succeed in destroying it, then the whole Waycircle would probably shred apart."

"Can you block it?"

Again, Thom shook his head no. "I'm curious where it goes, but that can wait. We need to pursue her now."

"I just saw those awful goats with her," whispered Adele, pointing.

Thom saw them too now, four-legged shadows following her like pet dogs. "The goats are a bother, but at least they don't fling fire or swing swords. Ignore the goats; we need to stop her and get the queen away from Ned and his father."

"We'll celebrate our success with goat stew," chuckled Marcus, leading them in pursuit.

* * *

Narissa made no effort to hide her movements, walking boldly across the rolling grassland toward the original archway. As she strode, she created a Wizard Light and sent it straight up into the air, where it hung like a beacon. She created a second one and set it to float just ahead of her as a light for her path. The reason for the first light became apparent, as horsemen came riding to her. The six knights came, as well as two men from the group that had fought earlier. Those last two brought along a collection of riderless mounts.

While Thom and his companions watched from afar, Narissa chose a horse for herself and mounted. Ned and Joseph set the queen across another empty saddle and starting tying her in place.

Thom, Adele, and Marcus sped up, too desperate to try hiding their passage.

Ned and Joseph finished securing the bound queen to a horse and then also mounted. Narissa motioned to her men and they set off, never looking back at the three trying to catch up with them.

Marcus stopped chasing, realizing it was hopeless now, but Thom strode right past him, refusing to give up. Thomas didn't look back, but he heard Marcus and Adele following. He crafted a Wizard Light as he walked, not daring to stop even for that. He made it in his hands and then sent it to float just ahead of them. Once the light revealed more of the grassland, Thom started running. Marcus and Adele also sped up.

No matter how hard they ran, they were no match for a horse's gait. They lost sight of Narissa and her guiding light, but they pressed on. Thom kept the lead, for he was the only one trained to hear magic. The Sorceress Narissa wasn't shy about using her skills, so he was able to hone in on her that way.

* * *

When they finally caught up with her, Narissa was kneeling near the Waycircle's original archway. Two men held up lit torches, for the Wizard Light was gone. Thom could tell that she was in the middle of crafting another enchantment, for he could hear new elements starting to blend in the bowl in front of her.

Ned and his father stood over the bound queen to the right of the archway, near the outer ring of evergreens. The six knights were off their horses and standing guard in a semi-circle around their leader.

The horses waited off to the other side, their reins secured to tree branches in a copse that jutted out from the Waycircle's tree-lined lip. The pair of goats grazed nearby.

Thom had extinguished his Wizard Light some time ago, when he first spotted the torchlight in the distance, so they had walked the last distance in the dark. He stopped now that he could see the enemy clearly, as did Adele and Marcus. Thom took off his pack and squatted over it, rummaging for his mixing bowl and his magician's box. He needed to prepare some magic. His work was noisy to any who could listen with their inner ear, but the sorceress' work was much louder.

As he worked, the other two watched their enemies.

"The men are light-blinded," observed Marcus. "They keep turning to look at her, so the torches rob their night vision. We should be able to sneak up on them with ease."

"What is she trying to do?" asked Adele.

Thom had been wondering the same thing. A quick glance showed her now touching the archway, smearing it with some concoction. He continued his work as he answered. "The archway's shimmer has dulled and darkened. I think she's somehow closing the Waycircle's entrance."

"That is our only exit," protested Marcus. "I've no desire to use any doorway she's made. We need to stop her before she finishes this mischief. Not only do I want to kill her and rescue the queen, but I also want to be able to walk out of here. I'll do what I can to get you close, Thomas, but you need to deal with that magician quickly."

The merchant's guard turned to Adele. "Ware the knights' armor. Your arrows won't penetrate their helms or chainmail shirts, so aim for the face, lower torso, or limbs. Are you ready?"

She nodded.

Marcus looked at Thom.

The apprentice had just finished mixing magical powders in his small bowl and had poured the mixture into one of the vials he had emptied. He was trying something new; it was a desperate move and dangerous, but he saw no other way he could even hope to best the sorceress. He needed something unexpected. There was one more element that needed to be added and then the magic would become active, becoming a Twist of Air. Francis had mentioned this trick of withholding the last element and the sorceress obviously did something similar; he just hoped he could finish the enchantment when the time came.

Thom met Marcus' eyes and nodded his readiness, though he didn't feel ready. They understood this would be their final confrontation. They had to stop the sorceress now, or die trying.

Eric Loren

TWENTY-NINE

Torn Veil

Marcus chose their approach, circling the guards and then coming at the last man on the right, closest to the Waycircle's tree hedge and near where the fake clergymen guarded their captive. The nearest man was no knight, just one of her two remaining mercenaries. Marcus motioned for Thom and Adele to wait as he slipped up and cut the man's throat. The fellow made no noise as he fell, for Marcus surprised him by sneaking up while the man was looking toward the center of the Waycircle. The three of them were past the guard line before the others realized what had happened. When they did, it was a mad rush at Thom and his companions even while Ned and Joseph sought to keep them away from the queen.

Adele let loose arrows, aiming at the sorceress. She struck the woman in the back, but Narissa didn't falter in her magic. Adele also struck one of the torchbearers in the neck and he collapsed, dropping his torch.

Marcus turned to fight off the knights as well as he could.

Thom now had to make a choice. What enchantment would he use? If an arrow lodged in her back was not enough to distract Narissa, then a Wizard Light would fail too. He hastily pulled out his magician's box and pulled out three elements and then shut and shoved the box back into his knapsack. Not worrying about the waste, he dumped the contents into his palm, mixing it with his other hand. His hand tingled and warmed as the elements mixed into the Fire Starter enchantment. Before it could do more than blister his hand, he flung the powdered mix at the small fire burning around the fallen torch. The fire surged in size, green grass shriveling and then bursting into flames.

Thom didn't have much more time, for the knights were almost on him.

He took out the vial he had already mixed and poured it into his hand, adding the final element and his spit, stirring it all with his finger. With the Twist of Air, he sent the flames racing toward Narissa. The remaining torchbearer dropped his torch and fled the advancing fire.

Thom kept at it, pushing the flames toward the sorceress, convinced that she would have to break from her magic to deal with his attack. But Narissa didn't react as expected. Not until the flames were at her feet did she move, and then it was to let go of the stone archway with one hand, reach into a pouch on her belt, and throw some powder behind her back. The flames died as if a flood had just saturated the area, giving an angry hiss and sending up even more smoke.

Thom knew that he had failed again when he saw only angry embers and that the sorceress had both hands on the archway stones again. The gray shimmer was nearly gone. It was becoming as dark as night within the stone opening, for she was turning it inactive, closing the opening.

Adele cried out. He looked over and saw her arm bleeding and a knight standing over her, ready to give the killing blow.

He ran toward her, yelling a challenge to the man, but the knight stayed focus on his prey. Just when the man's great sword reached the apex of his swing, the knight staggered and looked around with a puzzled look. It was then that Thom saw the small dart sticking out of the man's neck. A dryad arrow.

More of the knights fell to the poisoned arrows and then one hit Narissa and she finally staggered away from the archway, her enchantment disrupted.

Shrieking in rage, the woman tore the dart out of her arm and tossed it aside. She then clawed into her arm around the wound and ripped out a chunk of flesh, leaving her arm blood-soaked. She turned to face the attacker. Reaching into a belt pouch, she pulled out a handful of premixed elements and tossed them in a sweeping motion. Thom heard a grating jumble of magical sounds and then a sudden scream of wind filled his ears and battered his body. Everyone was thrown away from her. The windblast didn't last long, but it threw everyone off their feet.

Narissa picked up a dazed dryad from among the charred grasses and dashed the tiny woman against the archway behind her. However, that was the sorceress' downfall. Not only had her enchantment been interrupted, but now she had crushed a magical being against the weakened entryway.

Thom felt the release of a different magic, of something stored in the dryad's nature. He then heard a terrible ripping sound as the blackened glimmer inside the archway parted from top to bottom. The Road of Leaves stormed through the opening, a roaring wind and a squall of debris that dwarfed the sorceress' little gust.

Narissa spun in sudden horror and then staggered back from the sudden onslaught.

Thom would have been blown away if he had not already been knocked down. As it was, he lost sight of the sorceress as a flood of leaves roared into the Waycircle. The shifting Road of Leaves now howled through, devastating what had been a refuge from its nightly fury.

He saw Adele crawling against the storm and realized she was heading for the queen. He wanted to help her but he needed to finish off the sorceress first. He rose to his hands and knees and aimed for where he had last seen Narissa, in the middle of the torrent of leaves. For some reason, he didn't trust the dryad poison to finish her off.

He found the sorceress still standing against the wind's onslaught, even though she had been pushed back some distance.

She saw him crawling and yelled at him. "You! Who are you, that you can withstand me? You should have died many times already."

"I'm a mere apprentice," he yelled back, uncertain if she even heard. He remembered something Francis had told him and repeated it to her. "I don't fear you, for you can only kill me."

He struggled to his feet as leaves whipped by. He raised his sword in defiance, challenging her to attack.

She pulled out a vial of powder and tried to pour it into the hand on her wounded side, but the wind whipped the elements away, leaving her palm empty. Frustrated, she tossed the glass vial into the wind and let her damaged arm flop back down her side, blood running from where she had gouged out the poison.

Another dryad suddenly came at her, more blown than running. He must have been clinging to the perimeter trees near the archway, before releasing himself into the torrent of leaves. The tiny man had an arrow in his hand that he planned to jab into her since he couldn't shoot in this storm, but she stepped aside and struck him as the wind blew him past. He crumbled to the ground near Thom. Dead in his failure.

Thom fell back to his knees next to the tiny fellow, unable to keep standing in the gale.

The sorceress turned away from all of it, striding off toward the new archway she had built. Somehow, she was able to stand and walk where everyone else faltered.

Thom realized that she meant to abandon the Waycircle. He yelled after her. "Are you so afraid of a mere apprentice? Why do you run away from me?"

She looked over and he thought she laughed, though the sound was lost in the wind's fury. She yelled back at him. "You are dead already, so why should I bother? I'll let the Road kill you."

Eric Loren

THIRTY

Swirling Leaves

Sorceress Narissa then strode off, pushed by the wind but not staggered by it.

Thom was suddenly afraid that she planned to destroy the whole Waycircle once she arrived at the new archway. If he didn't stop her, then it could mean the end for everyone still alive in this refuge, including Francis, Queen Guinevere, the dryads, and sweet Adele. It was up to him to prevent such a catastrophe.

He crawled over to the dead dryad and retrieved the tiny arrow the man held, careful not to touch the poisoned tip. He fumbled another arrow out of the man's quiver and then fought his way to his feet. Turning his back on the maelstrom, he staggered after the sorceress.

It seemed like the wind no longer tried to push him over. Instead, it hurried him along as if carrying him in pursuit. Leaves were everywhere, making it hard to see.

He suddenly worried that he might get pushed right past her, missing her among all the airborne debris. It seemed he was getting pushed more toward the hills and not the distant archway. He tried to slow his pace, to fight across the rushing air, but it was to no avail. Thom was barely able to keep his feet under him as the wind carried him onward.

And then he saw her. Narissa strode directly ahead of him, ignoring the leaves and twigs that constantly struck her in the back.

Thom lost his feet and tumbled into a dip in the ground. He sprang back up, the tiny arrows still in each fist and their tips still fresh with poison. He looked for her and saw that the sorceress had also stumbled, although she had not fallen.

A branch flew by Thom's head, an end knocking him in the shoulder. He stumbled but kept his eyes on her. The branch hit her as well, directly in the back, and she staggered. She did not look back though, which was good, for then she would have seen him. He pushed on, determined to catch up and stop her.

As he pursued, he saw two others fighting their way through the wind, one person leaning heavily on the other. They were just ahead of the sorceress. It took a moment for him to recognize who they were. Adele and the queen.

When he saw Narissa swerve toward them, he tried to yell out in warning, but his words were shredded by the roaring wind. He ran, trying to save them, but then he fell. When he rose, he saw it was too late. The sorceress had them now.

He kept going.

"Close enough, apprentice!" Narissa yelled, holding a knife to Adele's throat. Adele was still trying to hold up the queen even as Narissa threatened her. The sorceress apparently knew of his affection for the maiden. "Turn around or she dies!"

Thom stopped, the wind buffeting him and trying to push him on. "Let them go!"

She smiled and pricked Adele's neck. "Turn around! Go back into the wind!"

He saw the fear in Adele's eyes and the hopelessness in the queen's. Guinevere was too weak to help Adele. What could he do?

Adele cried out as the sorceress cut her a second time, her neck now blood-stained.

"Oh God, help them," muttered Thom as he turned around and tried to walk into the wind. It pushed back, not wanting to let him go in that direction.

When he faltered, she yelled after him. "Keep going! If you turn around, I will kill her!"

He didn't doubt that she would. A sob caught in his throat and tears filled his eyes. He dared not look back. Head down, he trudged into the fierce windstorm.

He didn't even see the cloud of leaves racing his way until it engulfed him and spun him around. The wind grabbed him and threw him back toward the sorceress. Thom could see nothing through the debris, as twigs and leaves clawed at his exposed skin and grit filled his eyes. He tried running to keep his feet under him, but only touched the ground every third stride.

The wind carried him across the open ground and threw him into the queen, ripping her out of Adele's grasp. Both queen and apprentice tumbled into a pile. When Thom stood up, he saw Adele still in Narissa's grip.

"I warned you, apprentice. Now she dies and it will be your fault."

The sorceress meant to cut open Adele's throat, but just then a branch hit her from behind. She stumbled and lost her grip on Adele and her knife.

Thom lurched forward to get between Adele and the magician.

Suddenly the leaves began to whirl in a circle, enclosing Thom and Narissa within a swirling wall of flying debris. The air calmed within the circle but he could hear the roar from the wall of wind. The whirlwind also roared with the sound of magic, but unlike any magic he had ever heard. At first he thought it was her enchantment, but her confused look told him that was not so.

She focused on him at last and yelled over the roar, "The Road will not protect you, apprentice. You will die tonight."

"So be it, but I will die trying to stop you." He ran at her.

She formed a fireball and threw it hastily. He dove out of the way and it slammed into the leaves racing around them. The leaves caught fire and became a whirling wall of flame.

"Oh God, help!" he yelled, not caring if she heard. He had lost one of the dryad arrows in his dive, so when he stood up he shifted the remaining poison arrow to his left hand and unsheathed his sword to hold in his right.

She laughed contemptuously, creating another fireball.

Desperate, he threw his sword at her. It spun through the still air, wobbling. She stepped aside and it missed her, landing in the spinning wall of burning leaves instead. The winds picked it up and it joined the swirling debris.

She threw the second fireball and this time hit his side, flames splashing over his arm.

He cried out in agony but couldn't stop to extinguish the fire. Instead, he ran at her again. His sword was out of reach, for he saw it whipping around the whirlwind in the midst of the burning leaves. He had only the little dryad arrow, a mere oversized dart to use against the powerful master of dark magic.

Yet he ran at her, desperate to get close enough to use the tiny arrow. He ignored the flames eating at his sleeve. His focus was on her.

She formed a third fireball, but before she could throw this one, he collided with her and plunged the dryad arrow into her neck. Thom fell to the ground and tried to smother his arm, while she staggered back. Her last fireball fell to the ground and her hands went to her throat as she gasped for breath.

With a look of horror, she tried to yank out the poisoned dart, but her shaking fingers kept missing. She stumbled away from him and stepped back one step too far. The spinning winds caught her.

Narissa tried to fight against the pull and for a moment stood there in midst of the whirlwind, defiant of death. The burning leaves hit her and she let out a silent scream as she caught fire, then Thom's sword came whirling around and buried itself in her chest. She collapsed then, and the wind whipped her body airborne.

As suddenly as it had appeared, the whirlwind dissipated, the burning leaves scattering and many of them falling into a small stream. The sorceress' body thudded to the ground, lifeless now but still smoldering.

The winds returned to pushing in one direction again.

Thom just lay there, dazed and in pain. At least his clothes no longer burned.

Adele pushed her way through the wind to his side. "Thomas! Thomas! You live!"

He sat up as she wrapped her arms around him. He felt her lips on his and, for a moment, the agony lessened under that sweet ministration. She was crying.

He put his good arm around her and let his own tears flow.

THIRTY-ONE

Seeking Shelter

When a twig slapped his side, Thom remembered the storm roaring past. The wind buffeted his body, howling its continued fury. He looked around and noticed the charred and bloody remains of Narissa. He also saw the queen still lying where she had fallen during the final conflict. He remembered that their rescue was not yet complete.

He leaned close to Adele's ear. "We need to get the queen out of this wind." He considered going through the new archway but he had no idea where it led. That left only one other possible refuge. "We need to carry her back to the hills, to the ravine we hiked down."

Adele nodded her understanding. They helped each other stand in the wind and went over to Guinevere. They found her weak but coherent.

Thom spoke to her, "Your majesty, we need to get you to safety. Can you walk?"

"I will do what I can, great wizard," she replied, letting them help her to stand.

"I'm no wizard," replied Thom, feeling the need to correct her. "I am merely a magician's apprentice."

She gave him a weak smile. "If that be true, then I am merely a simple noblewoman."

He chose not to argue, for she was the queen. Her very clothes announced her great place in society, though the dress was now dirt smudged and torn. The arm he held was covered in rich fabric with gold embroidery, even in the darkness he could see that much. No crown sat on her disheveled hair, but the strands whipping past his face were long and rich even if they were gray-streaked. More than the clothes, her very bearing spoke of her status. He used his good right hand to grasp her arm, for his other side throbbed in agony from the burns. Adele had an arm around the queen's narrow waist, letting the noblewoman lean on her.

Looking about through the blowing debris and darkness, he did his best to judge the direction they wanted and then aimed them that way.

As they passed the sorceress' corpse, Adele told him to stop. She had Thomas take the queen's weight for a moment as she went over and, using both hands and great effort, pulled the sword free then gave it back to him.

He let Adele take the Guinevere's weight for a moment as he sheathed the sword with some embarrassment. Whether it was the hand of God or the Road's fury that gave Narissa that final stroke, he wasn't certain. He simply knew that it wasn't his hand that impaled the sorceress with it.

* * *

The Twin Hills appeared ahead, black against the night sky. Thom had not been far off in his choice of direction but they still had to trudge around the one hill's base. They passed an area of corrals and pens and then came to the mouth of the ravine, Thom paused.

"My queen, can you now bear more of your own weight? If so, then Adele will help you the rest of the way. A friend lays injured not far from here and I would want to rescue him."

"Go, young man, and rescue your companion. Maiden Adele and I will fare well in the meantime."

Thom looked to Adele. "If you can, climb to where we left Jake. That should be deep enough into the canyon. The winds will grow through the night, so find the best shelter you can. Be wary of your surroundings, for the storm may rip up trees and tumble boulders. I just hope this will prove to be enough shelter for us to survive."

"Go rescue Francis," encouraged Adele. "We'll be fine."

* * *

It proved a boon that they had not moved Francis away from all of the dead or else he would never have found one injured man in this howling night. As it was, it took some searching to find the area, for distances were deceptive in the storm. When he finally staggered on the monk, he found him awake but weak.

Francis saw Thomas. "What is happening, mage?"

"The sorceress is dead and the queen safe, at least she is if we can protect her through the night. The archway barrier tore and now the Road is whipping its leaves through here."

Francis chuckled, his relief evident. "A sorceress defeated by an apprentice. I want to hear that story in full."

"Maybe tomorrow, but now we need to get away from here. Can you stand?"

With Thom's help, he was able to get to his feet. His wounded side still wept blood. He almost fell when a strong gust buffered him, but Thom held him up. Together, they staggered toward the hills, with Francis using his cudgel as a walking staff.

They had made it about halfway when a horse and rider appeared out of the darkness.

Thom tried to fumble free his sword, afraid of another attack, but then he recognized the rider. Marcus.

"Thomas! You live! Where is Adele?"

"She leads the queen to where we left Jake. We hope to shelter in the ravine."

"What of the sorceress?"

"Dead."

"Good. Help Brother Francis up and I will carry him to safety."

Thom thought it a good idea, but Francis resisted. "No, go help Adele with the queen. Thom and I will make our way out of this storm together."

Marcus raised an eyebrow in surprise, eying Thom's side. Apparently, the darkness didn't hide all of Thom's wounds. "You magicians and monks are hardy folk. Very well, I'll go help with the queen. Hurry to follow after, for I would hate to lose the two of you."

He rode away, leaving the monk and the apprentice to struggle after him. The two held tight to each other and made their way toward shelter.

* * *

That night, trees toppled and winds roared even in that sheltered canyon. Though exhausted, no one slept much due to the windstorm's noise. They found a place between great boulders to lay Francis and Jake. The rest of them huddled there too: Thomas, Adele, Queen Guinevere, Marcus, and one horse. They spent the rest of the night that way.

Only with the arrival of dawn did the winds cease. As the noise died away, they all fell into an exhausted sleep, not awakened until they heard the yells of a rescue party. Knights and pixies entered the devastated Waycircle, led by Thomas' own master, Levitanus.

Eric Loren

THIRTY-TWO

Rewards from a King

King Arthur recognized everyone who had fought to save his wife and to spare one of the ways to Camelot. Light filtered through a stained-glass window high above him, coloring the hall but adding little warmth to the huge space with soaring ceilings. He stood in that light beam and it seemed as if the king glowed. He gave thanks to all those who had fought on the Road of Leaves, including those who had died. He did not speak long but it was heartfelt, then one of his men stood and recited to the audience a summary of the heroics each in the party had done.

Thom stood in awe with his companions in the audience hall, in front of the now seated king and queen. Beside him stood Adele, Marcus, Jake, Francis, Geoffrey, and two pixie elders representing their fallen comrades. All of them were dressed in fine clothes, although Thom's outfit was simply the formal attire of a magician's apprentice- a dark gray robe- but his new boots were of expensive leather and under his robe his shirt and trousers were of a fine weave. His left arm was in a sling from the attack, but the pain of the burns was a mere throbbing now and easily ignored, especially in this splendid setting.

Trying not to be too obvious, he looked at Adele, gorgeous in a flowing light blue dress that complimented her eyes. He wanted to look longer, but his attention was expected to be on the man reciting their acts. Even Francis wore a new garment rather than the faded grayish-black robe he had worn on the Road, and the fresh black of his Benedictine order made it almost a match of a wizard's robe but for the lack of any ornamentation.

The official reciting up front mentioned Thomas' name, drawing his attention back to the dais. Hearing the man speak such high praises of his deeds, he wanted to object. He was no hero. The account seemed exaggerated to make him sound braver than he was. But he dared not interrupt or argue; he knew enough to realize that this was the king's declaration and to argue would sound ungrateful or worse. Instead, with blushed face he accepted the words shared.

When the man finished, he beckoned Thomas forward and to the right, where another official held up his reward of coins and jewels and the grant of an estate. Thom walked over woodenly, numbed by the attention, and accepted the offered riches with an embarrassed thanks. The official had already moved on to reciting the deeds of Guide Jake, so at least the attention was off Thom as he bowed to the king and then returned to his place among his companions. His eyes swept over the hundreds of people in attendance for the ceremony and he felt even more out of place. These were lords and ladies, rich merchants and powerful knights. He was just a mere apprentice who certainly didn't belong in their midst, let alone receiving praise in their presence.

Thom stood in his designated place and half-listened as the list of Jake's deeds continued, but his thoughts kept going to the riches he had just been handed. He was still a magician's apprentice and his master surely wouldn't tolerate any frivolous spending by him, so what could he do to at least keep his newfound wealth safe until his studies were completed? And what was the name of the estate the king had given him? He was embarrassed to realize that the name had already slipped from his mind.

He had no idea where the announced lands were located and had no idea how he would ever be able to claim them or what he would do with the lands, for he still had years of studying ahead of him as Levitanus' apprentice. As he watched Jake go up for his rewards, Thom decided that he would seek his master's advice.

Over the next hour, all of his companions were well rewarded. Jake received a hefty coin purse and the title of Assistant Master Road Guide. Marcus gladly accepted the coins offered to him, but politely refused the chance to join the king's service. Because Francis' vow of poverty, his financial reward went to the Saint Barnabas monastery, but he was also granted access to the royal library to read whatever texts he wanted as often as he chose. Lord Geoffrey was given a senior squire position at court. He was barely able to control his excitement; a celebratory yell slipped out, which he quashed, but the smile stretching across his face never stopped.

Finally, the official recited Adele's heroic acts and she was called forward to her own treasure and the awarding of an estate. As she stepped up to receive those gifts, the queen spoke up for the first time, offering Adele a place among her court, which she accepted with a relieved smile. Thom was overjoyed that she would have a place, since the noblewoman she had been serving was now dead.

Following the rewards, they were led into the dining hall for a grand feast. Music and laughter filled the hall as abundantly as food and drink filled the trestles. Thom had to do everything with his right hand, for his left was in a sling, but there wasn't much to do besides lift his mug and use a fork or spoon.

An attendant had been assigned him and the fellow even cut Thom's meat for him.

The feast was all a wonder to Thom. The only thing that would have been better would have been sitting next to Adele, but she was at a table close to the king's party, the same one where they sat Lord Geoffrey, for they now saw her as minor nobility.

Thom's seat was further away from the lords and ladies, at a table among the honored merchants and traders, but at least he was next to Francis, Jake, and Marcus.

He saw the archbishop of Camelot in the hall, sitting at the king's table next to the abbot of Saint Barnabas, and it made him wonder what had happened to Ned and Joseph. Their bodies were never found, so they must have fled through Narissa's archway. The goats had also vanished, to Thom's disappointment. He would rather have seen them as part of tonight's feast, preferably well-roasted and quickly consumed by others. He wouldn't have touched the meat himself, though, for they would have given him a sour belly for certain.

* * *

Much later, as the celebration was waning toward midnight, his master Levitanus gathered the group in an otherwise empty sitting room, motioning them each to take a seat. Just as they settled onto the padded chairs and settees, another wizard swept into the room. It was Merlin. The man was tall, thin, and intense. His white hair was set off by his spotless black robe. His face showed wrinkles, but they made him seem wiser rather than older.

The leader of the magicians' guild nodded at Levitanus and then swept his sharp gaze over all of them. "I do not have much time. I came here to update his majesty and then I must return to the Road's repairs, but I wanted to take a moment to thank all of you for your good deeds. If you had not interfered, the sorcerers would likely have seized the Road of Leaves and redirected it to their own purpose. We, the remaining Founders, owe a debt to you and will reward you as we can, apart from what the king has already done."

Francis replied before he could say any more. "I, for one, want no rewards from you. I parted with your guild years ago and have no desire to be entangled in it again."

Merlin smiled, but it only touched his mouth and not his eyes. "You were once one of us, Francis. If you return to the guild, we will forgive your past and complete your training…"

The monk raised a hand to end the pleading. "Never. I serve a far better master now, so why would I want to return to your shadowy ways?"

Merlin raised a haughty eyebrow, obviously offended. The weak smile was now gone. "You think that your current master is greater than us? Any wizard outshines your abbot and you lie to claim otherwise."

Francis smiled. "Oh, I seek to obey my superior as a good monk ought, but that is not the master I meant. I serve someone who is far above any fallible man and I find that service suits me. Will you also claim to be a better master than God?"

Merlin frowned but said nothing.

Francis' smile faded as his look hardened. "The guild plays at enchantments while ignoring the so-obvious truth. You claim that magic and sorcery are very different, but I know better. Unless you actively resist its pull, you will slip into that darkness. All magicians experiment with the forbidden arts, for the lure is too great. I know that from my years spent at Clas Myrddin. You cannot deny it. Oh, you justify it. You will argue that a particular magical being was misclassified and is really just a mindless magical animal, but it will still be murder. You will claim the being volunteered to be a victim, like the elderly pixies do to help maintain the Road. But even then, some of their remains are salvage for personal gain. I have seen the pixie powder in too many magicians' boxes. Maybe you will not do the actual killing, but you will buy their powdered remains. The magic is just too tempting, especially after learning the greater spells.

"Magic leads to sorcery as surely as dusk leads to full night. That is the danger in which you dabble. That is why I have renounced magic and turned my back on it. I have broken from its hold and I call on all of you to do the same."

Thom was shocked at what his friend was saying. He knew the monk had renounced magic but he hadn't been aware of the strength of his hatred for it. He wondered how much of what Francis had said was true.

Merlin's glowered now. He stalked across the room to stand over the seated monk. "You are a fool. No one in the guild is a practitioner of the dark arts. To claim otherwise is to slander us. Have you already forgotten whom you were fighting on the Road of Leaves? But enough of this. I will not argue with you. Out of here, Brother Francis. You have forfeited your last chance to rejoin our ranks and someday you will rue your stupidity at rejecting us."

The great wizard stepped back as Francis rose to his feet. The monk looked at everyone, but especially at Merlin, Levitanus, and Thomas. "And you have rejected my urging to flee magic, which makes all of you magicians even bigger fools. I pity you."

Francis turned his back on the Merlin. He gave Thom a slight nod and a sad smile, then he walked out.

Thom watched his friend leave and wondered if he should have gone with him.

Into the awkward silence, Levitanus stepped up to Merlin's side. He was shorter and a bit heavier, though he appeared just as ageless. "As we were saying, we are truly thankful for what all of you have done."

"That man's hypocrisy is infuriating," stated Merlin, obviously still dwelling on Francis. "He claims magic anathema and yet it is obvious he must have crafted some of those enchantments that defeated Narissa and the others, for a mere apprentice does not have such skills." He looked at Thomas. "Is that not true, young man?"

"Those were all my enchantments," replied Thom. "He taught me many of them, but I was the one who did the crafting."

Merlin gave Levitanus a puzzled look. "You still have him dressed as an apprentice, but some of those were master-level enchantments. No apprentice can do them, no matter how good the instructor."

"He is talented and a diligent learner," replied Thom's master.

"There is more to this story," stated Merlin, "and you will need to explain it all some day, Levitanus. For now, have him moved up to journeyman in the guild's records, for that is his skill level. Understood?"

"I am not yours to order around, Merlin, but I will do as you requested."

The two wizards locked eyes for a moment, until Merlin nodded and then swept his gaze over the others once more. "I must be going, for I am needed back on the Road of Leaves. I will leave it to Levitanus to explain more about the guild's rewards for each of you."

Eric Loren

THIRTY-THREE

Rewards from a Wizard

After Merlin left the room there was silence for a time, then Marcus cleared his throat. "Pardon my rudeness, Wizard Levitanus, but what could you offer me besides more coin? I have no desire to be the guild's guard any more than I do the king's men."

Levitanus nodded his understanding. "And yet you still need a new employer because you lost your last one for helping us. Tomorrow, I will take you to meet someone who is interested in hiring you. I think you will find the position intriguing."

Marcus smiled. "I'm always willing to hear a proposition, but I promise no commitment."

"Fair enough. The king has graciously provided you a room for one more night, so I will meet you at Castle Camelot's front gate at noon to take you to meet him."

"Agreed." Marcus stood and gave the wizard a slight bow of respect and then left.

Levitanus turned to Lord Geoffrey. "Young man, you were brave to protect the freed prisoners even while injured. For you, the guild offers a chance to train with our guild guards in the art of hand combat, which could be useful even to a future knight. Do you accept?"

Geoffrey smiled broadly. "Yes! That would greatly help when I need to fight the bullies… to protect the less fortunate and such."

"Good. The guild arms master will send word to the castle's squire master and they'll arrange your schedule. For now, you should get to your quarters because it is late, but expect your training to start within a week or two."

Geoffrey thanked him again and hurried off, which left only Jake, Adele, and Thom with the wizard.

"I should get to bed as well, because I'm riding to Rowan Gate in the morning," said Jake, standing up. "I'm guiding masons down the Road for more repairs to an archway. There isn't anything else you magicians can do for me. I'm a simple man and the king's reward is more than enough."

Levitanus nodded understanding. "Nonetheless, we are in your debt, Guide Jake. If ever you have need, call on the Keeper of the Road for help and it will be provided."

Jake gave him a slight bow. "Thank you, sir. Hopefully, it will never come to that but it is good to know that I have an ally on the Isle of Sun."

As he left, Levitanus turned to Adele and Thomas who were sitting near each other. She sat straight on a settee while he perched on the edge of the chair placed next to it. "Lady Adele, you will now be considered among the nobility since the king gave you a rather large estate and the queen has taken you into her band of ladies, but we perceive that there are still gaps in your education. Most of the ladies-in-waiting aren't as accomplished in archery and combat as you, but they know how to host a gathering and what is expected when managing a household and so much more. Such training is not a specialty of our guild, but we do have on retainer a woman who works with our apprentices and journeywomen of noble bearing. We offer her services to help fill in those gaps caused by your previous employer's neglect. We hope such outside help will make your transition to court easier. Will you accept our offer?"

Adele gave him a warm smile. "Yes. I will admit that fitting in at the queen's court is one of my great worries and your offer has alleviated some of that. Thank you so much."

Levitanus smiled back and clapped his hands. "Good!" He looked over at Thomas and said, "To your feet, young man. We need to escort this young lady to the queen's wing."

"Oh, there's no need," argued Adele, standing. "I have spent time at court before with my old mistress. I can find my way."

"It is late, my lady, and even in the king's castle not all corridors are safe when so many of his guards are rough men. We will escort you, if only to alleviate this old man's concerns." Levitanus held out an arm to her. "Shall we?"

Adele smiled again and rested her arm on his, walking beside the wizard. Thom strode behind them, finding himself a bit envious of his master.

They made their way through Camelot Castle's maze of rooms and corridors and at last to the guarded doors of the queen's wing of the vast castle. They exchanged farewells and then Thomas and his master went to the castle's stable, where a carriage awaited them. Thom was surprised that it bore an emblem of the magicians' guild. The driver wore a uniform that included a red cape with golden-colored embroidered emblem that matched the carriage.

"That is the uniform of the guild guard," stated Levitanus, answering Thom's unasked question. He climbed into the carriage, sliding his staff into a holder that was specifically designed to hold a magician's staff. As he beckoned

Road of Leaves

Thom to follow him in, he placed his fine-leather knapsack at his feet and settled into the padded seat. "Sometimes being a part of the guild has its benefits."

Thom sat down next to his master, setting his own knapsack on the floorboards. He was surprised that the guild would send a carriage for them. "Are we going to Clas Myrddin now?"

"Of course. I am too old to seek out a tavern this late," laughed his master. "I am no admirer of the guild house since it is solely Merlin's dream, but it will provide us with warm beds and decent meals. You stayed long enough at the Camelot Castle while they tended your burns; it is time for you to be among your fellow magicians."

The driver took them out the castle's gate and down the slope into the city. Camelot Castle sat in the western section of the Camelot city so the guild house was to the southeast from there. Due to the late hour, the streets were empty and they made good time.

* * *

Clas Myrddin towered behind high walls. They drove along the cobblestone road that circled the guild house until they came to the main entrance. The night watch had heard their approach and were already pulling open the massive iron-bound gates.

The home of the magicians' guild was more like a soaring castle than a *house*, with many towering spires that Thom could only half-see in the darkness. The highest one, known as Sky Tower, reached so far up that it pierced the dome of magic that covered the king's city. The pinnacle of Sky Tower was hidden in clouds for it was the terminus of the Road of Clouds, a highway only the strongest of magicians could travel. As the carriage waited for the gates to fully open, he stared up at the clouds that covered the turret and then radiated out in a line heading off to the northern horizon.

"It is a majestic sight at dawn and sunset," noted Levitanus. "The Road of Clouds often captures the glow of the sun, especially when it is either pointed north or south."

"It moves?"

"All the Roads move, but this one does so at the whim of the magicians traveling its length. It may stay in the same place for a week or month, or it may shift by the hour. It is also the most fragile of the four Roads."

Thom had to think a moment to remember the fourth path: the Short Road. It was the one that moved every month, linking Camelot to a different city each time. It was that Road the city's residents used to trade and to spend their required time away, since being too long inside an enchantment will make a person or mundane animal unstable. Some called the it the King's Road because it allowed Arthur and his court easy travel to various parts of his realm far quicker than either the Road of Leaves or the Road of Waters.

The gates were opened wide by the red-caped guild guards and the carriage pulled in to a cobblestone courtyard and came to a halt before the keep's great doors.

"Usually, we would have driven to the more modest stable entrance, but I wanted you to see the grand entrance on your first visit here," said Levitanus, motioning for Thomas to exit the carriage.

Late as it was, most of the windows in Clas Myrddin were dark, but the lanterns at the grand entrance were lit and a man was already awaiting them at the just-opened door.

The elderly man bowed as the two approached. "Welcome back, Founder Levitanus. When I heard you were in the city, I had your rooms cleaned and the fires set."

Thom still had a hard time grasping that his master was one of the three Founders who created the Roads and the enchantment covering Camelot. Since Francis had mentioned it on the Road of Leaves it had seemed unreal, for his master seemed too plain and humble for such an exalted title. It had been a secret from Thom but here even the servants used the title.

"Thank you, Cleo, but what are you doing manning the door this late? Surely Merlin hasn't demoted you to night doorman."

The man smiled as he closed the door behind them. "My role has not changed, but it isn't often that I can welcome you to Clas Myrddin, since you so rarely come here. I couldn't resist the opportunity."

"And of course, you anticipated that I would have the driver use the main entrance. More than once I have thought this place misnamed. It is more your house than Merlin's. Clas Cleoddin has a nice sound to it."

The man wasn't about to argue with a wizard, so he politely smiled as he gestured for them to follow him through the dimly lit halls. As they walked, Thom pondered how the man acted toward Levitanus. He was obviously fond of Thom's master but also very respectful of him. He named him Founder just as Francis had, although his master had never used that title himself during the ten years Thom had lived with him.

As they walked, Levitanus kept the conversation going. "Cleo, this is my latest student: Thomas of York. He is exceptionally bright and skilled."

"Good to meet you, young man. I have already heard some tales of your bravery on the Road of Leaves. Well done, that. It would have been horrible if the sorcerers had succeeded in redirecting that way or, worse, collapsed the whole enchantment. You did well."

"Thank you," replied Thom.

Cleo led them along long wide hallways where the tile floors echoed their footsteps. They saw no one else until they took a richly carved stairway that led to the next floor of the keep. At the top of the stairs they passed a pair of guild guards who stood straighter at their approach and acknowledge Thom's master with a respectful nod.

"Who else is in residence?" asked Levitanus as they continued along a carpeted hallway.

"Only the council," replied Cleo, "and half of them will soon join Founder Merlin on the Road of Leaves. There is talk of involving journeymen in the repairs and even using apprentices for some of the mundane tasks. It seems that the Road's enchantment is quite tattered, but I do not need to tell you that, do I?"

"From what I saw and heard, it will take much work to restore the route."

They finally stopped at an ornate door that Cleo opened and then bade them to enter. "You will find your bed turned down, the fires stoked, and a tray of food in case you are still hungry after the king's feast. Also, there is a present that Founder Merlin left for the young man. He said it is his reward and his due for his service to the guild."

Levitanus frowned at that last information but only thanked Cleo for his service.

Thom entered a large sitting room behind his mentor, amazed at the rich furnishings and the very size of the place. His master's cottage could fit in here with space to spare and there were more rooms beyond this one.

"Please close and bolt the door, Thomas," said Levitanus as he shrugged off his knapsack onto a side table near the door and leaned his master's staff against the wall.

Thom did as asked and then followed his master toward the crackling fire. Resting over a chair next to the fire was a dark blue robe and a journeyman's staff.

Levitanus sighed, looking older in the dancing light as he stared at the displayed items. "Merlin is determined that this be your reward. They are yours Thomas, for you have proved yourself worthy of the promotion, but you may rue the expectations that come with the position."

"I am a journeyman now?" he asked, uncertain.

"The robe does not make the man. You will have to work hard, as you have already shown yourself to do, and while here at Clas Myrddin you will get much grief for being so young. There will be jealousy and disbelief among the other journeymen, for most do not attain the rank until they are a decade or more older than you." He looked up from the robe and met Thom's gaze. "You are skilled enough to be a journeyman; I have no concern about your abilities. What I worry about is your maturity to handle the scrutiny and, frankly, viciousness that will come your way now."

"I will do my best to not disappoint the guild," Thom replied.

Levitanus smiled with a touch of sadness. "The guild is not *that* important, Thomas. Rather, do not disappoint yourself. You are a talented magician and, more importantly, a good young man."

His master turned to look silently into the fire for a moment. Thom wanted to pick up his new staff and try on his new robe, but he sensed that his master was troubled so he just stood there and waited. Finally, Levitanus sighed again and looked back at him. "It is late; I am going to bed. You can take your new belongings into your room and try them out, but no magic tonight. Leave that crystal unkindled. We will talk more in the morning."

His master pointed out the door to Thomas' room, asked him to leave the fire burning but to extinguish the candles, and then Levitanus went into his own bedroom and shut the door behind him.

For a moment, Thom just stood there in the quiet room, not sure if he should be dancing with joy or mourning. He was happy but also concerned that his master seemed so worried about his new position. What was ahead of him?

Finally, he decided to do the practical first. He snuffed the candles, grabbed a plum from the fruit bowl, then gathered his new robe and staff and went to his assigned room. Once he had the door shut behind him, he had his own, muted celebration.

WAYS OF CAMELOT
4-Book Arthurian Fantasy Series

1- Road of Leaves

Thank you for reading the first book in the Ways of Camelot series.

2- Road of Waters

Available **August 15, 2023** in paperback and e-book

3- Camelot of the Roads

Available **September 15, 2023** in paperback and e-book.

4- Road of Clouds

Available **October 15, 2023** in paperback and e-book.

Eric Loren

About the Author
Eric Loren

Eric is an American author of fantasy, science fiction, and dystopian novels.

His writings include the Ways of Camelot series, the upcoming Tag Warren series, and the Cirian War saga.

The son of immigrants, he can speak his parents' tongue, though with a decidedly American accent. He studied our collective past and our present (holding a degree in both History and Religious Studies), and still enjoys learning about the world's diverse cultures and beliefs.

Eric currently lives in California, enjoying the sunshine and natural wonders of that unique state. He is married to his beloved Amy and has two wonderful sons.

Learn more about Eric at his website:
http://ericloren.com